The Augustus Conspiracy

THE AUGUSTUS CONSPIRACY

Anthony Nagle

2003
Galde Press, Inc.
Lakeville, Minnesota, U.S.A.

The Augustus Conspiracy
© Copyright 2003 by Anthony Nagle
All rights reserved.
Printed in the United States of America
No part of this book may be used or reproduced in any manner whatsoever without written permission from the publishers except in the case of brief quotations embodied in critical articles and reviews.

First Edition
First Printing, 2003

Cover designed by Gordon Robinson Associates, Minneapolis

Galde Press, Inc.
PO Box 460
Lakeville, Minnesota 55044–0460

In appreciation for their loyalty and support…
William G. Nagle
Ronald D. Guernsey
Dr. Ellen B. Buchanan
Lawrence "Butch" Lambert
Nickie J. Dillon

...the study of history is the best medicine for a sick mind, for in history you have a record of the infinite variety of human experience plainly set out for all to see, and in that record you can find for yourself and your country both examples and warnings; fine things to take as models, base things rotten through and through, to avoid.

Titus Livius
From The Founding of the City
Circa A.D. 10

Prologue

Rome
The Palatine

Mario's running shoes hit the ground with a squish. It was drizzling as he looked up the rope to see his brother starting down the ancient masonry wall. "Hurry up, Figlio. It will be light soon. We don't have a lot of time." Figlio dropped from the rope next to his brother. They knelt behind a marble column on the infield grass. The floodlights from the palisades, reflecting off the high, jagged walls of the Palace of the Emperors, cast eerie shadows across the Palatine Racetrack.

"Okay," Mario whispered nervously. "You go first. Run to the end of the racetrack. There's a portico to the left side of the wall. Wait for me there."

Figlio jumped up and sprinted across the wet grass. As Mario watched his four-teen-year-old brother disappear into the darkness, he could envision the Roman Emperor Domitian and his guests seated in the observation deck overlooking the long, oval stadium. They were cheering for their champion, who had just won the eight-lap chariot race.

Figlio's stringy, black hair was matted to his face. He reached the cave-like opening in less than a minute. He was breathing heavily—not so much from the running as from the tension coursing through his body. He turned, put both hands on his knees and squinted back at the shadows—his eyes searching the arena for his brother. He heard Mario's heavy footfalls racing across the sodden, grassy infield. A silhouette at first, the lean, brawny form of his seventeen-year-old-brother took shape as it emerged from the darkness.

Mario came to a stop underneath the portico's overhang. "How long will it take to get to the room with the scrolls?" Figlio asked with a nervous whisper.

"A few minutes. We're not far from it now. Turn on your flashlight. Let's go—follow me and stay close." They entered a tunnel leading to musty-smelling rooms under the Palatine that gladiators once used to dress for battle in the nearby Colosseum. Darkness shrouded the empty cavern. Figlio's trembling worsened as they wandered through a maze of chambers, over dirt-covered mosaic floors that depicted ancient gladiators battling lions and tigers.

"There it is," Mario said excitedly, pointing the beam of light to a small hole in the foundation wall of the ancient Roman stadium. He fixed the light at the wall and moved toward it.

Mario removed the rocks and debris piled against the wall, revealing a small crawlspace. "The racetrack wall butts up against the foundation wall of Augustus's palace. Last week I cut through the two walls. I found this room. It must have been a secret chamber that Augustus used." They crawled through the hole and landed in a large, open room beneath the Imperial Palace, built by Augustus Caesar in 3 A.D. "This is it. See, a secret room. No doors. Augustus must have had a passage that only he knew about."

"What do you suppose he used it for?" Figlio asked.

"Who knows. But Augustus knew what he was doing when he built it. It's been hidden from the archeologists and succeeding emperors for over two thousand years."

"And then the amazing Mario finds it," Figlio joked, feeling a little less tense.

"Shut up."

"Let's get the scrolls and get out of here. This place is starting to give me the creeps."

"Okay. They're on the far side of the room. See…" Mario swung the beam of light to the other side of the room.

"Wow!" Figlio exclaimed as he took in a small library filled with rolled parchments. "There are so many. How are we going to get them out of here?"

"We'll take as many as we can in our backpacks. We'll have to make another trip."

Figlio rolled his eyes. "If you think I'm coming back here, you're crazy."

"Okay, okay. C'mon, let's get started."

Mario started putting the ancient parchments into Figlio's backpack.

Figlio suddenly froze in his tracks. He turned, then grabbed Mario's arm.

"What?"

"I heard something."

Mario's first reaction was to chastise Figlio for being afraid, but then he heard something out of place. There were voices coming from the dressing rooms. He snapped off his flashlight. Figlio did the same. Mario crawled on his knees across the dusty floor, careful not to make a sound. He reached the far wall and looked through the crawlspace toward the maze of rooms on the other side. There were two flashlight beams—coming toward them!

"What do you see?" Figlio whispered.

"Shit. We were followed," Mario said as he strained to get a better look. The men stopped and one pointed his flashlight at the other. "They're not security guards." Guards would have merely chased them off.

"I thought you said nobody knew about this place."

Mario didn't answer. He concentrated on the two forms in the passageway.

"Hush! There's two men standing in the tunnel. One's got a gun," Mario whispered with a tremble in his voice.

The two flashlights started coming toward the boys again, then stopped. The men did not know which way to turn. They had reached the end of the labyrinth. Mario held his breath, hoping they would not see the hole in the wall. Despite the cold, sweat poured down his face. He whispered in Figlio's ear, "There must be another way out of here. Augustus had to have had a way in and out. In the far corner of the room there's a marble block. Maybe it covers a tunnel."

Mario moved very slowly through the pitch-black chamber. Turning on his flashlight would give away their position. He blindly walked toward where he remembered seeing the small marble slab. Reaching out, he encountered the foundation wall and moved his hand along it. Figlio held on tightly to Mario's shirt. Mario's foot struck something. "I think this is it." Groping for position, they slid the marble rectangle from its place. Mario pointed his flashlight where the slab had been, revealing a crawlspace just wide enough for one person..

"Let's go," Mario said softly.

Mario entered first. Figlio took hold of Mario's pant leg and followed him. They wiggled in, pulling themselves forward on their elbows. The air was rancid; cobwebs stuck to their faces. Figlio's throat was dry; dust clogged his nose and mouth. He could not breathe. The tunnel started to swirl. He felt dizzy and nauseated. Finally, he let out a loud gasp trying to suck in air. The noise penetrated the darkness. Mario and Figlio froze in their places.

"Over there! They're over there!" a deep voice cried out.

The boys quickened their pace. "I see it. There's a wider opening ahead," Mario squealed. "This must be the tunnel Augustus used to get to Livia's apartment. It's about three more meters." They moved as fast as they could, clawing the loose gravel with their fingers.

Suddenly, Mario's head broke into the open. It was Augustus's tunnel. He pulled himself from the crawlspace, landing with the palms of his hands on the muddy surface. He inhaled the fresh air, coughing out the dust. He turned and pulled Figlio out of the narrow opening. He looked back down the shaft and saw the beam of a flashlight coming at them. They turned and sprinted down a long, dark tunnel that ran the length of the Palatine. They found themselves standing in the pit of a well, surrounded by scaffolding.

Mario tried to organize his thoughts. Where were they? His panicked mind tried to form a picture of the ruins above; from the Imperial palace, they would have run under Hadrian's castle, then under the Temple of Augustus. That would leave them in the vicinity of Livia's manor. "Figlio. Climb up the scaffolding. When you get to the top, look to your right. You should see a temple with a headless statue sitting on a throne. It's the Temple of Cybele. Run toward the temple then go to your right. There's a stairway that goes up to the garden. We can hide in the garden."

Figlio agilely climbed the scaffolding. He reached the top, spotting the Temple of Cybele not ten meters away. The headless marble statue of the goddess startled him. He darted toward the temple, then spotted the concrete stairway to the right. He bolted for the stairs.

Mario reached the top of the well and looked back down. The flashlights were coming closer. He jumped from the lip of the well and saw a pile of marble rocks, discarded by archeologists. He picked up a chunk of marble and walked back to the well. Looking down the shaft, he saw two sinister faces looking up at him. He clutched the rock with both hands, then raised it over his head. The lead man reached into his coat pocket.

Mario thrust the marble block down the shaft with all the strength he could muster. The first man ran for cover, but the second stood flatfooted. The sharp edge of the rectangular slab blasted through his skull. He dropped lifelessly to the floor.

The other man rushed to his fallen comrade, his face flushed with anger. He lunged for the scaffolding. Mario quickly turned away and bolted toward the Temple. As Mario looked back at the well, he ran head-first into a large metal sign, falling to the ground and sliding on his stomach into a pile of dirt. Mario picked himself up and saw a flashlight coming over the top of the well. He scurried toward the stairs, slipping again on the wet gravel. Suddenly, a piece of the temple wall exploded inches from his head.

"Figlio, get down!" Mario yelled from his prone position. His younger brother stood waiting at the top of the hill. Figlio cried out, then dropped to the ground.

Mario looked up to see his brother fall. "Figlio, Figlio!" Mario cried in panic. He scrambled up the stairs, bullets whizzing past his head. Figlio was lying on the ground, clutching his leg, wincing in pain. Mario hoisted him over his shoulder and jogged across the wet grass. There was no time to run to the end of the garden, so he raced behind the lush evergreens surrounding the perimeter.

"Mario…Mario!" Figlio whispered, his words coming slowly between gasps for breath. "I'm okay. I think I can walk…put me down. Hurry up, Mario!"

Mario did as his brother asked, setting him gently on his feet. As Figlio stood testing his leg, Mario peeked through the grass. He spied the beam of a flashlight going straight up from the summit of the hill. Mario's mind raced, trying to find a way to safety.

"Figlio, I have an idea. Run to the observation deck at the end of the garden. Hide behind the walls. I'll try to distract him. Go, now!"

Figlio nodded. He started to run, limping from his wound, toward the portal at the end of the Farnese Garden, which overlooks the reflecting pool of the Vestal Virgins in the Roman Forum twenty meters below.

Mario walked slowly behind his brother, leaving heavy footprints in the sodden grass. At the end of the garden Figlio turned right and limped into the shelter of the portal. Mario went straight ahead and hid behind the trunk of a sprawling oak tree. He waited for what seemed like hours. Finally, he saw the flashlight coming toward him.

The man stopped. He had lost the footprints as the grass turned to a paved walkway. He waited, hoping to hear a sound that would betray the boys' hiding place. The only thing the man heard was the rustling of the leaves as a gentle breeze wafted through the Palatine. He pointed the flashlight beam in several directions, looking…looking. Mario pressed himself against the tree. He looked up to the sky. The clouds were clearing; the sun was about to rise. *Please, Saint Anthony, do not let him see my shadow.*

The man shrugged and spun to the left. He walked cautiously to the west observation deck overlooking the ruins of the Forum. Mario took a deep breath and listened as the man's footfalls became less distinct. He counted to ten very slowly, then slipped from the cover of the tree, the tips of his running shoes falling silently on the walkway. He slipped behind another tree, then slowly peeked around its base. The man was leaning over the guardrail, shining his light down the Palatine Hill. Mario waited, calculating the distance between himself and the lone gunman.

The man leaned back, satisfied that the boys did not escape down the hill. Mario bolted from behind the tree, racing at the man's back. He bent his elbows and brought both hands up. He slammed the palms of his hands squarely into the man's broad shoulders. The impact lifted the gunman over the guardrail and into the air. Mario watched as he plummeted toward the Forum, twenty meters below. The look on the man's face would haunt him for the rest of his life. It was a face frozen in terror—the helplessness of a man who knows he is about to die.

The gunman's body slammed into a raised, grassy knoll below. The sound of his neck snapping echoed through the early morning dawn of the Roman Forum. Three Corinthian columns cast their eerie shadows across the intruder's corpse as the sun rose over the Palatine.

Mario stared down from the observation deck in a trance—the gunman was lying spread-eagle under the columns of Castor and Pollux. But, it wasn't the dead man that he saw. It was two youths, dismounting from white stallions, spears in their hands, leading their horses to drink at the nearby Fountain of Juturna.

The legend of Castor and Pollux shot through his mind: The two boys, the same ages as he and Figlio, were riding at the head of the Roman Cavalry in 500 B.C., leading a brigade of Roman soldiers against the Etruscans and the Latins. At the moment of battle, the boys appeared in a vision to the citizens of Rome and foretold a Roman victory. Then they vanished.

Mario's stomach tightened. He did not believe in coincidence. The dead man lying at the ruins of the Temple of Castor and Pollux had to be a harbinger of something to come—an omen that portended a great victory. An unfamiliar energy from ancient Rome and the reality of the moment clouded his thoughts.

Mario turned away from the temple, feeling scared and alone. He ran back to the portal and called out to Figlio, his voice trembling.

"Mario, over here," came his brother's hoarse reply.

Mario walked into the shadows of the observatory to find his brother lying on the ground holding his leg and grimacing with pain.

"What happened, Mario? Are we safe?"

"It's okay. They're gone." He had killed two human beings.

Mario saw the blood from Figlio's wound. "Your leg, Figlio. Let me look at it."

Mario ripped Figlio's bloody pant leg where the bullet had torn a neat hole. He winced as he aimed his flashlight on the ugly gash. Figlio's leg was beginning to swell.

"My leg is getting numb, Mario. I can't feel anything." Tears were forming in the corners of his eyes.

Mario pulled off his T-shirt and twisted it into a tourniquet. He wrapped it around his brother's wound and tied the ends tightly to stop the bleeding. "Okay. Let's get you out of here. Put your arm over my shoulder. We'll go out through the aqueduct." Mario helped Figlio to his feet.

"Those men, Mario. How did they know?"

Mario grimaced. "I don't know. I don't know."

"What about the rest of the scrolls?"

"I'll come back later and get them. First, we're going to get your leg fixed."

Figlio looked into his brother's eyes. A smile formed on Mario's lips.

"What is it, Mario?" Figlio asked, his voice still filled with trepidation.

"I was just thinking," he said as they crossed the lawn of the early Farnese Garden.

"Thinking about what?"

Mario didn't answer. It was the irony, the irony of the past forging into the present: On this very spot, Romulus and Remus, orphaned brothers raised by a she-wolf, founded Rome in 753 B.C. Now, thirty centuries later, he and his brother had found one of Rome's best-kept secrets.

Book One
Chapter 1

Washington, D.C.
Spring 2000

Sam Harrison rounded the Washington Monument, shielding his eyes from the sun with his hand. He jogged down the hill past the Vietnam War Memorial and up the steps to the Lincoln Memorial. Muscles burning from the steep climb, he stretched for a few moments and then he ran down the steps back toward the Washington Monument. He pushed the timing button on his watch as he slumped to a halt. Satisfied, he decided to quit, but the nagging sense of guilt from the previous evening would not leave him.

"Four years sober…damn," he swore under his breath. The notice he'd received from the Internal Revenue Service two days earlier had unsettled him. A large capital gain that he'd failed to report had surfaced and the IRS wanted their due.

A black limousine pulled alongside him as he walked toward Constitution Avenue. The driver was Pug Williamson, personal chauffeur of CIA Director William G. Bannistar. A window lowered and the chauffeur leaned across the seat. "Mr. Harrison, I figured I'd find you down here. Mr. B. wants to see you, pronto."

Sam Harrison, CIA Deputy Director, climbed in, a look of disgust on his face. The only time he had to himself these days was Sundays.

"You mind stopping at my townhouse so I can change into something more appropriate?"

"Mr. B. told me to get you to his house right away. He said he didn't care what you look like or what condition you're in. Something's come up. It's *big*."

"What's so important that Bill wants to see me on a Sunday?"

"He wouldn't tell me. You know Bannistar won't tell me any Company stuff. But I got it on the q.t. he's got a meeting at the White House tonight with the President and the Secretary of State…"

"Warner Van Clevenson."

Sam's primary responsibility was gathering intelligence on terrorist activity and drug trafficking—most notably, Osama bin Laden's activity in Afghanistan and heroin traffic from the Middle East. For the past two years he had earned high marks from the Director and from the President for keeping CIA Drug Ops one step ahead of the drug lords. But bin Laden was another problem altogether. He seemed to be able to vanish and reappear at will.

It took Pug the better part of half an hour to get through Georgetown. At last they reached the Director's house on Dexter Drive. Thick elm trees surrounded the property, and a well-maintained garden ran from the front door all the way to the side of the house. The lawn looked like a putting green manicured to perfection. Sam knew that an elaborate security system was concealed in the lawn. Even though Sam enjoyed a comfortable lifestyle, he felt a sense of inadequacy every time he laid eyes on Bannistar's estate.

Pug stopped the car and hurried around to open the door for Sam, who climbed out, stretching his legs. A butler opened the front door and ushered Sam into the foyer. Wealth oozed from every corner—the lush carpet, the elegantly furnished living room, the early American portraits that hung in the corridor. Bannistar was one of the many people in Washington political circles who had been independently wealthy before taking their current jobs.

The butler escorted Sam to Bannistar's office. Bannistar was sitting at his desk, an unlit cigarette in his hand. The room smelled of stale smoke.

Bannistar showed all of his sixty-two years. His thick, gray hair was disheveled and heavy bags hung below his dark green eyes. Sam had to wonder why a man like Bannistar bothered with government service. What was in it for him? Certainly not the money. It had to be the power.

"Better take a look at this," Bannistar blustered, oblivious to Sam's running gear. He handed Sam a slip of paper, then snapped a silver cigarette lighter and lit a Marlboro. He inhaled deeply.

Sam scanned the page. He dropped into an overstuffed leather chair. He felt like he'd been kicked in the stomach. A cloud of pain washed over his face. He tried to hide it but did a poor job. He took a deep breath.

"Any other details?"

Bannistar hesitated. "Sorry, Sam, I was thinking about what Rham did to the last three agents that were compromised…"

Sam took another deep breath. Abdul Rham, the most powerful mullah in Afghanistan, had buried three CIA agents alive. It was his way of sending a message to the Agency: Anyone you send to my country will never leave alive.

"What about Libra?" Sam asked, trying to sound factual, but his tone betrayed him.

"I don't know any more than what's in that message. I think we can assume that Rham killed her. I hate to lose a good agent, but the risk comes with the territory. Libra went in with her eyes wide open."

Bannistar stood up and walked to the patio doors. He looked out at the gardens surrounding the flagstone patio. "Libra was close to getting the name of Rham's key distributor in Europe, and more importantly, she was drawing a bead on bin Laden. Three years of good, hard intelligence work down the drain. Shit."

"But there's a possibility she got out…with the information?"

"Maybe, but I wouldn't bank on it. Rham's too damn smart and too damn ruthless. The Taliban don't respect their own women. Shit, there's no way he'd respect one of ours. I can only imagine what he'd do to an American spy."

"I guess you're right," Sam replied slowly, his head ringing from the previous night's bout with Johnny Walker.

"But that's only part of it," Bannistar sighed. "The President called. He's been tipped off to a heroin shipment coming into the country. It hits the streets soon. And whoever he gets his information from says it's large and that there's more on the way."

"Afghanistan?" Sam asked, suddenly at full attention. He'd be on the hot seat for not ascertaining the information first.

"He didn't know for sure. But that's where he thinks it's coming from. Libra hasn't given us any names in Europe, so I have to assume that that's where the heroin is coming from."

"And bin Laden has contacts or distribution points other than Europe. Rham may want alternatives since we shut down his routes through Pakistan and Russia. He relied heavily on those routes and, at the time, didn't have any other way to get his drugs to America. Maybe he's not taking any chances this time around."

Bannistar shrugged. "That's a possibility. Especially if Rham thinks that he's on the ropes. Before you got here I spent some time reviewing the file on Afghanistan. Rham is responsible, according to Libra, for coordinating these terrorist cells bin Laden has set up through a group called the Shura Council. Apparently Rham's credibility is being scrutinized by some of the Council members because he's been careless lately with drug shipments. Libra seemed to think Rham was on his last leg and running out of cash. The other mullahs in Afghanistan are closing in on him— they want his poppy fields—and even his own people are questioning his competence. That, coupled with the fact that we intercepted his last two shipments with a street value of roughly twenty million, has to have lightened his pocketbook."

Bannistar changed the subject. "There's another problem—the DEA. They're on my case along with President Smithson. My opposite number over there is in bed with that moron Van Clevenson at State. They want to put the CIA out of business."

Sam was uncomfortable discussing the power jockeying inherent in Beltway life. "And this has something to do with your meeting at the White House tonight?"

Bannistar nodded. "Smithson's on the warpath. Crime is at an all-time low and the drug problem is suddenly manageable. He's scared shitless that this new wave of heroin will boost crime and hurt his ratings. He wants answers. And right now, I don't even know what the questions are. So that's why I called you. I need to buy some time. We have to find out what's really going on with Rham and bin Laden. I can't walk into the Oval Office with a pocketful of theories. I need facts." Bannistar took a hard pull from his cigarette. The stress lines on his forehead deepened. "I want you to go to Europe. See if you can pick up any pieces Libra might have left behind. I can stall the President for a while, but you'll have to work fast. Smithson's got a short fuse."

"Jesus, Bill, I don't even know where to start." Sam glanced down at the transmission that had been sent by Libra's contact in Europe. "The message, 'In the mouth of the wolf'—what's it mean?"

"Not sure. It was her signature for letting us know that the mission was compromised. Might be a place to start. I'd suggest you check Libra's files to see if there's any connection to the note and where it may have originated."

"That's a tall order, Bill. No one knows the identity of her contacts or where they're from. She kept a tight reign on her operatives."

The phone interrupted the conversation. Bannistar picked up the receiver and grunted into the mouthpiece. He listened thoughtfully for a few moments and then nodded at Sam, letting him know that the meeting was finished.

Sam turned and quietly left the room.

Pug looked on from the limousine as Sam slowly climbed the steps to his N Street townhouse. The drive from Bannistar's had been solemn. Sam hadn't said a word.

Pug shook his head and frowned as Sam disappeared through the front door. He knew a lot more about the inner workings of the CIA than he let on, but his interest was more along the lines of who was sleeping with whom. He remembered rumors circulating about Sam's affair with the mysterious agent known as Libra. Female agents were an anomaly and the intrigue surrounding Sam's clandestine activities were more than Pug could stand, but he resigned himself to the fact that Sam was entitled to a private life. He shrugged and headed back to Bannistar's.

Sam walked through his sparsely furnished living room and into the kitchen. He opened the refrigerator and reached for a beer, all his guilt from the night before dissolved with the news of Libra's apparent demise. He drained half the can in one swallow, then walked back to the living room and slumped down on the sofa.

He tried to put Afghanistan and Libra into perspective, attempting to separate his feelings from the situation. A monster like Rham wouldn't think twice about killing a double agent who had betrayed him. He tried not to think about the torture she must have endured. Rham would certainly have tried to pry information from her, and his sadistic methods of counterespionage were legendary.

He drained the last few ounces of beer, then slowly walked up the circular staircase to his second-floor office. He pulled a large oil portrait of Newport Harbor away from the wall, revealing a gray metallic wall safe. He swung the portrait back to the wall and stared at it. Libra had given him the portrait shortly before leaving for Afghanistan as a remembrance of their weekend there together. He didn't want to think about it.

He punched a six-digit combination into the LED on the side of the platinum-colored box. Two beeps sang from a micro speaker and a small green light flashed as the door sprung open. Sam reached in and pulled out a thick manila folder. Neatly typed on the folder's tab was Libra's real identity, which had been altered in all computer files to protect her cover. He set the folder on the desk, sat down, and flipped it open.

His eyes scanned the initial interview sheet. He had written it years ago, following their first meeting on her college campus in upstate New York:

Graduated cum laude, Phi Beta Kappa; captain of the women's lacrosse and squash teams. Honor Society, Drama Club. Major: Languages; speaks five fluently (not counting English)—Russian, Italian, Spanish, French and German.

She was damn good, far better than any agent he had recruited. He tried not to second-guess himself, but couldn't help feeling that he should have known better than to send one of his best agents on a suicide mission, even though she had almost pulled it off. Somehow she had convinced one of the world's biggest rogues that she was a disgruntled international journalist. Her dark coloring, auburn hair and high cheekbones allowed her to pass as Middle Eastern. The Company had made arrangements for several of her articles, many critical of the CIA, to be published in respected magazines throughout the world under the byline of her cover identity, Sunkara. One of her articles even showed up in *The New York Times* Sunday magazine. The article, a treatise on how the CIA had actually put the Taliban in power, achieved critical acclaim.

Sam memorized the street address and her mother's name. He would break the news to her family himself. He'd take the early morning shuttle to Newark, rent a car and drive out to Chatham. *God, what am I going to tell her mother?* Sam considered a series of vague explanations, but none of them seemed appropriate or believable.

Chapter 2

Kabul, Afghanistan
Sunday, Before Dawn

Rham's snoring was making her crazy, but it was the least of her worries. She was, for the first time since gaining acceptance in Afghanistan, scared for her life. She started second-guessing her judgment for creating such a dangerous assignment, then selling it to her superiors, especially Sam. Her fear started to turn to anger. *Calm down. Find a serene place.*

Libra forced herself to a meditative state. Her thoughts turned to escape. Her brother's words came to her: "Believe in yourself and you can do anything." A smile crossed her lips.

Rham's snoring had faded into the distance as she plotted the events that would help her regain freedom. She started to slip from the bed.

Rham stirred. "Is something wrong, darling?" he asked sleepily as he propped himself on an elbow. "You can't sleep? Have the boy prepare some warm milk."

She ran her hand gently across his cheek and forced a smile to her lips. "Milk just might do the trick. I'll have Jamillur prepare some."

"Ah, yes, my darling. It was a wonderful evening. Too much lamb has, I'm afraid, left me drowsy. But I would be more than happy to accompany you."

"No. Go back to sleep. It will take only a few minutes. I'll be back shortly." *Paranoid asshole.*

Rham nodded and rolled back into a heavy sleep.

With little effort, she mused, she could puncture his larynx and suffocate him. It would rid the world of a major nuisance. But killing him now would jeopardize her chances of getting out of the country alive. Rham's bodyguard would surely check on him as soon as she left the room. If he found Rham dead, he'd gun her down without a thought.

She glanced down at her watch: 4:55. Time was in her favor. Rham himself had removed her first obstacle. Had he not suggested that she go to the kitchen, he'd be alarmed if he awoke and she was not lying beside him. The past few days he wouldn't let her out of his sight. Everyone in the palace was suspicious about American spies.

Libra slipped to the side of the bed and sat upright. Rham stirred, then rolled over to face her. She froze on the edge of the bed, not daring to breathe. He started snoring again. She exhaled softly and walked to the bedroom door in her bare feet, not making a sound. She eased the handle of the door, then ever so slowly pulled it open. She peeked down the hallway. Rham's bodyguard, a bearded man in his late thirties, was sprawled across a worn leather couch snoring shamelessly, an AK-47 draped across his chest.

Libra brushed quietly past the anemic-looking thug and down the circular staircase into the kitchen. As she peeked through the kitchen-door window, she undid her robe, revealing her slender body through the thin nightgown. She untied the ribbon in her hair and let it fall around her shoulders. She opened the door.

The young guard's attention was caught by the soft glow from the door behind him. He turned to look. He could not believe his eyes. Abdul's mistress. She was even more beautiful than he had imagined. He had had fantasies about this woman ever since Rham had made him the night guard. He could not take his eyes from her naked body. She was motioning to him to come into the house. What good fortune!

She held a finger to her mouth, indicating that he should be quiet. He nodded eagerly and stepped into the kitchen, removing his tunic as he entered the room. Her face came close to his; he could smell her sweet perfume.

"I need you to help me, Jamillur," she whispered.

"Anything." The young soldier was dizzy with lust.

"Abdul told me to tell you that you are to prepare some warm milk for me as I am finding it difficult to sleep. Will you be kind enough to warm the stove while I get the milk and a pan? I will give you a nice surprise for your efforts."

"But, of course, madam. It would be an honor."

He turned his back to her, bent over and started warming the wood stove. "These stoves are difficult. They are so much work. It was much better before the Russians left and we had gas burners." As he started to stand up, she took a large iron skillet from the counter, raised it above her shoulders and brought it down on the young soldier's head. The pan made a dull thud as it reverberated off his skull.

Jamillur did not collapse as she had expected. He turned slowly, eyes wide. He looked up at the beautiful woman, bewilderment masking his face.

Just as Libra was about to bring the pan down on the boy again, his eyes rolled back and he collapsed in a heap. She quickly removed his clothes. Jamillur's uniform fit perfectly, except for the boots. They were too big, but they would do. Jamillur apparently had not had the benefit of a shower in some time, but that would enhance her credibility.

She grabbed Jamillur's AK-47 and then hurriedly pushed her hair up under the filthy white turban. She walked into the brightly lit backyard attempting to emulate Jamillur's patrolling stride as she headed for the pool of sport-utility vehicles in Rham's parking lot.

Libra headed toward a large, black Land Rover. She looked at her watch: 5:10. She would arrive at the airport in time to make the early morning flight to Istanbul. The key to the Rover was in the ignition and the door was unlocked.

"Jamillur," came an angry voice from the far end of the driveway. "Get back to your post."

"Shit," Libra swore under her breath as she froze in place.

The soldier's heavy boots crunched the driveway gravel as he marched closer. He reached out a meaty hand for Libra's shoulder, but before he could spin her around, the muzzle of an automatic weapon smashed into his eye, quickly terminating any disciplinary action that he had in mind.

Libra lifted the guard's body in her arms and heaved it into the back of the vehicle. She hurriedly jumped behind the wheel, started the engine and hit the accelerator. Lights suddenly went on all over the house. "Damn," she swore loudly as she spun the wheel.

Plumes of dust and gravel flew into the air as she headed toward the entrance of Rham's palace. As she turned the Rover onto the main road, Rham, bodyguard at his side, came storming out the front door. The guard raised his AK-47, then let go a long burst of 9mm ordinance.

The bullets bounced off the Rover, useless against the bulletproof glass and reinforced steel.

Libra punched the padded steering wheel and swore. Her plan was falling apart. While the Taliban were centuries behind the times, they did have cellular phones that would alert the guard posts on the way to the airport.

Afghan Ariana had one flight to Istanbul, at 6:00. There were no other options.

Libra felt a pang of lost confidence. She did not have the necessary papers to get past the Taliban guards at the airport, and the flight would surely be full. Things did not look good. She should have killed Rham when she had the chance. Now he would probably end up killing her. She guessed that she had about a five- to ten-minute head start. They probably wouldn't try to chase her since there were too many back roads and places to hide. No, they would anticipate her heading for the airport.

Rham's guards would have orders to shoot on sight. There was no way to bluff her way through the airport. She'd have to shoot her way out. This was turning into a suicide mission; she knew the odds were stacked in Rham's favor. Well, better to go toe-to-toe with Rham's goons than have to suffer the kind of torture he would undoubtedly inflict if she were caught alive.

Libra pushed the Rover down one dusty trail after another for the next fifteen minutes. The Khyber Pass was the only other way out of the country. She would never get past the Afghan and Pakistani checkpoints—not without papers, and certainly not in Abdul Rham's vehicle. She fought the pitted dirt trails for another ten minutes; the Rover rounded a sharp curve—five minutes from the airport. She saw the oncoming headlights of another vehicle. The trail was barely wide enough for one vehicle, let alone two. This could be trouble. She flashed her high beams hoping to stun the other driver. The other vehicle flashed its bright lights in response. She gunned the engine, picking up speed.

As Libra bore down, her headlights picked up a lone driver in a dilapidated pick-up truck. He had stopped and was parked to the side of the trail. She sighed in relief. She jammed on the brakes and brought the Rover to a screeching halt.

She lunged out of the Rover, the AK-47 clutched in her hands. She rushed at the truck. An old man was shaking violently behind the steering wheel.

"Out of the truck," she screamed.

The man was trembling so fiercely that she thought he would fall. He lifted his bony hands high in the air.

She sized the man up. About her size. "Take off your robe and throw it to me. Move!"

"You...you would take the clothes off the back of a poor, old man?" he stammered. "Please, have mercy on my poor soul," he pleaded with wide, sorrowful eyes.

She felt pity for the old man. His robe probably represented the better portion of his meager wardrobe and he probably lived in the truck. She thrust her free hand in the pocket of Jamillur's baggy pants. She was not surprised when it came out with a roll of twenty-dollar bills. Rham paid his guards well. American twenty-dollar bills were the standard barter in the drug trade.

"I need your truck. You can pick it up later at the airport. Here, take this," Libra said as she peeled away half the roll. "This will buy you a dozen new robes." She thrust the wad of twenties at the old man. His eyes widened in pleasant surprise and his trembling stopped. He bowed graciously as he snatched the money. He pulled the long robe over his head and handed it over.

"May Allah bless you," he said, bowing in gratitude.

"There is one more thing I want you to do."

The man looked up. He said nothing, but his suspicious, droopy eyes asked what he was to do.

"The four-wheel-drive over there," she said, pointing her gun at the Rover. "It belongs to Abdul Rham. If he catches you in it, he will kill you."

The old man swallowed hard. Clouds came across his face, fear returning to his eyes.

"There is a can of petrol in the back and what's left of Rham's personal guard. If you value your life, this is what you will do…" Libra gave instructions. "Then, when you fetch your truck, you will find these under the visor." Libra held up the remaining twenty-dollar bills in her hand.

"But how will you know if I do what you ask? What would prevent me from just running off with your money?"

"I will know," she said with a clear, icy look and a chilling tone. The old man sensed that the consequences for not doing what she said would come back to haunt him.

Two minutes later, Libra backed the old pickup down the trail in the direction from which it came. The old man held his bony hand in the air, waving. As he watched his truck fade into the night, a pale glow broke the darkness of night as it shrouded the dilapidated vehicle.

Libra checked her watch: 5:45. It took less than five minutes to reach the main highway. Now, the next obstacle: getting past the checkpoint at the main terminal.

Libra cursed every time the truck went over a bump. The shock absorbers were useless. A guard shack suddenly appeared in the distance. Beyond it she could see the lights from the main terminal. She reached to her right, then popped open the glove box. The old man's papers were right where he said they would be.

She counted three cars waiting in line to clear the airport security as she slowed the dilapidated truck. She grabbed the AK-47 and put it between her leg and the door. Adrenaline started pumping through her veins. Under Taliban rule, Afghan men all wore beards. If the guard got a look at her face, it was all over.

Libra checked the rear-view mirror. From out of nowhere, two jeeps filled with Rham's elite guard pulled up right behind the truck. They were waving their hands, yelling at her to stop. Three soldiers, their automatic weapons at the ready, jumped off the jeep, then sprinted toward her. She looked out the windshield; two more guards, their weapons in firing position, were coming straight for her. She felt her hand clutch the Russian assault weapon. It was hopeless. At least she would die knowing that she rid the world of some of Rham's terrorists.

#

THE WHITE HOUSE
SUNDAY EVENING

"I don't have the answers," Bannistar answered the President. "We lost our agent who was working undercover in Afghanistan. Sam is on his way to Europe to see if he can pick up the pieces."

President Jeffrey Smithson leaned back in his chair and stroked his chin in deep thought. Sitting next to Bannistar, the Secretary of State, Warner Van Clevenson, inwardly reveled with satisfaction.

Van Clevenson had a reputation for playing hardball and controlling his department with an iron fist. He was the only Democrat in Smithson's cabinet, and he had no tolerance for anyone looking better than he did in the area of foreign relations.

State had been trying for months to shut down the CIA. With its forty-billion-dollar budget, incompetent field agents and scandals like Aldrich Ames, the Agency had cost the United States dearly while producing only useless information. Bannistar presented a particular threat to Van Clevenson. Bannistar had accomplished what no other director had—he had made the CIA efficient. He had recruited highly proficient people and increased the effectiveness of the agents who were not reassigned.

The President leaned forward, directing his attention to Van Clevenson. "How reliable is your information?" he asked, referring to the drug shipments about to enter the country.

"My sources are solid. I think we can expect major inflows of heroin and cocaine over the next two months." He cast a side glance at Bannistar, who was struggling to control his anger. Drug information was his domain and Van Clevenson had been holding out on him.

"Bill, you have any further thoughts?" the President asked, looking down at a document on his desk to avoid eye contact with Bannistar. The President was clearly displeased.

"I need more time. We suspect the distribution channels from Afghanistan have been rerouted through Europe, but I won't have anything more until Harrison has a chance to evaluate the situation."

"I understand that Harrison has fallen off the wagon," Van Clevenson cut in.

The President shot a surprised look at Bannistar, who was now blindsided for the second time. Bannistar's face flushed a bright crimson. *The asshole really likes to hit below the belt.* He took a deep breath. "I'll personally vouch for Sam, Jeff. His sobriety is not the issue here."

"It's an issue if he's your point man in Europe," Van Clevenson retorted. Bannistar did not react.

"Okay, Bill, get me answers. I want daily reports." The President turned to the Secretary. "I have a meeting with the Russian Ambassador. We'll talk later."

Bannistar and Van Clevenson stood and left the Oval Office. In the corridor Bannistar said to Van Clevenson, "That was a cheap shot about Sam. In the future, if you have an issue with one of my people, talk to me, not the President."

"Well, Bill…" Van Clevenson began, in a condescending tone. Bannistar walked away before he could finish.

Chapter 3

Kabul Airport
Sunday Morning

Libra inched the AK-47 to her lap. One of the guards in front of the truck stopped dead in his tracks. He pulled a walkie-talkie from his belt, put it to his ear, then started nodding furiously. He collapsed the phone, waved his arms, then shouted something to the other guards.

The guard said something to the driver of the first car waiting in line to clear security. The driver nodded, then pulled his vehicle to the side of the road. The second car, the one immediately in front of Libra, followed suit.

Libra turned her head away from the window as the two guards went running past the truck. She let out a long sigh. The guards didn't give her a second look. Libra checked the rear-view mirror. The two guards were climbing onto one of the jeeps behind her. Then, in unison, the jeeps made a U-turn and headed back down the highway.

The two cars in front of her started to move to the gate. Libra slipped her weapon to the floor of the truck. Two more hurdles, the guards at the security gate and getting on the plane.

The first car cleared the security gate. She watched as the second car cleared security as easily as the first. The guard was relaxed. She readied the old man's papers as she approached the gate. Then fate intervened: Another guard came out of the guardhouse, walked up to his companion and slapped him on the shoulder. The two men looked at each other, then broke into fits of laughter. Libra glanced at the old man's papers one last time.

One of the guards looked up. He gave the truck a long, hard stare. Libra's heart jumped to her throat. She reached down for the rifle. Suddenly, a loud explosion rocked the early morning quiet.

#

The clock on the mantel struck 7:00 as Sam cracked open another beer and looked at the documents on his coffee table. He reached for his remote and turned on CNN. His thoughts and emotions were in turmoil. Libra was missing and presumed dead, and he didn't have a clue as to where he would start picking up the pieces left by her contacts.

He turned on his home computer. Work would help shake the anxiety. *"In the mouth of the wolf."* Who the hell uses an expression like that? Somewhere in Europe. Shit! Werewolves, wolves, timber wolves, jackals... He ran his hand though his hair trying to think of a starting point. He sent an email to Research at Langley requesting information on the encrypted message, knowing full well that he would have to wait until morning before he got any kind of an answer. He opened his Encarta Encyclopedia and keyed in the word "wolf." A long menu danced down the left side of his monitor. The first country on the menu was Afghanistan. He double-clicked on the country's name only to learn that wolves were an endangered species in Afghanistan. *Shit...everything's an endangered species in that godforsaken country.*

He continued his search through European countries trying to find a reference to Libra's last transmission. Most countries in Europe had wolves and most of the wolves were making the endangered species list. He searched for another two hours, then fell asleep in front of the monitor just as it flashed on Italy.

# # #

It took the old man several minutes to move the dead guard from the back seat of Rham's Rover to the driver's seat. He reached in the back, then lugged the heavy gas can to the hood of the truck. He followed the woman's instructions to the letter. He dumped several gallons of the volatile petrol on the hood, then saturated the interior with what was left. He backed away, struck a match and threw it on the hood. Flames jumped into the dawning sky as he trotted to the cover of a large rock.

Five minutes later a military jeep came storming down the dirt road. The driver, one of Rham's soldiers, stood up, grabbing the windshield with both hands. His eyes bugged at the sight of Rham's Rover on fire. He picked up a cellular phone and barked something incomprehensible into it.

The old man watched as the flames leapt from the hood of Rham's Rover to the interior compartment. Within minutes, three more jeeps filled with Rham's soldiers showed up. The soldiers charged out of their vehicles and raced toward the burning vehicle. They arrived just as the flames ignited the gas tank.

The old man put a hand over his mouth to keep from laughing as the guards dove helter-skelter for cover as a spine-tingling explosion and bright orange flames filled the air. The old man could hardly contain his excitement; he silently clapped his hands and roared inwardly at the sight of Rham's bullies groveling for safety.

# # #

Libra pulled the sleeve of the old man's robe over her wrist and held the papers vertical to the window. If the guard forced her to look at him, she'd blow his head off.

"Get moving, old man, or I'll arrest you for interfering with official police business," the guard bellowed, then returned to his chatter with the other guard.

"Right away, you sanctimonious asshole!" Libra muttered under her breath. She hit the accelerator and headed for the terminal. She parked the truck, then put the keys with the rest of the twenty-dollar bills up under the visor. She grabbed the AK-47 and jumped to the ground. She slipped the gun under her robe.

She looked back at the guard shack and saw dark, oily smoke billowing into the predawn light. A smile crossed her lips, thinking about the old man—he had come through.

She figured she had about twenty more minutes before the guards discovered that the explosion was a red herring. When they realized that the body in the Rover was Rham's guard, they would be back at the airport looking for her with a vengeance.

Libra slumped over and trudged toward the terminal. She entered the building. It was packed with travelers waiting for the flight to Istanbul. Her watchful eyes panned the faces of the weary passengers, searching for a mark that would get her on the plane.

Afghanistan did not issue computerized airline tickets—there were no computers. The Russians took all the hardware with them when they left the country in 1989. To get a seat on a flight, one simply paid cash at the ticket counter, then received a blue plastic-coated boarding pass. The only thing standing between Libra and freedom was that pass.

The passengers were already lining up to present their passes to an agent in a wrinkled blue blazer and gray slacks, standing behind a podium.

A telephone buzzed. The agent turned, picked up the receiver and nodded copiously.

The agent hung up, then, in a loud voice, addressed the passengers standing in line. "Ladies and gentlemen, may I have your attention, please. Due to a mechanical difficulty, the flight to Istanbul has been delayed. I will inform you when the problem has been corrected."

Mechanical difficulty, my ass. Someone figured out it wasn't me roasting in Rham's Rover.

She moved slowly through a throng of milling passengers and approached the podium.

"Excuse me, sir," she said in a disguised voice. "Would you let an arthritic old man board the plane a little early?"

The agent ignored her as he impatiently sifted through a pile of official-looking documents. She repeated the question in her own voice.

The agent looked up, surprised. "You will have to wait your turn, just like…"

He didn't finish the sentence. Something jammed painfully into his rib cage. He looked down. An automatic weapon was pressed into his side.

"With a pleasant smile, you will nod your head and escort me to the plane. If you decide not to do what I ask, this weapon will blow your stomach halfway to Pakistan," Libra said in a polite but forceful voice as she looked into the agent's eyes with a cold stare.

The agent had an abrupt change of heart. He nodded nervously, forcing a ridiculous smile to his lips. He unlocked the ramp door and escorted Libra across the tarmac to a Boeing 727.

"Okay, up the stairs," Libra ordered the agent as they reached the rear boarding steps.

"But, sir, er, madam," he corrected himself, "I do not think…"

"Up the stairs," Libra ordered again, waving the gun under his nose.

The man frowned, then turned and climbed the stairs. Three shabbily dressed stewards snapped to attention when they saw the agent enter the cabin. Their eyes widened when they saw the armed figure behind him.

"The three of you—out of the plane, now! Move!" Libra barked.

The young men flew down the stairs. "Now," pointing the gun at the agent, "move to the cockpit."

The man did as he was told. Libra pushed the lever by the rear exit, raising the stairs. She followed the agent down the aisle.

When they reached the cockpit door, Libra ordered the man to knock and yell to the pilot that he had the paperwork for the flight, then retreat from the doorway.

He followed her instructions. The door was opened by the flight engineer.

"Back to your seat," Libra ordered the man, a savage look on her face.

The flight engineer spun on his heel and returned to his seat.

"Start the number one engine, now," she bellowed at the captain.

The captain, a seasoned veteran, started to say something, but thought better of it when he saw the determination in her eyes. The enormous gun she was pointing at his flight engineer convinced him that this was no time for negotiation. His trembling hand flipped a switch, starting a motor under the right wing.

The airport was suddenly flooded with light. Through the cockpit window Libra saw six heavily armed jeeps starting down the main runway from the far end of the field. "Damn-it-all! Get that engine started or your engineer is a dead man," she screamed at the pilot, thrusting the gun in the face of the skinny young man.

"Madam, I'm working as fast as I can," the captain argued with a cracking voice. "It will take a few moments for the first engine to start. Then it will take a few more minutes to start engine numbers two and three."

"I don't have a minute. I want this plane rolling as soon as number one kicks over," she screeched. Libra's eyes watched the oncoming jeeps with trepidation. "You see those soldiers coming down the runway? They could not care less about you and your crew. They'll blow us all to kingdom come if you let them get close enough."

The captain had an unsettling feeling in his stomach. The woman was right. Abdul Rham's men would not hesitate to blow up the plane to get what they wanted.

"You two," Libra yelled at the first officer and the flight engineer, "out of your seats, now."

The two men stripped off their headphones and jumped up.

"Get off the flight deck! Move! You, too," she barked at the agent.

The three men hastily retreated to the main cabin. Libra followed them, then pulled the lever on the main cabin door and pushed it open. "Get off the plane. Jump. Go on, move it," she ordered.

The first officer walked to the edge and froze when he looked down at the fifteen-foot drop to the tarmac. Libra jammed the butt of the weapon into his back. He landed on the asphalt with a sickening thud. The flight engineer, deciding that it was better to land on his feet than on his head, rushed past the woman and leaped into the air. The agent followed.

Just as Libra secured the door, she heard the whine of the number one engine. She hurried back to the cockpit, then jumped into the copilot's seat and put on the headset. "Take that runway," she ordered, pointing to a second runway in the opposite direction of the oncoming jeeps.

The pilot turned and looked at Libra with desperation in his eyes. "That's impossible. It is too short for this aircraft."

"If we use the main runway, Rham's men will blow us to bits. Unless you've got a better idea, I'd suggest you get moving."

Blood drained from the pilot's face as he pushed the throttles and headed for the shorter runway. Rham's guards were within thirty seconds of firing range.

The plane jolted forward as the number two engine engaged.

"How much runway does this thing need to get off the ground?" Libra demanded.

"At least nineteen hundred meters. This runway is only sixteen hundred meters," the pilot answered.

"Was the baggage loaded?"

"No."

"Fuel?"

"Yes, of course. We are carrying sixty-two thousand pounds, a full load."

"Look, you can make a straight approach. That'll give us a few more meters. Hit the throttles hard. Move it!"

The pilot shot a belabored look at Libra. "But the jet blast...the people in the terminal?"

"Fuck the people in the terminal. They're not stupid. They'll figure it out. Get moving!"

The number three engine turned over as the pilot rammed the throttles forward.

The 727 lurched forward, gradually picking up speed. Libra took one more glance at the oncoming jeeps. Flashes from the muzzles of their automatic weapons told her they had opened fire. She shuddered at the prospect of a bullet puncturing one of the fuel tanks. Sixty-two thousand pounds of fuel suddenly igniting could be pretty ugly.

As the plane barreled down the runway, the pilot started mumbling something in Arabic. His knuckles were white as he clutched the stick. "It is going to be very close," he blurted into the headset, switching to English. "We have used up half the runway. Our ground speed has to be 195 kilometers per hour before we can lift off."

Libra looked at the ground-speed indicator. *Shit, we're not going anywhere near fast enough.* Every muscle in her body tightened. The old 727 was vibrating badly from the stress.

The end of the runway was rapidly approaching. "Come on, baby, get up, get up."

The pilot jerked the stick toward his chest. The plane shuddered violently, then as if on command, it lifted from the tarmac. Sparks flew off the plane's tail as it dragged the runway. They cleared the runway with a meter to spare.

"That was a little close," Libra said as she slumped back in her seat. "Nice job. I didn't think we were going to make it."

The pilot turned his chubby, mustachioed face to Libra. "To say the very least, I had my doubts that this plane could perform beyond its specifications. Another testimony to your American Boeing plane builder."

Libra let out a short, hesitant laugh, partly from nervous tension and partly from relief.

"What's your name?" she asked.

"Mohammed."

"Call me Rebecca. You're not going to be on a short list for a promotion at Afghan Ariana."

"Oh, well, these days nothing is certain in Afghanistan. I had been thinking of flying for another carrier anyway. I guess, Madam Rebecca, that you just helped me make up my mind."

"You have family?"

"My wife was killed by a Russian mortar in 1987. We did not have children. And my parents died long ago."

"I'm sorry about your wife. And I'm sorry to put you through this. I may be able to help you when we get to Istanbul."

"You are an American?" It was more a statement than a question.

"Yes. I work for the government. I might be able to pull some strings for you. You are a damn good pilot. I doubt that there are many like you who could get this tank off a short runway the way you did."

"I would be thankful for anything you could do."

"Well, let's get to Turkey first. We're not out of the woods yet."

At thirty-three thousand feet Mohammed set a course for Turkey and switched on the automatic pilot. "Now, if you will excuse me for a few moments, madam, I must attend to some personal business." His face flushed a bright crimson.

"Where the hell do you think you're going?" Rebecca asked, surprised by the pilot's sudden burst of bravado.

The pilot didn't answer. He walked off the flight deck.

Then Rebecca realized that in all the excitement the pilot had lost control of his sphincter muscle.

Book Two

Chapter 1

Sorrento, Italy

High in the Apennine Mountains overlooking the Bay of Naples, Count Alfredo Montefusco steepled his bony fingers in front of his face as he listened intently to the woman sitting across his enormous oak desk. He glanced up at the pictures hanging on the walls of his lavish office—Churchill, Roosevelt, Stalin and Mussolini. They were either shaking his hand or had an arm around his shoulder. All of them were smiling broadly for the camera.

He nodded his approval as the woman, dressed in a tailored, light blue Cassini suit, rattled off profit and loss figures for the last quarter of his multidivisional corporation. Her round, full lips, high cheekbones and aristocratic nose reminded him of her mother, his wife of fifty years who had died two years earlier. The loss of his companion had been devastating. His slate-gray eyes watched adoringly as his hand-picked successor handed him a detailed spread sheet.

"And Afghanistan?"

The woman's crescent brown eyes lit up. "A gain of almost fifty-two million—measured in American dollars."

Alfredo Montefusco leaned back in his padded leather chair. "Do these figures include the last shipment?"

"No, Father. We will not have those numbers for another two weeks; however, we anticipate that the second shipment will be more profitable than the first."

"And our relationship with Signore Rham?"

Ramona Montefusco shrugged and gave her father a disgusted look. She considered the Afghan leader a mental eunuch.

"Good. Then I think it's time we considered the possibility of a hostile takeover of Signore Rham's operations," the Count said, rubbing a finger across his thin mustache. He was already processing his plan.

"You already have a strategy for this takeover?" she asked, playing along.

"Right now, our friend Signore Rham is vulnerable. I received news late this afternoon that the CIA has had a mole in his operations for the past two years…"

"How does that make him vulnerable?" Ramona interrupted.

A broad smile lightened the Count's face. "The agent was a woman."

Ramona understood the implications immediately. Rham would lose face among his generals, and, more significantly, among the terrorist leaders who sent people to his training camps. A CIA agent penetrating Rham's operation was bad enough, but a woman! Rham would become the laughingstock of Afghanistan.

"Did the agent learn that Tri-Color Industries now controls Rham's shipping lanes?" A hint of concern was evident in her voice.

The count thought for a moment. "Signore Rham has assured me that no one—and he emphasized 'no one'—knew of the new arrangement he made with us for his heroin shipments. However, I would like to think of myself as not being that much a fool to believe a man who was compromised by the Americans."

"And what of this woman? Did Rham eliminate her?"

"Unfortunately for all of us, no. She managed to escape. It will be important for us to learn how much this woman knows. She could be a liability."

Ramona thought in silence, a disturbing look on her face. "Is there anything else that I should know?" She sounded impatient.

"According to my sources in Washington, Rham lost his last two heroin shipments to the Americans. The CIA estimates that the street value of those shipments was two hundred million dollars. So Signore Rham will come under heavy scrutiny by his military and by his other distribution channels."

"And what do you have in mind?" she beamed, her impatience turning to excitement.

The Count smiled, then shrugged. "A rather simple plan to eliminate Signore Rham and take over his heroin production. I think that you can handle it as easily and as efficiently as you have handled similar situations." Training his lovely daughter to run the day-to-day operations of Tri-Color Industries had certainly paid off.

Ramona raised an eyebrow.

"It must appear that Rham is trying to further his cause in the jihad—his ridiculous holy war—by perpetrating acts of terrorism against Israel and the United States."

Ramona listened with fascination as he laid out more details of derailing the Afghan despot. She felt almost sexually aroused at the anticipation of the power she would enjoy by adding yet another sector to the corporation founded by her father more than fifty years ago.

"It must appear that Rham is responsible…"

A knock on the door interrupted him. "Yes. Please come in, Ronaldo."

The door swung open and a trim man dressed neatly in black and whte walked into the room. "Bernardo, sir. He is on the telephone. You asked me to interrupt you if he should call."

"Yes. Thank you, Ronaldo." The Count dismissed him with his eyes as he reached for the telephone. "Excuse me, my dear, this will only take a moment," he said to Ramona.

"Yes, Bernardo," he said, pressing a button and putting the receiver to his ear. He listened to an excited voice on the other end of the line. "Very good, Bernardo. And how long will it take to tunnel through the mud? I see. Very well. You will call me when you have reached the temple." He leaned forward, about to conclude the conversation, when his eyes narrowed and his brow furrowed. "And when will we know if it is authentic?" He listened to the response, biting his lower lip. "No. For now, do nothing. We will let them do the work. Call our people in Rome and instruct them that they are to keep an eye on the boy and the man, day and night. Report back to me the instant you know something."

Ramona patiently watched her father. She knew that the call had something to do with his interest in Roman antiquity. She found his hobby, or obsession, of unearthing Roman relics dull and counterproductive. Roman artifacts had nothing to do with the corporation's businesses—unless, of course, the stockholders considered the red ink that the company spilled supporting her father's expensive hobby.

It had taken Ramona many years to come to terms with her father. He had the manners of an Italian gentleman, yet he could be absolutely ruthless with an adversary. She had watched him order the deaths of his enemies without so much as a second thought. He considered political leaders self-serving, self-righteous liars. Yet he was a champion of Italy; he had practically built the National Archaeological Museum in Naples single-handedly with his generous contributions. He had negotiated with museums all over the world for the safe return of Roman artifacts and, in many instances, paid huge ransoms. In some cases, where museums refused to separate themselves from a Roman trophy, he resorted to other means, usually unpleasant, to ensure the return of what he considered Italian property.

The Count put down the telephone.

"Something important, Father?"

"Ah, yes, yes," he replied, not trying to hide his excitement. "I will spare you the details, my dear, but suffice it to say, I think we may have an opportunity to vastly increase the stockholders' value in the company. Perhaps this will change your thinking about my hobby, as you refer to it."

"If I may, Father, can you finish the outline for the Afghanistan project?" she asked.

"Of course. Please forgive my drifting. Here is what I have in mind…"

Chapter 2

Washington
Other than the flickering glows from the television screen and the computer monitor, darkness filled the study. Sam snored softly, his head resting on his folded arms. The ringing of a telephone burst through his alcoholic haze.

Sam blinked and shook his head. He reached for the phone.

"Yes."

"Sam. It's Bill. Turn on CNN, then get back to me." The line went dead.

"CNN? CNN? Shit, it's already on," he mumbled to himself.

Sam reached for the beer on the end table and drained what was left.

The blond anchorwoman was speaking. "We have just received word in our Atlanta studios that an Afghan Ariana plane was hijacked by a lone gunman late this afternoon, 6 A.M., Afghanistan time. For a full report, we go now to Sid Meekan, standing by in Istanbul."

Sam watched as the anchor was replaced by a map of Afghanistan, Iran, and Russia. An inset of Sid Meekan appeared on the map.

"At 6:15 this morning, a hijacker believed to be an American woman, disguised as an Afghan patriot, commandeered Afghan Ariana Flight 600 as it was about to board passengers for a flight to Istanbul. The woman's identity and her motive are not known at this time. Also, it's not clear if she's part of a terrorist plot…"

"What the hell…!" Sam shouted.

"The plane is being monitored by international tracking stations and is now over Iran." An arrow with a trailing dotted line from Kabul appeared on the screen and pointed at the center of Iran.

Sam jumped out of his chair and fumbled through a stack of newspapers piled on the worn couch. He tossed the papers to the floor and grabbed a cordless telephone that had been buried underneath. He punched in a number.

"Yes," came Control's laconic voice from Langley, Virginia.

Sam gave his clearance identification. "Put me through to Cen Ops."

A click registered in his ear as his call was transferred to Central Operations. "Yes," came a sterile male voice.

"What have you got on the Afghan Ariana hijacking?"

"Just watching it on CNN. Why? You know something we don't?"

Jesus, the best spy organization in the world and we're getting our information from Cable News Network. "That may be one of our agents! Transfer me to Golden at the Istanbul station."

Sam heard more clicks and pauses as the call bounced off a satellite miles above the earth. Sam paced the room. "Mr. Golden's office," came a young, male voice.

"This is Sam Harrison, Deputy Director. I need to speak to Brad right away. This is an emergency!" Sam looked at his watch. It was 1:10 A.M.—8:10 A.M. in Turkey. Brad was an early riser—he should be in his office.

"Stand by," came the official-sounding response.

"Sam. What's up?"

Sam recognized Golden's mellow voice. "Can you get the Air Force to escort the hijacked Afghan plane to Attaturk? I strongly suspect that the hijacker is one of our agents."

"I'll have to pull some strings. May take a while."

"Pull 'em fast. If the Iranians intercept her first, we're going to have an international mess on our hands."

"Hold the line." Golden put Sam on hold.

Sam felt his muscles tense up as he waited. He reached for his beer. It was empty. He tossed it at the wastepaper basket. The can hit the rim of the basket and clanked to the floor. Five minutes later Golden returned to the line.

"I'm still trying, Sam. Looks like it's going to take a while. Got some red tape problems with this one. I'll have to call in a few markers. You'll owe me big-time for this one, pal." He disconnected.

"Jesus," Sam uttered to the dead line, "everybody in the government is running around with both hands on their butts."

# # #

ROME

Mario Mignini dragged his foot along the roadway to balance his bicycle. He sped down the hill from Via dei Pilarra and turned right onto Via Nazionale in the heart of downtown. A small Fiat slammed on its brakes and swerved toward the oncoming traffic to avoid hitting him. The driver stuck his head out of the window and shouted. Mario looked back over his shoulder to see the man gesturing with his left hand. He laughed as he peddled on toward Trajan's Column.

He dismounted at the guardrail overlooking the ruins of the Forum. He hiked up his green book bag, then pulled it off his back and placed it gently on the ground.

He leaned the bike against the wall as he wiped his face with the bottom of his T-shirt.

Mario's eyes danced from worker to worker in the large, rectangular mall lined with massive Corinthian columns. There were only five people working, restoring the columns to their original color. A look of concern washed over his face. *There should be six workers! Where is she?*

A young woman with silky brown hair strolled into the Forum from one of the arcades directly below him. "Maria!" he shouted as he leaned over the railing.

Maria stopped, turned and looked up at Mario. She shielded her eyes with her hand. A smile flashed across her pretty face. She had high cheekbones and round, hazel eyes. "Hi, Mario. You're early today, my friend!"

Mario's heart fluttered. "What is your question today?" he asked.

"Who was the first Roman to have two names, a first name and a last name?" Her eyes sparkled as she watched Mario's reaction.

"Oh, that's an easy one. It was Scipio Afracanus," Mario answered with melodramatic disappointment.

"And how did he get the name?" Maria shot back with another smile.

"The name was given to him by the Senate because he defeated Hannibal on the plains of Zama, in Africa, in 202 B.C. By defeating Hannibal, Scipio rid Italy of their longtime menace. The Senate, to show its gratitude, gave Scipio the name of the country where he defeated the Carthaginian general."

"Very good, Mario. You amaze me with your knowledge of Roman antiquity."

"Next time, make the question harder, okay, Maria?" he asked with a puppy-dog look.

She laughed. Mario was smitten by her happy eyes and her friendly demeanor. In his seventeen years, she was the prettiest woman he had ever seen.

"I brought an extra bottle of soda for my break today, Mario. Would you like to come down and join me? I'll introduce you to my colleagues, who are also experts on ancient Rome."

Mario's heart raced and his eyes widened. It was the first time Maria had invited him into the Forum. "Yes, yes. I…I would like that very much," he stammered. Then his face flushed with disappointment. "Oh, I can't. I almost forgot—I have to meet someone on the Palatine in just a little while."

"Where is that brother of yours that you talk so much about?" Maria probed, not wanting to let her new friend get away so easily.

"You mean Figlio? He is at catechism lessons. Today is his second-to-last day. Well, I must go now, but I will see you Monday, Maria." Mario waved, swung his bag over his shoulders and peddled toward the Victor Emanuel Monument with its towering pillars.

He whistled as he wove between the long line of stalled cars on the Via dei Fori Imperiali. He looked up to see shimmering waves of heat rising from the Colosseum.

He turned right at the Temple of Augustus and coasted to the entrance of the ancient Roman Forum. He jumped off and chained the bicycle to a rack. He sprinted through the guardhouse that served as the entrance to the ruins, ignoring the ticket agent.

Mario was well known to the employees at the Forum. He had shown up so frequently over the years that they started to wonder if he had come with the property. When they learned that he was training the new tour guides on the history of the site, they stopped charging him admission.

Mario strolled to the decaying stone walkway that once served as the main thoroughfare of ancient Rome and waved at a guard. He jogged right at the Arch of Titus, then climbed the steep walkway that led to the summit of the Palatine, the Palladium, home of the emperors.

Sitting on a park bench adjacent to the Farnese Garden, a lean, muscular man with chestnut-brown hair dropped a cigarette to the ground and stubbed it out under a Gucci loafer. He looked up to see Mario walking in his direction. A crooked, sardonic smile crossed his lips as he nodded at the boy.

Mario approached cautiously and asked, "You are the *tambarolo?*"

The man nodded and looked casually in the opposite direction. Satisfied that nobody was within earshot, he removed his dark sunglasses and looked up at Mario.

"Come, Mario," he said in a falsetto voice. "Sit here next to me."

Mario took a deep breath, hoping he did not appear nervous. He looked around the gardens, trying to avoid unnecessary eye contact.

"You have brought the item that we discussed on the telephone?" the man asked pleasantly.

"Yes. It's in my bag," Mario answered with a stern look. He had practiced in the mirror for over an hour the night before. He did not want to give the impression that he was a novice at this sort of thing. "And you brought the money?"

"Here." The man reached down under the bench and pulled up a book bag identical to the one Mario had on his back. "Inside, there's an envelope. Count it."

Mario's eyes widened as he slipped the envelope from the bag and counted ten crisp one-hundred-thousand-lira notes. He tried to stop his hand from trembling as he thumbed through the money, but it was no use. He had never seen this much money.

Mario handed his bag to the man, who lifted the flap to see a dried, cracked sheepskin scroll. A badly damaged wooden handle protruded from the end. The man quickly closed the flap and nervously looked around.

"When can I get the rest of the money?" Mario asked in his best negotiator's tone.

"Mario, Mario," said the man, with a smile. "You must trust me. This is my business. Without friends like you, I could not survive. Please, consider that we are partners."

Mario was swayed by the man's friendly approach; his eyes were bold and honest and his face reflected a sense of genuineness. Mario wanted to trust him, but his inner signals flashed a warning: *How do I trust a smuggler?*

"Meet me here tomorrow at the same time. If, as you say, the article is genuine, I will bring the rest of the money. And you, my young friend, bring more like this one and you will have all the money you need." The man put his sunglasses on, pulled them to the tip of his nose and gave Mario a condescending look.

"Okay," Mario said, his voice cracking.

Mario stood up, grabbing the bag with the envelope. He slung it over his shoulder and walked briskly down the Clivus Capitolinus, the ancient tunnel made of brick and mortar built by the early Romans as a passageway to the Forum. Was he betraying his beloved Eternal City? Or was he simply doing what he had to do to survive in an unforgiving world that had made orphans of him and his brother?

Mario found himself at the steps leading to the temple of another orphan—Romulus, the founder of Rome. His body trembled with shame. *Forgive me, Romulus. On the very spot where you and Remus founded the City, I betrayed you.*

#

The Ghetto

"*Boungiorno*, Mario. Are you going to work the summer?" asked the woman on the front steps. She was holding a small baby.

Mario shrugged. "I don't know yet, Signora Antonioni. There are not many jobs available." He hiked past the woman and up the stairs of the dilapidated apartment building. He jogged up three flights, then shoved a key in the door on the third-floor landing.

"Did you get it?" Figlio asked as Mario closed the door behind him.

"Yes." Mario pulled the bag off his back and removed the envelope. He set it on the table.

Figlio's eyes widened as he counted the notes. "Mario, this is a lot of money! When will you get the rest?"

"Tomorrow afternoon. They want to test the manuscript to see if it is real," Mario answered as he slumped into a chair.

"What are we going to do with all this money?"

"Put it in a bank."

"Huh?" Figlio was bewildered.

"This money is for our future. You want to spend the rest of your life being poor? I'm going to open savings accounts for you and me. Half the money will go into each account."

"Oh," Figlio responded with a disappointed look.

"How is your leg?"

"It itches, and you made the bandage too tight. How many more scrolls are there?"

"There are ninety-eight books still missing. They have to be near the ones I found last week. I am going down there again to look for them when it's safe," Mario responded wearily. "If I can find the rest of them, we will have plenty of money."

"Oh," Figlio answered. He trusted Mario implicitly. When his older brother set out to do something, he didn't quit until it was accomplished. "So when will you go get the rest of the scrolls?"

"After I get the rest of the money from the *tambarolo*. And when things die down in the Forum. The police are watching the place because of the men who tried to kill us. Did you notice anybody unusual hanging around?"

"No. I haven't seen anybody that looks suspicious. You think we should find another place to live for a while?"

"I don't know. I'm not sure what to do. But I know one thing—I don't want to run into any more people like we did on the Palatine."

Chapter 3

Somewhere Over Iran

"We are entering Iranian airspace, madam," the pilot said to Libra. "This could be risky. The Iranians do not think much of Afghanistan. If they know this is a hijacking, it would give them extreme pleasure to take us into their control."

"Look, we've made it this far. We'll make it the rest of the way."

"What's the plan when we get to Istanbul?"

"There's an Air Force base outside Istanbul, Incurcik. We'll land there. How's the fuel holding out?"

"The fuel is good. The headwinds favor us. We will have no problem reaching Turkey."

Libra could see the Iranian desert through the cloudless sky. She had ordered the pilot to maintain radio silence since taking off from Kabul. She figured the world would know by now the plane was hijacked. She didn't want to make radio contact that might let others know she was a CIA operative. She'd let the media do her work for her.

The pilot's voice broke into her thoughts. "Fighter jets, at two o'clock. They are Chinese-made Jian 7s, the equivalent of the Russian MIGs."

"Are they Iraqi or Iranian?" Libra asked.

"Iranian."

The fighters pulled alongside the 727. The pilot of the lead plane signaled for them to follow.

"What do you think?" Libra asked.

"I do not know," the pilot responded. "But I will hold this course. Maybe they will warn us before they start shooting."

"What a comforting thought." She raised her middle finger at the Iranian pilot.

The Iranian fighter pilot broke into their frequency. "Afghan Ariana. You are invading Iranian airspace. We know you are commandeered. We are informing you that you are now property of the Iranian People's Republic. You will follow us to Tehran, where you will not be harmed. I am to assure you that the Iranian government will provide for your safety."

"Yeah, right!" Libra blurted. She turned to the pilot. "Stall the son of a bitch. We should have help soon. Our side is not going to want an international incident."

The captain shot her an uneasy glance. He thought for a few moments before he answered the Iranian fighter pilot. "The hijacker has an explosive device. He has threatened to blow up the plane if I comply with your orders."

"You've been through this before?" Libra asked with a smirk. "Besides, what's this about a man holding an explosive device?"

The pilot shrugged.

There was a long pause while the Iranians tried to figure out how to respond.

"They are checking with their superiors. They will probably threaten to shoot us down, but if they know that you are an American, they may hesitate."

Finally, the Iranian pilot broke in: "We have orders to shoot you down if you do not follow us. I repeat: We will shoot you down if you do not comply with our demands."

"He's bluffing," Libra said. "Tell him you'd rather take your chances with me."

The pilot took a deep breath, then switched on the frequency. "My captor, an American, has informed me that he will die for the glory of Allah and the jihad before he will permit you to even get into position to fire your weapons."

"I hope they believe it," the pilot said to Libra in a doubtful tone.

"They will. They train plenty of their own terrorists. To die for the jihad is an honor."

There was another period of dead air.

The pilot started to chuckle.

"What's so funny?"

"I have to laugh—those Iranians do not know that they are being tricked by a woman."

Suddenly the Iranian fighters peeled off. In the distance Libra could see two black specks coming toward them.

"They are probably getting into position to launch a rocket," said the pilot, perspiration breaking out on his forehead.

Just then two American F-16 fighter planes roared over them. The Iranian MIGs had peeled off to the south. The F-16s pulled alongside. A friendly voice with a deep Southern drawl came over the radio: "This is Colonel James S. Frank at your service, ma'am. If you'd kindly follow us, we have a warm reception waiting for you at Incurcik Air Force Base." The pilot saluted smartly through the windshield.

"I can't believe it," Libra said, returning the American's salute with a friendly wave. Tears came to her eyes. For the first time in almost three years, she started sobbing.

#

KABUL
SUNDAY AFTERNOON

The room was deathly quiet. Abdul Rham bent over the Formica-topped table, face buried in his hands. He tried to calm his rage. He had just ordered three of his guards shot for their miserable attempt at finding the woman who had been his mistress. He looked up at his captain of the guards, Ali Mohammidi.

"Do we know who she was?" Rham asked with a scowl.

A knot formed in Mohammidi's stomach. He was terrified. When he answered, would he too face the firing squad? Mohammidi considered lying, but he couldn't think of a lie that his leader might believe.

"An agent of the United States, a CIA operative, Your Excellency." Mohammidi tried to control his shaking hands.

Rham let out a long sigh. He knew his days as the most powerful mullah in Afghanistan were numbered.

"You, as captain of the guards, were in charge of security. Were you not?"

Mohammidi nodded, his eyes bulging.

"And you only found out this day that the woman was a CIA agent?"

"Yes, Excellency. She had us all fooled. I conducted a thorough background check on her shortly after she moved in, just as you requested. Even our allies confirmed that the woman was a journalist." Mohammidi relaxed a bit. Rham would remember his painstaking work.

Rham pointed a finger at Mohammidi. He tried to speak, but the fury in his chest cut off the words. He reached for the Glock .38 holstered at his side.

Mohammidi didn't dare speak.

Rham sat in silence for over a minute, then emptied the pistol's chamber into his captain of the guards.

Chapter 4

Palatine Hill
Monday Morning

"Hurry up, honey. The kids are starving and my legs are killing me." The American stood between her two daughters at the north end of the Farnese Garden.

"Just one more shot of you and the kids with the Forum in the background. It's such a clear morning, might as well take advantage of it," retorted the small, wiry man as he focused his Nikon camera. "Okay, smile…say c-h-e-e-s-e!"

The younger daughter leaned against her mother and smiled. The older daughter, disgusted, forced herself to smile. The man snapped the picture, then pulled a red bandanna from his pocket and wiped his bald head.

"Okay, let's get some chow. Sweetie, why don't you go on ahead with the kids. I want to get some shots of the Forum. I'll catch up to you. Won't take but a minute."

The woman was only too happy to oblige. She whisked her daughters toward the exit.

The man removed the film from the camera and replaced it with a roll of high-speed, high-density Kodachrome. He twisted off the 35mm lens and replaced it with a long, high-powered telescopic lens, then expertly attached an automatic winder. He walked to the edge of the sixteenth-century portal and posed as if to shoot the buildings in the Roman Forum. Then he abruptly spun to his right and raised the camera: *Click, click, click, click, click.*

In less than two minutes he had close-up photographs of a boy and a man exchanging green book bags.

The American removed the film, detached the telescopic lens and winder and slipped them into a leather carrying case. He snapped the 35mm lens back in place, then walked out of the portal past the man and boy sitting on a park bench.

"Did you get your pictures?" his wife asked when he reached them at the exit.

"Yep. Sure did. Good day for shooting."

# # #

OVER SOUTHERN FRANCE
MONDAY AFTERNOON

"Ladies and gentlemen, this is your captain speaking. In a few minutes we'll be passing over the Swiss Alps. There have been reports of heavy turbulence in the area, so we'd like to ask that you return to your seats and fasten your seat belts. According to the computers here on the flight deck, we should arrive in Tel Aviv at six-thirty local time. We'll try to keep the flight as smooth as possible for you, so please, lean back and enjoy the ride. Thank you for flying with El Al." The captain replaced the microphone.

"Captain, we have a fire in engine three," the co-pilot said in a calm, steady voice.

The captain, through years of training, didn't even think; he instinctively shut down number three engine and engaged the automatic fire extinguisher.

"Negative, captain. It's not working. We still have fire."

"Shut down number four and close all fuel lines," the captain ordered the young co-pilot, whose tanned face had turned ashen. The captain's pulse rate doubled. He looked at the fuel gauge; over 300,000 pounds of highly volatile kerosene filled the three tanks of the Boeing 747-400.

"Mayday. Mayday. This is El Al Zero-Zero-Five-Seven Heavy, we have a problem."

"Geneva tracking. Go ahead, El Al Zero-Zero-Five-Seven Heavy."

"We've got a fire in our number three engine. Request emergency landing instructions for the nearest runway."

"Standby, El Al," the voice of the Geneva tracking station controller announced as he watched the green blip that represented El Al Flight 0057 begin flashing, indicating that there was an emergency in progress.

The controller cleared all the traffic near the El Al plane. He summoned his supervisor, standing at an adjacent computer screen.

Ten seconds later the controller was back to the captain. "El Al Zero-Zero-Five-Seven Heavy, nearest landing is Geneva International. Turn to vector Two-Niner-Seven and descend at your discretion. We currently have you passing through thirty thousand over Salins-les-Bains, France. Copy?"

"El Al turning to vector Two-Niner-Seven. Estimate direct approach in twenty-five minutes. Please have emergency equipment standing by."

"Affirmative, emergency equipment now rolling. Will advise runway number momentarily."

The captain turned to the first officer, "Start dumping fuel on the port side. We're too heavy to land. Also, tell the flight attendants to prepare the passengers for an emergency landing."

The captain picked up the microphone. "Ladies and gentlemen, our number three engine has quit on us, so we're making an intermittent landing in Geneva, Switzerland. There's no need for alarm; this aircraft was designed to fly on three engines. We apologize for the inconvenience. Please pay close attention to the flight attendants, who will instruct you in emergency landing procedures."

"El Al Zero-Zero-Five-Seven Heavy, we have you at twenty-two thousand feet, nineteen minutes to touchdown," the controller's even voice echoed in the captain's ears.

"Copy that. We're still on fire. Extinguishers not working. Repeat: still on fire, extinguishers not working," the captain said in a matter-of-fact tone.

The ground controller shot a worried look at his supervisor, who was monitoring the situation over his shoulder. "Tell them to use runway Two-Niner," the supervisor said, unmistakable angst in his voice. "That'll give them plenty of rolling room once they're on the ground."

"Where did Zero-Zero-Five-Seven originate?"

"Amsterdam," came the reply.

"She's going to be heavy with all that fuel. Even if she manages to dump, she's going to have plenty left over. I'll get emergency on runway Two-Niner."

The controller adjusted his microphone. "El Al Zero-Zero-Five-Seven Heavy, approach runway Two-Niner, from south. Turn to vector…" The controller stopped in midsentence. The blip representing the Boeing 747-400 had disappeared from his screen.

"El Al, do you copy?"

No answer.

"Say again, do you copy El Al Zero-Zero-Five-Seven Heavy?"

No answer.

"How many people on the plane?" the supervisor asked.

"Over three hundred…"

#

INCURCIK AIR FORCE BASE
OUTSIDE ISTANBUL, TURKEY
MONDAY EVENING

Libra awoke rigid and sweating, hair matted to her face. She looked around at the unfamiliar surroundings. A sparsely furnished room; furniture that looked as if it had been purchased at a garage sale. Then she remembered. She let out a sigh.

She had had the recurring dream again; he was sticking the needle in his arm, his eyes were rolling up inside his head as if he were about to die; his body was going into convulsions. He looked up at her and slurred her name, spittle coming out the side of his mouth. It was grotesque. His clothes stank—he had not bathed in days.

She shook the images from her head. Footsteps started tapping on the linoleum floor, coming down the hallway. She saw the silhouette of a man on the other side of the frosted glass door. The door swung open. A familiar face.

"Well, it looks like you're no worse for wear," Sam Harrison said with a smile as he approached her bed.

"Jesus. What the hell are you…"

"We got the news late last night," Sam interrupted. "I called Golden right away. He somehow managed to persuade the Air Force to escort you back here. Glad to have you back in one piece."

"It's good to be back…in one piece," she answered with liquid eyes. She reached out and pulled Sam to her. They embraced for several moments. Finally, Sam pulled away, embarrassed. He turned the conversation to Rham.

"I need to ask you some questions about Rham. We've got reports of heroin coming into the United States. The President is on Bannistar's case to determine the origin. Both he and Bannistar think it's coming from Afghanistan. Can you shed any light on the subject?"

Libra paused. "Not really. Ever since you picked off his last two shipments, Rham tightened security. He wouldn't even let his top lieutenants in on his new routes."

"New routes?"

"Yeah. He started testing the new routes shortly before the last shipments were intercepted—the shipments that normally went through Iran and Russia. He'd been pretty loose with his information up to that point. That's why Apollo was able to get the word out, but it cost him his life. I still don't know what happened to him."

"Any idea what the routes are, and who the new mules are?"

"No, not for sure. He's not shipping the dope through Pakistan—it's too difficult to get it through the Khyber Pass. The Pakistanis wouldn't allow it. But right off the top of my head, I can't think of anything."

"Think back. Is there anything—anything at all—that you can remember that might indicate who's smuggling the heroin?"

Libra paused, her eyes narrowed in concentration. Finally, she shook her head. "Right now, it's hard for me to focus. Too much has happened the past twenty-four hours. Sorry, Sam, but my mind's a little sluggish."

Sam changed direction. "Did our taking Rham's last two shipments hurt him at all?"

"Hardly. Rham's got an endless supply of poppy fields, cheap labor and very little overhead. His biggest expense is transportation. Losing two shipments didn't put a dent in his pocketbook. Right now, his biggest concern is establishing new lanes to Europe and America."

"What about his training camps?"

"Very intense, and business is booming. He's operating twenty facilities simultaneously. His clientele comes from all over the world—South America, Egypt, Russian spin-off countries, even the United States. I'm concerned, Sam. Those terrorists could do a lot of damage. Like the World Trade Center bombing a few years ago and the embassies in Africa."

Sam's throat went dry. Rham's camps had been financed, in part, by the CIA and Saudi Arabia, when America was supporting the Afghan rebels against the Russians in the 1980s. Now the poison winds were blowing back in their faces; Afghanistan was using American hardware to train terrorists to attack American interests.

"Why don't we continue this over dinner?" Sam asked.

Libra hadn't eaten in over twenty-four hours. "I'll take you up on that. I could use some decent clothes, too. The only thing they had for me to wear is an Air Force uniform. Oh, Jesus, Sam, I almost forgot—what happened to the pilot?"

"We're working on that. Needless to say, they'd lynch him if he ever showed his face in Afghanistan. I don't think he'll have a problem finding another job. Anybody that can take a thirty-year-old 727 off a five-thousand-foot runway shouldn't be out of work for too long."

Libra pulled herself out of the bed. "See if you can find me some decent clothes, will you?"

"Oh, one last question. Apollo's last transmission was in some kind of code. We were able to understand the meaning—that is, that you were compromised. But I think he was trying to tell us something with the words."

"What did the transmission say?"

"'In the mouth of the wolf.'"

Libra cocked her head in thought. "I don't have a clue what he meant. But I agree with you that he was trying to tell us something about the location of Rham's new distribution routes. You have Langley check it out?"

"Yeah. They came up empty, too. I thought you might have an idea of what it means because of all the languages you speak."

"Sorry. Doesn't ring a bell."

"I'll see what I can do about getting you something better than an Air Force uniform."

# # #

Kabul

Monday Afternoon

A sleek Gulf Stream jet with green, yellow and white markings glided toward its final approach at Kabul International Airport. The plane landed on the main runway, then taxied to a private hangar to the west of the main terminal. A tall, well-built man with a ponytail strutted off the plane's steps carrying an olive-green duffel bag.

"Bernardo?" a lanky, bearded man toting an automatic rifle on his shoulder called out.

Bernardo gave the man a quick nod. He was escorted to a waiting black Rover and whisked away. Thirty minutes later he was walking up the circular staircase in Abdul Rham's palace.

Rham stood to greet the athletic figure, a translator standing at his side.

"Shall we get right to business?" Bernardo asked, his voice dry and precise.

Rham nodded with hard, cold eyes.

Bernardo set the oversized bag on Rham's desk. He pulled the zipper down the long side, revealing piles of neatly wrapped twenty-dollar bills. "A small down payment and demonstration of good faith for the next shipment."

Rham snapped his fingers. An aide lifted the bag off the desk and disappeared into an adjoining room.

"As you know, the American government has had uncharacteristically good luck the past two years; their drug enforcement agencies have limited the amount of narcotics flowing into the country. My employer has devised a plan to change that; to disrupt the American government in a way that will enable us to increase our market penetration in America and in Europe. The plan will be of enormous benefit to you." Bernardo gave Rham a calculated look.

Rham's granite face was stern. "What is this plan?"

"It calls for you, through your training camps, to play an important role in creating a conflict between the United States and their ally, Israel. With your well-trained terrorists, you will further your cause in the jihad."

Rham dropped his military demeanor as he listened to the Italian describe the plan. He could see his credibility restored and his cause gaining momentum. But Rham wondered if the Italians knew how desperate he was for cash. The drug shipments the Americans had seized badly strained his cash flow, primarily because he had been siphoning off most of the profits from earlier shipments to fatten his Swiss bank account. He wondered how the Italians could have found out, especially since he had done such a good job conning his people into believing that the lost shipments were a mere inconvenience.

Twenty-five minutes later Bernardo concluded his presentation. "In addition to the plan I just laid out for you, Your Excellency, another diversion should be mounted in several major cities in the United States. We will leave the details to you, as this is your business. My employer is ready to reward you with an additional payment of…" Bernardo scratched a number on a small notepad and handed it to Rham.

Rham looked at the number and tried to appear indifferent, but his eyes betrayed him. "I will accept your offer," he said in his best autocratic tone as he extended his hand to Bernardo.

Bernardo gave a sardonic smile as he took the Afghan leader's hand. Ramona Montefusco would be pleased that Rham had taken the bait; the pompous ass had walked right into her trap. The Montefuscos had been right; the Afghan was desperate. He was also an imbecile. Bernardo shook his head, wondering how such a jackass ever managed to gain control of a country.

# # #

Sorrento
Monday Afternoon

The phone buzzed. Count Montefusco looked up from his work and reached for the receiver.

"Yes."

"The manuscript is authentic," came the voice in Italian with a heavy American accent. "The boy transferred it to the *tambarolo* about half an hour ago. What are your instructions?"

The Count leaned back in his chair, smiling. "For now, follow the boy. He will lead us to the rest of the missing manuscripts. Once you have found where they are hidden, make sure the boy is not able to tell anyone else. As for the *tambarolo*, follow him to see where he sells it. We may find even more treasures. Once you learn the identity of the buyer, terminate the smuggler and return the scrolls to Rome."

"Very well." The line went dead.

The Count leaned back in his chair, stroking his chin. This was indeed a magnificent find, right where the world would least suspect, yet right where they should be. When the boy led them to the rest of the documents it would be a major victory for Italy. He would demonstrate to the world that his nation's heritage was not to be treated with indignity.

They are fools, all of them.

CHAPTER 5

INCURCIK AIR FORCE BASE
MONDAY EVENING

"I just learned that Rham has put a half-million-dollar bounty on your head," Sam said. He looked up from his legal pad to see Libra putting down a tray filled with eggs, toast and greasy potatoes.

"Cheap bastard. I should fetch double that!"

"It's still a big enough number to attract the attention of some noteworthy hit men. You're going to have to lie low for a while."

"How'd you find out?"

"I just got off the phone with Control. Bannistar left the message. Who knows where he got the information. Probably CNN."

"So, what's our next move?"

"Not sure. Right now I need to ask you some questions about Rham. You up for it?"

"I think so. My mind's cleared a bit. The shower helped," she replied as she flicked a spec of lint off the freshly starched Air Force blouse. "Don't suppose you found a place that would deliver a size six dress?"

"Not at this hour. The stores are all closed. We'll get something in the morning."

"Jesus, it feels like morning. How long was I asleep?"

"About twelve hours, according to Golden. Must have been all the excitement."

"Back to Rham." Libra shoveled a forkful of eggs into her mouth.

"Why don't you start with everything that happened to you for the past couple of weeks. Don't leave anything out, no matter how trivial it may seem to you."

Libra shrugged. "Okay. Let's start with Rham's activities after you guys bagged his last two drug shipments."

Sam nodded.

"Things started to get icy. I wasn't sure if he was on to me or if he was concerned about losing his routes. The prospect of setting up new routes had to be unnerving. Our conversations were perfunctory; meaningless to the point of why-even-bother. There was one thing for sure: he suddenly came up with a major dose of lockjaw. That's unusual for him, since he's normally verbose, especially about his drug operations. Every night at dinner he'd blabber on about how he was outsmarting the world's drug police."

"Was he still buying your cover at this point?"

"I think he wanted to believe I was who I said I was, but he was starting to question it. If it hadn't been for the planted stories, I would have been a suspect long before I was."

"So you'd extract information from Rham at the end of the day. How much of it was believable?"

"Well, after separating his macho bullshit from reality, most of what he'd tell me was plausible. I'd check out the information as best I could, but my capacity to do any serious snooping was limited, for obvious reasons. The stuff that checked out, I'd pass on to Apollo, who I presume got it back to Washington."

Sam nodded gravely, thinking of Apollo's fate. "So, go on…"

"As I said, things were getting pretty chilly between the two of us. We'd sit at his table just staring at each other."

"What was Rham's reaction to the two intercepted shipments?"

"He was furious, but his anger was misdirected. He thought the Iranians or the Russians hijacked them, so I was off the hook, at least for the time being."

Sam shot Libra a crooked smile. "That was one of our better moves: disguising the pirates as Russians."

"Rham raised hell with his contacts in Iran and Russia for two full days. They finally got it into his thick head that they weren't the ones responsible for stealing his heroin, but he still doubted the Russians. He harbors a lot of resentment toward them for what they did to Afghanistan. Nevertheless, he started to think that he may have a leak inside his own company. That's when everybody became suspect." Libra took a long sip of the lukewarm coffee.

"That's when he started to consider you a mole?"

"Again, I'm not positive. He'd always had his own spies within the guards, but he never really relied on them up to this point. With the shipments compromised, he started to lean on them. He had his lieutenants scrutinized; shook up the processing plants; had a couple of soldiers shot; then replaced his Commander of the Guards. Had the poor bastard tortured, then shot. With that kind of scrutiny, you know he had to be thinking that I might not be who I said I was."

"Any ideas on the last transmission from Apollo? The message 'In the mouth of the wolf'?"

Libra thought for a few moments. "No, not really. I thought about it and I agree that he was trying to tell you something, but it sounds by the tone of the transmission that he was not certain that it would get to you, so he tried to disguise the message. He probably knew he was being watched."

"I suspect that he was on to the new distributor and was trying to tell us who he is."

Sam paused for a minute, thinking of his next line of questioning. He dreaded what he was about to ask, but he had to put his feelings.

"What about the intimate part of your relationship?" Sam wasn't sure he really wanted to know the answer.

"If you mean, did I get any information from him while I was sleeping with him, the answer is no," Libra declared defensively. Her stomach tightened at the memory of lying next to the repugnant man.

"I'm sorry," Sam offered, "but I needed to ask."

"No need to apologize. I can understand how you feel. It's painful for me to talk about it. You know why I chose to get involved with Rham, but let's not go into that now."

Sam didn't know what else to say. The silence made Libra uncomfortable.

"For what it's worth, I can't remember a two-year stretch when I had more headaches than I did the last two years," she added with a dry smile.

"Thanks. Well, let's go back to the new routes you mentioned earlier," Sam said, avoiding Libra's eyes. "That may be the place to focus our energy."

"I agree, but there's not much to tell you that you don't already know."

"How did you find out about them in the first place? The new routes, that is."

"Dumb luck. I walked into Rham's office late one afternoon and I caught him in one of his rare good moods. He had been talking on the phone to somebody—I was afraid to ask who—and I overheard him say that the two lost shipments were temporary. He had found another source; a 'better mule,' as he put it, to get the heroin to America and Europe. This 'mule' had the capacity to handle every bit as much as the Iranians and Russians."

"You remember any names?"

"If I heard a name, I would have remembered it. All I got was the tail end of the conversation. I remember walking into his office just as it ended. I was afraid he knew that I overheard him. But then we started talking and he never brought it up."

Sam jotted down more notes on the legal pad. "Jesus, I feel like we've covered everything, but we're coming up empty."

"So what do you do for fun in this town?" Libra asked with a wide grin. "I haven't had a night out in years. What do you say we go to Istanbul and do some touristy things?"

"Dressed like that?" Sam gave Libra's Air Force uniform a look. "Besides, there's bound to be a hit man lurking in the shadows, just begging for you to show your face. That half-million Rham has on your head scares me."

"Oh, screw 'em, Sam! Jesus, after two years in Afghanistan and a rather nasty escape from Rham's palace, a night on the town is nothing. I'm willing to risk it. What do you say?"

Sam put his pencil down gently and thought for a moment. "Tell you what, I'll split the difference. How's about we sneak out of here and go for a walk through the Blue Mosque? At least that way you won't be as easy a target as you would be downtown."

"Sounds good to me," Libra responded with new-found energy. "I'd just as soon forget Afghanistan ever happened. By the way, how's your recovery going?"

Sam hesitated. "I had a slip a couple days ago. It's a struggle."

"What happened?"

"It's a long story. I'll fill you in tonight."

"You okay with going into town and not drinking?"

"If you'll be my parole officer, I think I can risk it."

# # #

Istanbul

The military-issue car, an old Dodge, stopped at the entrance to the Blue Mosque. The four spires at the corners of the Mosque gleamed in the spotlights against the clear starlit sky.

Sam and Libra walked the perimeter. The dark waters of the Sea of Marmara reflected the moon's pale light in the distance below. A luxury liner sat in the harbor, its running lights bouncing off the water. The couple walked arm-in-arm across the garden path leading away from the Mosque, the warm breeze lifting Libra's spirits.

"If somebody told me two days ago that I'd be looking at this magnificent view, I would have said they were nuts."

"I can imagine," Sam said. "Any regrets?"

"I don't know if I'd call them regrets, but it's something that I certainly never want to repeat. There were more times than I care to admit when I asked myself why I was there in the first place."

"Why did you do it? You didn't have to, you know."

"I'm not sure, Sam..."

"Your reasoning at the time was that you wanted to get the drug dealer responsible for killing your brother," Sam said gently.

Libra felt her spine stiffen; clouds of sadness washed across her face. "Yes. I wanted to avenge Chet's death."

"Chet was your oldest brother?"

"Yes, my only brother. There were just the two of us. He always looked out for me; kept me out of harm's way. He died from an overdose of heroin in his senior year at Boston College. I still have horrible nightmares about it. I remember telling myself that I would track down the bastards responsible for manufacturing the heroin, and the son of a bitch who beat him up and injected him. I wanted to kill all of them." Libra felt a tightness in her throat; tears welled in the corner of her eyes.

"Sorry. I didn't mean to open an old wound."

"No reason to apologize. It helps to talk about it."

"How did he get hooked?"

Libra thought for a moment, not sure how much of Chet's story to reveal. "I never told you this, Sam, but on my seventeenth birthday an intruder broke into our house. Thanks to Chet, I was spared. But the guy loaded Chet up with heroin, then kidnapped him. He took Chet to New York and forced him to deal drugs. It took the police six months to find him in some crummy section of Queens. The bastards that took Chet turned him into a junkie."

"You weren't able to rehabilitate him?"

"We tried. God, he was in so many treatment programs. Unfortunately, none of them stuck. He'd get out of one program, stay clean for six months, then he'd be back on the junk."

"I'm sorry."

"Thanks," Libra replied, her arms crossed and eyes on the ground. "I vowed the day he died that I would do everything in my power to fight the drug pushers."

"Well, you've done yeoman's duty. You mind if I change the subject?"

"Not at all. Thanks for listening. What's your next question? Probably something about Rham."

"Why didn't you kill him—Rham, I mean. Why didn't you kill Rham?"

Libra thought for a moment. "I almost did. Yesterday. I had the opportunity, but then I figured he was my insurance policy, so I decided not to."

"What do you mean?"

"If one of the guards had stopped me trying to escape and found Rham dead, they would have killed me instantly. If I did get caught, and Rham was alive, I'd deny that I was trying to flee the palace. They wouldn't have dared harm me; I was Rham's woman."

Another pause. They walked silently across a marble walkway.

"Does Rham have any opposition in Afghanistan?" Sam asked, hoping to help her remember something more.

"Yes. There's the Intellectual Party, and they're gaining strength. Afghanistan has been through a lot the last fifteen years. The Russian occupation left the country in shambles. My God, Sam, people still sleep on rocks and live in mud huts. Then the Taliban took over and turned Afghanistan into a rogue country—training terrorists, exporting heroin. The Intellectuals want to restore the country to what it once was. I suspect that my escaping is going to weaken Rham considerably. He'll lose the support of his army and the countries that support his camps."

Sam's mind was roaming.

"Sam." Libra suddenly grabbed his coat sleeve. "What's that?" Her eyes widened as she pointed her finger at a bronze bust at the end of the walkway.

Sam looked ahead at the plaque. "I think that's Constantine. The Roman emperor who split the Roman Empire into two…"

"No, no. That's not what I mean. Look at the bust, the head. There was something…" Libra lowered her head into her hands, trying to think.

After a few seconds, she raised her head and looked at Sam. "The night that I overheard Rham talking on the phone, later, before we went to bed, there was a gold medallion with a bust like the one there. You know, it was one of those old Greek or Roman pieces. The kind of medallion that's sort of oblong, never quite round, even though the head is perfectly minted in the center of it."

Bingo, thought Sam. "You think there's a connection?"

"Maybe. I could be over-reaching, but it's a thought. You think it might be something?"

"I don't know, but let's check it out to be sure."

Chapter 6

Rome
Monday Afternoon

Ramona Montefusco leveled her eyes at the short, wiry American sitting directly across her mahogany desk. It was not the man himself that annoyed her, but rather the fact that he was an American. They were pushy, loud and arrogant.

"Am I to understand that two of our best men were killed by a teenage boy on the Palatine last night?" she asked, her eyes narrowing.

They were on the top floor of the tallest building in downtown Rome. The man chose his words carefully as the woman's eyes shifted to a number of photos spread across her desk.

"Yes. I don't have all the details, but suffice it to say that the police removed the bodies from the Forum this morning, before the tourists showed up."

"Who gave the orders for these men to follow the boys into the Forum?"

"The Count," the American offered slowly, cautiously. In his two years of under-the-table employment with the Montefuscos, he considered his balancing act nothing less than spectacular. He pocketed sizable sums of money from both Ramona in Rome and the Count in Sorrento.

Montefusco blinked in disgust. Her father's obsession with Roman antiquities was getting out of hand. He was making mistakes like he had never made in the past. She found herself having to check his work all the time, something that was unheard of in the past.

"Is there any way the police can connect the dead men to us?" she asked.

"No. The police have no idea who the men were or what they were doing in the Forum. My informants have told me that the whole matter is being kept off the record. It is the high season and they do not want to scare away the tourists."

"Very well." She gave the informant a thoughtful look. He was so terribly ugly, poor soul. He had bushy eyebrows, a bald head, veins that ran through his bulbous nose, a mouth that could probably swallow an orange whole, and dark baggy circles under his eyes. "You have done well. Just a few more questions and I will not take any more of your time."

The man nodded attentively.

"To whom did the *tambarolo* sell the scrolls?"

"The University of Paris. They paid handsomely for them, I am told."

"Why do you think that the University of Paris would pay such a high price for them?"

"We are not sure if it's because of their value as classical literature or if it is because of what's written on them. Apparently, the scrolls may contain sensitive information about the Roman Empire that has never surfaced."

"Please find out, right away. You will let me know the minute you have learned something."

"Of course," the man said as he started to rise from his chair.

"This is for your trouble," Ramona stated, close to smiling. She handed the man an envelope stuffed with one-hundred-thousand-lira notes.

The man clicked his heels, did a half-bow, then left the office.

"Signora, your morning papers," a voice came from behind her.

"Thank you, Guido," she said without turning.

The man set the papers on her desk.

Ramona Montefusco's eyes caught the headlines as the man left the room. An El Al Boeing 747 had crashed in western France. "Perhaps I was a bit too hasty about Father," she said softly.

# # #

ISTANBUL

TUESDAY MORNING

"Golden's managed to find a sketch artist. We want to try a composite drawing of the medallion you mentioned last night," Sam said. "It might give us a clue as to where the drugs are being shipped from."

Libra nodded.

"She's meeting us in ten minutes in Golden's office." Sam put down his coffee.

"Sam, there's not much about that medallion that I can recall," Libra said. "How come Golden's not going to use a computer? You know, like the police use, with all the different noses and eyes?"

"We thought about that, but the computer doesn't have any icons that would represent a two-thousand-year-old Roman or Greek. Golden's got someone he claims is better than a computer anyway. You about ready?"

Libra swallowed the last of her coffee and nodded.

They walked down a long, gray corridor. Sam stopped at a frosted glass door marked with Golden's name. He twisted the handle and waited as Libra walked through.

A male receptionist, pounding something into a computer, abruptly stood up. "Mr. Golden's expecting you, Mr. Harrison. He said to tell you to go right in when you arrived."

They walked into Golden's office. Libra was taken aback by the stark contrast between the Station Chief's office and the rest of the building. It had modern furniture, a large mahogany desk, and reasonably fashionable industrial-grade carpeting. A trim man with wire-rimmed glasses stood up from behind the desk. Libra guessed he was in his mid-forties. He had neatly trimmed gray hair, wide brown eyes and teeth out of a toothpaste commercial.

"Ah, Sam. Libra. Welcome. Hope your accommodations are satisfactory?" he said politely to Libra. She nodded and thanked him for his hospitality.

Sitting in a large leather chair, with an easel on her lap, was a short, dark woman in a long paisley dress. She had short black hair, full lips and deep-set, black eyes. She looked up at Libra and smiled hesitantly.

"This is Solmaz Cliek," Golden said pleasantly. "She will be sketching the medallion you saw at Rham's palace."

Standing at attention next to Solmaz was a young man in starched Air Force blues. Libra presumed he was a translator.

Libra took a chair to Solmaz's left. "If you will bear with me for just a minute," Libra said to Sam and Golden. She placed her hands on her knees, closed her eyes, then took three deep breaths. She forced her brain into a meditative state.

The eagle circled the palace, looking down from the puffy white clouds. She descended in long, circular patterns, landing on the balcony railing outside Rham's bedroom. She fluttered her wings, then leaped forward to the dictator's chest of drawers. The eagle stood on the top of the bureau looking down at the face of a gold medallion. The face of a warrior; bold, sharp eyes; chiseled jaw; long, flowing hair that fell around his shoulders.

The eagle flipped the medallion on its backside; a pattern, five figures in the form of a phalanx charging forward. The eagle froze the picture in her mind, then flew out of Rham's palace. She looked back to see the house shrinking in the distance.

Libra's eyes fluttered open. "Okay. I'm ready."

As she described the medallion to Solmaz, she was taken aback by the woman's ability to translate her words into an exact replica of what she was describing, without erasing any of the lines or asking questions. In less than thirty minutes the woman had drawn the medallion precisely to Libra's specifications.

Libra looked up at Sam and Golden. "I can understand why you don't use a computer." She took the sketch from Solmaz's hands and looked at it intently for a few moments.

Libra turned to the translator. "Ask Solmaz if she has ever heard the expression, 'In the mouth of the wolf.'"

Solmaz smiled, then nodded her head in response to the question.

"She says that it's an Italian expression that her grandfather used to use with his friends. It means 'good fortune.' It correlates with the story of Romulus and Remus, who founded Rome. They were raised by a she-wolf on the Palatine Hill."

Golden turned to the translator, amazed at how clear the drawings were. "Ask Solmaz how she was able to draw the pictures so precisely on the first go-round."

The translator turned to Solmaz. She listened with clear, understanding eyes, then smiled when the translator finished. She gave her answer slowly and directly.

The translator nodded his head with a befuddled look on his face. He glanced back at Solmaz, who nodded her head and smiled.

The translator looked at Golden. "She says that…well, sir…I think I understood her words; that is, well, what she said, Mr. Golden, is, 'I rode on the eagle's wings!'"

# # #

ROME

Despite Mario's admonition to stay off his feet, Figlio paced nervously around the small kitchen. Mario had been gone for over three hours. He had left the apartment shortly before midnight to finish what they had started on the Palatine.

"Oh, what will I do if Mario gets himself killed?" he said out loud to a faded green wall. "I will have no one to turn to." Nervous panic consumed him.

Suddenly he heard footsteps coming up the stairs. He rushed to the door and peeked through the peephole. When he saw his brother on the landing, Figlio ripped open the door.

"Mario, did you find the rest of the scrolls?"

Mario walked through the door. His clothes were caked with mud. A broad smile crossed his lips.

"Yes. And something even better—help me get the bag off my back and I'll show you."

Figlio pulled the book bag off Mario's back. He handed it to Mario. Mario opened the flap and pulled out a dried leather pouch.

"Gold coins! Six of them."

Figlio's eyes widened as Mario dumped the coins on a card table in the middle of the room.

The boys studied the strange markings on the coins. "Do you think they are worth much, Mario?"

"Probably not, but the gold will be worth something. Plus, I found three more scrolls!"

Mario pulled the old sheepskin parchments from his bag and showed them to Figlio.

"Is it more Livy?"

"Maybe. I'll have to check. But this time I got everything that was left in the emperor's private room."

"Were you followed?"

"I don't know, but I took precautions. Nobody could have followed me. That's why I took so long to get back. But to be safe, we'd better find another place to live for a while."

"But where?"

"I have an idea."

# # #

Istanbul
Tuesday Afternoon

The light in Golden's office was getting feeble. Sam flipped on a desk lamp as he pored through a stack of faxes from Athens, Rome and Langley. "Athens and Rome are no help," he said to Libra. "Langley says that the medallion didn't come from Greece or Italy. Says here that the etchings on the medallion appear to be from Carthage, sometime during the third or fourth centuries B.C. Also, they don't think it's a medallion. It's a coin."

"Where exactly was Carthage?"

"North Africa. What's now Libya. Home of the notorious Muammar Qaddafi. Two thousand years ago, home of the notorious Hannibal."

"What does Carthage have to do with Rham?"

"Good question, but I think we'll need a historian to figure it out."

"Any confirmation on Apollo's last transmission from Langley?"

"Yes. Fortunately, one of the researchers is an Italian-American. Says that the term '*En bocca el lupo*'—'In the mouth of the wolf'—is an Italian expression meaning 'Good Fortune.'"

"So Solmaz was right."

"Yes."

"Italian. Hmm. Think Apollo was trying to tell us that Rham's connections have something to do with Italy?"

"Possibly. They couldn't find anything else with that kind of reference. The way it works—the expression, that is—is that one person says to the other, '*En bocca el lupo!* The other person replies, '*Che crepi el lupo!*' meaning, you put something in the wolf's mouth and the wolf can't get you. Bottom line is that it's some form of Italian slang that means 'Good luck to you!' Doesn't make a lot of sense to me, but then, I'm not Italian."

"You think Rham might have made connections with the Italian Mafia?"

"It's a distinct possibility. But the Mob in Rome is not big on drug running. I have a connection to one of the dons in Rome. I could check with him. I doubt he'll tell me much, but he owes me a favor. Maybe it's time to collect the marker."

"What's your connection?" Libra asked.

"You don't want to know. Trust me."

"Okay. But what would a Carthaginian coin have to do with all this?"

"Don't have the foggiest idea. Langley is still studying the history of the era and the coin to see if there might be a fit."

Libra rolled up the magazine, then started tapping it on her forehead. "Do they have any pictures of Carthaginian coins on file?"

Sam fumbled through more pages. "Apparently not…yes, here it is." He pointed his finger to a sentence toward the end of the transmission, "'We're not able to find pictures in any world publications of the coin (composite picture) you faxed earlier today. Suggest you contact Professor Thomas H. Wotherspoon, Chairperson Classics Department, Colby College, Waterville, Maine. He is considered the foremost authority on classical numismatics.' Can't believe that someone makes a living studying this kind of thing. Sounds horribly dull."

"Let's give the guy a call. It should be just about lunch time in Maine."

Sam picked up the phone and asked the operator to connect him with a Tom Wotherspoon at Colby College in Maine. The operator said she would call him back when the connection was made.

Five minutes later the base operator was on the line announcing that she had a connection. "Go ahead, Mr. Harrison."

"Yes, I'm trying to reach Professor Wotherspoon. Is he available? This is quite urgent."

"I'm sorry, but Mr. Wotherspoon is on vacation until the end of the month. Is there a message?" The woman's voice was indifferently polite.

"This is an emergency. Official government business. Can you tell me where I can reach the professor?"

There was a pause and a click. "Kenneth Winston speaking."

"Yes, Mr. Winston, my name is Sam Harrison. I'm with the Department of State." Sam looked at Libra and shrugged. "We need an ancient coin identified. We think it may lead to a ring of international drug smugglers. Washington has suggested we contact Professor Wotherspoon as he is an expert in this area. Can you tell me where I might get in touch with him?"

Libra recalled Sam telling her to use the truth; it was always the best weapon in these kinds of situations. If you had to lie, make the lie as small as possible so you don't get tripped up on it later.

"Yes, yes." Sam scribbled on a notepad. "Thank you, Mr. Winston, you've been most helpful."

"What'd he say?"

"He said that Wotherspoon is in Venice, staying at the Hotel Danieli. He'll be there until tomorrow night, then he heads to Paris. He gave me the number of the Danieli and the number of the Hotel Tremoille in Paris should we miss him in Venice."

Chapter 7

Venice, Italy
Wednesday Morning

The green copper dome of the Basilica of Santa Maria della Salute and the Pala d'Oro Tower stand as the Custom Points where the Grand Canal empties into the lagoon of the Adriatic Ocean. Directly across from the Grand Canal, behind rows of sleek, black gondolas, stands the majestic Hotel Danieli, with its rustic-colored façade and regal entrance.

Tom Wotherspoon, a tall man with pepper-and-salt hair, gray eyes and a ruddy complexion, was on his way out of the front entrance with his wife Martha when he heard his name called out. He turned to see a young man holding a slip of paper.

"Professor Wotherspoon, I am terribly sorry, but this telephone message came for you last night. We were so busy with the new arrivals that we overlooked it until this morning. I hope you will accept my apology." The man's melancholy eyes told Wotherspoon that he was sincere.

Wotherspoon looked at the note. There were two messages, both from the same person with a return telephone number in Istanbul. He did not recognize the name Sam Harrison. The second message, however, caught his eye: "Found ancient Carthaginian coin. Will meet you at the Hotel Tremoille, Paris, Thursday, 8 A.M."

"Carthaginian coin? Interesting," Wotherspoon mumbled as he headed for the exit.

"What was that all about?" Martha asked.

"Who knows. First it was Professor Rinot calling from Paris about some missing Livy parchments that supposedly turned up; now it's somebody I don't even know calling about a Carthaginian coin. Why does this type of thing always happen on vacation?"

"That's the price you pay for being a legend," Martha said with mock sarcasm.

"Well, I'm not going to worry about it until tomorrow. Today, we're going to enjoy our first ride in a gondola," he said as they headed out into the sunshine.

#

Air France Flight 102
Istanbul to Paris

"You see this?" Sam nudged Libra's hand. He was holding the front page of the *International Herald Tribune*. A black-and-white picture showed debris from the El Al Flight 0057 explosion scattered across a vineyard in western France.

Libra removed her headset and shook her head. "We were so busy trying to track down that coin and Tom Wotherspoon that I didn't pay any attention to the news. What's it say?"

"An El Al Boeing 747 en route to Tel Aviv from Amsterdam apparently exploded in midair. The last transmission from the pilot indicated that one of his engines was on fire and that the plane's built-in fire extinguisher had failed. The fire ignited some 300,000 pounds of fuel. No survivors. There were 354 passengers and 12 crew members on board."

The captain of the Air France A-300 Airbus announced the route and flying time to Paris.

Sam continued. "It's going to be a while before they can determine the cause of the engine fire because there wasn't much left of the plane. Debris was scattered over a fifty-mile-long strip. Boeing refuses to speculate."

"Any mention of foul play?"

"Doesn't seem to be. There's a transcript of the pilot's last conversation with ground control. They were trying to make an emergency landing in Geneva; the pilot's transmission sounds routine, for an emergency."

"You think there may have been a bomb on board?"

"Hard to say. But, I have an inclination to discount that theory. El Al has the tightest security in the world. It'd take an act of God to get a bomb on one of their planes. Why?"

Libra sighed. "Rham's training camps were experimenting with new ways to blow things up; buildings, tunnels, bridges, and *airplanes*. You think it's a coincidence that an Israeli jet blows up in midair the night after Rham finds out the United States has had a mole planted in his operation for over two years?"

"He wouldn't have had the time to retaliate that fast."

#

Paris, France
Wednesday Night

Bill Bannistar didn't like getting phone calls in the middle of the night. "Damn-it-all, Sam, I'm not going to open a can of worms by getting involved in the El Al thing. Every indication points to an engine malfunction, not a bomb. I simply don't want to discuss it any further. Get the drug routes. I've got the President all over my ass on heroin shipments."

"Bill, I just…"

"Sam, that's final," Bannistar's voice roared through the phone. "You've been out of the field too long to make that kind of judgment." He hung up.

Sam shook with anger as he walked away from the phone. He wanted a bottle of Johnny Walker Red.

# # #

NICE, FRANCE
WEDNESDAY NIGHT

Professor Jean Claude Rinot stepped off the Train Grande Vitesse—France's high-speed train—onto the platform, looking for a taxi. The long ride from Paris had left him exhausted and agitated.

Ten minutes later, he walked through the front door of the Hotel Negresco.

"Professor! It is nice to see you again!" The concierge's face beamed as he recognized Rinot immediately.

The professor deposited the contents of his valise in a large safe-deposit box in the Negresco business office, then walked to the elevator in the lobby. His reflection in the polished brass doors alarmed him. His eyes were bloodshot and his face looked drawn and haggard.

The elevator doors opened on the third floor and he walked slowly to his room. He tipped the porter and walked out onto the balcony. He inhaled the salty sea air as he scanned the panoramic view of Nice. It was his favorite sight—strollers on the Promenade des Anglais, the moon's pale light reflecting off the rippling water in the Bay of Angeles. He felt the stress begin to drain from his body.

# # #

Rinot checked himself in the full-length mirror as he tugged a black cummerbund around his waist. His thoughts suddenly turned to Monique; his expression turned to sadness. She was such a joy! Why did she have to die so young? His thoughts went back to their honeymoon night in this very room thirty years ago.

He arrived at the Chanticleer precisely at nine. The maitre d' greeted him by name, as if he were a long-lost friend. Rinot, still a bit weary from the train ride, marveled at how the people at the Negresco treated him almost as if he were a part of their family. He felt energized again as the maitre d' escorted him to his table.

"We have reserved your table, Professor Rinot," the maitre d' exclaimed as he pulled back the chair for the professor. *The finest restaurant in all of Europe, and they have taken the time to remember our favorite table. They are so kind. I must thank*

Mme. Soulnaire for her thoughtfulness. Everyone from the wine steward to the chef greeted Rinot and took a few moments to chat with him. The meal was exquisite. He dined slowly, drinking in the atmosphere.

Chapter 8

Paris

Thursday Morning

The taxi pulled up in front of the Hotel Tremoille. Sam paid the driver, then waited on the sidewalk as Libra walked around the cab to his side. A doorman smiled, tipped his hat and opened the door.

Sam approached the concierge. "Would you please connect me with Professor Tom Wotherspoon's room?" he asked.

The concierge, a heavy-set man in his mid-forties, glanced at Sam. "You are Mr. Harrison?"

"Yes," Sam responded, a bit surprised.

"Professor Wotherspoon is waiting for you in the restaurant."

"What does he look like?"

The concierge let out a short chuckle. "You will recognize him." He raised his hand above his head in a parallel position, indicating that Wotherspoon was tall.

The restaurant was filled with tourists, mostly American and Japanese. Sam noticed a tall, trim man sitting alone reading a newspaper. "That must be Wotherspoon," he said.

As they approached the table, Wotherspoon looked up. "You, ah, Sam Harrison?"

"Yes, and this is my colleague, Rebecca Arnason," Sam answered as he extended his hand.

"Please, sit down. Have you had breakfast?" Wotherspoon asked in a cultivated, New England accent.

Libra nodded. "Coffee is all we'd care to have, thanks."

"Well, whatever this coin is, it must be pretty important for you to fly all the way from Istanbul. By the way, who are you with?" Wotherspoon asked, more an afterthought than genuine curiosity.

Sam pulled a leather packet with a government insignia on its cover from his coat pocket. He presented it to Wotherspoon. In it was a card that identified him as a representative of the State Department.

Libra watched as Wotherspoon barely glanced at Sam's ID, which the embassy had forged the previous night. He turned his eyes to Libra as she reached for her pocketbook. "That's okay, one is enough. I think I can trust you," he said to Libra with a wink and a boyish smile. Libra guessed Wotherspoon was in his middle sixties.

"Now show me the coin." Wotherspoon was not able to contain his curiosity.

"Well, we don't exactly have the coin, Professor. What we have is a picture, or an artist's rendition, to be precise." Sam pulled the Xerox copy from his briefcase. He handed it to Wotherspoon, who slipped on a pair of reading glasses.

"We were hoping you could identify the coin and the face that adorns it," Sam stated flatly.

Wotherspoon studied the picture. Nobody spoke for two or three minutes.

Wotherspoon finally looked up from the drawing. "Your message said that this was a Carthaginian coin. How did you know that? And why is it so important to learn the coin's origin?"

"I can't tell you that now; it's classified. However, I can tell you that Washington ran the picture through their computers to try to determine if the coin was Greek, Roman or Persian, but they couldn't come up with a match. The coin's makeup indicated that it originated in Carthage. Washington suggested we contact you because of your qualifications in this field."

"Have you actually seen the coin?"

"I haven't, but Rebecca did."

Wotherspoon turned to Libra. "Where'd you see it?"

Libra shot a glance at Sam, who gave her a slight nod. "Afghanistan," she answered. "Why is that important?"

Wotherspoon shot a doubtful look at Libra. "Afghanistan?"

Libra nodded.

"Hum. Well, I suppose that's possible."

"Please, Professor. Don't keep us in the dark. We're as interested in why it turned up in Afghanistan as you are," Sam interjected.

"Let me back up for a moment," Wotherspoon said, leaning forward, webbing his fingers and putting his elbows on the table. "Incidentally, the detail in this drawing is simply remarkable. That's what prompted me to ask whether or not you had actually seen it. At any rate, I believe, based on the detail, that this is a Carthaginian Cresa…"

"Believe? Professor, you're not sure?" Libra interrupted.

Wotherspoon was not used to being challenged. "Yes. You see, no one in modern times has actually seen a Cresa. Except, of course, for you. The only modern-day reference to the coin comes from a manuscript published by James Browning in 1906. As a matter of fact, only two copies of Browning's work exist; one at the Library of Congress and one here in Paris, at the University. At any rate, the coin was believed to have been minted by Hannibal—you, no doubt, know who he was! The story, according to Browning, was that Hannibal minted the coins prior to ravaging Italy from 219 to 202 B.C."

"So is this a picture of Hannibal?" Libra pointed to the drawing.

"Yes; that is, if this is a Cresa. And it certainly appears to be. You see, on the back side is a drawing of Hannibal's elephant brigade. Hannibal was a master strategist when it came to battle formations. General Patton, for example, studied Hannibal's elephant tactics in World War II. Patton used the same phalanx as Hannibal, only with tanks, to defeat Rommel in North Africa. Presumably on the same battlefield where Hannibal was defeated in 202 B.C. by the Romans."

"You said a moment ago, Professor, that Hannibal had the coin minted, implying that there may be more of these things floating around?" Sam cut in.

"Yes. Please forgive the diversion. According to Browning, Hannibal made thousands of them to bribe the tribes of northern Italy. He thought he could convince the nomadic tribes to turn against Rome and join his regiments. You see, Hannibal and his father were obsessed with conquering Rome. They came very close to succeeding."

"Why didn't they?"

"The strategy nearly worked. Hannibal made it all the way from the north of Italy to a village just outside Rome. He engaged and defeated the Romans at Cannae, which was just outside the city limits. If he had marched on to Rome, he would have won the war and conquered the Romans. But he stopped to let his soldiers rest after a fierce battle in which some 30,000 Roman soldiers died. That gave the Romans time to regroup. The Roman army caught Hannibal and his troops by surprise. They slaughtered the resting Carthaginians. Hannibal won the battle, but lost the war."

"Hannibal must have been toting around a substantial sum of loot."

"That's correct; however, the coins never surfaced. Furthermore, you've got to remember that all this is hypothesis. There's no hard evidence that Hannibal had the coins with him when he invaded Italy. There is only a passing comment by one of the Roman historians, Livy, that Hannibal bought the loyalty of the Latin tribes in the north. And keep in mind, Livy wrote about the Hannibalic wars over two hundred years after they ended."

"Presuming that he did, and I'm asking for a best guess, what do you think happened to them?"

"That's a hard one. As you're probably aware, old Roman and Greek coins have survived for centuries, in great quantities, but not the Cresa. It disappeared off the face of the earth. That is, if it ever existed at all. However, Rebecca's report would add some validity to the theory that it does exist. The other possibility is that the coins were melted down, then turned into another form of barter or made into Roman coins by the later emperors."

"So Hannibal's gold, if it did exist, was lost somewhere between Carthage and Italy?" Sam asked.

"That would be my guess. Yes."

Sam bowed his head in thought.

"But remember, Carthage was a superpower in those days. The Carthaginian Empire itself spanned all of North Africa and Spain. It was a power to be reckoned with. That's a lot of geography, but it's unlikely that they found their way to Afghanistan. Unless…"

"Unless what?" Libra broke in.

"Unless someone from Rome took them there. After all, the Roman Empire did extend as far east as Afghanistan."

Libra flashed an uneasy glance at Sam.

"There is one other thing," Wotherspoon said, almost off-the-cuff, "that I think you should know. And I apologize for not mentioning it sooner. However, the coin made me lose my train of thought."

"What's that?"

"I got a call from Professor Jean Claude Rinot the day before yesterday. He heads the Classics Department at the University of Paris. Apparently, someone has smuggled what he claims to be a portion of the lost work of Titus Livius—or Livy, as he's better known in modern times—out of Italy. There have been hoaxes regarding the lost works of Livy in the past. In the 1950s, for example, several of Livy's lost works turned up in Rome; they had been mysteriously discovered in the vicinity of the Black Sea. The Roman government's Historical Society paid hundreds of thousands of dollars to the man who 'found' them."

"So what happened to them?"

The professor chuckled. "They were forgeries. Shortly after the Italian government purchased the manuscripts, which were authenticated by some of the best Latin historians in academia, carbon dating was introduced and it turned out that the parchment that the supposed original works were written on was manufactured in 1945! The Italian government and academia had egg all over its collective face."

"They ever catch the guy who authored them?" Sam asked.

"Never did. But he must have known Livy's works inside out and backwards to fool the best minds on Roman antiquity."

"How did he pull it off without getting caught?"

"Whoever it was, he was good. As I recall, he had an intermediary, someone who was independent of the whole situation, to do the dirty work. The intermediary disappeared shortly after he collected the money."

Libra jumped in. "Doesn't it seem a little strange, Professor Wotherspoon, that some of Livy's lost works turn up at the same time that this Carthaginian Cresa surfaces? Didn't Livy write at length about Rome's war with Hannibal?"

"That's correct, and it is a rather unusual set of circumstances." Wotherspoon became contemplative for a moment.

Sam broke the silence. "Why was Rinot calling you?"

"He wanted to verify the type of coins that were used for barter during the reign of Augustus. You see, Rinot wanted to be absolutely sure that the Livy manuscripts are genuine this time."

"Do you know if he had the parchment tested by carbon dating?"

"As of our conversation he hadn't had them tested."

"Did you ask him why not?"

"Yes. Rinot is a bit eccentric. I think that he wanted to enjoy the manuscripts as if they are the originals before having them tested. Apparently he got them just before leaving for vacation and didn't have the time to get them to a lab. If they are Livy's works, he can be the first to translate them. It would be quite a coup."

"Where can we find Rinot?"

"Normally right here in Paris, but as I mentioned, he's on vacation the next couple weeks, somewhere in southern France. One of the Riviera cities; Nice, I think."

Just then, a woman's voice rang out behind Libra. "Good morning!"

Wotherspoon stood up, followed by Sam, as his wife approached the table.

"Please don't get up," the woman said with a friendly smile.

"Martha, this is Sam Harrison and his colleague, Rebecca Arnason. They're from the State Department. Sam's the one who left the message about the coin."

After exchanging pleasantries, Martha excused herself to get in the buffet line.

"We won't keep you any longer, Professor. We appreciate your giving up some of your vacation to help us out," Sam said, rising from the table.

"May I keep this?" Wotherspoon asked, referring to the drawing of the Cresa.

Sam hesitated. After thinking for a moment, "What if I send you a copy at Colby College when we're through with the investigation? I certainly understand why you'd want it; however, I'm a little concerned that if the picture gets into the wrong hands it could jeopardize our work. I'm sure you understand," Sam offered apologetically.

"Certainly. Here's my card," Wotherspoon offered. "It was nice meeting you, Rebecca."

Libra smiled at the professor and nodded. She and Sam headed for the front of the hotel.

As the doorman stood aside to let them pass, a man lying on the roof of the adjacent building propped himself up on the parapet and lifted his powerful rifle into position. He sighted the cross hairs of the telescopic lens on Libra's heart. He squeezed the trigger.

# # #

Nice

Thursday Morning

The breeze off the Bay of Angeles lifted the curtains, letting the sunshine into the room. Rinot woke with a start. He looked at the digital clock. Nine o'clock! He felt a twinge of guilt for sleeping so late. But it was a holiday. He opened the curtains to a beautiful Riviera day. Quickly, he showered and dressed.

Rinot returned to the hotel following a ninety-minute walk around the city. He stopped at the safe-deposit boxes and removed his notes, a stack of papers some six inches thick. He rode the elevator to his third-floor room, then called room service and ordered his usual light lunch with tea. He unzipped a leather bag and removed a laptop computer. He neatly piled the papers next to the laptop, then opened a new document.

He had been working for half an hour when he heard a knock on the door. "Room Service," came the cordial voice.

Rinot opened the door and a waiter, a large man with a ponytail, pushed a food trolley into the room. "You wish me to serve you, monsieur?"

"No, I will serve myself, thank you." Rinot signed the check. He poured himself a cup of tea and resumed his work.

"Let's see, Marcellus sacked the Temple of Siracusa in 212 B.C. That would mean…" A searing pain rushed through his chest, then down his left arm. He let out a cough and tried desperately to inhale. His chest muscles tightened. He couldn't breathe. Panic seized him. He tried to reach for the telephone, but he was paralyzed. He tried to scream, but he couldn't form the words. Darkness engulfed him.

Two minutes later, a knock on the door. "Room Service, Professor. I have your tea." The waiter pressed his ear to the door. He slipped a key into the lock and entered the room.

The waiter rushed to Rinot's body, then took his wrist and felt for a pulse. Satisfied that there was no heartbeat, he picked up the teacup and pot and replaced them with fresh ones. He poured half a cup, placed it next to Rinot's head, then picked up the professor's notes and covered them with a sterling silver serving tray on his trolley.

The waiter lifted Rinot's head, then gently placed it on the writing table next to the computer. He dumped the appropriate files from Rinot's computer onto a diskette, then pushed the computer off the table. It crashed to the floor, destroying the hard drive, the screen and the remaining files.

The man carefully replaced Rinot's head on the table, allowing his left arm to drift over the smashed computer. He stepped back and inspected his work. A look of satisfaction came across his face.

The waiter picked up the tray with the soiled teacup and teapot. He put Rinot's valise on the lower shelf of the trolley, then started for the door. As if he had forgotten a minor detail, he put the tray back on the bed, then picked up Rinot's navy blazer, which was lying in a heap on a chair. He rummaged through the pockets. Finding what he was looking for, he picked up the tray and walked out of the door.

As he stepped into the corridor, he looked back and said, "Yes, Professor. I will tell the switchboard that you do not wish to be disturbed. Thank you, Professor," he said politely, but his ruse was short-lived as the shrill ring of the telephone echoed through the room.

The waiter pulled the door shut. He pivoted on his right foot, looking anxiously up and down the long hallway. Seeing no one, he walked down the hall pushing the trolley as if he were on his return trip to the kitchen. He glanced at his watch. Twelve-thirty. He had one hour to get to the airport and take the only flight of the day back to Rome.

Chapter 9

Rome—The Palatine
Thursday

Mario pushed the ten-thousand-lira note under the glass partition. An old man looked up, surprised. "Mario, Mario," he shook his head. "You know that your money is no good." The man looked around, his sunken eyes nervously scanning the sparse office in the cinderblock building. He motioned Mario closer.

Mario felt his stomach tighten as he leaned forward.

"You know what they found in the ruins Monday morning?" the man whispered through a circular hole in the Plexiglas window.

Mario shook his head, fear pinching his throat.

"Two bodies; one on the Palatine, the other in the Forum," he said in a hoarse whisper.

Mario blanched. "No!" he exclaimed in mock surprise. "Do they know who the men were?" he asked as if he didn't have a clue. Suddenly, he realized his mistake; how would he know the bodies were men?

"The police said there was no identification on the bodies. They found one man by the Temple of Castor and Pollux. It looked like he was pushed off the deck. What a mess, Mario! The other, and this is a strange thing, they found him at the bottom of the well near the Temple of Cybele. His skull was smashed in by a big stone. You weren't wandering around the Palatine again on Sunday night, were you, Mario?"

"Oh, no," Mario's voice rose an octave, "Figlio and I, we, we were with friends who are visiting from Sicily."

#

Mario drifted through the Forum. The midmorning heat was unbearable, but he hardly noticed. He was lost in remorse. The columns of the old Roman temples stood high against the puffy, white clouds.

"*There were two brothers. Much like you and Figlio. They also lost their parents,*" the priest's words abruptly rang in his ears. "*They were cared for by a she-wolf until they were able to fend for themselves.*"

"*But the other brother, Remus. What happened to him, Father?*"

"There was a fight. Remus tried to kill Romulus. But he failed, and Romulus killed Remus. The lesson of the story is that you must always honor your little brother, Mario. It is now your responsibility to take care of Figlio."

The priest's words sent a shiver down his spine as he trudged through the humidity.

Mario wandered aimlessly. He passed the Temple of Castor and Pollux, then abruptly snapped back to reality; he was standing where the man had fallen to his death. Suddenly, he remembered: The *tambarolo!* He was late!

He quickened his pace, sprinting through the headless statues of the Vestal Virgins; past the Round Temple of Romulus; under the decaying Arch of Titus, and up the steep incline to the Palatine. He stopped at the spot where he was supposed to meet the man with chestnut-brown hair. He was out of breath. *The man was not there.*

# # #

Paris

Thursday Morning

The marksman squeezed the trigger on his Heckler & Koch pistol and fired three rounds in rapid sequence. Each bullet found its mark; the first sliced through the heart; the second severed the spinal column; the third blew away the chest bone.

"There will be no bounty for you today, my friend," the man uttered to the lifeless body. He did not know why he was to protect the American woman from Rham's assassins, but he never questioned orders.

The man, in his early thirties, with thick, black hair and a bushy mustache, holstered the Heckler & Koch. He buttoned his tweed sports jacket so that the gun could not be seen.

Two hundred feet away, on Rue de la Tremoille, Sam and Libra walked hurriedly toward Avenue George V, each lost in private thoughts. The day was bright, the air thick with humidity.

"We need to track down this Jean Claude Rinot," Libra finally said, watching the barges floating down the Seine. "Right now, I'm trying to figure out if we're after drug smugglers or errant antiquity dealers. My senses tell me that the two are related. I don't believe in coincidences."

"I'll try to find out where Rinot's staying in Nice. When I get his location, I'll fly down and interview him."

"Based on what Wotherspoon had to say, I think Italy would be a good place to start looking for the mules. You think the Sicilian Mafia is moving Rham's drugs?"

Sam was about to answer when a taxi pulled up in front of them. They climbed in the back seat.

"No, it can't be," Sam said as they situated themselves in the back of the cab.

Libra gave him a look that said, "How can you be so damned sure?"

Sam looked out the cab window as they crossed the George V Bridge. He avoided her eyes. Two years ago, after Libra left for Afghanistan, the American government systematically eliminated most of the Sicilian drug lords. It was sensitive information, as the government had formed their own counter drug terrorists—illegal as hell—to combat the drug smugglers in southern Italy. The President had approved the clandestine division out of desperation. He'd had enough of America's drug problems and decided to take matters into his own hands. At the time, Italy was the major source of heroin coming into the United States.

"American Embassy," Sam told the driver.

Ten minutes later the cab pulled up to the American Embassy. Sam and Libra scurried up the front steps.

It took Sam a little over an hour to learn that Professor Jean Claude Rinot vacationed at the same time, the same city and the same hotel every year. "Well, at least the guy's consistent," Libra shrugged as she dialed the number of the Hotel Negresco.

"Professor Jean Claude Rinot, please. This is Paris calling with an urgent message for the professor," Libra said in flawless French.

Two minutes later the hotel operator was back on the line announcing that there was no answer.

"Would you have Professor Rinot paged, please," Libra's voice was demanding.

"One moment, please," came the polite reply. The operator put Libra on hold.

Five minutes later, Sam watched as Libra's face changed from impatient exasperation to melancholy surprise. "I see. Yes." Libra listened to the voice on the other end of the line, nodding her head slowly, her clear brown eyes distant. She replaced the receiver and turned to Sam.

"Rinot's dead."

\# \# \#

KABUL
THURSDAY AFTERNOON

Moman Jasuri drove the big Rover over the rut-strewn, dirt road. In every direction the tall poppies were all that he could see. Occasionally he would pass a field where laborers toiled, scraping the brown granules from the poppy shoots into large burlap sacks. He pulled into Rham's parking lot, screeching the big vehicle to a halt, dust flying high in the hot sun. He grabbed his AK-47 from the passenger seat, fearful it would be stolen if he left it behind. In Afghanistan guns, drugs and currency were all common barter.

He hurried up the front steps to Rham's palace. The new security guard recognized him immediately and let him pass to the flight of stairs to Rham's second-floor offices. The inside of the palace was dimly lit, the carpet threadbare, and the wallpaper yellowed with age and cigar smoke. Rham's assistant greeted him at the landing and ushered him into Rham's office.

"Your Excellency. You called for me?" He snapped to attention.

"Yes, Commander. Sit down, please," Rham said as he relit his cigar.

Jasuri sat in the chair that faced Rham's desk, setting his weapon on the floor. Although it was cool in the office, Jasuri could already feel the beads of perspiration on his forehead. He had been summarily dismissed by Rham in their last meeting, shortly after Rham had gunned down his predecessor, Ali Mohammidi. He anticipated another confrontation and he did not want to suffer the same fate.

"I have an important mission for you, Commander. You must not fail." Rham cast an ominous glance at Jasuri.

"Yes, Your Excellency," he replied, swallowing hard.

"As you are aware, preparations for a major attack on the United States have been in progress for some time. I am pleased with the work you have done in preparing the men for this assignment. I am so pleased, in fact, that I am making you the commander of the mission. You will leave tonight. Our agents in America have made all the necessary arrangements. You must not fail, Commander Jasuri," Rham repeated.

Jasuri's eyes widened in apprehension.

"Safe houses have been established in each city. All arrangements for passports, necessary papers, travel documents, credit cards and so on have been made. You will instruct your men accordingly." There was a hard tone to his voice.

"When do you wish the bombings to happen, Your Excellency?"

"The explosions are to take place simultaneously. You will be given twenty-four hours notice. It will be within the next six days. You are to assemble your men at once. Maps of each building are now at the camps. You will have detailed floor plans and a complete report on the security in each building."

"And escape routes?" Jasuri asked.

"Yes. It is important that everyone escape," Rham mumbled unconvincingly.

"Yes, Your Excellency. And how powerful are the bombs we are to use?"

"Very powerful, C-4 plastique—more so than the one used in New York. It is important that the Americans focus all their attention on the bombings. The damage must be devastating," he finished with a ruthless stare at Jaṣuri.

Jaṣuri bowed in grateful appreciation as he stood to leave Rham's office. *This was truly a great honor. To do the work of the jihad!* Allah had blessed him.

#

PARIS

THURSDAY AFTERNOON

"Dead?" Sam repeated. "How?"

"The woman on the phone didn't know. She said a porter found him slumped over the reading table. She said it looked like he'd had a heart attack," Libra said.

"That's it? No other details?"

"No. The porter apparently found him when he went to his room to tell him about our phone call. They just discovered the body, so they don't know anything. Jesus, Sam, suddenly we've got all these events cropping up. I don't believe it could all be random. Somebody's pulling a lot of stings and killing a lot of people to get to…to get to whatever."

"What do you mean?"

"An El Al plane falls out of the sky the day after I escape from Rham's palace; a rare Carthaginian coin is discovered in Afghanistan; Livy's missing books surface after two thousand years, and the leading authority on Roman antiquities dies a day or two after he gets his hands on them. Something's going on; I think these events are connected."

"So what are you thinking? That Rham's behind it all?"

"Not Rham. He doesn't have the gray matter to pull off something this elaborate. But whatever it is, he's somehow connected to it. Even though there's no hard evidence to prove any of it, my intuition tells me that we've stumbled onto something bigger than Rham's drug routes."

"You think there's somebody else controlling these events?"

Libra thought for a moment. "I know this may sound far-fetched, but what if those Livy transcripts had something to do with the whereabouts of Hannibal's gold? Think about it. Livy writes in detail on Rome's war with Hannibal; why wouldn't he mention Hannibal's financing his campaign in Italy? He only mentions it in passing, according to Wotherspoon. Shit, that was one hell of a long campaign—seventeen years. It seems odd that Livy doesn't mention the Cresas in his works."

"Maybe he did. Maybe those are part of his lost works?"

"No." Libra bent her head in thought as she paced. "No. All of Livy's writing on the war with Hannibal survived intact. That I do remember from my Western Civilization classes."

"How do you know that?"

"It just came back to me. I had to read the whole damned story of Hannibal crossing the Alps in Western Civ at William Smith. And I remember Professor Burrall telling the class that all of the books that Livy wrote—I think there were about a hundred forty—the books on the war with Hannibal made it to modern times complete. And if we're to trust Wotherspoon, Livy didn't mention the gold, except in passing."

"Hmm. Interesting point. I hadn't thought about that. So if I'm reading you correctly, the newly found Livy books might shed some light on the whereabouts of the Carthaginian gold. It would be one helluva stash, worth millions by today's standards. That might explain Rinot's death."

"What doesn't figure is why Livy would fail to mention something as significant as a major haul of gold, gold from a wealthy competing empire that disappeared some two hundred years before he wrote the book."

"Maybe he thought that it was unimportant in the overall scheme of things. Hell, Hannibal was a major threat to the existence of the Roman Empire. Perhaps he overlooked Hannibal's financing the war in favor of the Romans winning it?"

"Nah. Doesn't fit. What I remember about Livy's writings was that he was very detailed in almost every aspect of the war with Hannibal. Seems to me he even made a reference to a Roman general's sacking a Greek temple somewhere in Sicily. The general, whoever he was, toted off massive quantities of gold."

"How the hell did you remember all that?"

"My classics professor made a big deal about it in class one day. As I recall, he had authored a paper on the subject. His theory was that this event was the beginning of the end of the Roman Empire."

"So what else did he say about it?"

"Well, the gist of it was that the Romans started bringing the captured Greek artifacts back to Rome. This upset the religious beliefs and practices of the Romans. Can't remember why. But the long and the short of it was that Rome started becoming corrupt; hence, the beginning of the end."

"Right." Sam shook his head in disbelief. "What it doesn't explain, however, is the El Al crash or Rham's new drug routes."

"Sure it does. Right now we don't have the connections. Trust me, Sam, all this shit is connected."

"Well, you're going to have a hard time convincing Bannistar. Judging by his reaction to the El Al crash, I'm not sure he's going to be overjoyed at hearing that we're on the trail of nonexistent terrorists who didn't blow up a plane, and the murderer of a French professor who died of a heart attack."

"Screw Bannistar. There's something going on, and we're in a position to find out what it is. Have you lost your touch? I think you've spent too much time behind a desk."

Sam tried not to react. She was baiting him and he knew it. He took a deep breath and turned from the window. "That was a cheap shot. Look, I'm not disagreeing with what you're saying. What I'm trying to get across to you is that Bannistar ain't buying it. He's going to be all over my ass wanting to know about the heroin shipments. When I tell him what we've found, he'll think we're nuts. Shit, he'll probably reassign us to the Metropolitan Museum as custodians."

"Calm down, Sam. I wish you'd trust my instincts. There's too many similarities in this whole mess for them to be mere coincidences."

There was a pause. Sam took another deep breath.

"Sam, I'm sorry for the desk remark. It was unkind." Libra's voice cracked.

Sam walked over and held her in his arms. She pressed tightly against him. "Forget it. I probably have been behind a desk too long. Washington has a tendency to isolate you from reality. You lose focus, perspective, and everything else rational."

"Just hold me. I want this to be over."

Libra pulled back and looked into his eyes. Their lips met; softly at first, then harder until passion overtook them.

Chapter 10

Paris

Friday

Sam strolled into the embassy restaurant. The tables were covered with fresh white linen and bouquets of colorful flowers. On the walls were antique French prints of Lafayette, Washington, and a few others he didn't recognize. Waiters in white half-coats and dark slacks hovered about.

Libra looked up; her eyes sparkled when she saw Sam walk to the table. She was looking through a stack of photographs. "Let me use your pencil," she said.

Sam pulled a mechanical pencil from his shirt pocket and handed it to her. "What are you doing?"

"These came in last night from Bannistar. The FBI is looking for international terrorists who might have entered America illegally. He wants to know if I'd seen any of these handsome dudes in Afghanistan. They're not exactly GQ suit studs."

Libra started sketching a beard on the picture of the man in front of her. "Hmm…this guy could very well be… ah, yes, Mr. Moman Jasuri…in drag no less."

"Who's he?"

"Rham's new right-hand man. Oversees the training camps, the drug operations, terrorist activities. A jack-of-all-trades when it comes to terrorist activity. A very nasty dude. Rham has likely promoted him to Captain of the Guards. His predecessor, Ali Mohammidi, is probably on the other side of the sod by now. I'm sure Rham had him executed for letting me get away. I'd better get this to Bannistar right away. If Jasuri is in the United States, he's not there on a spiritual retreat."

"Well, you're right about Rham not being smart enough to orchestrate whatever's going down."

"Why's that?"

"Sending a man you can identify to America. That wasn't very smart. You think someone is setting Rham up?"

"That would be my guess. But who?"

"Anyone else in there you recognize?" Sam gestured at the pictures.

"No. I've never seen any of them, but then again Rham didn't exactly let me wander around the camps."

Sam summoned a waiter with a wave of his hand and asked him to fax Jasuri's picture to Bannistar.

"What time is your plane to Nice?" Libra asked as she put aside the pictures.

Sam glanced at his watch. "Hour and a half. I hope to hell you're right and I'm not off on a wild goose chase."

"Don't worry. If Rinot's death wasn't from natural causes, I think we're on pretty firm ground, at least as far as Bannistar's concerned. Did you tell him?"

"You kidding? Bannistar would shit if he knew what we were up to. Jesus, running around the south of France looking for Carthaginian treasure." Sam rolled his eyes. "How about checking out Rinot while I'm in Nice? He may have left something in his office, or at home."

"There's one other thing. Before you got up this morning, I had Research run a passenger list of the El Al plane. There was an MI-6 agent on board."

Sam stopped his fork halfway between the plate and his mouth. "Why was he going to Israel?"

"Haven't gotten that far yet. But I do know that our British cousin was based in Rome!"

Sam fell silent as Libra sipped her coffee. "The guy had to have been on to something. An agent isn't going to go from Rome to Amsterdam to Tel Aviv when he can go directly from Rome. He was trying to cover his tracks."

"Well, he was pretty sloppy if he was trying to cover his tracks. He filled out paperwork with the airline because he was carrying a weapon. If someone was trailing him, it wouldn't have been too hard to figure out he was a spy."

"Jesus, that doesn't make any sense." Sam looked puzzled. "You got any more surprises for me?"

"Nope. That's the last one," Libra said innocently.

"Well," he sighed, "I hate to admit it, but that would add credence to your theory that Rham's drug runners are somehow tied to this Livy thing. But I'll suspend judgment until we have more facts."

"As long as I'm going to do some snooping, I'll need a gun. Mind if I borrow yours while you're touring the French Riviera?"

"Of course. Walk with me to the front door. I'll give it to you there so we don't have to show it off to the embassy staff. You expecting trouble?"

"Well, there's the bounty Rham has on my head, but that's not what's bothering me. I have the sense that there's someone following us."

"When did it start? The feeling, I mean."

"When we left the hotel after talking to Wotherspoon. Do you have an extra for yourself?"

"Shit, no. I have been tied to a desk too long. It never occurred to me to bring two. Look, you take it. If I get into trouble, I'll talk my way out of it."

"You silver-tongued devil, you."

Sam stood up to leave. Libra swallowed the rest of her coffee and followed him to the front door.

"See if you can come up with why the agent was on his way to Tel Aviv," Sam stated.

"I'm one step ahead of you, Sherlock," Libra replied with a wide smile. "Should know something later this morning."

Sam pulled a Glock .38 from his belt holster and handed it to Libra. He kissed her on the cheek, then stepped through the heavy wooden doors to a waiting limousine.

Libra put the gun in her pocketbook, then went back to the restaurant and started thumbing through the Paris telephone directory. To her surprise, the professor's phone number was listed and his address was two blocks from the embassy. She also looked up the address for the University of Paris. Then she found the phone number for the Minister of Information at the Louvre and committed the numbers to memory.

Libra returned to her room and changed quickly. She slipped on a pair of pleated black slacks, a matching turtleneck sweater and black running shoes. After tying her hair into a ponytail, she strapped a money belt around her waist, tucked the Glock into the belt, and pulled the sweater down over it. Lastly, she put a set of burglar's tools in her sleeve. She walked out of the embassy.

As she walked toward the professor's address, she had the sense that somebody was watching her. Looking back over her shoulder periodically, she saw nothing out of the ordinary. But she had learned long ago to trust her inner signals, and they were flashing danger. Taking no chances, she hailed an oncoming cab.

"Where to, Madame," the driver asked.

"The History Department at the University of Paris." She gave the driver directions.

As they drove past the Embassy, she concentrated on unusual movement from the sidewalks. Again, nothing seemed out of place.

After driving for five minutes, Libra ordered the driver to stop. "Let me off on the corner."

"But, Madame, we are still a long distance from the University."

"Just let me out on the corner," she ordered.

She handed the driver one hundred francs, then jumped out of the cab and ran down a flight of steps leading to the Metro. She purchased a ticket from an automatic vending machine and took the next train to the station closest to Rinot's apartment block. She hadn't noticed anyone following her, but her inner senses continued to warn her that there was danger lurking nearby.

Back at street level, the sidewalks were practically empty. She was astonished by the size and beauty of the professor's building. It was not the kind of building she expected a college professor to live in. She walked past the front entrance. A doorman and a security guard were posted in the lobby. Trying to con her way past them would be useless. She had to find another way in without being seen. Her eyes panned the building for an underground parking garage. She spotted it halfway down the block.

Libra casually strolled to the end of the block and waited. Five minutes later she heard the gears of a garage door opening. A jet-black Jaguar emerged from under the building. As the Jaguar turned, Libra sprinted down the driveway, ducking under the garage door as it was closing.

She looked around. No one was in the parking area. She walked to the entrance and slipped a set of burglar's tools from her sleeve. She jimmied the lock and pushed back the door. She walked to the elevator and pushed the button for the sixth floor.

When the elevator stopped, she paused and listened at the door. Her proximity sense told her that the corridors were empty. She was taken aback by the luxurious décor of the hallway. Soft hues of pink and green covered the walls and the carpet was plush.

She checked the numbers of the apartments, which were on gold-plated signs at eye level to the right of the doors. Each resident's name was written in script just below the number. She found unit number 602, with "Jean Claude Rinot" stenciled beneath. She felt her pulse quicken as she walked to the door, then gently knocked. She waited for a few moments then knocked again.

No answer.

She shoved the burglar's tools into the keyhole. The door sprang open, revealing an expansive living room. Potted plants were placed throughout, making her wonder when the next watering would be. A housekeeper probably maintained the apartment when Rinot was away. Hopefully, not while she was there. She looked around. Oil portraits from the Renaissance hung in heavy wooden, gold-leafed frames. Seventeenth-century wrought-iron lamps adorned the antique end tables. There was an almost uncanny sense of balance to the room.

Libra started her search. She turned to her right and walked to the end of a short corridor, where she found the master bedroom. As in the living room, the bedroom furniture was expensive and the room neat and orderly. A four-poster bed, complete with canopy; a walnut seventeenth-century armoire; and a large, very old dresser. On the dresser was a color photograph of a woman. Libra picked up the gold picture frame and stared at it. Brunette hair, dark moon eyes that sparkled, high cheekbones, and a full rounded mouth.

Libra replaced the picture, then checked for a hidden wall safe. Not finding one, she turned to the walk-in closet. She had never seen so many high-quality suits in one place. She pushed the hangers aside, looking for a safe. There wasn't one.

Libra walked back into the hallway. She turned toward the living room. The door to the next room was locked. She picked the lock, then let out a gasp as the door swung open. Books lined every wall from floor to ceiling. A large, antique desk, with a high-powered reading lamp, occupied the middle of the room.

She picked the lock on the desk in under five seconds. Rummaging through the professor's papers was tedious, compounded by the fact that Libra wasn't sure what she was looking for. She used up valuable time sifting through letters and personal effects. The desk revealed nothing. She turned to the bookshelves.

Libra removed sections of books looking for a wall safe. She worked for two hours, removing three books at a time and replacing them carefully. Her efforts were futile.

She walked back to the dining area and checked behind the portraits hanging on the walls. No safe. She sensed that she had missed something; something right under her nose.

As she put her hand on the door latch, she remembered something…the photograph in the bedroom! Libra sprinted back down the hallway. She picked up the picture, analyzing it with a different perspective. The portrait was slightly crooked against its shiny gold frame. She loosened the thin metal clasps holding the backboard in place and slid the cardboard sheet out of the frame. Taped to the inner facing of the backboard were two jackets of microfiche.

Microfiche! Copies of manuscripts would be bulky and difficult to hide. But microfiche could be hidden anywhere. She admonished herself for wasting so much time.

She slipped the jackets into her money belt, then carefully replaced the backboard in the frame. Libra checked to make sure the picture was aligned properly with its gold frame. She rushed out of the bedroom to the living room.

A feeling of relief washed over her as she headed for the door. Then her breath caught in her throat. The doorknob was turning.

# # #

NICE, FRANCE

Sam jumped out of the taxi and jogged up the steps to the entrance of the Hotel Negresco. He walked into the lobby and across the polished marble floor.

"I'd like to talk to the hotel manager," Sam said, rather loudly, to the man at the reception desk. "This concerns the death of Professor Rinot."

A look of consternation washed over the clerk's face. He clearly didn't appreciate the matter of Rinot's death broadcast to the wealthy clientele. "May I have your name, please?"

"Of course. Sam Harrison with the American Department of State." Sam flashed his phony credentials.

The man nodded obligingly then picked up a phone and said something in a hushed voice. He turned back to Sam. "Madame Soulnaire, the proprietor, will see you right away. If you would please wait here in the lobby, she will be here momentarily."

It took Mme. Soulnaire only moments to reach the lobby. The hotel did not want this inquisitive American on the loose any longer than necessary.

Sam was startled by Mme. Soulnaire's striking beauty. At sixty years old, she had an aristocratic face, opaque blue eyes, high cheekbones and long, perfectly coiffed gray hair. Her shapely figure, too, did not escape his attention.

"Monsieur Harrison?" she said with a pleasant smile. "Would you be so kind as to join me in my office?"

"Certainly," he replied, noticing that she did not extend her hand. He couldn't decide if this was a snub, or if French women simply did not shake hands with men.

Sam thanked her for seeing him without an appointment. She gestured for him to take a seat.

"Would you care for coffee or tea?"

"No, thank you. Your time is valuable and I'll try to be as brief as possible."

"Then, how may I help you, Mr. Harrison," she asked pleasantly. Her English was slightly accented but otherwise flawless.

Sam sensed that she would not fall for a phony explanation. "I'm with the United States Government. Professor Rinot was working on a project for the University of Paris. The project may have direct implications to drug dealers who are smuggling vast amounts of heroin into the United States. I'm concerned that the professor may have left behind some very sensitive papers that could lead us to the smugglers."

"Drug smugglers? I can hardly believe that Professor Rinot was mixed up in that kind of thing."

"Not directly, Mme. Soulnaire. We think that he may have been an unwitting victim of someone who was after some recently discovered manuscripts," Sam replied.

"I see. That makes more sense. Exactly what kind of papers are you looking for, Mr. Harrison?" A puzzled look replaced the austere front that she had been showing.

"I can't be more specific as the documents are classified."

She paused momentarily. "I do not recall seeing anything except his smashed computer. Strange… It did not occur to me that he might have notes. I was the first one in his room, after the porter found him. There was nothing on the desk where he was working. We did not even find his valise…his safe-deposit box was empty also."

"Did he normally keep his valuables in the safe-deposit box?"

"I presume he did. He took out one of the larger ones when he arrived. We weren't able to find the key to the box in his room. We had to have a locksmith open it. Just this morning, in fact. It was empty. The manager informed me that the professor had removed his valuables from the box after returning from his morning exercise, shortly before he died."

Sam digested what Soulnaire had told him. "Please indulge me for a moment, Mme. Soulnaire. Think back to the professor's computer that was destroyed. Can you describe what you observed?"

"It seems that it was badly damaged, but I doubt that it was beyond repair. Does that help you?"

Sam considered what she had told him. A computer that fell from a desk would be damaged, of course, but *badly* damaged was another matter.

"When you say it was badly damaged, could you give me more detail?"

"Yes, certainly. The screen was shattered, which one would expect from a fall. But it is curious; the keyboard was smashed in. I hardly think that would be caused by such a short drop."

"Did you notice if there was a floppy disk in the A drive?"

"No. I did not look. At the time I was more concerned about the professor and the proper care of his belongings, which have been returned to his family in Paris."

"I assume that the computer was returned also?"

"Actually, no. We did not return the computer because, in its damaged state, we thought that it might be too painful for his family. So we sent it to the morgue along with his body. Do you suspect foul play, Mr. Harrison?"

"Possibly. But I can't be sure until I know exactly what caused his death."

"Well, from all appearances, as distasteful as these things are, he died from heart failure."

Sam thought for a moment. There probably would not be an autopsy. Rinot's death would be dismissed as unfortunate, not as a murder. He decided to approach it from another angle.

"Did Rinot eat anything in his room?"

"Hmm…wait one minute, let me check."

She walked to her desk and picked up her telephone. "Yvette, would you check yesterday's receipts. See if Professor Rinot ordered Room Service. Thank you. Hold for one moment, please." She cupped her hand over the phone and turned to Sam. "The professor had lunch delivered to his room."

"Can you get the name of the person who delivered the meal?"

She nodded, then spoke into the phone. She waited for maybe a minute. "I see," her eyes narrowed and her face became taut. She put down the receiver.

"It would seem that no one on our staff delivered the professor's meal."

# # #

Paris

Libra sprinted back to the master bedroom and dove under the bed behind the lace skirting.

The door to the apartment opened slowly, and a black-haired man with a heavy mustache entered. He turned to the hallway, his eyes taking in every detail. He entered the bedroom, walked to the closet and sifted through Rinot's clothing.

Libra silently reached for the Glock.

The man grunted in dissatisfaction. He walked to the armoire. He opened it and started flinging Rinot's clothes around the room. He pulled out two drawers, then dropped them on the floor. He checked for false panels. Finding none, he turned to the chest of drawers and started the procedure again, tossing the clothing and drawers haphazardly on the floor.

He's got to be looking for the manuscripts, Libra thought. *Shit, this guy is stupid. Nobody hides anything in such an obvious place.*

A baritone voice uttered something in Italian. Books started falling noisily to the floor. The man was in Rinot's study. *The asshole is going to get us both caught.* Silently she dragged herself from underneath the bed.

Libra tiptoed to the hallway. Holding her breath, she peeked into the library. She saw the side of the man's face as he tore open a book, then let it drop to the floor. He was large, over six feet and built like a powerful athlete. Strangely, he was dressed like a college professor himself, with a tweed sports jacket and smartly pressed dark slacks. She considered slipping out of the apartment, but reconsidered when she reasoned that this guy might be able to shed some light on Rinot's death and the missing Livy works.

Libra waited until the man turned his back to the door. Clutching the Glock in her hand, she rushed at the intruder, then shoved the barrel of the gun into the lower right-hand corner of his head. She had no way of knowing that the same man had saved her life the day before.

She barked at him in Italian: "Make the slightest move and you're a dead man!"

The man spun around with lightning speed, knocking the Glock from Libra's hand, sending it bouncing off a rack of books. In what seemed to be the same motion, he thrust his right hand into Libra's chest, pushing her violently across the room. She tumbled to the floor, somersaulting into a sitting position, her back to the wall.

She had underestimated the intruder. He was a professional.

Libra rolled to her right, thrusting her right leg at the man's knees. She hooked the back of the man's leg. He cried out in anguish, then buckled sideways and hit the floor with a thud.

Libra, on her hands and knees, scurried across the room toward the Glock, but the man was too fast. He grabbed her leg with an outstretched hand. It felt as if she were caught in a vice. The pain was excruciating.

Libra looked back at the man. His right arm was rising, coiling to strike her with a karate chop.

With her free leg, she smashed her foot squarely into his mouth. Blood spurted as teeth cracked and fell to the floor. His grip loosened. She yanked her other leg free as the man writhed in pain, then she lunged for the Glock.

The man, dazed by the blow, struggled to right himself, then reached back inside his coat and pulled out a snub-nosed revolver. He tried to align Libra in his sight. He squeezed the trigger. A bullet whizzed past Libra's ear as she stood to position herself. The man repositioned the revolver for a second shot, but before he could get the round off, two slugs from the Glock tore through his heart. The impact propelled him back into the bookshelf. His lifeless eyes stared at Libra, a mask of surprise shrouding his face.

Libra caught her breath as she looked down at the ugly blood stain spreading on Rinot's antique carpet. She searched his pockets for identification and pulled a billfold from his inside jacket pocket. She flipped it open. An official CIA identification looked back at her. "Son of a bitch," Libra swore. She stuck the wallet in her belt, then headed out of the apartment.

The gunshots would not go unnoticed. It would be only a matter of minutes before the police showed up. There was no time to cover her tracks.

Libra sprinted to the end of the hall, opened the door, and checked the corridor for traffic. The hallway was empty, so she walked casually to the fire exit. She was trained long ago as an agent not to run from a crime scene—it only attracted attention. Reaching the exit, she bolted down six flights of stairs and into the street.

She walked casually across the street and into the lobby of the Hotel de Suede. The concierge—typically Parisian—never looked up from his desk.

"Do you have a phone that I may use to place a local call?" Libra was as nondescript as possible.

"Yes, to the right of the lobby," he said, eyes on his paperwork.

Libra walked slowly to the phone and dialed the emergency number listed above the phone. A man's voice answered. Libra spoke rapidly, altering her voice.

"Yes…yes, there are gunshots coming from one of the apartments, on Rue de Suede, number 25." She hung up the phone.

#

NICE

The shrill ring of the phone disrupted the conversation. Mme. Soulnaire's face took on a look of agitation. "Yes," she answered.

"It is for you, Mr. Harrison." She extended the phone to Sam.

Sam put the phone to his ear. "Can you talk?" It was Libra speaking in Italian. Somebody was within earshot—somebody she didn't want eavesdropping.

"Not really. What's up?" Sam responded in Italian.

"We seem to have a lot of company all of a sudden…" She told him about the incident in Rinot's apartment. Sam listened patiently, but his stomach was churning.

"Did you find out if Rinot was murdered?"

"It looks that way." Questions flooded Sam's mind, but he knew he couldn't ask them now.

"I've got to get out of Paris. The heat is going to get turned up and I don't want to be around when it happens."

"Meet me at the D'Inghilterra," Sam said casually, referring to a hotel in Rome. He handed the receiver to Mme. Soulnaire.

"Please accept my apology for the interruption. That was an important call. Just a few more questions, then I'll let you get back to work. Did anyone remember who took the food to Rinot's room? Did they get a description?"

"I am afraid not." Now it was her turn to blush. "I would appreciate it if you would keep this information confidential, Mr. Harrison. I'm sure you can understand how upset the guests would be if they learned that there was a breach in our security."

"Of course." Sam didn't let on that the information from Libra would ultimately lead to questions regarding Rinot's stay at the Negresco. When the press got wind of the story, Mme. Soulnaire would wish she worked for a different property.

"Well, thank you for your time, Mme. Soulnaire. You have been very helpful. I'm sorry I had to visit your fine hotel under these circumstances." He stood to leave.

"Please feel free to visit us again, Mr. Harrison. I'm sorry that I could not give you more information about Professor Rinot's death." This time she extended her hand. "Can you find your way to the lobby? You'll have to excuse me, but I'm suddenly feeling somewhat faint."

As Sam walked out, she reached for the phone and dialed a number in southern Italy.

#

ROME

TRAJAN'S FORUM

A torrential rain flooded the grassy area surrounding the marble platform in Trajan's Forum. Maria shivered as she watched lightning flash against the low, dark clouds. There was no use trying to make it back to her apartment. She had an uneasy feeling in her stomach. The other workers had left over an hour ago, before the storm hit.

"Maria!"

Mario's voice. *Where? No. Can't be.* Nobody would come out in this downpour. Her mind was playing tricks on her.

"Maria!" Mario's voice came again through the sheets of rain.

She walked out from the overhang holding a red poncho over her head. Rain obscured her vision. She could make out Mario's lanky form leaning over the railing. Behind him, another boy. They looked like drowned rats.

"Mario, what are you doing out here in this miserable weather?" she yelled up at him. She could hardly hear her own voice against the downpour.

"Maria, I need to talk to you."

"Well, get down here out of the rain. You'll catch your death."

Mario and Figlio scurried to the end of the block, at Trajan's Column, and bolted down the cracked marble steps into the Forum. They hustled under the overhang out of the rain. Their T-shirts stuck to their skinny bodies. Mario wiped the water from his arms with his hands. Figlio rubbed his hands through his hair, trying to get the water out.

"You two ought to have your heads examined. Out in this rain, honestly," Maria said. "Why did you come here?"

Mario looked at her with sullen eyes. He swallowed hard. "We are in trouble and we need your help."

"What kind of trouble?"

"We think that someone is trying to kill us."

"What? Who is trying to kill you?" Maria asked.

"We, that is…well, we don't know," Mario stammered.

"Well then, let's try *why* is someone trying to kill you?" she said, still not believing a word.

"Maria, we need a place to hide. We thought you might be able to help us."

Maria thought for a moment. She hardly knew Mario. If he was in some kind of trouble, what would she be getting herself into?

"Mario, you're not leveling with me. What's going on? Tell me the truth."

Now it was Mario's turn to hesitate. Did he dare tell her about Livy? He felt as if he didn't have any other options. Despite his street-smarts, he had difficulty lying to people.

Mario inhaled deeply, then tried to get the truth out. "Well, Maria, you see…Figlio and I found one of Livy's lost works. It's on a scroll and somebody followed us and tried to take it from us…"

Maria looked at Mario with disgust. "C'mon, Mario, you expect me to believe a story like that?"

"I didn't think you'd believe me, so I brought the scroll with me for you to see. You are an archeologist and you can read the classics, so I'm going to show you. Please look at it. You will find that it's real. Figlio, get the scroll out of my book bag."

Figlio unhooked the back of Mario's book bag, then pulled out a neatly rolled sheepskin scroll tied with a leather cord. He handed it to Mario.

"See for yourself, Maria. We are very serious." Mario extended the scroll to Maria. She hesitated, and then took the scroll in her hand.

"If this is some kind of joke, Mario…"

Maria unraveled the scroll. "This is in remarkably good condition for something that's supposed to be over two thousand years old."

Maria looked at the Latin script. Her breath caught in her throat. On the upper right-hand corner was the signature of Titus Livius.

"Holy shit! Mario, this…this looks real as hell. How do you know it's not a forgery? You know, there have been forgeries. Where on earth did you find it?" Maria was talking rapidly, firing questions at Mario faster than he could field them. Finally Maria, catching her breath, exclaimed in broken Italian, "Oh my God…Oh my God…Oh my God."

Mario nodded.

"Mario, this is unbelievable! Do you realize that? These works have been missing since…Oh my God, Livy makes a personal reference to Augustus killing all those…Oh my God…this has to be real, nobody could make this up."

After several minutes, Maria pulled her eyes up from the scroll. She swallowed hard. "Mario, Jesus, I'm sorry I doubted you." Her hands were shaking. "Have you read this?"

Mario nodded, not sure if he should say anything just yet. He had little experience with women, and her behavior was beyond his comprehension.

"Do you realize that this might change history's perception of the first emperor of Rome? Mario, we have to get this to the proper authorities."

Mario was in no mood to discuss the proper disposition of the scroll. "We can't do that right now, Maria. The rest of Livy's books are still where I found that one. If we act too soon, they might fall into the wrong hands. There are some things we need to do first. If you can help Figlio and me, I will tell you the rest of the story and then I think you will agree that turning the scroll over to the authorities is not such a good idea right now."

Maria looked at Mario suspiciously. "What do you have in mind?"

"Figlio and I need a place to hide for a while. We can't go back to our apartment. It's too dangerous. We are asking you to help us. That's all I can say now."

Maria thought for a few moments. "Okay, Mario. I'll help you, but when you're out of trouble we turn the scroll over to the government."

"Thank you, Maria," Mario said, visibly relieved.

Maria looked at Figlio. "Figlio, I'm so sorry. Where are my manners? I've heard so much about you from your brother. By now you know, I'm Maria." She extended her hand. Figlio shook it awkwardly. "You two can stay with me in my apartment. It's on Via Veneto. But I have one condition," she looked sternly into Mario's eyes.

Mario nodded. Right now he didn't have a lot of bargaining power.

"We keep the scroll for now. And I get to translate it. But we keep it a secret. Nobody—and I mean nobody, other than the three of us—knows about the scroll. Deal?"

Mario just kept nodding. Right now, he couldn't have asked for a better deal.

Chapter 11

Chicago, Illinois
Saturday Morning

Moman Jasuri hung up the secure telephone in the basement of a rundown single-story house on the south side of Chicago. He climbed the wooden stairs into the small dining room and out the side door of the house to a dilapidated garage. He entered to find two men dressed in blue coveralls, working on a white 1998 Ford Taurus. The car had been stolen the night before and the license plates changed to look like official government plates.

One of the men, a clean-shaven Libyan, looked up as he balanced the car door on its hinges. "The bomb will be ready. The explosive has been planted in the car, and the timing device is being installed under the dashboard."

He showed Jasuri how to work the timer. It would be set for 5:15 P.M., the height of rush hour. All Jasuri needed to do, after he parked the car, was flip a switch to start the timer.

Operatives in Detroit, Boston, and Washington were in place. The phone call only one-half hour ago revealed that the bombing plans were perfect. Two of the men had been stopped by airport security, one in Detroit and the other in Washington. But their identities held up.

Jasuri rehearsed what he would do: At precisely two o'clock Monday afternoon, he would drive the car to the Sears Tower tenants' parking garage. He would park the car on the second deck. He would initiate the timer, ride the elevator to ground level, and get a taxi to O'Hare airport. At O'Hare he would board an Alitalia flight to Rome. By the time his flight was taxiing on the runway, the bomb would explode.

Satisfied that his plan was foolproof, he stepped outside and looked into the sky. A slight breeze from Lake Michigan warmed him as he raised his hands in supplication to Allah for making the jihad against the American infidels a triumph.

Jasuri's reverie was abruptly ended as a bullet from a high-powered rifle penetrated his right eye.

#

Paris

Libra replaced the receiver in the lobby of the Hotel de Suede. Whoever killed Rinot didn't find what they were looking for in Nice. Otherwise they wouldn't have bothered searching his apartment. And a CIA operative, to boot. Someone had gone to a lot of time and expense to plant a mole inside the Company. She turned her thoughts back to the meeting with Tom Wotherspoon. Rinot had told Wotherspoon on the phone that he had what he thought were the original Livy books, or at least some of them. He was planning to have the parchment authenticated scientifically—which would mean that he had put the original Livy documents in a safe place until he returned from holiday.

Libra hailed a taxi and took it to Rue Scribe #11, American Express. At the American Express building, she entered a phone booth and dialed the Louvre Department of Ministries. Her call was answered on the tenth ring.

"Yes," Libra said. "I'm trying to locate a company in Paris that does carbon dating. Can you recommend a firm that provides this service?"

The man on the other end of the line was happy to oblige. He gave Libra the name of a company on the outskirts of Paris. Libra thanked him and hung up. She walked up the circular stairs to the American Express travel desks. Finding an open queue, she purchased first-class airline tickets to London, Amsterdam, Frankfurt, and Rome.

She walked out and across the street to L'Opera. It took only moments for her to find a taxi. She ordered the driver to Rue Rivoli, the shopping district.

When they reached the busy street, Libra pulled out three one-hundred-franc notes and told the driver to be back in an hour.

Libra went into a large department store where she picked clothing, luggage, and accessories. Explaining to the clerk that she was leaving the country within hours, she changed into a navy blue Chanel suit.

Libra ran out the front door to find the taxi waiting. She gave the driver the address of the Classics Department at the University of Paris. There was a chance Rinot had left the scrolls in a secure location at the University. If he had, it was unlikely that he had told anyone.

At the University, Libra gave the cabdriver another 300 francs and asked him to wait.

Libra walked down the corridor of the two-hundred-year-old Classics building. She passed Rinot's locked office, then turned into the reception area. Two secretaries looked up as Libra walked into the room. One got up and walked to the counter.

"May I help you?" she asked.

"Yes. I'm with United Press International and I'm doing a story on some ancient transcripts that were recently recovered. I understand that a Professor Rinot is a leading authority on the subject and I was wondering if I could interview him." Libra noticed a walk-in safe at the far end of the room. The heavy steel door was open.

The woman hesitated and a sad look washed over her face. "I'm so sorry, apparently you did not know, but Professor Rinot died from a heart attack only yesterday."

Libra anticipated the response. "Oh, I'm terribly sorry," she said. She thanked the woman for her time and walked out of the office into the hallway.

The receptionist had shown no sign of recognition at her mention of "ancient transcripts." The originals might be in that safe. She had to find out.

Libra started to formulate a plan.

Sorrento

"We have had good results in America, father," Ramona said with uncharacteristic enthusiasm as she sat on the far side of Count Montefusco's office. "All of Rham's terrorists have been disposed of and there will be no resistance to our plan for taking control of his operations."

"Well done, my dear. Do you anticipate any other problems?"

"No. All of our people have successfully left the country, with the exception of our best agent, who is completing the last phase of the operation—eliminating the director of the Central Intelligence Agency. It will be assumed, of course, that the Director's death was a result of Rham's retribution."

"I see some concern in your face, however," the Count remarked.

"It has to do with your antiquities business. We have had a setback."

"Yes?"

"One of our men has been found shot to death in Professor Rinot's apartment."

The Count paused for several moments, considering the consequences. "Who killed him?"

"The woman agent. The one who fooled Rham."

"Hmm, this woman appears to be very resourceful. What do you think is motivating her?"

"She seeks revenge for the death of a brother who died at the hands of an American drug dealer."

The Count thought for a moment. "There is a Chinese proverb, 'When seeking revenge, first dig two graves.' She will make a mistake. When she does, we will deal with her."

"You do not want her terminated?" Ramona asked with a raised eye brow.

"Not yet. She is a professional. There is no sense in wasting more of our people. Unless I miss my guess, she will find what she is looking for and save us the trouble. Continue to have her followed."

"Why, Father, are these ancient transcripts so important? Surely it cannot be for their literary value. We have much more to gain from Rham's operations than from some ancient writings. Why put such time and effort into such a high-risk operation?"

The Count paused, reflecting on how much he should divulge. "There is a possibility that the writings of Livy could offer us enormous profit, but at this point I'm not certain of their monetary worth beyond their historical value."

"I'm not sure what you mean."

"In 217 B.C. there was a Roman general named Marcellus who was ordered to take the Greek city of Siracusa in Sicily during the war with Hannibal. Marcellus was successful, after a long campaign, in securing Hannibal's treasury. There was a great deal of gold stored there. It has never been recovered."

"I see," Ramona said.

"Have our people been able to locate the two boys?"

"These brothers are a nuisance. They have gone into hiding, and they have eluded our people in Rome. Perhaps we were too hasty in killing the smuggler who purchased the scroll from the older of the two?"

"Yes, that seems to have been an error in judgment on my part. I had not anticipated that the smuggler would find a buyer as rapidly as he did."

"You did not think that anyone would believe the discovery of the Livy works?"

"Precisely."

"You did too good a job fooling the scholars with your fake Livy scrolls many years ago?"

"Yes, yes. Had I known then that it would make scholars very skeptical today, I would never have done it, but who would have thought that the originals would surface? It would seem that we do not do well with CIA agents and teenage boys."

"I can assure you that the woman and the boys are merely inconveniences and that they will not give us any more trouble."

"What do you have in mind?"

"I have a plan that will lure them into a trap. When the trap is sprung, I will turn them over to you for final disposition."

"Very well," the Count finished with a slight smile.

#

Paris

Libra walked toward the south entrance of the Classics building as though she were late for an appointment. Holding a large shopping bag, she checked her watch. It had taken only an hour to find an automotive supply store and purchase half a dozen emergency flares. She had changed back into her black walking outfit.

She entered the building and turned to the women's lavatory across the hall from the business office. The lavatory was empty. She took three flares, lit them, and dropped them into a garbage container. The room started to fill with dense, white smoke.

Libra opened the door to the hallway and kicked a rubber doorstop between the floor and the door. Smoke from the flares started filling the corridor. Libra sprinted to the reception area. Stopping at the door, she shouted with as much alarm as she could muster, "Fire! The building's on fire! Get out, now!"

The secretaries practically tripped over each other as they bolted for the exit. After the secretaries ran out, Libra sprinted into the safe. *What am I looking for?* she asked herself as she scanned the shelves. All she could see were ledgers, a money box with a small amount of cash, record books, student grade books. She grabbed a footstool to get a better look at the shelves above her line of vision. Nothing unusual. She turned to look on the opposite wall. There! Underneath a green plastic tarp…something. Libra jumped off the footstool and moved it to the other side of the floor. She climbed back up and lifted the green canvas cover. Two scrolls; the wooden handles were badly damaged. They had to be the Livy books.

Libra grabbed the tarp, wrapping it around the scrolls. She lifted the bundle and put it under her arm. It was surprisingly light. She put the tarp into the shopping bag that she had carried into the building. She stopped at one of the desks, picked up a steel wastebasket and emptied the contents on the floor. It took her less than ten seconds to light the remaining three flares and throw them into the wastebasket. Smoke billowed through the office. Libra opened a window, letting the smoke pour out. To anyone walking by, the Classics building appeared to be on fire.

Libra bolted down the corridor to the exit on the south side of the building. She suspected the two secretaries would be standing outside the main entrance watching and waiting for the building to erupt in flames. It would be only a matter of minutes before the fire department showed up. With a little luck, the secretaries would not notice the missing scrolls until the next day—if they had even known that they were there.

# # #

"Where to now?" the taxi driver asked.

Libra gave him the address of the firm that conducted carbon dating tests on the outskirts of Paris. "After I finish my business at the next stop, I will need you to take me to the airport. Here is a small retainer. The balance will be paid when we get to Charles de Gaulle." She handed the driver five one-hundred-dollar bills.

They rode in silence for the next hour. The taxi pulled up to a small office building. "I will be approximately one hour. Please wait here as I am on a tight schedule."

The driver nodded and opened the newspaper.

Inside the building was a counter with two linoleum-top desks behind it. She could hear machinery whirring in the back room. A man in a lab coat sat behind one of the desks, talking on the telephone. Old black-and-white pictures of somebody with Charles de Gaulle hung on the dirty, green walls. The man hung up the phone and walked to the counter.

"Yes? May I be of service?" he asked.

"I hope so," Libra responded. She extended her hand. "My name is Barbara Prendergast, with United Press International."

The man extended a beefy hand. "I am Guilliam Setterant. I am a lab assistant here."

Libra put her briefcase on the counter along with the shopping bag. "I'm doing a story on ancient Roman artifacts, and I would like to learn more about carbon dating. Monsieur Grey at the Louvre gave me your company's name. He said you do excellent work for them."

"Ah, yes. Monsieur Grey. We do all the testing for the Louvre and the University," the man responded, wiping the edges of his bushy mustache.

"May I have about ten minutes of your time to ask you some questions for the article I'm researching?" Libra asked.

"Certainly. Perhaps you would like to come into the lab to see how the process is done?"

"Thank you. I would like that." Libra followed him around the counter and through a door into the back room. The room was as immaculate as the front office was filthy. The walls were covered with white ceramic tile. Testing machines of all kinds filled the room. Six men and one woman, all in white lab coats, looked up from their work as the two entered the room. They nodded and smiled in her direction.

The man escorted Libra to a machine at the far end of the building and proceeded to explain how it worked—how the paper to be tested was prepared and where it was put in the ovenlike opening.

"I wonder if you would be kind enough to test a document that I brought with me. I do not have much time as I must catch a plane in two hours to Rome. Would it be too inconvenient for you to test this scroll? I would be happy to pay a premium if you could." Libra knew the lie was weak, but she had little to lose.

The man thought for a second. "It is highly irregular to run a test without a purchase order."

Libra handed him a wad of rolled up 100-franc notes. "Would this suffice as a purchase order?"

The man saw that the other technicians were not paying any attention to the transaction.

"Ah, yes, but of course."

The man performed the process he had just explained. He walked over to a printer and picked up the report.

"Yes, Madame, you will be happy to know that this parchment is over two thousand years old. The exact date would be 20 B.C." He handed Libra the report and the scroll.

"You have been most helpful. Thank you so much for your time," Libra said, as she headed for the door.

#

ROME

Figlio shielded his eyes from the sun as he watched the tourists at the outdoor restaurants surrounding the piazza of the Pantheon. He sat on the stairs of the fountain. Mario was late. This was not like him. Nevertheless, the thought of his older brother brought a smile to his face.

Mario had been more than a brother. He had been a father and mother rolled into one. Figlio could hardly remember his father, and the only thing he remembered about his mother was that she was very pretty. Even though it had been years since the accident, he could picture her as though it were yesterday.

His parents had gone out that night. It was their wedding anniversary. They lived in Palermo then. There was an explosion. The police said it was a car bomb. It was a mistake. The Mafia, they said, planted a bomb for the mayor, who was running a campaign against crime and against the Mob. His parents were innocent victims. Figlio remembered the somber face of the policeman who came to the house that night.

Mario had cried all night, vowing revenge against the people that killed his mama and papa. They moved to Rome, to be taken care of by the priests in the mission. Every month an anonymous donation was made to the orphanage. The donation always came as a remembrance to his mother and father. Mario said it was Mafia guilt money. As time went on, Mario's anger diminished and he turned his attention to raising his brother.

Now Figlio was worried. Ever since the men tried to kill them on the Palatine, he feared for their lives. These men would kill them at the first opportunity.

Through the crowds he saw Mario dodging pedestrians on his bicycle. He stood up and waved. Mario saw him and turned his bicycle toward the fountain. He jumped off the bike and sat down next to Figlio.

"Did you have any luck with the *tambarolo*?" Figlio asked, sounding a bit anxious.

"No. I must have called two dozen times. No answer. The telephone just rang and rang."

"What about the library?"

"I found the names of museums that might buy the Livy scroll and the coins. Now all I have to figure out is how to approach them. This will be no easy task. I don't speak French or English and our best prospects are in Paris and London. I don't even know how to get to those places!"

"Is there anyone who can help us?"

"I have some ideas, but I don't like them."

"Let me hear them, Mario," Figlio said with boyish interest.

"Well, one, we could go to the *padrino*," Mario said.

"You mean the Mafia?" a wide-eyed Figlio loudly exclaimed.

"Hush! Not so loud, Figlio. It's only a thought. They owe us. Maybe they can make the connections for us. One favor, that's all," Mario said with a shrug.

"Mario, Mario." Figlio shook his head in disgust. "There is no such thing as one little favor. Once you're in, you're in. For life!"

"I didn't think you'd like that idea much," Mario said. He felt stupid for even suggesting it.

"You said you had a couple of ideas. What is your next idea?"

Mario approached what he was about to say very cautiously. He knew his next idea would upset his brother. "Well, Figlio, look at it this way: We have been resourceful enough so far. Am I right?"

Figlio didn't trust his brother's tone. "Why don't you just tell me your idea, Mario? You don't need to soft-sell me. I probably won't like it anyway, so let's hear it."

"Okay, okay," Mario said, raising the palms of his hands. "I propose we get on the train, go to Paris, and sell the scroll and the coins to the museums ourselves."

"What? You are crazy, Mario. And what about Maria? Remember, you said she could translate the scroll before we did anything with it."

"All right, all right. I did say that, but Maria will go back to America when the summer is over and we will never see her again."

"But you promised…"

No response. Mario simply stared at Figlio, trying not to snicker.

"Mario, you are crazy."

"Look, Figlio. If we could find what the archaeologists could not find in hundreds of years, we can find out how you go about selling ancient artifacts. Besides, I have a plan. I will find out how the smuggling is done. Then how to approach the museums. And sell the scrolls!"

"Do you really think you could do that?"

"I think I can. Besides, Figlio, who would suspect that two boys had found one of Rome's best-kept secrets? I don't think anyone will bother us. I think the problem will be when we find a buyer. Then, our ages will work against us."

"Mario, I'm afraid. We've been chased and shot at. Someone tried to kill us. Our lives are in danger because of these scrolls. I am scared to get on a train and go halfway across Europe and get involved in something we know nothing about. Can't we just stay here and wait for the *tambaroli?* I don't want to leave Rome."

"You make a good point, Figlio. But what else can we do? I can't find the *tambaroli.* They've disappeared. We have enough money to last for about a month without going into the savings accounts. Don't you see, this is our chance to have enough money to live decent lives. I am sick and tired of being poor. I want a better life for you and for me. This is our chance."

After a long pause, Figlio said, "I don't know, Mario. It's too scary. I would rather wait. Going to some foreign city…" He let the thought trail off.

A slight smile crossed Mario's lips. He knew his brother had no choice but to follow him on his newest adventure. Besides, he had seen Castor and Pollux in the Forum. He suspected that this was part of the new life the vision prophesied.

#

Monte Carlo

Sam did not notice the beautiful Mediterranean coastline rushing by the train window. A legal pad on his lap, he attacked the problem logically, trying to fit the pieces of the puzzle together:

Chronology of Events
1. Apollo sends message, "In the mouth of the wolf."
2. Libra sees Carthaginian Cresa in Afghanistan.
3. El Al plane crashes in France with an MI-6 Agent based in Rome.
4. Lost works of ancient Roman historian Livy discovered.
5. Rinot murdered while translating the Livy works.
6. An Italian attempts to kill Libra in Rinot's apartment in Paris.

Sam looked over his notes, seeking a common denominator. It became apparent that his notes had ties to Italy. He turned his attention to Rinot's murder. Why? Someone knew Rinot had the manuscripts. They either wanted Rinot out of the way so he wouldn't divulge what he had translated, or they wanted the manuscripts.

Whoever killed Rinot might have wanted the manuscripts to fill in some missing pieces regarding the Roman Empire. *What if the manuscripts Rinot had in his possession told only a portion of Livy's story? What was on the microfiche Libra found in Rinot's apartment? If she can get her hands on the originals before leaving Paris, we'll have more to go on. Perhaps they'll lead to the drug operations. Libra may be right; the two just could be tied together.*

As the train sped toward the Italian border, Sam broke out in a wide smile. He remembered the name of a dear, old friend. A friend who owed him a favor. A friend who could help. Now, if he's still alive, it was time to collect the favor.

Chapter 12

Langley, Virginia
Saturday

William Bannistar bent his tall frame into the back seat of the Cadillac limousine. Pug took one look at his face and realized the guy had had a tough day. He knew well enough to leave Bannistar alone when he was in one of these moods. Pug put his foot on the accelerator and drove the car away from CIA headquarters.

Bannistar mulled over several annoying developments. Sam had not checked in. What agitated him even more was Sam and Libra's purchasing airline tickets to various cities throughout Europe. This was characteristic of agents going to a deep cover. The airline tickets were meant to throw off anyone trying to trail them. Something, or someone, had them spooked.

The second enigma confronting Bannistar was a missing researcher, Salvatore Sangi. The man had vanished. Bannistar discovered that the man was missing when he called down to Research for background on the Livy books. Sangi would have executed the order for the department and analyzed the data. But he was gone! A call to his home revealed only that he was not there. A subsequent search turned up nothing unusual.

Bannistar's thoughts were interrupted by the realization that the limousine was going faster than usual. He leaned forward and pushed the Plexiglas partition to the side.

"Aren't we overdoing it a bit, Pug?" Bannistar asked wearily.

"We've got a problem, Mr. B. The brakes aren't working. I think somebody's been fooling around with the car."

Bannistar noticed the red speedometer needle passing through 70 mph. "Did you try turning off the ignition?" Bannistar asked, his eyes wide open, adrenaline replacing his fatigue.

"Yes, sir. But somebody has rigged the damned thing. It won't turn off. It just keeps accelerating. I've already tried to call for help, but the cellular phone is dead."

The speedometer was approaching 80. "We're gonna have a big problem in about two minutes, Mr. B. We're coming up to the Susquehanna Bend," Pug said referring to a steep, winding hill on the freeway, bordered on one side by a sheer granite wall and on the other side by a fifty-foot drop to the Potomac River. "I've got an idea, Mr. B. Fasten your seat belt."

Just then, one of two forty-foot semitrailers, which had been traveling single file in the slow lane, pulled into the passing lane. The other tractor-trailer increased its speed so that it pulled parallel to the first trailer. They blocked both lanes of the highway. Pug sped toward them at 85 mph.

"Get the tag numbers of those damned trucks, Pug. They're going to try to force us off the highway. Oh, shit, never mind. The tags are fake anyway," Bannistar said with resignation.

"Hang on, Mr. B. Here we go." With that, Pug jammed the gearshift lever into Park while pressing his foot on the emergency brake. The big Cadillac bucked, and a loud pulverizing sound came from underneath it. The transmission's gears meshed against one another. Suddenly, the transmission seals blew open. The emergency brake failed to catch. The momentum of the heavy vehicle snapped the brake cables in two.

Pug steered the limousine toward the guardrail. Sparks flew as metal scraped metal. The Cadillac made a sickening, screeching noise as it bounced off the guardrails. It rebounded back into the passing lane. The trucks applied their brakes. They were trying to force the limousine off the road and over the cliff.

Pug fought the wheel, turning the car back toward the guardrail. "It's working, Mr. B. We're starting to slow down. But hang on. At this speed we may end up under one of those trailers."

"Damn it, Pug, stay clear of those fuckin' things. They've probably got an explosive rigged in the back. If we get stuck under one of them, we'll be blown to kingdom come!"

The limousine hugged the guardrail. It was closing in fast on the trucks. Pug looked at the speedometer. "We're down to 50. Jesus, I think we're gonna make it," Pug snorted, tension easing from his voice. "Those semis can't hit their brakes; they'll jackknife. They've got to maintain their speed."

"Good," Bannistar barked, looking out the rear window. "I hope you've got the Smith & Wesson on board, Pug. My guess is that we're not out of this yet."

Pug hit a button under the driver's seat. The seat cushion from the passenger side popped up, revealing a pump-action shotgun. "If somebody is following us they're going to get an assful of lead."

The Cadillac was slowing…20 mph…10. Finally, the big car came to a stop. It was pinned against the guardrail, less than an eighth of a mile from the hill overlooking the

Susquehanna Bend. Pug grabbed the shotgun, then pulled a .357 Magnum from the glove box.

"You stay down, Mr. B. I'll take care of the backup." Pug had looked forward to this day for twenty-five years. The Company had trained him for this type of action in the unlikely event that someone might try to kill the Director.

Pug scrambled across the front seat, let himself out and positioned himself behind the rear fender of the limousine. He looked back up the highway. His stomach tightened when he saw it—big, black Mercedes 520-SEL.

Pug could see the driver gritting his teeth and clutching the steering wheel. Two more motherfuckers in the back. The rear window started to slide down. The prick was aiming an AK-47 at him! "Okay, you miserable bastards, come and get it."

He guessed the Mercedes was moving at 65 mph. The car was in the passing lane but starting to shift to the near lane. Little wind. The parkway was empty; there were no other cars in sight.

Pug extended both arms, ignoring the cramp in his leg. He lined up the barrel of the .357 with the man's head and squeezed the trigger. A thundering blast rang in his ears. When his eyes focused, he saw that the round had found its mark; the bullet had blasted through the gunman's forehead and out the back of his skull. The AK-47 clanked to the concrete and somersaulted toward him.

The dead man's accomplice then slid across the seat to the window. He pointed an Uzi at Pug. Pug ducked down behind the fender as a spray of bullets washed over the trunk.

Pug aimed the Smith & Wesson, then cocked it into the firing position. A second wave of bullets came in two short bursts, then stopped.

Pug jumped up from behind the Cadillac. His reflexes responded automatically as the Mercedes sped by. Another thundering roar rang in his ears. He looked in time to see the Mercedes being driven by a headless, bloody torso.

The Mercedes buckled to the right. Its tires could not hold the road. It flipped over. Pug watched as the Mercedes disappeared down the side of the hill.

Pug turned and glanced back down the highway to make sure there were no more assassins on their way. A black-orange ball of flame leapt into the air from below the hill, followed by a blistering explosion. The acrid stench of burning oil and smoke filled the air.

"Was that the best you could do?" Bannistar asked with mock severity as he climbed out of the rear door. "I wanted those cocksuckers alive, damn it. They could have given us a lot of answers to a lot of unanswered questions. Jesus, Pug, why'd you go and incinerate them like that?"

"Friends of yours?" was all Pug could think to say.

Bannistar grunted, then let out a belly laugh.

# # #

ROME

The ten-hour trip from Nice left him exhausted, but he couldn't let the fatigue get in his way. His senses were alert. With the possibility of someone in the Company keeping tabs on him, he couldn't afford to let down his guard.

He looked at his watch. Midnight. Not too late. Probably just the right time. He walked up to a pay phone and inserted a debit card. He pushed the numbers into the phone from memory. Some things you never forget, he thought to himself. This phone number was one of them.

The phone rang three times before a deep baritone voice answered with a simple "Prego."

"*En bocca el lupo,*" Sam said softly into the telephone.

"*Che crepi el lupo.* Where are you?"

"Termini," came Sam's reply.

"A driver will pick you up out front in twenty minutes. What are you wearing?"

Sam told him.

The line went dead.

Sam picked up his briefcase and headed for the exit. Twenty minutes later a dark blue Lancer limousine stopped in front of the station. Sam climbed in the back seat before the driver could get out and open the door.

The driver wore a lightweight business suit—tailored and very expensive, not what one would expect to see a chauffeur wearing. He could have passed for a Wall Street broker, Sam thought. But when you work for the boss of all bosses in the Italian Mafia…

Sam's mind wandered as they drove into the night. He flashed back to his past relationship with the Mafia chieftain.

It was 1979. Don Portico's family was at war with the Fuminari family. The unwritten law was that individual family members were untouchable. They were never to be harmed, or held hostage, during times of interfamily disputes. The Fuminari family, in a desperate attempt to wrest control from the Porticos, seized Don Portico's ten-year-old son. They had him hidden in a warehouse in the shipping district of Rome.

Don Portico was beside himself. This was his only son, heir to the family empire. Don Portico put out a handsome reward for anyone who could provide information leading to the safe return of his Lorenzo. If his son was killed, he vowed holy vengeance and took a solemn oath to eliminate the Fuminari family.

Sam, then a young CIA operative, was meeting with a double agent from the Soviet Union two days after the kidnapping. The two agents met outside the very warehouse where the Fuminari family was hiding Lorenzo. Sam spotted two men entering the warehouse at three in the morning.

Curious, Sam followed the two men to a remote office, where he overheard one of them explaining that they were to kill the boy and dump his body in a place Don Portico frequented. Sam was acquainted with the Don, and he knew of the situation with the Don's boy.

He didn't hesitate. He took out a .22 caliber pistol and surprised the men as they were about to slit the boy's throat. He shot both men in the chest before they knew what was happening. He finished the job by putting a bullet in the head of each man. The Fuminari family would know the killings were done by a professional.

Sam returned Lorenzo to his father.

The Don's last words to Sam were, "I owe you more than a favor, my friend. I owe you a life." Now Sam was here to collect. He wasn't sure where to start, but the Don would get him the information he needed. Of that there was no doubt.

The car pulled up to a house on the outskirts of Rome. Don Portico was one of the wealthiest men in Rome, but no one would ever know it from this modest two-story, brick structure. The chauffeur ushered him through the front door.

Sam was greeted in the front lobby by a giant, at least six-feet-six-inches tall and weighing three hundred pounds. The man greeted Sam with a broad smile, then expertly frisked him for weapons. The giant was satisfied that Sam did not present a threat. He escorted Sam through the house to the basement and into a large office.

Don Portico was dressed in neatly pressed khaki pants, brown Gucci loafers and a blue golf shirt. His thick gray hair was neatly combed back. He looked much younger than his sixty-six years. He walked up to Sam and gave him a bear hug. "It is good to see you after all these years, my friend," he said, slapping Sam on the back with both hands. "You look good. You've been taking care of yourself, I see. Come, sit down. We'll talk about old times before we get to business." He picked up his phone and ordered refreshments.

Sam sat down and looked around the room. Beige plaster walls, a large oak desk, and two comfortable chairs. A large Persian throw rug covered most of the tiled floor. For a Mafia don's office it was sparse. Sam wondered how many men had been sentenced to the hereafter in this room. *If walls could talk...*

A man in a bone-white jacket brought in two glasses of wine on a silver tray. The Don took one of the glasses. The waiter turned and let Sam take the other. The Don lifted his glass in the air and said to Sam, "*Salute!*"

The two men raised their glasses and took a gulp of the wine.

"You are married now, Sam? With a few bambinos. No?"

"Not yet, Don Portico," replied Sam. "But the day is coming. And your son? He is well?"

The conversation went on like this for another fifteen minutes. The men laughed at past exploits, serious at the time but lighter in retrospect. Sam let the Don decide when it was time to discuss business. Eventually he did.

"Now, my friend. You have a problem. How may I help you? You know it is always more fun to chase spies than it is to do my businesses."

Sam told the Don everything. "We will need a safe house, a place where we cannot be found. We are being hunted by our own people as well as the police. And we will need somebody to translate the manuscripts."

When Sam finished the Don stood up. "Done," he said with a wave of his hand. "My driver will take you to an apartment not far from here. He will be at your disposal twenty-four hours a day. I will make arrangements to find a translator. Is there anything else?"

"One small detail, but an important one. I don't know if you can help me, but we'd like to find the *tambarolo* who smuggled the scrolls out of Italy. They could tell us who found them and where the rest are located. They can also tell us who has the other set. The information they have would be invaluable in resolving some unanswered questions."

The Don nodded; his eyes were chilling.

Sam stood up and thanked the Don.

#

Washington

"Well, why were the police bringing you home?" Dorothy Bannistar asked her husband, a look of horror on her face. She stood in the middle of the kitchen wearing a red wool sweater with dark slacks and black pumps. None of their friends believed she was sixty-five. Slim, blond, and tan, she looked ten years younger. She anxiously watched her husband take a bottle of Johnny Walker Red from the liquor cabinet.

"The limousine broke down on the GW Parkway. A patrol car stopped. The trooper delivered me here." Bannistar did not want to upset his wife with the details.

Because of the sensitive nature of what happened, the details would be kept from the press.

"That was awfully nice of them," Dorothy responded, relieved that it was nothing more serious. "I'll take one of those, too," referring to the Scotch that Bannistar was pouring. "Are you off the wagon again?" she asked with an arched eyebrow.

"Bad day. I need something to settle my nerves."

Bannistar reached in the cabinet for another tumbler. He poured the Scotch into a shot glass, and when Dorothy wasn't looking he downed it in one swallow.

"Here you are, honey." He handed Dorothy a glass filled with ice cubes and Scotch. "I didn't water it down, so take it easy." He turned to the door before she could scold him about his drinking. "I've got to make a quick call. Be back in a minute."

Bannistar picked up the secure line and dialed Control. The line rang once. Bannistar punched his code into the receiver.

"One message," the mechanical voice said. "Call Ambassador Lambert, American Embassy, Paris. Marked Urgent."

An operator at Langley scrambled the call to Paris. He waited as the phone rang. It was answered on the second ring by Lambert.

"Bill Bannistar, Larry. What have you got?"

"You missing one of your employees?" Lambert asked.

"Yeah. Disappeared a couple days ago. You obviously have something. What is it?"

"The Paris Police picked up a DOA in an apartment not far from the Embassy."

"Shit." There was a momentary pause. "Describe him."

"About six feet. One-seventy-five. Black hair. Brown eyes. No identification on his body."

"Give me the specifics."

"The police don't know what happened. They found him with two bullet wounds in the chest. Ballistics confirmed they were from a Glock .38. Police think that he got caught in the act of a burglary by another burglar. Indications were that there was a struggle. An anonymous caller, a woman, tipped off the police. You got any rogue agents on the loose?"

Bannistar ducked the question. "Whose apartment was it?"

"A professor of classical studies at the University who died of a heart attack yesterday in Nice. Any idea what he was looking for?"

"I'd rather not say."

"The police thought he might have been an American. That's why they called us. Wanted to know if anybody was missing. They thought, because he had no identification, that he might have been attached to the Embassy in some way. I just got back from looking at the body. I couldn't give them positive ID. How do you want us to handle it?"

"I'll have somebody from Langley call you right away for cleanup. Keep this under wraps. We've got something sensitive going on. Right now, I don't need any press. I've got enough problems as it is."

"Will do." Lambert hung up.

Bill Bannistar reached for his Scotch. He drained what was left in one long swallow. He reached for his briefcase and pulled out Salvatore Sangi's personnel file. He started thumbing through it. Joined the Company right out of college. Graduated top of his class at University of Virginia. Trained as a field operative, but opted for research and analysis. Performance reviews were good. Nothing that would indicate a problem. But if he were a mole, his record would be squeaky-clean. He made a note to himself to have Sangi's early background rechecked.

Moles. Goddamned moles. Shit. But who could he have been working for?

He picked up a legal pad and started listing the cities to which Sam and Libra had purchased airline tickets. Rome. It had to be Rome. He reached for the phone. "Get me Tim Benedict at the Rome station. I don't care if it's two in the morning over there. Get him the hell out of bed, and call me back," Bannistar roared into the telephone.

He waited nervously, puffing on a Marlboro and drumming his fingers on the desk. Fifteen minutes later, the phone rang.

"Mr. Bannistar," a groggy voice said. "This is Tim Benedict in Rome. I just got your message."

"Tim. We've got a problem. I've got two rogue agents on my hands." Bannistar gave a quick rundown on Sam and Libra. "My guess is they're hiding out somewhere in your back yard. Sam Harrison was stationed there early in his career. Start checking his known contacts. See if you can locate him. I need to get to him in a hurry. Call me back tomorrow and check in. Doesn't matter if you have anything or not. I want an ongoing progress report. They probably think the Agency has turned on them. If you find them, approach them carefully. They're spooked. They're not going to trust you or anybody else from the network."

"Got it," Benedict responded. "I'll have my people on it right away, and I'll call you tomorrow with a progress report." He hung up.

Bannistar then did what he had dreaded all day. He picked up the red phone to the White House.

# # #

ROME

The driver dropped Sam at an apartment building in the center of Rome. He took the elevator to the penthouse. The suite was lavishly furnished. Sam went to the window and pulled open the drapes. Below him was the Trevi Fountain, the marble statues bathed in light. The surroundings were even more magnificent than he had expected.

He sat down on the green silk sofa, took out a legal pad and started to formulate a plan. The first thing he would have to do is make reservations at Hotel D'Inghilterra. When Libra showed up, she'd have to be able to leave a message for him. Second, he had to find a lead to the *tambaroli*. Someone in Rome knew where the Livy manuscripts had been hidden for the past twenty centuries. Third, he had to find out if he and Libra had been compromised by the Agency—and if so, why.

What had happened to Libra? He'd half expected her to be here by now. But since he hadn't been able to communicate with her at the Negresco, he wasn't able to learn if she may have had other things to do, like tracking down the scrolls. The phone rang, interrupting his thoughts.

"*Prego?*" Sam said into the receiver.

"Everything is to your liking?" It was the Don.

"Perfect. You're a most gracious host."

"The airport and the train station are being watched by your people. You must have just slipped them when you arrived. They are watching for you and Libra, so avoid those places. Next, the people that you wanted us to find seem to have disappeared. The *tambaroli*, how do you say, smugglers?"

"That's correct."

"Well, the ones we know about are gone. We cannot locate them anywhere. This is curious."

"Anybody know why?"

"No," replied the Don. "They simply disappeared. And there is another disturbing matter. A week ago, there were two bodies discovered in the ruins. We are checking with the other families, but so far nobody knows who these men were, or why they were—how do your movies say?—*offed*."

"Yes, 'offed' is the word they use," Sam said with a chuckle. He liked how the Don tried to Americanize everything for him.

"These two men. Nobody knows who they were. Our informants at the police tell us there was no identification on the bodies. Their fingerprints are not on record. So the authorities are at a loss as to who these men were and what they were doing in the ruins at night. The investigation has been dropped because nobody came forward to identify them."

"How did they die?"

"One was discovered in the bottom of a well on the Palatine Hill, his head smashed open by a hunk of marble. The other fell to his death in the Forum. He was probably pushed from the observation deck on the Palatine, overlooking the old Forum. The man's neck was broken when he landed in the Temple of Castor and Pollux."

"See what else your men can find out about them. They may be connected with the rest of this."

"Certainly, my friend. Is there anything else I can do for you?"

"Not right now. I need to get some sleep. You might ask your men to keep an eye out for Libra. She hasn't shown up yet. I'm sure she'll be coming in from the airport or train station. Thanks for your help." Sam hung up.

# # #

Termini Station, Rome

The two brothers stood on the train platform awaiting the boarding announcement. They looked no different than the thousands of students that flooded into Italy this time of year.

"What time do we arrive in Paris?" Figlio asked.

"At noon tomorrow. We will try to find a place to stay, then we will see if we can get an appointment at the University of Paris."

"And what if they aren't interested, Mario?"

Mario shrugged. "Then we will find another."

As the brothers talked, something moved in front of them, casting a huge shadow. Mario looked up. In front of him was a giant of a man. He was smiling.

Mario's initial reaction was to grab Figlio and run. But there was another man standing to his right. There was a man standing next to Figlio, and two more men standing behind them. Mario's eyes followed the giant's hands. A raincoat covered his right hand. Under the raincoat he saw the muzzle of a gun pointed at his chest. The man motioned for Mario and Figlio to start moving toward the exit.

Chapter 13

Geneva, New York
Monday

Professor Tom Burrall turned up South Main Street, jogged past fraternity row and headed toward the Hobart-William Smith campus. He glanced at his watch. Just enough time left to shower and get to his eight o'clock class.

As the professor approached Cox Hall, he noticed a woman coming through one of the four massive oak doors, onto the concrete steps that jutted into the quad. *That's odd.* The building wasn't unlocked until eight in the summer. He couldn't help but notice how attractive she was. She looked familiar, but he couldn't quite place her.

He ran past the building nodding politely at the woman. She was wearing a William Smith T-shirt and black spandex running shorts with colorful Nike Airs. She started running toward him. As he jogged past the building, heading for Bartlett Hall, he was a little surprised to find her jogging beside him.

"Hi, Professor," the woman said in a friendly voice. "You probably don't remember me, but I was a student in one of your classes years ago. I've got a problem and I need your help."

"Oh, yeah," Burrall said between breaths, "what's that?"

Her best weapon was the truth, or at least a portion of the truth. "I have ten of Livy's lost books, and I need them translated."

"What?" Burrall started to laugh. He stopped in his tracks.

Libra focused her eyes directly on his. "This is not a joke, Professor. I have ten of the 'lost' books on microfiche. The originals are locked in a safe-deposit box in Paris. So far, the only other person to see the transcripts was Jean Claude Rinot. He was murdered because somebody wanted them."

"You knew Rinot?" Burrall asked in a raspy voice. He didn't look convinced. "I heard he died from a heart attack. You say he was murdered?"

"It was made to look like a heart attack. He was poisoned."

"How did you find this out?"

"I can't really tell you any more than that, Professor. It's classified information. That's why I need your help."

"Who are you with?"

"Central Intelligence Agency."

"No shit. You knew Rinot? He was the Godfather of Roman Studies."

"Not exactly. He somehow got his hands on two of the Livy scrolls. To the best of our knowledge, they were smuggled out of Italy about a week ago. But he died before he could translate all of them. We think whoever killed him wanted what was in the manuscripts."

"So why is the CIA interested in Roman history?"

"I'd rather not go into that right now, Professor; however, suffice it to say that whoever is behind Rinot's murder may also be responsible for smuggling drugs into the country. A lot of drugs. It's a major problem. If you can help me you'd be doing the country a great service."

"How do you know this?"

"All I can tell you is that a number of people have been killed, and we believe the killings are related to the Livy transcripts. That's why I want them translated."

After thinking for a few moments, Burrall said, "I'm sorry, but I've forgotten your name."

"Rebecca Arnason. You can check your 1982 *Echo and Pine*. My graduation picture is on page two-fifty-eight. I need your help, but what I'm going to ask you to do is dangerous. As I mentioned, people have died because of these manuscripts. I don't want to jeopardize you or your family's safety. If you choose not to work on them, I'll understand."

"If I do help you, what guarantee do I have that I won't be harmed?" Burrall asked.

"Is there a place we can talk? I need to go over the details with you. This is not a good place."

"Okay. I have a class at eight. I'll be finished by nine-thirty. Can you meet…"

"Professor, I don't think you understand the urgency of this situation. I'm running against the clock. There's no telling how many more people will be harmed because of these books. It's important that you look at this microfiche immediately. Can you find somebody to take your class?"

"Not at this hour."

"Then cancel it." Libra's voice turned hard.

The professor's face took on a look of horror. He cleared his throat. "One more question," he said, his voice trembling. "How do you know the manuscript is the original, and not a forgery?"

"Carbon dating verifies that the parchment, written on sheepskin, is two thousand years old. It was manufactured shortly before the birth of Christ. I've seen the documentation and talked to the people who did the testing. In Paris. The day before yesterday. Is that good enough?"

"For now, it's good enough."

"If I recall, the library has private screening booths. Let's go. We can talk there."

"Jesus, Rebecca. Hold your horses. Do you mind if I shower? Livy's waited over two thousand years. What's another thirty minutes?"

"All right. But hurry."

"I'll meet you in the library as soon as I finish. Should take me only twenty or thirty minutes. I'll call the administrator and have her tell the students the class will be rescheduled."

"If it's a class on Roman history, Professor, you'll have a lot more to tell your students. Trust me," Libra said, a faint smile crossing her lips.

# # #

The first frame of the microfiche showed something written in Latin, one language Libra hadn't mastered. The small letters were faded but legible. Considering it was over two thousand years old, it was in remarkable condition.

She heard the door open behind her. Professor Burrall walked into the room. He was carrying an old leather briefcase. "Okay. Let's see what you got."

Libra snapped off the projector. "Not so fast, Professor. First there are a few conditions."

"What are they?"

"I need you to work with me on the translation of Livy's works. It's important that you follow my instructions to the letter. Many lives depend on it."

"In what way? I don't understand."

Libra laid out a detailed plan for the professor, with very specific instructions on how he was to communicate information regarding the transcripts.

"Furthermore, until you're notified by me, and me alone, you are not to tell a soul about these transcripts. If anybody from the United States Government approaches you, you are to deny you have these. Understood? As I mentioned earlier, this is for your own protection."

"Agreed," Burrall replied, as he stepped toward the reader.

"Second. You will not receive any monetary compensation for translating the works. At least not from the government. Is that agreeable?"

"Yes."

Libra put a hand to his chest, gently holding him back. "One last thing…"

"What else?" Burrall asked, frustration in his voice.

Libra thought he'd agree to anything at this point…even paying to translate them. "You are not to divulge the contents of what you translate—to anyone. Your students, your family, the colleges, and especially the press. Is that perfectly clear, Professor Burrall?"

"Perfectly. Now may I begin, young lady? You, yourself, stressed the urgency of getting these things translated. So if there are no more conditions…" He let the thought trail off.

"Yes, Professor, by all means, begin."

The professor opened his briefcase and pulled out a legal pad. Everything in the room had disappeared except the Livy transcripts. He lost all track of time.

Libra felt a shooting pain in her temples. Her mouth dry, she propped herself against the wall, fighting waves of fatigue. I've got to press on, she thought to herself. This is the first tangible break in the case. She rubbed her eyes and shook her head.

After five minutes, Libra nudged the professor. "Professor Burrall. Have you found anything?" she asked, not trusting herself to say anything more.

"Oh, yes. I'm terribly sorry. This certainly appears to be Livy. The writing is consistent with his surviving books." He glanced up at Libra. "Are you okay?"

"It's jet lag. I think I need to lie down for a few minutes."

"You should find a nice couch just down the hall."

Libra's legs wobbled as she grabbed the door frame to keep herself from falling. She straightened herself and walked slowly across the carpeted hallway. She found the couch at the end of a row of books. Gratefully, she collapsed onto it and was sound asleep within seconds.

# # #

Two hours later, Libra awoke. She stretched, got up, and walked back down the hall to find Burrall hunched over a drafting table, staring at the microfiche in the reader.

"Are they what I described to you, Professor?" Libra interrupted him as she entered.

"Yes. At least they appear to be. I really won't know until I've read further."

"Can you say more about that?"

"Livy personalized history; that is, he wrote history like most modern-day authors write novels. Factual information, the detail of an event, is sometimes inconsequential to him. It was the ongoing history, the story, that was important. He really was trying to glorify Rome. By the way, are you feeling better? I'm sorry not to have asked earlier."

"Fine, fine. Tell me what you've translated so far."

"This particular book is about events taking place in Spain. Probably around 100 B.C. The Roman army suffered staggering losses in a battle with a rebel army from the Pyrenees. Livy then turns his attention to Rome and the election of the consuls. The Romans kept excellent records on their elected officials. But that's not what you're looking for. There's a lot of material here. It will take some time to translate all of it."

"How much time, Professor?"

"That's hard to say. It can take all day just to figure out one paragraph. Words carried different meanings two thousand years ago. As I mentioned, Livy had a tendency to accentuate the glory of Rome and play down the negatives; therefore, getting his precise meaning may take days, maybe even weeks."

"Shit. I don't have that kind of time," Libra blurted out.

"Well, I don't know what else to tell you."

"Somewhere in there, we think Livy makes reference to the location of a fortune in gold. A treasure. Probably spoils from a vanquished country. Is there any way you can scan the transcripts for this reference?"

"I'll try, but I can't promise you I'll find anything. I certainly can't find anything while we're talking. So if you'll excuse me, I'll get back to work."

Libra walked out of the room.

# # #

Libra looked at her watch. The professor had been working on the transcripts for five hours without a break. She decided to check on him. She walked down the library stairs to the closed room. The professor was still at it. She opened the door. He didn't look up.

"How's it going, Professor?"

"What? Oh. I didn't hear you come in. Slowly, I'm afraid. This will take much longer than I originally anticipated. So far, I haven't found anything that would even so much as hint at a treasure. Come closer. Let me show you what I've got."

Libra moved closer to the professor. She could see he had used up two full legal pads.

"The first set of microfiche is pretty routine stuff. I takes place long after the Hannibalic Wars. Livy writes about the peace in Italy and the surrounding countries. Elections, government business, that sort of thing. Now, there is one thing that's curious."

He had Libra's full attention. She nodded for him to continue.

"Livy wrote his books in sets of five; that is, every five books represent a ten-year period in Roman history. For example, from 220 B.C. to 200 B.C., Rome fought Hannibal. Livy covered this entire period in books 21 through 30. That is to say, two sets, of five books each, covered two ten-year periods. We were fortunate that the twenty books covering the war with Hannibal survived intact. Livy wrote one-hundred-forty-two books in all, covering a period from 753 B.C., the founding of the Empire, to 9 B.C., the period of Augustus Caesar. But only thirty-five of Livy's books survived. Some eighty-seven books are missing; that is, until now. You have given me the equivalent of ten books, or twenty years of Roman history. It will take several weeks, perhaps months, to translate what you've given me."

"I see," Libra said noncommittally.

"Well, the first piece of microfiche," Burrall continued, "represents Livy's books 51 to 55. The second piece of microfiche represents books 116 to 120. So you see, there is a significant time gap between the two sets. I scanned both sets for anything out of the ordinary, but, in truth, found nothing that we in modern times do not already know. However, I don't want to discount the fact that what you are looking for may very well be contained in one of these books. I simply will need more time to dig through all the material."

Libra, obviously disappointed, asked the professor for an overview.

"The first set of books is pretty boring stuff. He talks about the countries in the Mediterranean and how they struggled to rebuild from the years of war with Carthage. The second set is considerably more interesting. Livy talks at length about Augustus's plans to build Rome into a modern, cosmopolitan city. You may remember the saying, 'Augustus found Rome a city of stone, and left it a city of marble.' He goes on to talk about the many mystery cults that had cropped up in Rome, and how they disrupted the political and moral order of Roman society. One of the mystery cults, incidentally, was Christianity. That's when you came through the door."

Libra had to make a decision. She couldn't stay much longer. Within the next couple of hours, Washington would pick up her tracks.

"Keep working on them, Professor." Libra walked out.

Twenty minutes later, Burrall's eyes widened in disbelief at what he had just found. His breath caught in his chest. He turned to the door and called for Rebecca. She was nowhere in sight. He ran down the corridor and up two flights of steps to the reception area. She was not there. He rushed to the counter, described Rebecca, and asked the young man working there if he had seen her.

"Yes," he said. "I saw her leave the building a little while ago."

Burrall looked at his watch. Ten o'clock. He'd worked on the transcripts for thirteen hours. His eyes were weary from looking at the microfiche. He decided to call it quits for the day. He carefully put the microfiche in a manila envelope and placed it in his briefcase with his pages of notes. He trudged up the long flight of stairs to the main reception area, where he was let out of the building by a guard.

He was exhausted from the day's activities. He still could not fathom his good fortune. To have ten of the missing Livy books drop right into his hands was beyond his wildest dreams. He had seen what no other human being had seen for almost two thousand years. *In all probability, the last person to see what I have read today was Augustus Caesar. Incredible.* He was absorbed in thought as he made the five-minute drive to his house just off campus.

He climbed the stairs to the bedroom and changed into his pajamas. After brushing his teeth, he crawled into bed next to his wife. Sleep came in a matter of seconds. He dreamed there was a helicopter landing in his spacious back yard. Suddenly, Jane was shaking him, telling him to wake up.

He sat up, startled. He looked at his wife. "Jesus, Tom. I think a helicopter just landed in the back yard!"

He rubbed his eyes as he walked to the window in time to see a large man jump out of a helicopter, ducking down to avoid the wash from the rotor. The yard was flooded with light. He counted five Geneva police cars and three New York state troopers, their lights all flashing as they pulled around the helicopter.

"Jeeesuss! I knew it was too good to be true," Burrall said, remembering Libra's words about keeping his mouth shut. "So much for keeping a low profile."

"Are you Bill Bannistar?" a New York state trooper dressed in a gray uniform yelled as he crossed the driveway to the Burralls' back door.

Bannistar turned to see the trooper walking toward him. "Yeah. I'm Bannistar. What've you got?"

"There's an urgent call for you. I got 'em on the radio in my unit," the trooper said.

Bannistar and the officer walked to the car, its red lights still flashing. The trooper picked up the microphone from under the dashboard and spoke into it. "Okay. Patch the Bannistar call through." He handed the microphone to Bannistar.

"She's on a flight to L.A. as we speak," one of Bannistar's aides reported. "The flight left Chicago about an hour ago. She boarded in Rochester, then changed planes in Chicago. It's scheduled to land at LAX at 11:30 West Coast time."

"Okay. You sure she didn't get off in Chicago?"

"Affirmative. She boarded the flight in Chicago."

"Good. Get that plane isolated when it lands. Don't let it get to the gate. Call the airline. Get her off that damned plane, and call me as soon as you have her." He released the speaker button and tossed the microphone on the seat of the car.

Bannistar walked up the rear steps of the house to find a terrified Tom and Jane Burrall waiting at the door. *Time for some diplomacy.*

"Professor Burrall, my name is William Bannistar. I'm the Director of the Central Intelligence Agency. I'm sorry for all the commotion. May I come in and talk to you? It's regarding the young woman who was here this afternoon."

Chapter 14

Rome
Tuesday

"What took you so long?"

Libra crossed the lobby and entered the penthouse. She walked across a multi-colored Persian rug that covered part of the polished marble floor. French and Flemish paintings adorned the walls of the entry. The living room was enormous. The furniture looked as though it had been pillaged from Versailles. Seventeenth-century antiques. Wrought iron lamps. A silk sofa.

"Jesus, Sam. I knew you had good connections in Rome, but this...this place looks like it belongs to the Pope. I've never seen anything like it."

Sam took Libra in his arms. "It's a long story. I'll tell you about it shortly. Right now, I'm just glad to know you're safe. I was getting concerned when you didn't show right away. Bannistar's got the airport and the train station under surveillance. I thought they might have spotted you."

Libra looked up at Sam, a smile coming across her face. She kissed him gently. "Hopefully Bannistar's still looking for me in L.A.—I switched planes in Chicago to throw him off. I had no trouble swapping a flight attendant her uniform for a Chanel suit I bought in Paris. She got off the plane with the rest of the passengers. There were three guys watching the gate. Jesus, Sam, you'd think they'd be smart enough not to wear their Sunday best when they're on a stakeout."

Sam's eyes narrowed. "So Bannistar's covering his bases—he at least suspects we're in Rome,. He doesn't know for sure. Benedict must have set up the stakeout, which doesn't make a lot of sense. Unless it was an act, in which case he knows where we are and wants us to think we've slipped his dragnet." He crossed the living room, pulled the heavy drapes apart and looked down at the Trevi Fountain. "Hard to tell..."

"Who is Benedict? The Station Chief here in Rome?"

"*Si, bella signora.* With all the tourists hanging around the fountain, it's hard to tell if any of them are looking for us."

Years ago Libra and Sam had worked out a system where they seldom, if ever, told each other everything they had learned on assignment. If they were separated, or compromised, the danger of divulging too much information to the enemy became a significant liability. If, however, they kept what they knew separate until the appropriate time, all the information they collectively possessed could not be pried from them.

"Did you bring the microfiche?" Sam asked.

"Yes. Have you found somebody to translate it?"

"Sort of. First, let me bring you up to date on a couple of things you'll have to know." Sam filled Libra in on his meeting with the Don, the missing *tambaroli,* and the two dead men found in the Forum.

"You think it might have been the same people who killed Rinot?"

"No. From the description the Don gave, they were chasing somebody—somebody who was a little smarter than they were about the topography of the Palatine and the Forum.."

"That would seem to confirm that we're dealing with an unknown commodity. Does the Don know who is smuggling Rham's heroin?"

"No, not really. But whoever it is, they're causing the Mafia some headaches. All the *tambaroli* have disappeared. The Mob uses them to smuggle illegal items and deliver information. Whoever it is, they're pretty gutsy. Messing with the Mob is risky business."

"I can't believe that the Don isn't aware of the narcotics moving through Italy to Europe and America."

"Well, if he is aware of it, he's not letting on, not that he would anyway, but I got a sense that he's clean on this one," Sam argued. "Come with me. We have a couple of guests who arrived just before you did. I think they can shed some light on the situation."

Libra followed Sam down the long corridor, past several lavishly furnished rooms. They came to a locked door at the end of the hallway. Sam pulled a key from his pocket and opened the door. "Ever see a master bedroom locked from the outside? Obviously, a Mafia floor plan."

The door swung open. Libra looked in. In the middle of the room sat two young boys, bound to heavy wooden chairs with rope and gagged. They craned their necks to look at Sam and Libra. Lying on top of a large, wooden bureau were two scrolls, identical to the ones Libra had stolen from the University of Paris.

Libra stopped in front of them, looking Mario directly in the eyes. She turned to Sam. "They're just boys! How on earth did they end up here?"

"The Don's men tracked them down early this morning. They were on their way to Paris, apparently to sell those scrolls. The Don's men brought them here for safekeeping. Don't ask me how the Don knew where to look for them, let alone find them."

"What have *they* got to do with all this?"

"That's what we've got to find out. I think there may be a connection between these two and all the killings."

Libra walked up to Mario and removed the gag from his mouth. She did the same for Figlio. In Italian she asked, "What are your names?"

Mario looked at the floor. "My name is Mario Mignini and this is my brother, Figlio."

"Well, Mario and Figlio, I'm Libra and this is my friend Sam. Let's see if we can't get this rope ußntied," she said gently.

Sam walked over to the boys, took a penknife from his pocket and cut the ropes.

"I'll bet you two are thirsty. How about some water?" The boys nodded eagerly. Libra headed for the kitchen.

Mario and Figlio rubbed their wrists. The rope had left deep bruises.

Libra returned to the room a few minutes later carrying a silver serving tray with two crystal goblets and a chilled bottle of San Pellegrino. "This is the best I could do on the spur of the moment."

Mario and Figlio gulped the water and looked up expectantly when they finished.

Libra chuckled and poured another round. The boys were warming up to her nicely. "Where do you boys live?"

"In the ghetto," Mario replied.

"And what about your parents? Don't you think they'd be worried about you?"

Sadness washed over their faces. Libra knew she had asked the wrong question. "Your mother and father, they are no longer with us?"

They nodded solemnly. "I'm sorry, Mario and Figlio. I know how hard it is when you lose a family member. I lost my brother not too long ago. It was very painful. Maybe we can talk about that later. Right now, Sam and I need your help. We are trying to find out why people are being killed. We think that the two men who were found in the ruins last week worked for the killers. Can you tell us what happened that night? And, please, don't be afraid, we are not going to turn you in."

Mario and Figlio exchanged fidgety glances. "You promise that you will not tell the police?"

"You have my word, Mario."

"We don't know who the men were. We were on the Palatine looking for more of the Livy scrolls when the men suddenly appeared. They chased us, with guns. I didn't mean to kill them, but if I didn't, they would have killed me and Figlio. One of the men shot Figlio in the leg."

Libra addressed Figlio. "Let's take a look at your leg."

Figlio rolled up his pants leg, revealing a neatly wrapped bandage. "It is not bad at all now. It doesn't even hurt when Mario pours the peroxide on it."

"Well, you've had expert medical attention, I see," she said, looking at Mario; his face was turning crimson. "We'd better have a doctor take a look at this anyway, just to be sure, but it looks like it's healing nicely. Let's get a fresh bandage on this." She motioned to Sam.

"So the men chased you on the Palatine. How did they know you would be there?"

"I think they followed us from our apartment."

"Why do you think they were following you?"

"Because of the scrolls. Somehow they knew I found the lost works. I think they thought if they followed us we would lead them to the hiding place." Mario reached for another glass of water.

"How do you suppose they knew you had them?"

Mario shrugged. He looked at Figlio, who said, "I didn't tell anyone."

Libra let the question go. "Tell me, Mario, why did you sell the scrolls to smugglers rather than turn them over to the authorities?"

Mario took a deep breath. "Because Figlio and I are poor. I wanted the money so we wouldn't have to live in poverty the rest of our lives. The Italian government will not pay anything for Roman artifacts."

"What did you do with the money?"

"I put it in the bank."

Sam returned carrying a blue metal box. "There should be something in here to dress that wound." Libra took the box and began the task of applying a fresh bandage.

She turned to Mario. "Where did you find the books of Livy?"

Mario hesitated. "If I tell you that, what do Figlio and I get in return?"

Libra cast a quick glance at Sam. The boy had a lot of moxie. Sam gave her a deadpan nod.

"Tell you what. If you will tell us where you found the scrolls and help us translate them, Sam and I will make a handsome contribution to your savings. How does that sound?"

"What is 'handsome'?" Mario asked, puzzled. Figlio looked on with a big grin.

It was all Libra could do to keep from laughing. "Your years on the streets have taught you well, my young friend. Tell you what, we'll start with a million lira and double it if you do a satisfactory job helping us translate what's written in the scrolls." Libra didn't really know if he could translate the ancient Latin, but she sensed that he could.

Mario knew better than to accept the first offer. If Libra was willing to render that much for openers, she had to have more in reserve. "Two million to start and double that when I get finished translating the scrolls."

"Okay, it's a deal." Libra stuck out her hand. Mario shook it with a haughty look on his face. Figlio, not wanting to be left out, shook Libra's hand as well.

"I found the scrolls in the foundation wall of Augustus Caesar's palace," Mario offered.

Sam and Libra shot Mario a look of disbelief. "You mean these things have been on the Palatine the last two thousand years and nobody found them?"

"Yes. Right under everybody's noses. They were sealed in the foundation wall in special compartments. Augustus must have wanted them hidden for some reason."

Mario explained how he had first discovered the scrolls: It happened on a dark night in the spring. He wandered alone through Hippodrome of Domitian. He was curious about the gladiators; he wanted to see where they prepared for battle. He stole into what once was an elaborate dressing room. The area beneath the hippodrome was still in good condition, considering it was over two thousand years old. The mosaic floors in colorful red, black and white tiles were dirty, but he could still see the many pictures on the floor: gladiators fighting wild animals, slaves, and other gladiators. The colorful murals on the walls also survived the centuries.

He had been searching for nothing in particular, but he came across a large crack in the foundation wall of the hippodrome, a crack that went all the way through the foundation wall and into a chamber of the Imperial Palace. Mario guessed the room was a secret antechamber, with false doors, so that no one but the emperor could gain access. Someone had piled rocks high against one of the chamber walls to hide its contents. Curious, Mario removed the rocks and found a hollowed-out shelf containing the scrolls. At the time, he had no idea what they were. He was more interested in the architecture of the room. He reasoned that this was where the great emperor Augustus came to read in private.

Mario went on to explain how he had found a crawlspace in the emperor's library that led into a nearby tunnel. This was the same escape route Mario and Figlio used the night the men chased them on the Palatine. Mario figured the tunnel was Augustus's private passageway because it passed under several important buildings and temples on the Palatine, then ended next to the house of Livia, Augustus's lover. Livia later became the emperor's wife, and the Empress of Rome.

Libra was enchanted by Mario's story. He obviously knew a lot about ancient Roman civilization. But she sensed he was holding something back. She wasn't convinced that he was telling her everything. A good negotiator never gives away all his options.

"Let's see, Augustus? Augustus? What was it about Augustus that I recall from my Western Civilization courses?" Libra chanted while Mario looked on. "Oh, yes, now I remember. Wasn't it Augustus, Mario, who was so popular with the Roman citizens that when his palace burned down the people of Rome each gave him a coin to rebuild it?"

"Yes, of course!" Mario responded too fast and too eagerly. "That explains the gold coins Figlio and I found in the wall." Mario tried to catch himself, but it was too late.

"Coins? What coins?" Sam came roaring out of his chair.

Kabul

"And everything is ready?" Abdul Rham asked, his voice pained.

"Yes, Your Excellency. There are three Rovers, and four of my best guards. They will escort you to the laboratory. They will not leave your side. Every precaution has been taken," the man said assuredly.

Rham walked out the front door and down the wooden steps, where four burly men with semiautomatic weapons awaited him. The four men huddled about Rham as he walked toward one of the waiting Rover 200s. He perspired heavily in the noonday sun. He had not slept well, and he felt irritable. Losing Moman Jasuri to the Americans was bad enough, but having his plot uncovered was more than he could endure.

I have lost millions to the Americans. They have taken my best men from me. The woman, she is responsible for everything that has gone wrong. The heroin shipments will be ready tomorrow. Then…then I will find a way to seek revenge against the Americans.

His thoughts consumed him as he stepped into the middle Rover. He told the guard to move over; he would drive today. The other guards piled into the Rovers in front and back of Rham's. He impatiently honked the horn, letting the lead car know it was time to go. They were heading to one of the laboratories in the mountains. This particular factory was experiencing a mutiny.

As the Rovers started to move toward the dirt highway, Rham noticed that his guard was frozen in place, staring fearfully at the floor. Rham followed his line of sight. A four-foot-long asp was draped across the floor of the vehicle, staring at Rham's foot.

Rham looked up at the Rover in front of him. It was applying its brakes. Rham slowly moved his foot from the accelerator to the brake, careful not to disturb the asp. In less than a heartbeat, the deadly snake lunged and embedded its fangs in his leg. He let out a loud wail. The Rover veered off the road and smashed head-on into a banyan tree. Rham was dead before the vehicle made impact.

Chapter 15

Rome

Tuesday

"Yes, there was a purse filled with gold coins," Mario confirmed regretfully.

Sam held out a piece of paper. "Do the coins look anything like this?"

Mario took the paper. "No. They are much different than the one in this picture."

Libra leaned forward. "Where are the coins, Mario?"

"I have them hidden in a safe place. You're not going to take them from me, are you?"

"No, Mario, but we'd like to take a look at them."

"These coins are not like any others I have seen, and I know every coin that was made during the Republic and the Empire."

Sam's ears perked up. "Say more about that, Mario."

"They have the bust of a warrior on one side and a battle formation on the other. They are made from gold."

Libra looked at Sam and said in English, "You think the coin I saw at Rham's was something else?"

Sam shrugged with a puzzled expression.

Libra turned back to Mario. "The coins you have may be Carthaginian, not Roman. They may have been minted by Hannibal before he attacked Italy."

"I didn't know Hannibal had coins made. Even if he did, why would they be in Augustus's palace? Hannibal invaded Italy two hundred years before Augustus was emperor."

"Maybe Livy recorded the answer," Sam interrupted. "How good are you at translating Latin, Mario?"

"He's the best in his class," Figlio jumped in. "Nobody is better at translating Latin than Mario."

Mario blushed. He was unaccustomed to this kind of praise, even from his adoring brother.

"Is that true, Mario?" Libra asked.

"Yes. I have translated all of Livy, uh, the Livy that exists," Mario's face contorted. "I think I can translate what's in the scrolls."

"First, let's get those coins, Mario." Libra patted him on the knee.

# # #

Positano

Approximately two miles south and east of Positano, in the blue-green waters of the Bay of Salerno, sits a tiny, rocky island left by the receding glaciers millions of years ago. Sitting on top of the granite island is a large, modern house with wide, open-air rooms. Expensive Corinthian leather covers the sofas and chairs, made especially for outlasting the summer heat and salty air.

Count Montefusco watched from the window of his office as a flock of gulls dove after fish. Intense confusion clouded his mind. He had been sure that the boy who had found the Livy scrolls would lead them to the rest of the missing documents. The *tambaroli* and the French professor were easily disposed of. Now another problem had arisen: Two CIA agents had somehow gotten into the picture.

He circled his large desk and removed a thin book from a drawer. There were only two copies like it in the world, one in Washington and one in Paris. The Count's book was the original manuscript, thought to have been destroyed many years ago. He opened to a carefully marked page and read for the hundredth time Browning's thesis on Hannibal and the Carthaginian Cresa.

"Hello, Father," Ramona said with a forced smile as she entered the room and kissed her father lightly on the cheek. She was wearing a red Ferragamo dress with black Gucci pumps. Her perfume, Shalimar by Guerlain, filled the room. "I have good news. Signore Rham met with a most unfortunate accident yesterday. It seems he was bitten by a serpent. Our people are in position and taking the necessary steps to secure control of the poppy operations."

"What is the timetable you have arranged?" the Count asked.

"We will be ready with the first shipment in less than a week. The profits from this shipment will be roughly one hundred million dollars. The tankers will all be in position by that time. I have seen to the matter personally, Father. Everything has gone as you predicted."

"Very well. Now I'd like to turn your attention to another matter." He picked up Browning's book. "There is a distinct possibility that we may be able to increase this quarter's profit even more than we had anticipated. That would make it the single largest quarter in the history of the corporation. Our stockholders will be pleased."

Ramona's eyes widened in anticipation. Already the stockholders were heralding her as the leading candidate for businesswoman of the year. Doubling the profits would certainly be an added dividend that she had not considered. "And what is that, Father?"

"In 212 B.C. a Roman general named Marcellus sacked a Greek treasury in Siracusa, Sicily. According to Livy, the historian, Marcellus made off with more treasure than all of Rome and Carthage combined. That treasure, believed to be in the form of gold coins, was never seen again. It is believed that Livy chronicled the events surrounding the disposition of the gold," he held up Browning's book, "documented here. All that we need to do is procure the scrolls."

"And how do we do that?" Ramona's large, dark eyes widened further.

"The two CIA agents are in Rome. They are believed to be renegades, thanks to our people inside their organization. I have been able to confirm that the woman did indeed steal the scrolls from the University of Paris..."

"That same woman who escaped Afghanistan?"

"That's correct. She and the bumbling bureaucrat she has with her will lead us to the scrolls. They are staying in the building across from the Trevi Fountain. It is owned by Don Portico, so you'll have no trouble finding a way to get her."

"I have an idea as we speak. Let me give it more thought. Wouldn't it be pleasant for you to have her as your guest here at the summer home?" Ramona teased.

The Count leaned back in his chair, steepling his fingers. "Hmm, I hadn't thought of that, but yes, it's a splendid idea."

"You expect trouble from the CIA?"

The Count let out a humph. "The CIA is harmless. Nothing more than an overgrown albatross, despite our failure to terminate their leader."

"Very well. And what do you intend to do with the agents once they have led us to the Livy chronicles?"

"Kill them, naturally."

Chapter 16

The White House

"So, that's about the size of it." Bannistar concluded his briefing on the situation in Afghanistan.

"Any idea who tried to run you off the road Saturday?" the President asked.

"Nothing. Their bodies were burned beyond recognition. All of them had traces of cyanide in their teeth, according to Forensics. They all had the death capsules installed in their third molars. We have no idea where they came from or who they were working for, so there are no dental records to check. Their fingerprints had been acid-etched, so we couldn't get a read on whether or not they had records. Interpol was no help, either."

"What about your two agents? They have any success learning who the new mules are?"

"I haven't heard from them. I think they're in Italy. Most likely Rome. But I'm not positive. They've gone into deep cover. I'm embarrassed to inform you that there may be a mole in the Agency. They know it, I know it, but we don't know who it is. We're doing a sweep of all employees right now."

The President paused, a disgusted look on his face. "What the hell is going on over there, Bill?"

"We're up against something new in terms of counterespionage. Whoever planted the mole is not, we think, a foreign government. I suspect that it's a clandestine organization based somewhere in Europe."

"For what purpose?"

"Don't know right now. It may have something to do with the drug operations. Drug running is a big business—no need for me to tell you that—and I think that whoever we're dealing with is well organized and is using every angle they can to ensure that they stay a going concern."

"How many people know about the mole?"

"You and me and three others at the Agency who can be trusted."

"I don't need to remind you, Bill, that if this information surfaces and the press gets a hold of it, we're going to have a major league scandal on our hands. My popularity ratings are running high, partially because we've been able to reduce drug-related crime in the country. But the ratings could go south in a Yankee second if the public gets wind of a drug mole in the CIA."

Bannistar understood the implications and it scared the hell out of him. He didn't need another embarrassing incident at the Agency to complicate his life.

"Well, you've got my assurance that we're doing everything that we can to root the mole out with as little publicity as possible."

The President nodded, looking unconvinced. He changed his direction. "What did you get out of that college professor in upstate New York?"

"We obtained copies of the text Libra left with him." Bannistar did not tell the President that his agents had stolen the microfiche from Burrall's home after the professor had denied having them. "Research has already started translating it. But we can't determine if there's anything of value in it."

"When will they know something?"

"A day or two. The text is relatively easy to translate. Research developed a software system, part of the Encryption and Forgery Division, that can translate ancient Latin into English. So it's just a matter of time, plugging the Latin version into the network. The documents, though, are lengthy, so even after they're translated we've got to go through the books with a fine-toothed comb to determine if there's something in them that can give us a clue to what's causing the commotion."

"I hate to ask a stupid question, but what do we know about Livy? I vaguely remember something about him from college."

"Livy isn't exactly a household name. I had to do some research myself to find out who he was. Augustus hired him to write the history of Rome. Apparently Livy was tight with the emperor. They were friends. He started writing for Augustus when he was thirty years old. Then he worked on the history of Rome for forty years. He was well-regarded in Roman political and intellectual circles. Livy's work was titled *From the Founding of the City*. It covers the period of history from the Roman Republic and the Roman Empire, starting in 753 B.C., then concludes sometime during Augustus's reign."

"I assume not all of Livy's history made it to modern times. So Rinot made a microfiche copy of the transcripts, then hid it in his apartment for safekeeping."

"Right. Only thirty-five out of a hundred and forty-two books survived antiquity, although summaries of most of his books made it."

"You have any idea what we're looking for in the transcripts?"

"Not really. But I think Livy may have known the ultimate resting place for a large hoard of gold. His works may provide specific information on where it was hidden. Livy says that a Roman general—name of Marcellus—ransacked a Greek treasury in Siracusa, Sicily, sometime around 200 B.C. Marcellus hauled off one hell of a lot of loot. Take a look at this."

The President put on his reading glasses, then picked up Bannistar's notepad. He read aloud in a monotone voice:

"'This, then, is the story of the capture of Siracusa. The booty taken was almost as great as Carthage herself, Rome's rival in power, which had fallen.'"

The President took off his glasses as Bannistar circled back to his chair. "Why would there be so much wealth in a small city-state like Siracusa?"

"Siracusa was in the middle of the major shipping lanes back then. It was a natural way station between Egypt, north Africa and western Europe."

"Let me see if I understand what we've got so far. Sometime around 200 B.C. there was a cache of gold that ended up in the hands of one of the Roman emperors—presumably Augustus—two hundred years after it was stolen from a Greek treasury. Research thinks it was hidden somewhere in Italy?"

"Yes," Bannistar replied. "And we believe that Livy's works have a road map, so-to-speak, to the gold's location. I know this sounds like a Robert Louis Stevenson novel."

"This is all very interesting, but what the hell does it have to do with Rham's heroin shipments?"

Bannistar sighed. "That's a good question. This may sound preposterous. Jesus, even I have difficulty believing that we're sitting in the Oval Office discussing the spoils of war that some Roman general plundered from the Greeks twenty-two centuries ago. But, if you'd bear with me for a moment, I think I can make more sense out of it. Rham is about to go belly up. He's strapped for cash. His last two drug shipments were siphoned off by our side, so he can't buy arms to run his terrorist camps. So somehow he gets wind of a rumor; there's a pile of gold buried somewhere in Italy. I think that's what we need to focus on, Jeff: where Rham is getting his information. If we can determine Rham's source, we can cripple his drug business once and for all. But if the son of a bitch does get his hands on the Marcellus treasure before we do, he's back in business. And this time, we won't have Libra sending back the play-by-play."

The President stroked his chin. "There's a part of me that thinks this whole thing is a wild-goose chase, Bill. But the way you present it, it does seem to have some validity."

"I think we can assume that somebody, most likely Rham, wants to get their hands on whatever Livy is talking about in those damned books. My God, we've got a planeload of people killed, a professor murdered, Sam and Libra in deep cover, and somebody attempting to blow me off the GW Parkway. Furthermore, consider that Rham has a number of his best terrorists in the United States, undoubtedly to blow up buildings in four cities, and some heretofore unknown organization knocks them all off before they can carry out their mission. I'm almost embarrassed to admit it, but whoever it was, they knew more about Rham's terrorist activities in this country than we did."

The President nodded. "What about the El Al crash? What's the connection there?"

"Not positive, but there was an MI-6 agent on the plane, and an hour after the crash, in his Rome apartment, they found an extremely rare coin. The coin—according to Tom Wotherspoon, the professor Sam interviewed in Paris—has a value somewhere in the neighborhood of a million bucks."

"Go back for a moment…back to the people who took out Rham's terrorists. These guys made it through our security, even though we were on alert. You think Sangi tipped them off?"

"Probably. But, again, I'm guessing. I didn't even know about Sangi until the day before yesterday. He was caught in that professor's apartment in Paris, presumably looking for the Livy books. I have to bet Libra got there before he did, or, more likely, at the same time. They must have struggled. Libra wouldn't have killed him unless she was threatened in some way."

The President leaned forward. "Bill, who the hell are these guys?"

"Whoever they are, they've spent a lot of time getting themselves into the Agency. I was probably targeted for extinction on the GW last Saturday because we're getting too close to them. Somebody, some organization—and I'm not sure it's a political organization—has spent a lot of time setting this thing up. And if it hadn't been for those goons trying to run me off the road, I would still be in the dark. Jesus, in my own fucking organization, no less. My concern is that the CIA may not be the only agency infected. This could be pandemic…"

The President changed the subject. "I'm curious about why Libra left the microfiche behind."

"I'm not sure. I think she was either trying to throw us off the trail, or she's trying to tell us something without blowing her cover."

"What do you mean?"

"Her track was too easy to follow, yet it was perfectly timed. A rogue agent would never have used credit cards so openly. She had to know we'd pick up her trail in a matter of hours."

"What do you think she's trying to tell us?"

Bannistar paused. "I'm afraid that's another piece of the puzzle I haven't been able to figure out. It's just a little too obvious that she wanted the microfiche to get to us. The question is, why?"

"Let's take a closer look, Bill. Why do you suppose Sam and Libra went into deep cover?"

"My guess is that when Libra ran into Sangi in Paris, she discovered his connection to the Company. The logical conclusion they draw is that the guy is a mole. If there's one mole in the Company, there's probably more, and they can trace Sam and Libra's movements. They may even think that I've sold them out."

"Well, it's a logical conclusion. Who would have thought that some unknown organization would have infiltrated the Central Intelligence Agency? They probably believe you're the brains behind it. So what are you going to do?"

"Right now, I'm a little low on options." Bannistar threw his hands in the air. "Wait…wait and hope for a break. If information about the scrolls leaks out, that would tell us there are more moles buried in the government."

"What are the odds that the El Al bombing was the work of this phantom organization?"

"I'd bet my next paycheck that they had a hand in it. The British agent apparently was on to them. Obviously, they want whatever secret they're protecting kept a secret."

"I need you to move fast." The President started to rise from his chair. "I'm getting heat from the Israelis to come up with suspects in the bombing. I'm also getting heat from the press."

"I'm moving on this as fast as I can, Jeff. But with no contact from Sam and Libra, I'm operating with a significant handicap."

"I understand. But I've got to maintain credibility with the electorate. Keep me in the loop. I want to be informed about any developments, day or night."

Chapter 17

Rome

"Can you talk about your mother and father?" Libra asked. She and Mario walked side by side in the Via San Vincenzo Lucchesi, two blocks east of the Trevi Fountain.

Mario told her his story. He stuck to the facts and showed little emotion.

"It must have been very hard raising a brother all by yourself," observed Libra.

Mario shrugged casually. "You get used to hardships if you understand that life is difficult. I often wonder what it would have been like if my mama and papa were alive today. And what about you? You lost a brother?"

"Yes," Libra answered. "It was very painful. I was about your age when it happened. A man broke into our house when I came home from school one afternoon. I was able to escape, thanks to Chet—that was my brother's name. But the man kidnapped my brother, took him to New York City and forced him to sell drugs, all the while loading him up with heroine and cocaine. By the time the police found Chet, he was addicted. He was in and out of drug treatment, but it never worked. While he was still in college, Chet died of an overdose of heroin."

"What kind of man would do something like that?" Mario shook his head.

"A very sick man."

"Was he caught, the man who kidnapped your brother?"

"No. The police were never able to find him."

"I am sorry for you."

"Thanks, Mario. Not a day goes by that I don't think about Chet."

"I know. I think about my mama and papa a lot, too. What do you do, anyway, Libra?" Mario asked, changing the subject.

"I work for an American company. We're trying to put the drug dealers out of business, Mario." Libra shifted gears. "How did you learn Latin?"

"The priests who ran the orphanage, they made me read the Latin books over and over. Livy, Plutarch, Seneca, Tacitus. It was hard work, but I guess that's what got me so interested in my country's history. Italy was once a very powerful country."

"Who was your favorite Roman?"

Mario paused. "I guess that I like Augustus Caesar the best."

"And why is that?"

"I think because of what he did for Rome. He did a lot for education and he built Rome into a very powerful empire. Did you know that he was the first emperor of Rome?"

"I may have. Didn't he come to power by defeating Antony and Cleopatra?"

"Yes. He defeated them at the battle of Actium in 31 B.C. Did you know that the name Augustus means 'consecrated or holy one'?"

"I didn't know that."

"Yes, it was the name given to him by the Senate after he defeated Antony and Cleopatra. But Augustus also had a ruthless side to him. He had three hundred senators and two hundred knights killed when he was part of the triumvirate in his rise to power.."

Libra started to make a connection. "Do you think Augustus could have withheld important information from the public or the Roman Senate back then?"

"Oh, yes. Even though he did a lot for Rome, he could be pretty nasty when he wanted to."

"You think Augustus might have kept Livy's works hidden for some political reason?"

"I don't know. He made a big deal back then of restoring Rome's moral virtues and such. Maybe he was 'talking out of both sides of his mouth,' as you say in America?"

They had been walking for about thirty minutes.

"Mario, I want you to turn right at the next intersection." Libra's voice had a ring of urgency.

"Huh?"

"Don't ask any questions. Just do as I tell you. I want you to get us lost, like fast." Libra had picked up a young man in the corner of her eye. He had been behind them since they got out of the limousine.

They turned right at the next intersection and for the next twenty minutes Mario took Libra on an odyssey through side streets, alleys, and five restaurant kitchens.

"It's okay now, Mario. We've lost him."

Mario shrugged, then started to point out landmarks, giving Libra a brief history of Rome as they dodged people on the narrow sidewalks. As he finished telling Libra why the Palatine was chosen as the original site for the city by Romulus and Remus, they arrived at the ghetto.

"This is where Figlio and I have lived since they let us out of the orphanage," Mario said, pointing to a rundown apartment building. It was drab green, old and filthy. It was streaked with black soot from the air pollution. The fascia had not been cleaned in years. On the front steps young women in loose-fitting dresses sat fanning themselves and the babies in their laps. The smell of garlic and onions permeated the air.

"How long have you lived here, Mario?"

"Almost a year. The orphanage was full and they wanted to make room for the younger children coming in. So the priests were able to get this apartment for Figlio and me."

Libra sensed that the apartment was being watched. "Is there another way in, Mario?"

Mario led Libra away into a building across the block. "There is an underground passage that connects these two buildings, but hardly anyone uses it."

Libra followed Mario down a long flight of steps and through a tunnel that reeked of urine and rancid air. They climbed another set of stairs that led to Mario's building.

As Mario was about to unlock his door, Libra's proximity sense alerted her to trouble. She stopped and grabbed Mario's hand. She yanked him back into the hallway, wrapping her hand over his mouth. "Be very still. There is someone in your apartment."

The blood drained from Mario's face.

"He knows we're here. He's stopped moving. He must have heard us talking," Libra whispered. "Give me your key, then go back down the stairs. Don't let any of those women on the front steps come into the building. Get them away. There may be trouble."

Mario nodded, then took off down the steps.

Libra pulled a Glock .22 from an ankle holster. The person in Mario's apartment would be ready. Chances were, he was armed as well. She needed to throw him off balance.

Libra pressed herself against the wall adjacent to the entrance. She took a deep breath. She reached out, careful not to get her body in front of the door, and inserted the key in the lock. She counted to three. She ripped open the door and dove to the floor.

A man, crouched in the center of the room, fired a pistol at the open doorway. Whap. Whap. Whap. A silencer muted the sound as bullets spat from the muzzle and embedded themselves in the hallway wall. Libra stood up and slammed the door before the man could attack from his position. Two more rounds ripped through the door, leaving clean holes in their wake.

Libra bolted up the stairs. He had one shot left. She needed to create another diversion.

She heard the door open. The man's footsteps clicked on the linoleum floor as he crossed the hallway. Libra hid on the fourth-floor landing. She waited, adrenaline sharpening her senses.

She peeked around the banister, down the stairwell. A heavyset man with black hair and a mustache was holding the gun in both hands. His arms extended, he pointed his gun up the stairwell. Libra pulled back. He walked up the stairs.

Libra listened for the man's footsteps. One more step and he'd be right in front of her. She could hear his labored breathing as he mounted the last stair.

In a catlike motion, Libra sprung from the landing. The man's head jerked up. His body stiffened. With blinding speed, Libra thrust the heel of her palm into the gunman's chest.

The man fell back, dropping his gun. It clanked down the stairs. His face twisted and he doubled over, letting out a stream of air. Desperately, he tried to fill his lungs. Libra slammed the side of her hand into his head. He crumpled to the floor like a sack of potatoes.

Libra grabbed him under the armpits, then dragged him down the stairs into Mario's apartment. She ran into the hallway, picked up the gun, and called for Mario.

Mario walked back into the apartment and saw the man lying face down on the floor. Libra was going through his pockets. "How did you do that?" he asked, astonished.

"Never mind that now. Go get the coins, and then get me some rope so I can tie him up. Hurry."

She checked his gun. She had been right—one round was left in the chamber of the Heckler and Koch 9mm handgun.

Mario came out of his room carrying the leather pouch and a bolt of clothesline rope. Libra took the rope and wrapped it around the man's wrists and ankles.

"Get me some water," Libra said as she turned the man over on his back.

Mario filled a cup with water from the sink. He brought it to Libra. She threw the water into the man's face. He started coming around, and found himself staring down the barrel of his own gun.

"Who do you work for?" Libra asked as she cocked the trigger and brought the gun up against his nostrils.

The man's eyes showed icy contempt. "Fuck you!" he spat back.

"My, my, aren't we testy this morning," Libra responded sarcastically. "Mario, go watch the steps."

Mario sprinted out of the apartment and waited on the landing.

Libra turned her attention back to the man on the floor. "Well, let's see if lowering your testosterone level will improve your manners." She holstered the Glock, wrapped her fist into a ball, then hit the man in the groin.

The man wriggled in agony and let out a painful yelp.

"You want to answer my question or would you rather be singing soprano in some boys choir?" Libra balled her fist to strike again.

The man caught his breath, coughed. "I am with the police department. I'm here to question the boys…"

Libra slammed her fist into the man's groin again, even more forcefully. "Right. And I'm Sister Rebecca from the Convent."

The man howled and withered into a fetal position. "*Basta! Basta!* Please, no more."

Libra let the man recover for a few moments. "Okay, asshole, let's have the truth. Who do you work for?"

"I don't know his name. He gives me instructions through an intermediary."

"How do you get paid?"

"A lockbox."

"Where?"

"At Termini Station."

Libra's interrogation was suddenly interrupted by Mario. "Somebody is walking up the stairs. By the sounds of the footsteps there is more than one."

"Is there another way out of here?"

"Yes. Through the roof on the top floor, there is a hatch."

"I'll meet you in the hallway. Hurry."

Libra looked back at the man, who now had a big smile on his face. "Well, it was a pleasure to have met you. Pity that we couldn't have spent more time together." She gave him a swift blow behind the ear, causing a brain hemorrhage and sudden death.

Libra sprinted out of the apartment. "Okay. Let's get out of here." She grabbed Mario by the front of his shirt and pulled him up the stairway. Two sets of footsteps were pounding up the stairs a flight below.

Mario pulled Libra up through the roof hatch by the arm. Hand-in-hand, they sprinted across a sea of flat roofs, waves of heat swirling around them.

After running for several minutes, Mario stopped to catch his breath. Suddenly, with no warning, Mario threw both of his arms around Libra. "*Grazie*, Libra. You just saved my life. If I had come back to the apartment alone looking for the coins, that man would have killed me, and Figlio too. I want to tell you something, Libra, but it is a secret and you must promise not to tell anyone. Okay?"

"Okay."

"The night the men chased Figlio and me in the Forum, I prayed to Saint Anthony; he is my patron saint. I asked him to protect me. He did. But then, after I pushed the man off the Palatine, I saw the two boys, Castor and Pollux."

"Castor and Pollux?"

Mario related the ancient story of the two boys, and how it was a vision from Saint Anthony. "Don't you see, Libra. Saint Anthony has sent you and Sam to watch over Figlio and me. This afternoon proves it, for you saved my life."

Libra was touched by Mario's enthusiasm. "You have a gift, my young friend. And I doubt that it is a coincidence that we are in each other's lives. We will learn from one another. Now, we must get back to the Don's apartment."

Chapter 18

Washington

Wednesday

No sooner had Bannistar settled himself into his padded leather chair than his secretary stormed into his office. Betty Andrews was an aggressive fifty-year-old woman with platinum hair.

"Yeah, Betty, what now?"

"Call Phil O'Brien in Research. He called an hour ago and said it was very urgent."

"Thanks, Betty." Bannistar dialed the researcher's extension.

"Yeah, Phil. It's Bannistar. What have you got?"

"Bad news, I'm afraid. Somebody has taken the Livy microfiche and deleted all the computer files. Including the backup."

Bannistar's face turned ashen. "How did it happen?"

"I don't know. I came in this morning and it was gone. Everything. The film, the hard copies, the backup discs. And it's been erased on the mainframe. It's as if it never existed."

"Have you mentioned this to anyone else?" Bannistar asked, his voice rising.

"No. You're the only one."

"Good. Keep your mouth shut. I don't want anybody knowing about this except you and me. That includes your boss. Keep him out of it. I want a list of everybody working on the project, and anyone you think may have known about the files."

"Yes. Yes, sir, Mr. Bannistar."

"I want a verbal report. My office at five o'clock. Nothing written. Got that?"

"Yes, Mr. Bannistar. Five o'clock. I'll be there, sir."

Bannistar hung up.

The Director leaned back in his chair, rubbing his face with both hands. He opened the middle desk drawer and pulled out a bottle of Maalox and took a long pull. *Libra knew that the Agency was harboring another mole.*

Bannistar pressed the intercom button on his phone, summoning Betty.

"Get me Phil O'Brien's personnel file. And get me the files of all the people working on the Livy thing. Be discreet. I don't want anybody to know about this."

"Right away, Mr. Bannistar."

Bannistar punched in the numbers for Control. "Get me Tim Benedict, Rome station."

# # #

Rome
Wednesday

"Don Portico, sorry to trouble you. Libra has come up with a theory that might help explain the missing *tambaroli*. I'd like to get your opinion."

"Hey, Sam, let's get something straight, huh? You and Libra are no trouble. It is my privilege to be helping you. *Capisce?* Now, my friend, what is it that you are looking for?"

Sam filled him in on Libra's exploits at Mario's apartment.

"I will see what I can find out." The Don hung up.

There was a knock on the door. Sam opened it to see a blindfolded, elderly man standing in front of him. The Don's chauffeur stood at his side, holding his elbow. He escorted the man into the living room.

The chauffeur untied the blindfold. "*Signore et Signora*, this is Professor Giorgio Rosolinni. He translates the Latin for you."

Sam nodded appreciatively and addressed their new arrival. "Come in, Professor. We have some very important work for you. Tell us a little bit about yourself."

The professor looked up to meet Sam's eyes. "*Signore*, I am retired from the University. I was on the faculty for thirty-five years as a professor of classics. For the last ten years, I chaired the department. I have written many articles, and I have written three books, all published, on Roman antiquity. I also have written a book about the lost continent at Thera…"

Sam held up his hand and broke in. "How do you know the Don?"

"My family owes a great deal to Don Portico. My family and the Don's have been very, very close for many, many years." The professor pulled a wallet from his coat pocket. "This is my daughter and her children, my grandchildren. Don Portico is their godfather! Don Portico asked me for a favor. How could I refuse?"

"Okay, okay. That's enough," Sam cut in. "Follow me, Professor. You have an able assistant."

The professor followed Sam down the corridor to a study. Mario was seated at a large mahogany desk, his head under a reading lamp. He looked up. Sam introduced the professor to Mario.

"Your assistant, Professor. I can assure you that Mario is well versed in the Latin classics. This is, no doubt, a great honor for the two of you to be the first translators of Livy's lost works."

Sam returned to the living room. Libra was sitting on the sofa with a legal pad and a book propped up against her legs.

"What are you doing?" Sam asked.

"Boning up on Roman history. Augustus Caesar, specifically."

"Learn anything?"

"It looks like Augustus was a typical politician despite all his good press. He pursued power ruthlessly. He made allies of convenience and turned on them to solidify his power. He avoided being seen as a monarch, styling himself as the 'first citizen of Rome.' He promoted the values of the earlier Republic. Augustus was a master at spin control. He knew how to endear himself to the people of Rome and the Roman Empire. I think that Livy may have written something about him that was not flattering, and Augustus made sure that the information was suppressed."

"So, you believe that Augustus conspired to keep Livy's history—and perhaps Marcellus's gold—to himself. Only he did too good a job. His secrets stayed hidden for centuries, until Mario, in his quest to better understand Roman history, stumbled across them."

"And someone else, also knowledgeable in the field of antiquities, who just happens to run a drug business on the side, learned about Mario's discovery."

"So how do we find out who the someone else is?"

"We wait. They probably know we have the scrolls. That means they'll come after us. In the meantime, we translate Livy's books to determine if we're right. Make sense?"

"I suppose…"

"Consider for a moment, Sam, that the men on the Palatine and the one at Mario's apartment were pros. But they made mistakes. In any case, I think somebody on the inside is tipping them off—they're always one step ahead of us."

"A drug cartel that has moles in the CIA? Knows our every move? That's a bit of a stretch."

"It makes perfect sense to me. Having a few people on the inside to pass on information about the DEA and the CIA would be one heck of a competitive advantage for an international drug runner. These guys have long arms and deep pockets. With the world in a state of relative peace, the drug lords have taken center stage and they're using every means at their disposal to make money."

"Okay, your point is well taken. Do you really think they'll come after us?"

"Yes. If I were them, I'd wait for us to make the next move. They want us to lead them to the rest of Livy's works, or to whatever we find in the books."

Sam mumbled something incomprehensible.

"Did you take a look at the coins?" Libra held the cracked leather pouch toward Sam.

Sam dumped the gold coins into the palm of his hand. He took one and set the rest on the coffee table. "Take a look at the face."

"Mario was right," Libra said with a low voice as she examined the face etched into the gold surface. "The head is different than the one I saw at Rham's. What's on the other side?"

"Nothing, it's just flat."

"Do you suppose that's Hannibal?"

Sam shrugged. "I don't know. We'd have to have somebody like Wotherspoon look at it to be sure. But even he wouldn't be able to make a positive identification."

"What if the coin I saw in Rham's room wasn't authentic?"

"What do you mean?"

"Well, suppose it was a knockoff. Somebody's idea of what a Cresa might look like?"

"Which would mean that whoever sent those guys after Mario and Figlio has an interest in Roman antiquity. That would attest to your theory that he's operating here or somewhere in Italy. Which part, though?"

"Somewhere in the southern part of the country would be my guess," Libra answered. "Drug traffic between Naples and Sicily is intense. I wouldn't be surprised if somebody in that area has made some kind of arrangement to smuggle Rham's heroin."

Libra stood and paced around the living room. "What if Augustus got hold of the gold, melted it down and had his own face engraved on the surface? That would explain a lot."

Sam was about to comment, but he was interrupted by the professor, who came storming into the living room, out of breath and very excited.

"*Signore et Signora,* please excuse me, but you must come at once. I think we have found something of importance," the professor exclaimed.

"Just a moment, Professor," Sam interrupted him. "Take a look at this and tell me if you recognize the head plate." Sam picked up the coin and handed it to the professor.

"I will need a magnifying glass. Please. I have one in my bag."

They followed the professor down the hallway to the study.

The professor opened his briefcase, pulling out a small magnifying glass. He placed the coin on the table and studied it through the glass for several minutes. Finally, he shook his head and turned to Sam. "I am sorry, but I have never seen anything like this. I cannot tell you where it came from or whose head adorns the surface. There can be little doubt, however, that it is an ancient piece."

"You think it might be the Carthaginian, Hannibal?" Libra asked.

The professor shrugged. "That is a possibility. But I have never heard of a coin with Hannibal's face on it."

"Thanks, Professor," said Sam. "What did you find that is so important?"

The professor deferred to Mario, who looked directly at Libra. "The manuscripts that you brought back from Paris on the microfiche are fake!"

Chapter 19

Rome
Thursday, Before Dawn

Benedict rolled over in his bed and grabbed the telephone. He glanced at the red numbers glowing from the digital clock next to the phone: 3:00.

"Yes," he said groggily.

"Tim, sorry to disturb you in the middle of the night." It was Bannistar on the line. "I need a rundown on the Mafia don, Don Portico. We think he may be hiding Sam and Libra."

"I'll get on it right away," Benedict replied. "Incidentally, Bill, we haven't had any luck in spotting either Sam or Libra at the terminals."

"Don't underestimate them, Tim. Libra ducked our surveillance in Los Angeles last week. Everything I've got points to Rome. Get back to me as soon as you find something."

"Will do." Benedict hung up and walked to the bathroom. He stretched in front of a full-length mirror. His attention was drawn to his forehead, where a new mole had begun to grow.

#

"A fake?" Sam's face twisted in astonishment.

"What makes you so sure?" Libra interjected calmly.

Mario shrugged. "It's not Livy's style."

"That's it?" Sam shot back. "Not his style!?"

"Yes. I know Livy, and this is not Livy."

Sam looked to the professor, who stood behind Mario with his left hand on the boy's shoulder. "He is right. This is not Livy. It is a reasonably good forgery. In fact, it was so good that it fooled the whole world forty-some years ago."

Libra was doing her best not to laugh. "Did you know?" Sam practically spat.

Before she could answer, the phone rang. Sam picked up the receiver.

He nodded his head several times then said, "Okay, we're on our way down." He looked to Libra. "The Don's men picked up a couple of thugs outside Mario's apartment about an hour ago. He's got them tied up in a warehouse not far from here."

Libra winked at Mario and Figlio as she headed for the door.

"*Ciao, la bella signora,*" Mario whispered.

#

The captives awoke strapped to heavy gurneys in a vacant warehouse. A man in a white laboratory coat squirted a syrupy liquid into the air from a long syringe. He injected the younger man first, then the older man. Their eyes registered nothing as they watched the man go about his work. As their eyes began to lose focus, they saw a woman in black, with long, auburn hair, coming through the door.

"As much as I hate to admit it, you were right again," Sam said to Libra. "These are the goons who were waiting for Mario and Figlio."

"Now let's see if we can get anything from them," Libra said.

"What did you use?" Sam asked the man in the laboratory coat.

"Amobarbital sodium. It is a hypnotic sedative, once used for anesthesia, but no more. The doses they received should make them eager to tell you anything you want to know."

"Yes. I know amobarbital sodium," Sam snapped. He turned to Libra. "These guys probably know no more than they have to." He switched on a portable recorder.

Libra started with the older man. "What is your name?"

"Alberto Pisquitini."

"How old are you?"

"Thirty," he responded, his eyes half-opened.

"Where is your home?"

"Amalfi."

Libra looked at Sam and the "doctor."

"Southern Italy, *Signora*. About two hundred kilometers from Naples," came the doctor's reply.

Libra addressed the younger man. "What were you doing at the piazza today?"

"Waiting for two boys."

"Why were you waiting for them?"

"Orders."

"Whose orders?"

The man hesitated. After several seconds, he said, "A woman's voice on the telephone."

"Whose voice on the telephone? Did the woman's voice have a name?"

"A woman," he repeated. "I do not know the woman's name."

"What were your instructions?"

"To capture the boys and take them to a place."

"What place?"

"The name of the place was to be given to us after we got the boys."

"Who pays you?"

"I do not know. We are paid in cash. It is left at a designated place."

"How do you get in touch with this person to let her know you have found the boys?"

"There is a telephone number."

"What is the telephone number?"

The young man gave her a telephone number. The number had a prefix that designated Rome.

"Is there a time when you are to contact this woman?"

"Yes. At midnight. We are to check in every day at exactly midnight."

"And is there a code you are to use when you check in?"

"Yes. My code is 'I am here in body and in spirit.'"

"And what is the name of the organization that gives you your orders?"

The man hesitated. He did not answer.

"The name, *Signore*. What is the name of the organization of the people who give you your orders?"

Libra held her breath.

The man rolled his head from side to side. His eyes opened wide. He was perspiring heavily. After several seconds he passed out.

Sam turned to the other man. "How much are you paid for delivering the documents?"

"Three million lira."

"And is the place where you pick up your money always the same?"

"No. It changes with every assignment."

"Where were you to be paid following this drop?"

"We are to pick up our money at a post office box at the main Post Office. Box number 4032."

"What happened to the *tambaroli?*"

Pause. "I don't know."

Sam turned to the younger man, who had regained consciousness. "Do you know who killed the *tambaroli?*"

"No."

"Who were the men who were killed on the Palatine a week ago?"

"Associates."

"What were their names?"

"I don't know."

Sam looked back at Libra. She shook her head. Sam turned to the doctor. "They're all yours." He wondered what Don Portico would do to these men. He doubted that it would be pleasant.

Sam and Libra walked out of the warehouse and jumped into the Lancer. They ordered the driver back to the Don's apartment.

An hour later, the driver stopped in front of the building. Sam and Libra hopped out of the car. As they walked across the sidewalk to the entrance of the building, Sam suddenly grabbed his left shoulder and lunged forward, hitting the wall before he fell to the ground. Blood blotted the back and front of his shirt.

Libra dove to the sidewalk, then crawled over to Sam. His face was screwed in pain. Libra could smell Sam's blood as it dripped onto the sidewalk.

"I'm okay," he muttered in a breathless gasp. "It just hurts like hell. I think the bullet went clean through. Where'd it come from?"

Libra scanned the building on the far side of the street. She could feel her heart pounding in her chest. An open window on the fourth floor.

The chauffeur emerged from the limousine, .357 Magnum in hand. "Give me your gun, and get Sam inside!" Libra took his weapon and crouched cautiously toward the street.

A figure appeared in the fourth-floor window: a bald man with telescopic rifle. Libra took aim and fired. The shooter cried out and dropped back into the room.

Libra spun around toward the building, using the limousine for cover. A car roared down the street. She turned, pointing the weapon at the oncoming vehicle. Something moved in the corner of her eye. She looked up at the window. Another man was pointing the rifle at her. She pivoted to fire at him—too late. A bullet knocked her to the ground.

Libra lay sprawled on the sidewalk, face down. The car screeched to a stop. Two men dressed in black jump suits and ski masks ran out, picked her up from the sidewalk and tossed her in the back of the car.

Chapter 20

Rome

"There you are, *Signore*," the doctor said as he applied the last of the white adhesive strips over the gauze covering Sam's wound. "You are lucky. The bullet went clear through your shoulder. Another fraction of an inch and it would have passed through your heart."

"Thanks. I appreciate all you've done. Now, if you'll excuse me, I've got to get back to work."

"Not so fast. Take two of these every few hours. They are for the pain and so the wound will not become infected." The doctor handed Sam a small brown envelope filled with tablets.

"What is it?" Sam asked with an involuntary, nervous smile.

"An antibiotic with codeine. I would advise you to keep your arm in a sling." The doctor folded his bag, then walked out the door.

Sam buzzed Mario on the intercom. "I need to talk to you for a few minutes."

"*Prego, Signore?*" Mario asked as he walked into the living room.

"Mario, I need to ask you some questions about the scrolls you sold to the *tambarolo*. I'm trying to figure out what these people did with them. Exactly whom did you sell the scrolls to?"

"I do not know the man's name, but he was *tambarolo*. You see, I made a deal with him. He paid me one million lira up front, for the first scroll, and he said if the scroll was genuine, he would pay me another three million lira."

"Did you notice anything unusual when you met him?"

"It was just a regular day on the Palatine—tourists wandering around taking pictures."

"Did you notice if anybody was watching you? Think carefully."

Mario cocked his head in thought. "Wait. Yes. There was an American family very nearby. The man was taking pictures of his wife and children at the Portico. He was funny looking."

"What do you mean?"

An embarrassed smile came to Mario's lips. "He was very ugly. He was thin and bald and had a great big nose. He was wearing these baggy short pants with black socks."

Sam's jaw tightened and he clenched his teeth.

"The man's children, Mario. Were they boys or girls?"

"They were girls. Two of them. One about my age, the other younger."

Sam swore under his breath.

"Oh, and another thing. The man stayed behind and took pictures of the Forum after his wife and daughters left. I thought that was odd."

"Do you think he got a picture of you handing over the scrolls?"

Mario shrugged. "He could have, but I was not paying attention."

"If he did get pictures of you, that might explain why those men tried to kill you on the Palatine. They wanted pictures so they could follow you to the rest of the scrolls. They were going to let you and Figlio do the dirty work, then take them from you."

They were interrupted by a ring of the telephone. Sam leaned over and picked it up. "Yes?"

"Sam. You okay?" It was Don Portico.

"Yeah, I'm fine," he said as a jabbing pain shot through his shoulder. He reached in his pocket for the drugs the doctor had given him.

"And they have taken Libra." The Don's voice was deadly serious.

"Yes. I think they took her out with a dart gun. It's unlikely that they would kill her just yet, but after they get what they want from her, she's expendable."

"I have all my people looking for her. The other families are looking for her too. Also, you do not have to fear leaving the apartment. The people who have been spying on you have been dealt with."

"Thanks, I owe you one," Sam replied.

"No, Sam. It is I who am indebted to you. I have my son because of you. You will always be a part of my family." With that, he hung up.

Sam turned his attention back to the boy. "Mario, tonight at midnight I must make a call to a contact that I got from one of the men who were hunting you. I have to tell the person that I have captured you and Figlio. Would you and your brother be willing to help? It may be dangerous."

"I would be happy to help. So would Figlio. What do you want us to do?"

"I'll let you know after I make the phone call. But now, I need to get some rest," Sam replied, his eyelids at half-mast. The codeine was taking hold, and he decided not to fight it. He leaned back on the sofa and was snoring softly before Mario stood up to walk back to the professor and Figlio.

# # #

Mario and Figlio tiptoed past the living room and out the front door to the elevator. "We'll go out the side entrance. From there it is about fifteen minutes to Maria's." Figlio nodded.

They walked out into the humid night air and started running. Mario took every back alley between the Trevi Fountain and the Via Veneto. Fifteen minutes later they were walking toward Maria's apartment building.

"You think anybody followed us, Mario?"

"I don't think so."

The two bolted up the stairs to Maria's third-floor apartment. Mario knocked on the door.

"Who is it?" Maria yelled.

"Mario and Figlio," Mario said.

She pulled back the chain lock and let the two boys in.

"Where have you two been? I've been worried sick about you," Maria scolded.

Mario swallowed hard, then told her what had transpired the past twenty-four hours. Maria watched him intently. Her face slowly softened as she listened to his story.

"So what do you want?" Maria demanded after Mario finished.

Mario hesitated. "I need the scroll."

"Mario, we had an agreement that only the three of us would know about the scroll until the appropriate time. I spent hours translating it. If I give it back to you now, I won't have the opportunity to finish. And there is some very interesting information in the scroll. Information that the world needs to know. Come into the study and I'll show you."

Mario and Figlio followed her down the corridor to her makeshift study. Maria pulled the scroll from a hiding place in her closet and rolled it open on her table. "I'll read you what I've translated so far. You're not going to believe this."

She started slowly: "'The religious problems consuming the Emperor's mind have become secondary with the rumors of vast riches taken from Siracusa by Marcellus over two hundred years ago during the war with Hannibal. It is widely rumored that the spoils of Siracusa are in the possession of the Emperor Augustus. Augustus has denied the rumors, but his credibility is now in question not only with the Senate, but the populace as well. There is no record that I know of to document this rumor, nor do I know how it started.

"'Roman law requires that even the Emperor must pay taxes to the State, even from spoils won in battle. In this particular matter, however, the spoils do not belong to the Caesars, but rather to the heirs of General Marcellus. It is not known how the spoils of Siracusa came to be in the possession of the Caesars, but by virtue of the immensity of artifacts taken from the Greek temple, it is widely held that this treasure of gold and Greek objects could easily finance an entire nation, and so there is wild speculation that my friend Augustus is withholding what rightly belongs to the State. This is tantamount to treason, but no one would dare challenge the Great Emperor on this topic and, so, the rumors persist. But, at the time I write, this is all a matter of conjecture.

"'Augustus's popularity does not seem to have diminished, even though I have stated that his intentions regarding the Marcellus treasure are in question. It was only a short time ago that the citizens of Rome, grateful to Augustus for all his accomplishments, contributed to the rebuilding of his home following a fire that destroyed the entire structure. The great Emperor would accept only one coin from each citizen, even though they offered more. This act of humility on the part of Augustus won him the hearts of the people in Rome and throughout the Provinces.

"'There are those who believe that the Caesars did come about the riches in a clandestine and ruthless way. The calamities that befell the Marcellus family are widely known. What is not known is that the disasters that befell this noble family were manmade rather than coincidences of nature. I will not elaborate further on this aspect of the calamities, because I have written about them in the history of the city one hundred years following the defeat of Hannibal. Nevertheless, the winds of accusation are blowing in the direction of this wonderful and noble family, the Caesars.

"'There are others who believe that in their gratitude to the Caesars, the Marcellus family bequeathed their fortunes to Julius Caesar, Augustus's predecessor. However, no will exists to document this theory. It is a little-known fact that, following the life of Marcellus, the Caesars provided many leniencies to the Marcellus family in the way of taxes and in the way of protection from enemies of the Roman Empire. But, as I stated earlier, all this is left to conjecture. There is no documentation that shows the Marcellus family left their estate to the Caesars when their lineage expired.

"'I do know, however, firsthand, that Augustus does have at least a major portion of the riches and gold taken at Siracusa. In deference to my friend, and sponsor, a man who has genuinely given me everything I posses—wealth, fame, recognition—I have omitted this from my earlier writings. I am including this information here in this last book of my history in the hopes of providing posterity a clear record of what transpired during the reign of Octavius, the first citizen of Rome. It is my hope that this last book will be revealed long after I am gone, and my friend Augustus is gone, so as not to shed a bad light on the good that Augustus had created for the nation. I believe I am doing what was in good conscience for the Empire and for posterity, so that history may objectively judge Augustus as a great leader.

"'For me, I do not absolve myself from complicity in this matter. It is with the fear of ostracism that I withhold this part of the history of the greatest Empire to ever rule the world. Because it is only a rumor, and because nobody can come forth with evidence attesting to fact, I felt it best to leave this information out of *From the Founding of the City*. But I can say, with certainty, that Augustus's intentions for the treasure were not self-motivated, but rather his intentions were to use the treasures to continue building one of the most majestic cities the world has ever known.

"'Now, as to where Augustus kept such vast fortunes so they would not come to the light of day, I will elaborate. For it is truly a stroke of genius by a man who transformed the city of Rome from one of brick and mortar to a city of marble. For too, it is this very Emperor who created Pax Romana, the longest period of peace and prosperity the world has ever known.

"'Before his gallant attempt to conquer Rome over two hundred years ago, the great Carthaginian general, Hannibal, entered into a treaty with the Greek state of Siracusa. At this particular time in history, Siracusa was a thriving seaport because it was here that all seagoing vessels, whether traveling east or west, had to stop to take on fresh supplies. Siracusa had grown to be a powerful nation in its own right.

"'Hannibal, in his mistaken belief that he would conquer all of Italy, deposited vast sums of gold—in the form of Carthaginian Cresas—with the Greeks at Siracusa before his monumental invasion of the Italian Peninsula. Hannibal was more than a little confident that he would rule all of Rome's provinces by the end of the war, so he strategically left the gold in the hands of the Greeks, to be reclaimed following his anticipated victory. I must speculate here, but I presume that Hannibal was going to use Siracusa as a power base for his new empire, so the gold, left with the Greeks, was for the purpose of establishing a Carthaginian treasury.

"'At any rate, it was Marcellus who spoiled Hannibal's plans by sacking the Greek temple that housed this immense fortune. As I stated earlier, I will disclose where the great Emperor Augustus hid the Carthaginian booty.'"

"Go on," Mario demanded.

"But that's all there is," Maria replied glumly.

"That's it? Livy doesn't finish and say where Augustus hid the Carthaginian gold?"

"Probably, but not in this scroll. Look here," she pointed to the end of the Latin text. "He must have finished what he was writing on another scroll."

Mario was abashed. "Oh, no! The two scrolls I sold to the *tambarolo!* One of them must have had the rest of the story."

"And the person who knows where the scrolls are has been kidnapped by the killers," Figlio added.

They were interrupted by a pounding on the door. Maria, Mario and Figlio looked at each other, terrified, as the door blew open and two brawny men barged into the apartment.

Chapter 21

Positano

Libra's eyes slowly fluttered open. She let out a low moan as she rotated her head from side to side. Her mind was sluggish, numb from a drug-induced sleep. It started coming back. "Shot," she whispered. "Shot in Rome." She shook her head, trying to loosen the sedative's grip.

She felt her body for wounds, but the only evidence was the stabbing pain in her left shoulder. *A stun gun. Drugs.*

Someone had put her in a very comfortable chair. She was not tied up. The room was lavishly decorated. Pink, floor-length drapes bordered the windows. Wood and dark leather furniture was in every corner. She saw a large canopy bed with a white silk comforter. The floor was polished marble with green inlaid patterns. The walls were covered with a rich-looking, floral-patterned paper. The only thing missing, she mused bitterly, was a little Pachelbel playing in the background.

Whoever her host or hostess was, they had taken the time to put a fresh bandage on the small wound. She suspected that it would not be long until her benefactor showed up. Her eyes searched the room for a camera. Intuition told her she was being watched.

A door abruptly opened and a tall, elderly man walked into the room. By the way he carried himself, she suspected he was used to being in a position of power. His face was pallid and his body very thin. He had long gray hair, neatly combed back on the sides, not one lock out of place. With his pencil-thin mustache, he looked a little like Vincent Price. He was wearing a silk burgundy housecoat with a navy ascot. Thin, tasseled loafers covered his small feet, and a Patek Philippe adorned his bony left wrist. *Probably cost in the neighborhood of ten thousand dollars just to dress this dandy up in the morning,* Libra mused.

He pulled up a chair, sat down, looked into her eyes, and smiled, exposing a set of perfectly straight white teeth.

"Welcome, my dear," he said coolly in flawless English. "I hope you have had a good night's rest. In case you were wondering, you will be my guest on this beautiful island. I hope you find your stay comfortable as well as enjoyable."

Libra kept her eyes locked on his, showing no emotion.

"Well, since you appear to choose silence over conversation, then permit me to introduce myself. My name is Count Alfredo Montefusco. You may call me Alfredo. I much prefer informality. Please correct me if I'm wrong, but you are the quite capable young lady they call Libra, an undercover agent for the CIA. Educated at William Smith College, a language major with honors. You achieved the top of your class at Quantico, Virginia, where you were trained as an agent. Your real name is Rebecca Arnason. Have I overlooked anything?"

"What do you want from me?" Libra asked in a soft, low tone.

"I thought we'd have a short, get-acquainted chat. But, getting back to your name. May I inquire how you came about such a delightful sobriquet?"

"It's a code name. I chose it because it is the astrological symbol for balance and cunning."

"You have chosen well. From what I know of you, you are very good at neutralizing your enemies. Incidentally, you owe me a favor. For saving your life."

"Is that a fact?"

"Last Thursday, in Paris, as you were leaving the Hotel Tremoille, there was an independent contractor perched on the building next door, ready to collect on Abdul Rham's bounty. The man who saved your life, one of my better employees, I'm sorry to say, is now dead. You killed him."

"You will have to be more specific. I don't keep track."

"In Professor Rinot's apartment."

"Your man suffered from intolerable manners."

"Yes, well, I will not debate the point. I have other things to discuss that are far more important."

"Things like bombing an El Al passenger plane with over three hundred people on board?"

The Count's eyes flashed. "Surely you do not think that I had anything to do with that tragedy?"

Libra paused. "Giving you information at no cost is of little benefit to me."

The Count was not accustomed to being challenged, especially by someone who had so few options. He kept his posture steady and unemotional, but Libra could sense vulnerability. "Fair exchange is no robbery. A give-and-take session is perfectly acceptable to me."

"What I think is unimportant; however, what the Israeli and British governments think is another matter."

"And why would they suspect that I had a hand in that horrible tragedy?"

"An MI-6 agent was on that flight. His home base was Rome. He let his superiors in London know that he had uncovered information regarding your activities," Libra lied. "It does not take a rocket scientist to figure out that you needed to have him silenced."

The Count cleared his throat in apparent discomfort. "I am afraid so, my dear. But the world believes it was Abdul Rham who sabotaged the plane."

"You must have had another reason to kill over three hundred people?"

"Yes, a very good reason. Unfortunately, the man knew too much. You see, he was one of my—how do you say in your spy language—a mole? We suspected that he was about to give the Israelis information that was detrimental to our operations."

"Operations?"

"In due time. Suffice it to say that I am a patron of the classics—Roman classics, to be specific. You see, I have dedicated the remaining years of my life to restoring many of the Roman and Greek artifacts to their rightful owners."

"So your organization uses antiquities as a cover for drugs and terrorist activities."

"Suit yourself with whatever definition pleases you. However, I think you will agree that the world's museums have raped my country for much too long."

"That entitles you to kill innocent people?"

"I will refrain from going into that matter further. I must turn the conversation back to you. Quid pro quo, I believe, was what you requested when we began this conversation. You see, my dear, you have caused me a great deal of inconvenience."

"You confuse inconvenience with incompetence," Libra focused on the Count's face, which had taken on a gray pallor.

The Count's hands shook visibly. He took a deep breath. "You do not have much leverage, as I am sure you're aware."

Libra watched the old man try to get control.

"What have you done with the Livy chronicles that you stole from the University of Paris?" he demanded.

Libra continued to provoke the old man. "How were you able to get a mole inside the CIA?"

The Count's eyes shifted anxiously. "It took me years to devise that plan, and had it not been for your good fortune in Paris, it would still be intact. But enough about that. You must tell me what you did with the original scrolls."

"You are certain that what I found in Paris were the original chronicles and not forgeries?"

"You have tested my patience long enough. The consequences that you will face for this insubordination will be severe. What do you know of Livy? It was a clever ruse you played on the unsuspecting professor at Hobart College. You delivered him the forgeries of the Livy books that I, myself, wrote in 1949. I'm surprised he did not recognize them as such. Now, for the last time, where are the scrolls you took from the University of Paris?"

Libra answered with a partial truth. "The originals, as I'm sure you know, are with my colleagues in Rome."

"Yes, I am aware of that," the Count said tersely, his body shaking with rage. "I must know the *precise* writings of Livy that you have in your possession. There is specific information in one of his books that I must have without any further delay."

"Specific information as in the location of the Carthaginian Cresas?"

"How did you know about the Cresas?"

"In point of fact, the coin does not exist."

The Count was at a loss for words. Finally he offered, "You apparently are not familiar with the work of Browning."

"I'm familiar with Browning. It apparently has not occurred to you that he perpetrated the same hoax on the world that you did some forty years ago. Browning was merely suggesting that Hannibal might have stored vast quantities of gold in Siracusa. He never knew for sure."

"And you do?"

"Yes. However, I am afraid I cannot tell you more because I see no benefit in doing so. As you said, the consequences for my insubordination would be severe. I see no reason to continue our conversation."

The Count had regained his composure, knowing he still had the upper hand. "Yes, well, please forgive me, for I have been less than polite. I can understand your need to rest. I have other matters to attend to as well. We will talk again soon."

Libra looked impassively at him.

"One more minor point. Since you are my guest, everything that you will need to enjoy your stay on my island is at your disposal. I am afraid that there is no transportation, except my own, to the mainland, so I would caution you not to try to leave."

Libra continued to look through the Count. He tried to hide his frustration with Libra's indifference, but his rigid expression and the lines on his face showed that he was annoyed.

"I'm sure that after you have spent some time on the island, you will be in a better disposition to discuss these matters in more detail. We will speak again tonight at dinner. My daughter Ramona will join us at that time. In the meantime, feel free to wander about at your leisure." He turned and walked out of the room. As hard as he tried, the Count could not disguise his anger.

Libra wondered how much time she had. Undoubtedly, they would eventually drug her to get the information they wanted. Once it was obtained, she would be expendable.

She got up from the chair and looked out the window. The ocean extended to the horizon. She saw the foamy white waves spraying a dense mist as they pounded a wide perimeter of jagged rocks. She slipped on a pair of deck shoes and walked out of the bedroom into a large, open hallway. As she walked down the stairs, she passed a large oil portrait depicting the Spanish Steps in Rome.

She walked through an expansive living room onto the terrace. Directly below her was a swimming pool. Her eyes scanned the horizon. She guessed it was two kilometers to the mainland. The ocean currents would be treacherous. She looked to the south and saw a village sprawling up the side of the mountain.

She walked down a flight of marble steps and wandered around the island looking for a place to jump. The island was about five hundred yards long and three hundred yards wide. Rocky cliffs, the shortest of which had to be over fifty feet, overlooked the sea on all sides.

Libra started to formulate a plan.

Chapter 22

Rome

Mario grabbed the scroll from the table and furiously rolled it in his hands. He bolted toward the window.

"The fire escape, Mario, take the fire escape." Maria spun on her heels and followed him.

Figlio lunged for one of the folding metal chairs tucked under the card table. He grabbed it and flung it at the two men. The chair slammed into the first man's chest, knocking him to the floor. The second man stumbled over his fallen comrade, then hit the floor with a grunt.

"Run as fast as you can," Mario yelled up at Maria and Figlio. "These men carry guns." One of the thugs was climbing through the window. Mario had already reached the ground. Maria and Figlio were close behind.

Mario snatched a wine bottle from a garbage can and pitched it at the man coming down the fire escape. The bottle missed its mark, but the shattering glass momentarily halted the man. Maria and Figlio followed Mario as he sprinted onto the Via Veneto.

They ran for fifteen minutes, taking every back alley Mario knew. When they reached the Trevi Fountain, Figlio turned to Mario. "It's a good thing we were so careful about not being followed." There was more than a tinge of sarcasm in his voice.

#

Washington

Bannistar stuck his head out of his office. "Betty, get me the President. Tell the switchboard that it's an emergency." He picked up his phone. The wait was short.

"Yeah, Bill, what've you got?" The President sounded tired.

"First the bad news. I just got off the phone with Incirlik. Apparently—and the reason I say apparently is because it's only a rumor—Abdul Rham is dead."

"What's so bad about that? That's the best news I've heard in weeks."

"There's more. We have no idea who took his chair, but whoever it is, he's shipping drugs like gangbusters. Afghanistan has drugs pouring out its seams. Shipments are coming into the country at a record clip. We haven't been able to isolate the entry points, but it looks like the heroin is coming in from just about every seaport in the country."

Bannistar continued: "Satellite photos, over the past week, show a dramatic increase in the training camp populations. The sites are overflowing with terrorists. And if that weren't enough, they've opened another five camps."

The President paused, then took a deep breath. "I think the best plan of action is to have you brief the Secretary of State in the morning. We'll have to figure out some kind of action plan to counter the flow. For the time being, I think it would be wise to get word to the DEA so they can alert the authorities in the major markets, and in Europe."

"That's being done as we speak," Bannistar responded.

"I'll have Van Clevenson call you in the morning. He's tied up for the rest of the day with a delegation from the United Nations—the Middle East situation—so I won't interrupt him. But I'll damn well make sure he clears his schedule tomorrow. I've got time available tomorrow afternoon."

"That'll work for me."

"So what's the good news? I could stand a big dose of that right now."

"The mole hunt is over. We've isolated them from the phantom organization. We've got Libra to thank for that. She set them up using that professor in upstate New York."

"What are you going to do with them?"

"Feed them misinformation for a while. Let them filter it back to the ringleaders. I'm hoping that will flush them out into the open."

"Have you been able to connect this organization with Afghanistan?"

"No, not yet. But I've got to believe that Sam and Libra are on to them. The problem is, they're still in deep cover."

"Keep trying. I've got a lot of confidence in your relationship with Sam. I don't believe he'll hold out much longer. The two of you are like father and son."

"Jeff, there is one other thing. I have an idea, but I'll need your approval. It's tricky and, after you hear it, I think you'll agree it's got to be off the record. If it's exposed, I'll take the heat and resign."

The President's voice turned deadly serious. "Okay, Bill. Let's hear it."

For the next five minutes, the President listened attentively to Bannistar's plan.

"What do you think?" Bannistar asked when he was finished.

There was a pause. "Well, you're right about the heat. I don't think anybody would look favorably on the U.S. Government working with the Mafia. If the press gets hold of it we're dead meat."

There was a long silence. Bannistar expected the President to kill the idea. "You know, it's so cockamamie that it just might work. Let me ask you some questions so I'm sure that I'm clear on what you're suggesting. You want to send your chauffeur and some chiphead to Rome because there's nobody else you can trust at this point?"

"Right. I'll spare you the rationale, but they're both well trained in what needs to be done. Plus Pug Williamson speaks Italian."

There was another long pause. "What the hell; it's so stupid nobody will believe it anyway. You've got my approval to go ahead. I don't want anybody to know about this except you and me. If we get caught…well, we'll cross that bridge when we come to it."

#

ROME

"Signore Sam. Wake up." Mario gently shook Sam's shoulder. Sam had been asleep for five hours. When they returned from Maria's apartment they didn't dare wake him.

Sam sat upright on the sofa, rubbing his eyes. "What time is it?" he asked, remembering the call he had to make.

"It is eleven-thirty," Mario responded. "I was afraid you were going to sleep past midnight, so I decided to wake you up. Do you want me to get you anything?"

"Some water, please."

Sam shifted his weight on the sofa. He thought about the call he was about to make. *Do I really want to get Mario and Figlio involved with this?*

Mario returned with a glass of water. Sam looked up into Mario's wide eyes. "Mario, I've been rethinking your involvement in this thing. It's too dangerous for you and for Figlio. I think I'd better handle it myself."

Mario's face registered a momentary flash of anger. "How will you fool these people then? You have to have my help. You can't do it yourself."

Sam hated to admit it, but Mario was right. Without him he'd lose the opportunity. If he didn't move tonight, then who knew what would be next? It was his only chance to get to Libra.

"Okay. You can go along. But not Figlio. One of you on my conscience is more than I can stand. Two would be unbearable."

"Ah, there is one other thing," Mario stammered, a sheepish look on his face.

"What?"

"There is another person."

Mario had no sooner finished when Maria appeared from the hallway.

Sam did a double-take. "Who is she?"

"This is my friend, Maria. She's from America, like you and Libra."

Sam shook his head and started to laugh. "Why not? Welcome to the party, Maria. I don't mean to be rude but, ah, how did you get involved in this, er…well…situation?"

Maria told him. She spared little detail.

Sam looked at Mario. His eyes registered chaos and confusion. "You mean there's another scroll?" He looked down, trying to hide his astonishment and disgust, while Maria put her arm around Mario's shoulder.

Sam sighed. "Maria, where are you from?"

"Connecticut. I'll be a senior next year at Wells College."

"I used to date a woman from Wells, long before your time. What are you doing in Italy?"

"I'm here on an archeological dig. It was coordinated by Cornell. It's part of my degree."

Sam turned to Mario. "About this other scroll. Where is it?"

"The professor is reading it in the study. He's checking Maria's work." He told Sam what they had learned from the scroll at Maria's and about the break-in at her apartment.

At this point, Sam wasn't surprised at anything. "For the time being, Maria, you'd better stay here. You'll be in danger if you return to work. Somehow we'll have to get word to your parents that you're all right." He forced a smile, then looked at his watch. It was almost midnight.

Sam thought about the drop. It would probably be at a place where he could be watched. Sam doubted they would transfer the scroll by car; too much traffic. They'd use an intermediary to pick up the scroll and deliver it to another intermediary. The key was to find the last drop spot.

"What is it you want me to do?" Mario asked.

"I'm not sure yet. Let's wait until we find out what the instructions are."

At midnight. Sam reached for the phone and dialed the number. It was picked up on the first ring, but no one spoke.

"I am here in body and in spirit," Sam said, in a low voice.

"Do you have the boys?" the woman hissed.

"Yes. Do you have the money?"

"It will be dropped at the Post Office box number you were given once we are satisfied that the merchandise is genuine. And the two boys?"

"They have been taken care of per your instructions. It will look like an accident."

"Put the merchandise in a shopping bag. Take it to the Antico Cafe at seven tomorrow morning. Go to the back room and take the table in the far right corner. Put the bag on the chair that faces the front of the cafe. Order espresso, then leave." There was a sudden click, and the line went dead.

Sam summoned Mario, Figlio and Maria.

"Do you know the Antico Cafe?" Sam asked.

"I know where it is. It is on the Via del Corso," Figlio said.

"Okay, here's the plan…"

###

Friday Morning

Sam walked into the open-air entrance of the Antico Cafe, carrying a plain brown shopping bag that contained a decoy scroll. Businessmen were lined up at the counter, drinking espresso and eating pastries.

Sam walked to the rear of the cafe. As he expected, all the tables were empty. After the businessmen left, the tourists and late-morning shoppers would fill this part of the cafe. He walked to the rear table as instructed. He put the shopping bag on the far chair, pushed it under the table, and sat down, facing the rear of the cafe.

No sooner had he sat down than a waiter was standing over him, asking *"Prego?"* Sam did not look up; he kept his face buried in the newspaper, hoping this was the first time the Antico Cafe has been used for this purpose.

"Espresso." Sam turned his face away.

As the waiter moved to the kitchen to fill Sam's order, Mario walked through the front door of the cafe and up to the cashier. *"Espresso et dolce,"* he said.

The waiter returned with Sam's order in less than two minutes. He wasted no time slugging down the espresso. He tossed some coins on the table, rose from his chair, and walked out. As he passed through the bakery, he saw Mario out of the corner of his eye.

Mario watched as the waiter hurried to Sam's table and lifted the shopping bag from the chair, then walked back to the kitchen.

About five minutes later, a young boy with a blue book bag hurried out from the kitchen, through the cafe to the front door. At first Mario thought nothing of it—just a boy on his way to school. Then it hit him. *There is no school—it's summer vacation!* He turned sharply and ran out the door.

Mario looked to the right and to the left. He cursed aloud. The boy was nowhere in sight, lost among the throngs on the sidewalk.

Mario dejectedly walked back down the Via del Corso toward the Don's apartment. Then he glanced up and saw the boy crossing the street at the Column of Marcus Aurelius, moving into the Piazza Capino.

Mario followed close behind, trying not to be obvious, but the boy never turned around. He turned left at Via della Scrofa, then left again at Via di San Agostino. He was headed for the Piazza Navona. Mario knew a shorter route, so he sprinted down Via della Scrofa, turning down a small alley between two government buildings. He arrived in the center of the Piazza Navona and looked toward the south entrance.

The boy entered the piazza, lazily wandering down Corso del Rinascimento. Mario walked into an outdoor cafe situated between the Fountain of Neptune and the Fountain of Rivers. He sat down at an empty table, keeping his eyes on the boy.

Mario ordered an espresso. The boy walked to a bench and sat down, putting the book bag next to him. He looked dejected as he crossed his legs and screwed his face into a pout.

A priest carrying a bag of popcorn and an attaché case sat down next to the boy. Mario guessed him to be no more than thirty years old. He had closely cropped blond hair and was very skinny. The priest said something to the boy and started throwing popcorn to the gathering pigeons. The priest put the popcorn aside and pulled what looked like a small Bible from the case. The boy moved closer. He looked at the open book in the priest's hands.

Mario snapped to attention. He anxiously watched as the boy reached for the book bag, unzipped it, and handed the scroll to the priest. Mario breathed a sigh of relief.

The priest took the scroll and slipped it into his attaché case. The boy zipped the book bag, and the two stood up, shook hands, and parted. The priest walked determinedly toward the Church of Saint Agnese in Agone, which faced the Fountain of Rivers. He walked through a set of doors and disappeared inside.

Mario sprinted to the church. The wooden pews were empty save for four or five worshippers, their heads bent in prayer. He did not see the priest anywhere.

Mario walked down an aisle to the right of the pews. A sign pointing to the church office was just ahead. He turned in the direction of the arrow and walked into a small, dimly lit church office. An elderly woman with gray hair and thick glasses scowled at him as he walked through the door.

"What can I do for you, young man?" she asked, sounding annoyed.

"I would like to see the priest. I need to confess a sin. I have done something very bad, and I need absolution right away. The guilt is tormenting me."

The woman's tone softened. "Please wait here. I will see if Father Morelli can see you."

Mario waited. In less than a minute the woman walked back into the room. "You may go in and talk to Father Morelli. But be brief. He has a very busy schedule today," she admonished him.

Mario walked through the office door into Father Morelli's office. In disappointment and shock, he saw that Father Morelli was at least sixty years old.

Chapter 23

POSITANO

The Count turned and summoned his valet. "Please summon our special guest, Ronolo." The Count's eyes tingled with fury. Tonight's affair would certainly be one of the most gratifying in his long, accomplished career. Seeing Libra humiliated then destroyed. It was an exquisite *coup de grâs*.

The valet did a half-bow and walked to the long stairway leading to the guest rooms.

The Count rubbed his bony hands together. The wine steward entered with a chilled bottle of Cuvee Dom Perignon. He poured the champagne into the four crystal goblets on the table. The Count positioned himself at the table so that Libra would sit between his daughter and himself.

The valet returned to the dining room, his face flushed with fear.

"The guest, Your Excellency, she is not in her room!"

"Well, she must still be wandering about the island. She cannot be far. Summon security and have them bring her to the dining room," he said with exasperation.

Ronolo did a half-bow and walked from the room.

The Count pulled the chair for Ramona. "Ah, a delightful fragrance, my dear. What is it called?"

"It is by Jean Pateau, Father. It is called, simply, 'Joy!'"

As the Count moved to take his seat, an exasperated Ronolo ran back into the room. He was out of breath. "Your Excellency. The woman is nowhere to be found on the island. She has vanished."

The Count's face turned a deep crimson. The veins in his neck bulged out. He took the napkin from his lap, raised it above his head, then slammed it on the table. No one, not even Libra, would dare an escape from his island. It would mean certain death.

As he rose from his chair the chief of security came running into the dining room. "Your Excellency, the woman is gone! We have searched every corner of the island. She is nowhere to be found."

The Count felt his chest tighten. Rage surged through his entire body. It would be the last time this woman would get the best of him. Through clenched teeth the

Count blurted out, "Find her. Bring her here to me." There would be no more games with the American woman. He would subject her to chemicals, get the information he needed, then kill her. Nobody had ever dared skip out on one of his dinner parties. Now this!

Chapter 24

Sorrento

Searing heat scorched Libra's lungs as she forced her eyes open. The room was a blur. She forced herself to breathe. The cool fresh air charred her chest. She rubbed her eyes, trying to figure out where the hell she was. She started coughing.

The last thing she remembered was being sucked under water by a riptide as she fought the waves. She remembered trying to signal a boat slowly transcending the isthmus between Capri and Positano. The jump from the cliff. Libra remembered the waves coming at her with numbing speed. The water felt like a concrete sidewalk when she hit it. She was knocked unconscious by the impact. She recalled coming to as her head bobbed above the waves.

"*Buonasera, Signora,*" came a voice from the bed next to her.

Libra rolled her head in the direction of the voice. A friendly face smiled back at her, a man about her age. His legs were in traction wrapped in plaster casts. His dark eyes sparkled, making Libra want to smile.

"Where am I?" Libra asked.

"You are in Sorrento, *Signora*."

"How long have I been here?"

"They brought you in about two hours ago. You have been sleeping ever since. They said you were nearly drowned in the ocean. They found you floating about a kilometer from the village. They said you were very lucky. If they had not found you when they did, you would have died."

"Jesus." There wasn't an inch of her body that didn't ache. "How did I get here?"

"The captain of the tour boat that runs between Positano and Capri. He left only minutes ago. He was hoping you would wake up before he left."

"Remind me to get his name before I get out of here so I can thank him," she mumbled.

A minute or two passed. "What happened to you? You look like you were hit by a truck."

"No, not a truck, *Signora*."

"Call me Libra, *prego?*"

"Ah. An unusual name, but it befits you."

"So they say."

"My name is Antonio."

"So what happened?"

"I was in an accident." Antonio looked away, grimacing at the memory.

"What kind of accident?"

"I was walking along the road between my home and the hotel where I am employed. I was hit by a large automobile and knocked me into the ditch. The car sped away after striking me down."

"Did they get the driver?"

"No. No one saw it happen."

Libra shook her head. "Was it really an accident, or do you think you were hit intentionally?"

"I think somebody wanted me out of the way. The only reason I can think of is that I overheard a very strange conversation one night while I was attending to some dinner guests at Le Sirenuse Hotel in Positano. You see, I am the head waiter there. I think someone at that table didn't want me repeating what I overheard."

"Really? What did you hear?"

"There were four men…" As Antonio began to describe the men, he stopped in midsentence. Libra's mouth had fallen open and a look of surprise filled her face. "Is something the matter?"

"No. Please continue."

"The men were dressed in very expensive silk suits, Armani, I expect. It is not unusual to see such wealth at Le Sirenuse. It is a very exclusive hotel. Anyway, one of the men was very demanding. He had a thick, bushy mustache and very oily skin. Anyway, they were talking about drug smuggling. A very unpleasant topic, I can assure you, but they had too much to drink and I think they said some things that they wished they hadn't said."

# # #

WASHINGTON

"…and you'll need to use the passcode, 'Tuscany is pleasant this time of year.'"

"Thanks." Bannistar committed the number and passcode to memory, picked up his phone, and repeated the number to Control, advising Control that he was moving to one of the secure rooms located deep in the bowels of the Langley complex.

The phone in the secure room was ringing when he arrived. He picked up the receiver and heard Control say, "It's ringing in Rome, Mr. Bannistar."

"*Prego*," the foggy voice of a sleepy-sounding woman answered.

Bannistar, in broken Italian, repeated the passwords. There was a pause and a click.

"*Buonasera,*" came the voice of a young man.

Bannistar was taken aback. He did not expect the phone to be answered by a teenager. He had anticipated someone older. "*Signore Harrison, per favore.*"

A pause.

"*Un momento, Signore.*"

Bannistar breathed a sigh of relief.

"Yes," came Sam Harrison's voice into the phone.

"Sam. It's Bill. We need to talk."

A five-second pause.

"Okay, Bill. What the hell is going on? And how did you get through to this number?"

Bannistar exhaled. He had always played it straight with Sam. He seldom pulled punches, even when the news was bad. "Jenkins White, he's the Ambassador to Italy, got me the Don's number. I don't know how he did it, and I'm not sure I want to know. Sam, we've got a problem…" Bannistar went on to explain the Salvatore Sangi situation and the missing microfiche. "They tried to kill me and Pug. Sam, I know they've got Libra, and you took a bullet in the shoulder. We think it was Benedict who found you after I told him you may be hiding out with the Italian Mafia. Benedict may be one of them."

"The Mob?"

"No, no. Benedict is on the payroll of the people who are causing all the problems."

Sam's pulse raced. He wasn't sure whether to trust Bannistar, but he was running out of options. With Libra gone, he had only the Don and his soldiers, but they were isolated to Italy and did not have the access to the kind of information Sam needed. After considering the situation for a few moments, he figured he may as well take another risk.

"Benedict *is* one of them. He's the one who set up the kid who found the scrolls. Benedict's a double. He's working both sides of the street. Unfortunately, we don't know who these bastards are or how they're connected to Rham."

"You know that the microfiche Libra found in Rinot's apartment was a duplicate of the dummy Livy books written in the fifties?"

Sam didn't say anything.

"Does she have the originals?" Bannistar asked.

Sam hesitated. He still wasn't sure if he could trust Bannistar with all the information. "I'm not sure exactly what we've got," Sam said, satisfied that he was at least telling the truth. Sam suspected that if Libra did have the originals, she hadn't told him where they were or how she got them.

"What do you have?" Bannistar sensed that Sam was holding out.

"It's a long story, but I think we've got one of the scrolls."

"What do you mean you *think* you've got one scroll? Do you or don't you?"

"Here's the problem: We're not sure if it's genuine. I think that's why they kidnapped Libra instead of killing her. There may be something in the damned thing about a lost fortune, in gold. Some Roman general sacked a Greek temple in Sicily two thousand years ago…"

Sam was complimenting himself on the half-truth when Bannistar interrupted.

"We know all that. Bring me up to speed on what you do have."

"What do you mean you know all that?"

"O'Brien dug it out of the library. Marcellus sacked the Greek temple."

Sam shrugged, then continued to fill Bannistar in on what Maria and the professor had translated. "We could use some help. I've got more than I can handle right now and it's going to take them weeks, if not months, to get all this shit translated. By then we may be too late to save Libra."

"I'll see what I can do. In the meantime, route all your calls to me through Control." He hung up.

Sam replaced the receiver. It started ringing as soon as he put the receiver down.

"I'm in the Sorrento hospital." Libra's voice was no more than a whisper.

"I'm on my way."

# # #

Libra did not hang up. She listened. Two seconds later she heard it, a soft click. Someone in the hospital was listening.

Libra dropped the phone, ran out into the corridor, slipped on the floor and slammed into the far wall. Pain reverberated through her body. A surge of adrenaline overtook the discomfort as she looked down the hallway toward the nurses' station.

The night nurse, a plump woman in her late twenties, stood behind the counter, telephone to her ear. She was talking in excited bursts. Libra sprinted toward her, her bare feet hitting the floor in quick thuds, the hospital gown coming untied. The nurse, panic spreading across her face, slammed down the phone and reached under the counter.

Libra could see the nurse's face, fear in her eyes, her mouth set, teeth clenched—a most dangerous foe. A cornered person, fearing for life, produced massive quantities of adrenaline. The most mild-mannered person could do unbelievable things with the strength that fear and the urge for survival wrought.

The nurse jumped up, brandishing a syringe with a long steel needle. She raised it over her head and let out a scream. She dove at Libra's chest. Libra anticipated the move and lurched to the right. The needle tore through Libra's hospital gown, barely missing her left shoulder.

The nurse toppled over the counter, her body teetering across the countertop, legs flailing in the air, chest and arms dangling toward the floor. Libra brought the side of her hand crisply down on the nurse's neck. The nurse let out a gasp. Her body went limp. The hypodermic needle dropped to the floor with a click.

Libra tugged the nurse's body from the counter. Her head bounced off the floor with a dull thud. Libra turned her over, grabbed her pudgy wrists, and dragged her down the corridor. She pulled the nurse into the room. Antonio looked up.

"What…?" Antonio's face turned gray.

"Never mind," Libra cut in before he could ask. "Close your eyes."

Libra lifted the nurse with a grunt. She was heavy, about 225 pounds. She set the chunky nurse on the bed. Libra threw off the loose-fitting hospital gown, then stripped the powder blue uniform off the nurse. She slipped it over her slender body.

Libra strapped the nurse to the bed, then stuffed the end of a towel into her mouth.

"Okay, Antonio, open your eyes," Libra said, catching her breath.

Antonio wished he hadn't. In the bed where Libra had slept for the past two hours, the night nurse was strapped down, wearing only a bra and panties.

"Is she…?" Antonio's voice trembled.

"No. She's just unconscious. She had a nasty fall to the floor. She'll come around in an hour or so. She'll have a monumental headache."

He breathed a sigh of relief and turned his eyes toward Libra. He started laughing.

"What's so funny?" Libra asked.

"Look at yourself in the mirror," Antonio replied, color returning to his face.

To her horror, the uniform was so big she looked more like a polar bear than a nurse. "Yeah, well, my shorts and shirt haven't dried out yet, so this is the best I can do."

Libra walked out into the corridor. She returned in less than a minute, pushing a wheelchair. "Okay, Antonio, you're going for a ride." With that, Libra pushed the wheelchair to the side of his bed and gently helped Antonio into it.

"Where are we going?" he asked, fear rising in his voice again.

"Somewhere where we can't be found."

"What is going on? I don't understand…"

"It has to do with those men you overheard at the hotel the other night. They're dangerous, very dangerous. Unless I miss my guess, they are the ones responsible for breaking your legs. I think their intention was to do more than break your legs, Antonio."

Antonio gulped. "Then what was it?"

"They want you dead," Libra said, trying not to alarm him more than he already was.

"You mean, just because I overheard a drunken conversation? That's why they wanted to kill me?"

"It may have been a drunken conversation, and one I'm sure those men wish never happened, but you heard things that could jeopardize their operations. Now, let's get out of here before her friends show up."

"But why didn't they kill me once I got to the hospital?"

"Unless I miss my guess again, Antonio, that nurse was about to give you and me both a shot of something that would ensure that we never talked to anyone."

"How do you know that?"

"I'll show you."

Libra pushed him down the corridor toward the elevator. She stopped at the nurses' station, applied the brakes to Antonio's wheelchair, and picked up the syringe from the floor. It had a strip of red tape wrapped around it.

"I don't think this was your penicillin shot."

Antonio strained his neck to look back at the syringe. He felt a lump in his throat as Libra put it into her pocket.

She walked around to the other side of the nurses' station and spotted another hypodermic needle as ominous as the one she had picked up from the floor. Only this one had a blue strip of tape wrapped around it. "Well, Antonio. Looks like we were both slotted for extinction," she said as she slipped a plastic sleeve over the sharp point and put it into her other pocket. She did the same with the first needle.

She suspected that one of the syringes contained lethal ingredients, the other some kind of chemical to knock her out. They obviously wanted Antonio dead, but the Count had unfinished business with her.

Libra pushed Antonio to the elevator door. She pushed the down button and waited. The elevator arrived and Libra pushed the wheelchair in.

The elevator stopped with a thump at the reception area. Libra wheeled Antonio to the hospital entrance. As she was about to open the large glass doors, a limousine carrying three men abruptly stopped in the driveway. She spun Antonio around and headed for a door marked "X-ray," hoping the men in the car hadn't seen her.

Libra had no sooner closed the door when she heard someone running down the corridor. She held her breath. The footsteps continued on down the corridor toward the elevator. She breathed a sigh of relief, opened the door, and peeked through the crack. No one in sight. She grabbed the handles of the wheelchair and spun Antonio around.

She pushed Antonio onto the driveway. The limousine was parked just outside the entrance, its engine idling. The driver was still behind the wheel. "This may be our only chance for getting out of here," she whispered to Antonio. "Try to act like you're in pain."

"I do not have to act. My legs are killing me."

She pushed Antonio to the rear of the waiting limousine and locked the brake on the wheelchair. She walked to the driver's window and knocked on the glass. She had to act fast. She didn't want the driver to think the situation through. If she acted like she knew what she was doing, he just might take the bait. The driver lowered the power window.

She figured her best chance to get the car was to disorient him. "I have the man. He is in pain. The others are getting the woman now. Get out, and help me get him into the back seat. His legs are broken." She moved away quickly from the window so he wouldn't notice the baggy nurse's uniform.

The driver opened the door and stepped out of the dark limousine. He turned his droopy eyes toward the nurse, and helped her lift Antonio into the back seat of the car.

"Now. Put the wheelchair in the trunk. And hurry. The men will be down momentarily."

The driver did as he was told. After he slammed the trunk lid down, Libra hit him sharply in the stomach. He looked down, trying to suck in air. Libra pulled a syringe from her pocket. The one marked with the red tape. She stripped off the plastic sleeve and turned to the driver, who was bent over in pain. She jammed the needle into his right buttock and emptied its contents.

Within seconds, the driver stood upright. He emitted a strange gurgling noise. He fell to the ground and rolled over on his back.

Jesus, Libra thought, *that was one hell of a shot*. She turned back to the limousine, reached in and pulled the cellular telephone from its mount next to the driver's seat. She pushed the redial button, then tossed the telephone into a garden filled with magnolias.

She got behind the wheel and turned to a wide-eyed Antonio. "Where is your family, Antonio?" Libra asked urgently.

"They are in Positano, about a half-hour from here."

Libra cursed under her breath. She knew Antonio's family would be watched. If they were taken hostage, they would ultimately be killed. She had to find a way to help Antonio get them to safety.

"Why are you asking, Libra?" The blood drained from Antonio's face. The thought of his family being in some kind of danger mortified him.

"Trust me, Antonio. We've got to get word to them that there may be trouble. They've got to get to a safe place, a place where nobody can find them. We've got to get to a telephone."

"But you just threw a phone away."

"I threw their cellular phone away so they wouldn't be able to trace the car. We can't use it."

Antonio thought for a few moments. "Turn right at the exit, and go up the winding hill. I know a place where we can hide and use a telephone at the same time."

Libra floored the accelerator. The taillights vanished from sight just as three angry-looking men walked out of the hospital.

#

Sam turned to the professor, Maria and the boys. "A package will be delivered here sometime tomorrow afternoon by special courier. I suspect it's the two scrolls you sold to the *tambarolo*. When they get here, start translating them immediately. We want to find out if Livy tells where the rest of the Carthaginian gold is hidden."

"Where are you going?" Mario asked.

"I can't tell you that now, but I don't want any of you leaving the apartment until we get back. The Don's men will see to it that you have everything you need to get those scrolls translated."

Sam grabbed a gym bag filled with Libra's clothes and headed for the door.

Chapter 25

Sorrento

The limousine made its way up a steep, winding hill overlooking Sorrento. "Turn left at the driveway, six meters ahead," Antonio shouted.

The tires screeched as Libra spun the steering wheel to the left. The car sprayed a plume of gravel as it sped up a narrow driveway built into the side of a mountain. Libra failed to negotiate the first hairpin turn and rammed the front of the car into a makeshift wall of railroad ties. The right headlight shattered, and the sound of punctured metal reverberated through the car. She slammed the limo in reverse, backed up, and aimed it back up the hill.

"You okay?" she yelled at Antonio, who had been thrown forward with the impact.

"I think so."

"Where are we going?" Libra cut the wheel sharply, narrowly missing another retaining wall.

"This road will take us to a parking lot behind the Hotel Bristol, which is at the top of the mountain. It is very dark in the parking lot. The parking lot is hidden by citrus trees and shrubbery. It will be difficult for anyone to find the car there."

"Don't be so sure. It took hardly any time for those goons to find me at the hospital. They'll have people looking for us within the hour, especially since we're in their car."

"We can hide in the hotel. My brother-in-law is the manager. I'm certain he will find a room for us."

"Thank God for small favors." The car came to the end of the narrow driveway. Libra's eyes scanned the top of the mountain, which was partially illuminated by the hotel's lights. A tall iron gate protected the hotel parking area. There was enough room for six cars. She could see three, well hidden by the darkness of night and an orchard of orange trees. There were no lights. Antonio was right. The area behind the hotel was secluded, dark, and well hidden. As she lowered the window, she could feel the cool breeze off the Bay of Naples and smell the perfume-sweet aroma of the citrus trees.

"There is an entrance to the hotel straight ahead," Antonio said, pointing to a large wooden gate approximately two meters past the parking area.

Libra inched the car to a small delivery area in the rear of the hotel. She could see a flight of stairs from a patio leading down to a restaurant.

She turned the engine off, jumped out of the car, and ran to the trunk. She lifted Antonio's wheelchair out, pushed it to the rear door of the car and carefully eased Antonio into it.

"Let's see if that brother-in-law of yours can get us in a room for the night. I don't think it's going to be easy. This time of year the hotel has to be full."

"That is not a problem. He always keeps one room vacant for emergencies. But the emergencies are usually his own. So he does not have to go home to a nagging wife, if you understand my meaning."

"Let's hope we're the only emergency tonight."

She pushed Antonio in the wheelchair to the top of the hotel steps. There were two flights leading down to the restaurant. She put the brake on the wheelchair and headed down the long flight of marble steps.

"I'm going to get help. What's your brother-in-law's name?"

"Dominic. His office is on the first floor. It is behind the registration desk."

Libra bolted down the two flights of stairs, stopping in a large foyer between the restaurant and bar. She spotted the elevator to the left of the bar entrance. She pushed the down button, then listened to the cables grind as the elevator ascended the six floors to the top of the building. The corridors smelled of disinfectant.

"I need to see Dominic, immediately! There is an emergency," Libra barked at the concierge, who happened to be standing in front of the elevator as the doors opened into a small reception area.

"*Si, Signora*. Right this way," he replied nervously, snapping to attention. He walked down a short flight of steps to a door marked "Employees Only."

He knocked on the door. Libra walked by him and pushed open the door.

A rotund man with a full head of black curly hair looked up from behind a small desk. The air in the room was stale. Piles of paper cluttered the desk. Dominic impressed Libra as a first-class slob.

She shut the door, leaving the concierge standing in the hallway. "Dominic, your brother-in-law, Antonio, is upstairs. He is on the patio in a wheelchair. His life is in danger. I need you to help me get him down and into a room, prego."

"Please, *Signora*. Slow down. I do not understand. What is going on?" His pudgy face was wrinkled with confusion.

"There's no time to explain. I need your help getting Antonio down the stairs from the roof. He is in a wheelchair, and I need to get him into a room," Libra said slowly, trying to convey a sense of urgency. *Not only was Dominic a slob, but a dimwit to boot.*

"Okay. I will follow you. First let me get a key. He can stay in my private room. I keep this room for nights when I'm too busy to go home. I was planning on staying there tonight. But if it is as you say…"

The two of them barely fit into the elevator. Libra squeezed to the rear. She guessed Dominic weighed three hundred pounds. The elevator struggled under his weight as it started to move. His breath reeked of wine and garlic. Libra tried not to breathe.

They walked off the elevator onto the sixth floor, and Libra jogged across the foyer and up the stairs to Antonio.

"Did you find Dominic?"

"You didn't tell me he was a bit heavy, Antonio. I hope he can help us get you down the stairs."

Just as she finished saying it, she heard Dominic's heavy wheezing behind her. For a three-hundred-pound man, he showed surprising agility. He took one look at the situation and started barking orders as if Libra and Antonio were his employees.

"I will push Antonio." Dominic lifted the back of the chair and easily maneuvered Antonio down the two flights of stairs, careful not to let Antonio's legs come in contact with the railing or the wall.

Antonio's eyes widened as he looked down the long flight of steps. Libra walked in front, guiding the wheelchair.

Dominic pushed Antonio to the elevator, Libra following close behind. They descended one flight, then walked down a linoleum-covered corridor. Dominic's shoes clicked on the polished floor as he gently eased Antonio to the end of the corridor, stopping at the last room.

"The best room in the house for my sister's husband," Dominic announced as he shoved open the door, revealing a large room with two double beds and a large balcony overlooking Sorrento and the Bay of Naples. The strong aroma of mildew made Libra flinch.

"I must leave for a while, but I will return in a few hours. I would appreciate it if you would let no one, and I mean no one, know that Antonio is here." Libra looked at Antonio. "Call your family. Don't tell them where you are. Tell them that they are in danger. They must find a safe place to stay. Instruct them to get out of the house immediately. Understand?"

"Yes. Right away, Libra. Where are you going?"

"Someone's expecting me at the hospital." Libra walked out the door into the corridor.

Dominic and Antonio looked at each other and shrugged.

# # #

SORRENTO

Sam and the Mafia driver pulled up to the entrance of the Sorrento hospital. There were three men standing at the front entrance. Two more men were in the middle of the driveway, lifting a body bag onto a gurney. Sam leaned forward.

"Do you have a gun?" he asked the driver as he removed his own service revolver from a holster on his belt.

The driver simply put his hand under his blue chauffeur's coat, pulled out a Walther PK .38 and raised it in the air for Sam to see. It looked more like a cannon.

"By the looks of things, my associate has already left the hospital. These guys just might be a little pissed. You'd better get ready."

"Not to worry, *Signore*. The car is bulletproof. They will do us no harm."

The biggest of the three men, with a bushy blond beard and hair tied back in a ponytail, walked to the driver's window. He was wearing a tweed sports jacket with a brown turtleneck and a faded pair of blue jeans. The man rapped his enormous knuckles on the driver's window, leaned down to get a better look at the driver and demanded in an angry tone that the driver get out of the car.

The driver gave no indication of being intimidated. He slowly glanced up at the man through the closed window. His steely eyes calm, he casually smiled at the thug and then, very slowly, brought his left hand up from the steering wheel and pressed his middle finger against the window. He punched the accelerator. The rear wheels spun against the slick asphalt, leaving a cloud of smoke as it tore away from the hospital entrance.

The big man had wrapped his hand around the door handle. He spun off the car in a 360-degree circle. He reached inside his coat and pulled out a pistol, took aim, and started firing. Sam looked back through the rear window to see the other two men in the center of the driveway, arms extended outward, bright flashes coming from the muzzles of their guns.

A barrage of bullets swept over the car. They pinged off the windows and fenders. It sounded like they were in the middle of a hailstorm.

The driver headed up the main road from the hospital. He sped up another winding hill, past a waterfall illuminated by colorful lights, a hotel set in the side of a mountain, and a hidden driveway.

Sam abruptly yelled at him to stop. The driver slammed on the brakes, throwing Sam forward. His head bounced off the stationary portion of the sliding window. He cringed as pain shot through his wounded shoulder.

"What is it, Signore?" the driver asked softly, oblivious to the fact that Sam had nearly come through the window.

Sam pointed to a car about to come out of a driveway hidden behind an old house. He noticed something unusual about it. Its headlights were out, one of them smashed in. Sam opened his door and ran across to the car. At precisely the same moment, Libra stepped out of the driver's side door.

"Nice outfit," Sam said as he noticed the baggy nurse's uniform. "What happened back at the hospital?" he asked.

"It's a long story. I'll give you the details later. I think those bastards back at the hospital may lead us to the bombers of the El Al plane. I was just going down there to see if I could tail them. Try to find out where their leader is."

"Follow us," he yelled, and spun around to the limousine. Sam walked up to the driver, who was gawking out the window. "You know a place where we can ditch that car?"

"*Si, Signore*. I know a place only minutes from here."

"After we get rid of that car, I want you to tail our friends from the hospital. Do you think you can handle it?"

"No problem, *Signore*."

He hit the accelerator and headed the car up the hill past the hidden entrance of the Hotel Bristol. Sam looked in the rearview mirror. Libra was close behind. They came to a fork in the road, and the driver steered the car to the left and into a restaurant parking lot.

"So, where do we ditch that car?"

"Here, *Signore*. Tell the *signora* to park it and leave the keys in the ignition. It will be picked up before the night is over. Trust me."

Sam wasn't sure if he was referring to his Mafia friends, or to the certainty of theft. He hopped out and ran up to Libra's car as it turned into the lot. He repeated the chauffeur's instructions.

Libra parked the car and jogged back to Sam and the waiting limousine. They climbed into the back seat.

"Where to now?" Sam asked. The driver was watching the road intently.

"We wait here. All the cars from Sorrento will have to pass in front of us regardless of the direction they are headed. The left fork in the highway takes you back to the village and on to Naples. The right fork takes you through the mountains to Positano."

Sam turned his attention to Libra. "What were you doing in the hospital?"

"It's a long story. Suffice it to say, I think I picked up the connection between Rham and the Livy books." She told Sam about Antonio and about her escape from the Count.

The driver's eyes lit up in amazement as he overheard Libra tell Sam how she had escaped the island. Sam abruptly closed the Plexiglas partition. She had gambled. On the south side of the island the cliff was only fifty feet from the ocean surface. The rocks were not as prolific below. The water looked deep and calm, so she decided to risk it.

"You were lucky that boat happened along when it did."

"No shit."

Headlights lit up the road. They all turned their attention to the approaching car. It was not the men. The conversation stopped. They could hear the low whine of the air conditioner as they sat in silence, their eyes glued to the black pavement in front of them.

For no particular reason, Libra's mind started drifting back to her basic training at CIA bootcamp, to some of the things they had told her to do if she was caught by the other side. The truth was one of your best weapons, they said. They wouldn't believe you anyway, so might as well use it. And the basic rule of lying: Never lie unless you absolutely have to, then make the lie as small as possible. Once you told a lie, it was too easy for the other side to trip you up if you forgot details of the lie later on. Furthermore, you had to make up more lies to cover the original.

Libra's thoughts were broken by the driver. "There is another car coming." They watched as a set of headlight beams rounded the corner as the car ascended the hill. The driver turned on the limousine's headlights. The driver of the oncoming car quickly turned his head, looked directly at the limousine, and squinted. He was blinded by the limousine's high beams. There was no mistaking him. Tall, bushy blond beard, hair in a ponytail.

"That's them," Sam softly told the driver.

The car took the right fork, toward Positano. The driver waited a few moments, then eased the car onto the highway with the headlights off.

Each time the car ahead disappeared from sight around a bend in the winding road, the driver accelerated. He slowed down as soon as he saw the taillights of the car ahead. There was enough light from the moon to illuminate the roadway. The only thing Sam worried about was a car coming from the other direction. It would either smash into them or give them away.

For fifteen minutes the process continued. Libra turned to Sam and whispered, "We must be getting close to the top of the mountain. My God, the elevation must be five thousand feet." She looked back down from the side of the road. She could see the lights from Sorrento below. "Jesus, Sam. This guy's good. He ought to train our guys."

The car ahead turned into a driveway about sixty meters up the road. The driver slowed the limousine and inched ahead. After no more than a minute, the taillights started moving, then seconds later disappeared behind a line of orange trees. The driver increased his speed. In less than a minute they pulled up to the driveway entrance, just in time to see the taillights disappear again as the car turned toward a gigantic villa hidden in an orange grove.

The driveway entrance was guarded by large steel gates. The perimeter of the property was surrounded by a high chainlink fence with razor wire coiled along the top. Ivy was woven throughout the fence, giving it an almost harmless appearance. The fence stretched as far as Sam could see. Behind the fence was a large orange grove. He could barely make out four chimneys jutting into the night sky. They made a dark silhouette against the star-filled sky.

"What do you want to bet that the other scrolls are somewhere in there?" Sam asked Libra. He turned to the driver. "Who does this place belong to?"

"I don't know, Signore. I'm sure if you ask at the hotel, they will be able to tell you. Do you want me to help you get inside the gates?" The driver appeared eager for some more action.

"No. I think we'd be outgunned. My instincts tell me there are more armed guards in there than the three of us could handle. Why don't you take us back to the hotel," Sam answered.

The driver shrugged in obvious disappointment.

Sam turned to Libra. "We can pick up a car in Sorrento in the morning and figure out a way to stake out this place. I'd also like to have a conversation with Antonio. He may be able to give us more information."

Libra quietly nodded while she formulated a plan of her own.

Chapter 26

Sorrento

Saturday Morning

A bright orange sun peeked over the mountains, extending its rays down the tree-covered hills, through the early-morning mist, across the Bay of Naples. Libra blinked back the rays. She couldn't sleep in the musty bedroom, so she had pushed two deckchairs together just outside, wrapped a beach towel around herself, and dozed off as the gentle breezes from the sea lulled her to sleep.

She rose and walked to the railing. The soreness in her body had not faded. Pain in her arms and shoulders throbbed as she scanned the horizon. She was awestruck by the panoramic beauty. In the distance was Mount Vesuvius, its perfectly sculpted form towering above the villages below. A large, puffy cloud stubbornly shrouded its peak.

She heard the clanging of a church bell. The village was coming to life. Fishermen were making their way to the sea, following narrow cobblestone streets to their small, weathered boats. Women carrying baskets of freshly baked bread walked briskly to their shops on the main thoroughfare. The Apennine Mountains loomed high in the background. Citrus groves covered their shady hillsides. Smoke from smoldering fires drifted lazily through the air.

A ship blasted its horn. Libra turned to watch an immense freighter steaming across the shimmering blue water to the port of Naples. "Peace and serenity," she softly mumbled to herself. She stretched her arms high into the air, loosening her sore muscles. She took a deep breath, inhaling the mild sea air. The beauty of the Amalfi coastline had a calming effect on her frazzled nerves.

The screen door opened and Sam walked onto the balcony wearing only a T-shirt and boxer shorts. "Pretty view," he observed.

"It's a fascinating country, Sam. This is the prettiest coastline I've ever seen. Much prettier than California."

"So beautiful that nothing more beautiful can be seen on this earth."

"Where did you get that line? Or did you make it up?" she asked.

"André Girde, the travel writer. I remember reading it before I took my first vacation here years ago. The Amalfi coast road is a scary trip. It's hard to keep your eyes on the road, the scenery is so beautiful. The road itself was built for post-World War II traffic. Now they've got everything from oversized tour buses to daredevil motorcycle racers. I remember seeing two buses sideswipe each other on a narrow turn."

"Was anybody hurt?"

"Nah. The buses never even stopped. They just kept right on going. Down there," Sam pointed to a small grotto below a towering rock wall, "is where Ulysses had to plug his ears to avoid hearing the seductive song of the sirens." Sam put his hand to his forehead, shielding his eyes from the sun. "And way down there, at the base of Vesuvius, is Pompeii."

"Tell me about Pompeii. Wasn't it buried in ash by the volcano? I remember seeing movies about it in elementary school. People buried alive, their bodies leaving imprints in the ash that perfectly preserved their dying positions."

"Right. It was during the first century, I think. Can you imagine what it must have been like? It happened in the afternoon. The historians said the sky was pitch-black from the smoke. The people of Pompeii had no idea what was going on—they thought the world was coming to an end. Just imagine this whole area," Sam said, spanning the bay with his arm, "engulfed in darkness in the middle of the afternoon. Waves so fierce that all the ships in the harbor capsized. Hundreds of people drowned trying to escape. When it erupted, it consumed all the oxygen for miles around. Hundreds more suffocated. Horrible way to die."

"If we have time, I'd love to walk around the ruins."

"You remember *Spartacus,* with Kirk Douglas?"

"Sure."

"Well, the real Spartacus hid in the lip of the volcano from the Roman army."

"Fascinating," Libra said. She turned and put her arms around Sam's neck. "All this luscious scenery…" She pressed her body to Sam's.

The touch of Libra's hands on his neck aroused him. He let go of her, leaned in the room and pulled the drapes, listening to the soft snoring coming from Antonio's bed. He turned back to Libra and put his arms around her. Their lips met.

Libra's soft moans coaxed him on. They held each other tightly, Sam kissing her neck and stroking her auburn hair. Libra wrapped her arms around him, pressing her body tightly to his.

"Oh, Sam…Sam…"

He gently pushed her terrycloth bathrobe off her shoulders, down her arms, letting it fall to the balcony floor. He tenderly kissed her neck, then slowly moved his mouth to her breasts. Her nipples hardened at his touch. Her hunger and desire rose. She felt a strong tingling sensation through her body.

Libra moved her hands to Sam's shorts, loosened them, and dropped them to the floor. She took his hand, turned him around, and led him to the chair that she had slept on the previous night. Libra mounted him, throwing her arms around his neck, meeting his lips with hers. She thrust her tongue into Sam's mouth. He moaned.

Libra closed her eyes and let the sensation fill her completely. Sam held Libra's hips. His eyes rolled back. They breathed in unison.

Libra whispered into Sam's ear. She held onto his neck with both hands, her fingernails digging into the skin, and thrust her head back. She let out a loud cry as she climaxed. Sam came at precisely the same moment, letting go a deep moan of satisfaction.

Libra held onto Sam, her head on his shoulder, their bodies entwined. Their breathing was steady…the breathing of two lovers released from their long-pent-up passions.

Several moments of silence followed.

"Know what I like best about our lovemaking?" Libra asked, looking passionately into Sam's eyes.

"No. What?"

"The way we climax together. It's always been that way, even when we first made love years ago. Do you know how many people have never experienced that?"

"No. I haven't exactly been keeping track of those sorts of things. I've had a few other things on my mind lately," he replied in mock sarcasm.

"I don't either. I'll bet it's a lot, though." They were quiet for a moment.

"Sam, I've decided to quit."

"Why?" A surprised look came over his face.

Libra sighed. "I've had enough. I feel as though I've gotten closure around Chet's death. For me, it's time to move on to something else."

"What brought that on?"

"The last forty-eight hours. I've been shot at, drugged, and held prisoner by a maniac. I've jumped off a cliff, almost drowned in the Bay of Naples, and a crazy woman disguised as a nurse tried to kill me with a lethal injection. Honestly, Sam, I don't know how much longer my luck can hold out."

"I think that would make most people want to quit their job."

"The other thing, Sam. It's waking up in the morning and looking at this beautiful country. You know, I wish I were just another tourist with nothing better to do than find a good restaurant. Think about it. Not having to chase drug dealers and spies day in and day out. Not having to worry about who's killing whom. Enjoying a cozy little breakfast together, sipping cappuccino at a sidewalk cafe, getting on a train and visiting Pompeii."

Sam did think about it. She was right. This was no life, especially for her. It was one thing to sit in an office in Washington all day, quite another to be out in the cold risking your life. "If you could wave a magic wand, what would you do?"

"What did you say? I'm sorry, Sam, I drifted off."

Sam repeated the question.

Libra thought for a few moments.

"When we're done with this project, or whatever you call it, I'm going to resign. I'm sure as hell not going to work for a while. Maybe travel. Take some postgraduate courses, possibly."

"What about family?"

"Yeah. That's on the agenda," she said with a sigh. "I've decided I want two kids, a boy and a girl. And I've got to get started pretty quick. My biological clock is on its last few hours."

"You want to talk about it? I thought we were going to save this conversation for Washington."

"Shit, Sam…I'm ready. When I woke up in that hospital last night, I realized how precious life is. I don't want to spend another second risking mine the way I have the past few weeks. The more I think about it, the more I realize how lucky I am to be here talking to you." She kissed him on the cheek, then gave him a quick hug.

"You've got a point." He inhaled deeply. "Okay, I'll make a deal with you. You see this project to its conclusion, and I'll ask you to marry me," he blurted out impulsively. Sam's face turned a bright crimson. He didn't believe what he had just said. He wasn't sure if he was more afraid of commitment or rejection.

"No deal." Libra flashed angry eyes at Sam. She got up abruptly and put on her robe. "I'm not making my marriage conditional on anything, especially this. You want to marry me, you ask me respectfully…and no conditions."

Sam held his breath and paused. "You're right. I apologize," he responded, genuinely ashamed. He'd taken too much for granted in their long relationship. "Let me rephrase the question. Will you marry me?" His face turned another shade of red as he sat in the chair with nothing on but a beach towel draped across his midsection.

"I'll think about it," Libra said, gloating over her victory.

Sam gazed blankly at the balcony floor. He wasn't sure if he was mad or relieved.

#

ROME

Figlio marveled at how well his brother, Maria and the professor worked together. They sat side by side, translating the scrolls that had arrived by special courier the previous afternoon. Not once did they have an argument. This was unusual for Mario. He used to fight with the priests constantly when they translated together, becoming angry and defensive when he was challenged. Even if he was wrong, Mario would never admit it.

"Figlio. Go get the professor. I think I have found something, but I need some help," Mario said, his voice ringing with excitement.

Figlio shuffled down the long corridor toward the kitchen. He found the professor in the kitchen, looking into the refrigerator. "Professor! Mario needs to see you. Can you come right away?"

"Yes, Figlio," he mumbled. "I will be down in a minute." He reached in the refrigerator and pulled out a plate of leftover lamb. "*Molto bello,*" he chirped.

"What have you found, my young student?" the professor asked between bites of lamb. He held the plate in front of Mario's face in offering. Mario declined with a wave of his hand. The professor offered the plate to Figlio, who reached across the table—cluttered with scrolls, notepads, dictionaries and an assorted variety of pens and pencils—and snatched a bite from the plate.

"We need your help with this particular passage. I can't quite make out what Livy is saying. There may be something meaningful in the text. I'm not sure. The matter is complicated by the fact that the writing has faded and the words are hard to make out. Also, this third paragraph is almost entirely rubbed out. It looks like the ages and the moisture have been unkind to this particular scroll."

The professor followed Mario's hands as he pointed to several faded lines on the scroll, which was spread across the desk and held down by a paperweight at each end. He picked up a magnifying glass and held it close to his eyes. After a few moments of observation, he reached for a notepad and scribbled several sentences with a mechanical pencil. He leaned back in his chair, bringing his hand to his chin. Several moments of silence passed.

"Did you come up with something?" Mario finally asked.

The professor leaned forward. "I'm not sure. I need to think about this passage for a few more moments."

"Perhaps I can help you?"

"Okay. You tell me what you think Livy is saying in these passages, and we'll compare what you say with my notes," the professor said.

Mario could not contain himself. Never had he had as much fun translating the classics as he did with the professor. "You must have been a great professor at the University," Mario said.

"Don't patronize me, Mario," the professor said with piercing eyes. "Let's see what you've got."

"Here, in this passage," Mario pointed at a line in the scrolls, "Livy says that the great grandson of Marcellus, the head of the family and a member of the Senate during the reign of Julius Caesar, was often remiss in tending to his responsibilities. The next line is not clear; I can't make out the words—they are too faded."

"Continue on with the next paragraph," the professor instructed, as he watched Mario struggle with the text.

Mario turned his eyes back to his notes. "Livy says that Marcellus—the great, great-grandson, that is—and his family were attacked—the text is not clear on who attacked them—while they were in the south on state business. But he does not specifically mention a city, at least in these paragraphs. Perhaps that's what's missing in the text that has been destroyed?" Mario looked up at Maria and the professor, then continued. "The attack on the family would be significant for two reasons: First, it was during a time when his duties required him to be on the Senate floor and, second, because it was widely held that Marcellus was plotting to overtake the government at Pompeii. The other factor that leads me to the conclusion that the gold may be in Pompeii is that it is not far from Sicily. It would have been a lot easier to move the gold there than to Rome."

"But Livy speculates that Marcellus—the younger—wanted to take the city for his own purposes, secede from the Empire," Maria interjected. "Do you think that would mean that Marcellus was going to use the gold to set up his own power base in southern Italy?"

"Possibly," the professor answered. "What I am having trouble with here is whether Livy is talking about theory or reality. You see, he's speculating. There was obviously some political intrigue going on during the reign of Julius Caesar and his adopted son, Augustus. If Livy is right, what he's saying is that Julius and Augustus were conspiring to eliminate the Marcellus family. Now, whether or not that is factual, I can't tell. There are no other records to indicate what was really going on."

Mario stopped. He thought for a moment, then answered the professor's thesis. "The rest of the paragraph and the following two paragraphs are not discernible. They are too weathered. Then Livy says—and this is what I do not understand—

that the ethical and moral fabric of society had decayed even further during the Imperial reign."

"That's what I'm talking about," the professor cut in. "He is distinguishing between the Roman Republic and Rome ruled by the emperors. Obviously, Livy was privy to inside information because he worked for Augustus and was close to the emperor. So these documents were probably hidden by Augustus so that the world would not know what he was up to. It looks like he had planned some kind of clandestine plot to usurp the Marcellus's family fortune."

Mario nodded, then continued. "He says, and I'm paraphrasing here, that Marcellus the younger was, in part, responsible for the decay that was instituted by Marcellus the elder two hundred years earlier. What does that mean, Professor?"

The professor stroked his beard. "Livy is referring to Marcellus's sack of the Greek Temple at Siracusa in 212 B.C. Livy argues that it was that event that precipitated the fall of Rome."

"I don't understand," Mario said.

Maria broke in. "Livy believed that the Greek artifacts brought back to Rome started the unwinding of *pietas*. That is, people no longer went to the Roman temples to worship their gods; they went to the temples to see the Greek treasures. In other words, the temples were turning into museums. This is important, Mario, because the strength of Roman society was based on a social order of importance: to the gods, first; then the state, second; the family, third; and the self, last. Self-indulgence was becoming the order of the day; it was becoming more important than a sense of duty to the gods and to the state. So religion, which was the bond that made the Roman Empire so strong, was coming undone. Am I right, Professor?"

The professor nodded with an approving look. "The Greeks had a profound influence on Roman art and culture. I think Livy may be overdramatizing the Greek influence on the Roman political order, but your point is well taken, Maria, and it may explain why Livy was so upset. Upset enough to write an addendum to his History."

Mario nodded.

The professor continued: "*Religio*—that is, the moral fabric of the Roman Empire—was deteriorating. Now, go back to the passage on Marcellus, the one where you say he and his family were robbed by outlaws. The way I translate the passage is this: Marcellus and his co-conspirators killed a party of—and I'm not sure of Livy's meaning here—legislators from the south."

Mario referred back to his notes, then to the original text. He took the magnifying glass from the professor and reread the passage. "No, Professor, I think that I am right on this one. Marcellus was killed, because Livy does not mention him again in the rest of the texts. And if I am right and he was killed, it would mean that someone else ended up with the gold."

"Hmm, perhaps you are right. Which would mean that the spoils taken from Siracusa would be somewhere in the vicinity of Pompeii, because at that time Rome was spending great sums to rebuild Pompeii following the earthquake that all but destroyed the city."

"Do you think that it still might be there?" Maria asked.

"There is a strong possibility that it is because there is still a large portion of Pompeii that has not been unearthed. The other possibility is that it is in Herculaneum, which was also destroyed by the earthquake."

"Why there?" Mario asked.

"Herculaneum is where the wealthy Romans went on holiday. It is very likely that Marcellus had a villa there, and it is a short distance from Pompeii. Only a small portion of that city has been unearthed since. It is still buried under the new city. It would be the more logical place for Marcellus to have hidden Hannibal's gold."

"Ooh," Maria cooed. "Do you really think there might be gold buried in Herculaneum?"

"We should find out soon enough," the professor answered. "If we can determine an exact location for Marcellus—Pompeii or Herculaneum—it would give us a good start on finding it. But remember, the gold may have been melted down and taken by someone else over the centuries. Besides, we're not really sure if there was that much gold. It's only a presumption on Livy's part."

"So what do we do about resolving the tenses?" Mario asked.

The professor responded with another question. "Is it possible that the manuscripts themselves have been so weathered by time that the original text has been distorted?"

Mario shot a puzzled look at the professor. "I don't know what you mean."

"See here," he said, pointing the tip of his mechanical pencil under the magnifying glass on the parchment, "the text has been distorted. The way the characters read it could almost be translated as was killed versus killed. You see, the expansion and contraction of this paper over the centuries has shifted the characters. Only slightly, but enough to change the meaning of what the author is saying. Does that make sense to you?"

Mario shrugged. "It looks as if you are right, Professor. I can't understand how I could have made such a simple mistake."

"It was an easy enough mistake, Mario. Anyone would have come to the same conclusion."

"A simple rearranging of the characters because of the condition of the parchment. I wonder how many true meanings are lost, how many things Livy wrote, mistranslated. What if…?"

"Regardless of the tense of the verb, you have come across something terribly important…"

The professor's words were interrupted by the distant ring of the telephone in the living room.

#

Libra walked back into the room from the balcony to find Antonio still asleep, snoring gently. Sam walked in behind her and headed for the bathroom. She gently nudged Antonio. "Antonio. Antonio, wake up."

Antonio's eyes opened with a start. He looked at Libra. A smile lit up his face. "I'm sorry I was asleep when you came back last night. Dominic gave me something to calm my nerves. I'm afraid it was very powerful. I went to sleep right away."

"Antonio, I have a friend I would like you to meet. He works with me. We are trying to find the people who broke your legs," Libra said.

At that moment, Sam walked out of the bathroom dressed in a pair of khaki slacks and a blue golf shirt. "*Buongiorno*, Antonio. I would like to ask you some questions about the men you saw at the hotel the night before your accident."

Antonio frowned. "But I do not remember much about it."

Sam knew that he would remember more than he thought. Questioning him would help him recall details that he had pushed to the back of his mind.

"Can you tell me a little bit about the men in the restaurant that night?" Sam asked gently.

Antonio's mind reflected back. The picture was becoming clearer now. "They were very drunk, and they were very loud. One in particular, a very sleazy-looking man, kept demanding more of this and more of that. He kept me running all night."

"Do you remember what they were talking about?"

"Yes. I got bits and pieces. You must remember that I was coming back and forth from the kitchen serving the meal. But I do recall them talking about finding a large sum of money. No, wait…" Antonio paused. "They were talking about digging. Yes, that's it. They were talking about digging treasure from the ground."

"Did they say where they were digging?"

"No. That's when I left the room to get more pasta. But I didn't take them very seriously. They were so drunk. I thought it was just drunk talk."

"Did they say anything else that you remember?"

"Yes. They talked a lot about drugs…heroin, I think. But in southern Italy it is wise to forget overhearing that kind of conversation. The Mafia does a lot of drug business here, so no one wants to even admit that they know anything about the Mafia. So I pretended like I heard nothing."

"Did you hear them mention any names?"

Antonio paused again. "Yes, but it was a name that I don't recall. It was foreign."

"Abdul Rham?" Libra cut in.

"Yes, yes, that was it. I remember now because at the time I thought what a funny name. Abdul."

"Do you remember what they said about Abdul?" Sam asked.

"It was funny. I couldn't figure out if this Abdul was a partner or an enemy of these people. Sometimes they talked about him like he was an ally. But I would no sooner return from the kitchen with the espresso, and they were talking like this man was their enemy."

"Anything else you remember?"

"If I think of anything I will let you know. I must have heard something important. Otherwise, why would they try to run me down with a car the next day?"

"How's about some breakfast?" Sam looked at Antonio with a smile.

"That I would like very much. But first, I need some help going to the bathroom," he said, his face turning crimson.

Libra picked up the telephone and called down to Dominic's office. He answered on the second ring with a groggy, nasal voice. He sounded like he had spent the balance of last night with his nose in a bottle of Chianti.

"Dominic, this is Libra. Would you be so kind as to bring us up some breakfast? Also, would you call the car rental agency in Sorrento and get us a car? We also need two pair of high-powered binoculars."

"*Si, Signora,*" Dominic yawned in Libra's ear. "I will take care of everything for you."

Chapter 27

Sorrento

Sam pulled up to the entrance of the hotel in a rented Fiat. Libra was waiting for him. She ran around to the side of the car and got in.

"Did you get Bannistar?" she asked.

"No, he was in a meeting. Wants me to call him tonight if possible." Sam headed up the hill to the villa where they had seen the limousine disappear the night before. The little car strained against the steep, winding road.

"Looks like a pretty elaborate security system," Libra observed as they drove past the villa. "What do you want to bet there are security cameras strategically located around the perimeter, and that the fence is electronically sensitive?"

"I don't think I'll take that bet. Let's see if we can find a place at the top of the mountain to set up shop. Should get a pretty good view of the place from up there."

As they drove past the entrance, the gates started to slide open. He drove slowly up the hill, hoping they had not been seen by whoever was coming out. Libra watched through the rear window. A long, black limousine pulled onto the coast road. It turned in the direction of Sorrento.

"That was the Count in the back seat," Libra announced. "That's the same limo we followed last night. You follow it, and I'll stay here and see if I can find a way to get in this place. It may be the opportunity we need to find out if the Count has anything to do with the drugs."

"Jesus, you think you can get past all that security?" Sam asked doubtfully.

"I don't know, but I'll sure as hell give it a try. At the very least, I'll be able to get a better look at the grounds and find out where they're vulnerable. If I can get in there, it would be nice to do it while the Count and his bodyguard are out!"

"Okay, I'll look for you at the top of the mountain when I get back." Sam made a sharp U-turn in the middle of the narrow mountain road. The limousine disappeared as it rounded a curve. Sam pulled the car to the side of the road. Libra grabbed a small Walther PK .47 from the glove box and took one set of the high-powered binoculars that Dominic had put in the car. She jumped out as Sam hit the gas and headed back down the mountain.

No sooner had Sam and the Fiat disappeared around a bend in the road than Libra heard the unmistakable sound of dogs padding to the fence, growling ferociously. Three Doberman pinschers spotted her through the fence. Their growling turned to loud, angry snarling and barking as their muscular hind legs propelled them high against the security fence. Their sharp white teeth flashed against the sunlight as they angrily snapped their mighty jaws at the intruder.

Libra instinctively backed away. The damned dogs would attract attention. The guards would know that someone was on the perimeter. She doubted that they would think she was a tourist out for a morning walk. It took her the better part of five minutes to reach the property line. As she jogged up the side of the mountain, she could still hear the angry barks.

Libra spied the summit of the mountain. It was no more than twenty meters away. She figured she could find a place at the top of the mountain that would look down on the villa. The air was thin, and she started to perspire even though there was a cool breeze coming from the ocean.

By the time she reached the top of the mountain her breathing was heavy and labored. Her heart was pounding. She gasped for air, but it was difficult to breathe given the altitude. Libra looked down the other side. The road to Positano snaked along the side of the hill toward a small village about two kilometers away. She stopped, collected her breath, and headed into the woods overlooking the villa.

Libra saw fires burning in several locations within the compound. Guards were burning broken branches that had been culled from the citrus groves. She counted eight men. The Doberman pinschers were frolicking among them, the intruder at the fence a distant memory.

Libra moved farther into the woods. The house came into view. A three-story brick villa. It was immense. Four red brick chimneys rested on the roof, scraping the blue sky above. "Jesus, the place could house a small army," she muttered under her breath. She raised the binoculars to her eyes, looking for a place to break in. She sensed that she was being watched.

###

The Count's car stopped at the Pompeii tollbooth. The driver, the man with a bushy beard and ponytail, grabbed the toll ticket from an automatic ticket machine, then sped toward Naples. As Sam pulled up to the tollbooth, he could barely see the back of the limousine in the distance. He grabbed a ticket from the machine, then floored the accelerator. Even giving it all the gas it could stand, the small car was no match for the limousine.

Sam pushed the Fiat for thirty minutes, weaving in and out of traffic. As he approached the exit for Ercolano he spotted the limo waiting at the tollbooth. Sam pulled onto the exit ramp. It took three minutes to reach the tollbooth. By that time, he'd lost the Count again. He cursed and drove aimlessly through the streets, looking in vain for the black limousine.

Sam wondered if they had spotted him on the road from Sorrento. Unlikely, he thought to himself. He crisscrossed the small city for another hour. Eventually, he came to the gates of Herculaneum, another ancient city buried by Vesuvius. What the hell, he thought to himself, it's worth a look. He pulled the Fiat into a nearby lot.

He reached in the glove box and removed a small caliber pistol. Grabbing the second set of binoculars from the passenger seat, Sam got out of the car and gave the keys to the attendant. He paid the admission fee and entered the four-thousand-year-old city.

Considering that Herculaneum had perished under torrents of mud from Vesuvius over twenty centuries ago, Sam thought it appeared to be in remarkably good condition. Many of the dwellings had been reroofed with ceramic tile that simulated the original roofs of two thousand years ago. The buildings themselves were well preserved.

An unshaven man wearing a shabby brown sports jacket with dark baggy pants walked up to Sam. "*Scusi, Signore.* You like to have guided tour of Herculaneum? Very cheap."

Sam looked at the man. "No, Signore," he said, and waved the man away.

Sam took the binoculars from the case and brought them to bear on the south end of the site. A construction shack marked "Tri-Color Construction" in bold black letters stood behind the concrete roadway. Sam's heart started to race. The limousine. "Ponytail" was leaning against the front fender of the car. Sam focused the binoculars and zeroed in on the big man.

No sooner had Sam set his eyes on him than the door of the construction shed opened and out stepped the Count, followed by a construction worker. Both men were wearing white hardhats with the Tri-Color logo embossed on the front. They walked toward the entrance of the ruins. The Count was clutching something in his right hand as he started walking down the gangway to the ruins. Sam adjusted the lens and refocused on the Count. Jesus, he was carrying the scroll!

Sam walked back to the entrance, where he purchased a glossy tour book. The Count and the construction worker were walking slowly toward the northwest corner of the ruins. Periodically, the Count would point up to the city of Ercolano. The construction boss looked up, too, then looked back at the Count. He nodded. They walked past the remains of several villas, then turned left on one of the stone streets and disappeared into a tunnel.

Sam turned to the foul-smelling tour guide. "Signore, I have reconsidered. I would like a tour after all."

The man snapped to attention. He rushed to Sam's side instantly, and chattered on as they strolled down the long, sloping path to the perimeter of the ruins. At the end of the path was a wooden walkway that descended into the ruins.

The guide (Sam had mentally dubbed him "Pig-Pen") gesticulated wildly each time he made a point. They walked slowly down the road. Pig-Pen stopped right in front of Ponytail.

Sam looked at Pig-Pen, nodding his head as though he were listening. Sam reckoned Ponytail was no more than two meters away. As bad as Pig-Pen smelled, he was providing a cover, Sam reasoned. Without the guide, he would be exposed.

Finally, Pig-Pen pulled Sam by the sleeve and led him to the wooden walkway. They walked down the planks to a street of gray-black stones. Sam turned his attention to the tunnel just ahead.

"Where does that tunnel lead?"

"The tunnel goes under the city of Ercolano. The construction workers use it to get to the rest of the ruins, which are still buried in the mud of Vesuvius. What you see here is only twenty percent of the city. The rest…"

Sam pulled a one-hundred-thousand-lira note from his pocket. Pig-Pen quit talking and stared at the note with unconcealed lust. "Would you mind getting me something to drink?"

The guide snatched the note from Sam's hand. "*Si, Signore.* I will return in a few minutes." He headed off behind a row of first-century townhouses.

Sam guessed that it was the last he would see of Pig-Pen. One hundred thousand lira would buy a lot of vino.

Sam walked on past the tunnel. He could see light bulbs strung across the ceiling of the cavern. Sam guessed he could see five to six meters inside. The Count was nowhere in sight. Sam walked through the villa garden. He shot a quick glance up the hill. Ponytail was still standing at the limousine, picking his fingernails.

Sam heard voices coming from the tunnel. He peeked up to see the Count and the construction worker emerge from the tunnel. They seemed to be in some kind of argument. They were no more than a couple meters away. His back was turned, so the two men could not see his face.

"But you said you knew the location…" It was a harsh, angry voice.

"It was the best we could do."

Sam turned and looked at the two men. The Count had the scroll opened, stretched out from the two ancient wooden spools in either hand. The worker was looking down nervously at something on the parchment. The Count was gesturing with his head for the man to take a closer look.

Sam's heart started to race. He'd wait until the Count started back up the wooden gangway. Sam hoped the construction worker would go back into the tunnel. He could snatch the scroll from the Count's hand while he was walking back to his limousine. He'd use his gun to neutralize Ponytail—one shot to the chest. It probably wouldn't kill him, but it would immobilize him long enough for Sam to get past him to the Fiat.

Sam waited a few moments, then looked back at the two men. The Count headed slowly for the gangway, while the construction worker walked back to the tunnel.

Sam turned and started walking behind the Count. The Count stepped on the plank and grabbed the rope railing with his right hand. He clutched the scroll in his left. Sam was less than a meter behind him. He took a long, quick stride. He had to make the snatch quick and sudden so the Count would not instinctively tighten his grip and tear the ancient parchment.

Then the Count did something that Sam had not anticipated. He turned around suddenly and looked directly into Sam's face. There was a sparkle in his eyes, "Ah, Mr. Harrison, there you are! We have been expecting you."

# # #

Sorrento

Libra counted eight men in gray work uniforms laboring in the compound. She focused her binoculars on one of the men. He wore a straw hat to protect himself from the afternoon sun. As he bent over, Libra saw a pistol strapped to his ankle.

Three Doberman pinschers, eight security guards, a razor-topped chainlink fence. To a casual observer, it looked impenetrable. Libra suspected she could crack it. First the dogs…

# # #

Herculaneum, Italy

"I believe this belongs to you," the Count said as he handed the scroll to Sam.

Sam looked at it in disbelief. Why was the son of a bitch handing it to him? And how did he know Sam would be there?

Sam reached in his pocket and pulled out the Beretta. He pointed it at the Count's chest and cocked the hammer.

"I'm afraid that won't do you much good, Mr. Harrison. Or may I call you Sam? If you would take a moment to look about, you will see my construction boss not more than a meter behind you with a Smith & Wesson .38 caliber pistol pointed at the middle of your spine. And up there," pointing to a restraining wall, "is Rondo. He is a crack marksman with a telescopic rifle. At this moment he has a nasty-looking weapon pointed directly at your head. I am told that those things do not leave much intact. And you've met my tour guide…"

Sam looked back. Pig-Pen! The foul-smelling "guide" walked from behind a retaining wall, a gun in his hand and a big smile on his lips. "Thank you for your gracious tip, *Signore*."

Sam's mind raced as Pig-Pen took his weapon.

"I would consider it an honor if you and your friend Libra would be my guests for dinner this evening," the Count declared with a pleasant smile. "Yes, Libra is at my farm as we speak. She's on a hill overlooking the orchard. I suspect she's trying to figure a way to break in. I doubt that she will have any more success than you did, however."

Sam walked up the planks to the car, followed by the Count and the guide. The Count, with a smile and a sweep of his arm, motioned Sam into the vehicle. Ponytail slammed the door behind him. The Count climbed in the other side.

"So how do you like what my construction company has done to this wonderful ancient city?" the Count asked pleasantly.

Sam tried to control his anger. "What is your construction company digging for now?"

"Not what you would suspect. And please, call me Alfredo. We are trying to locate a temple, actually. The Temple of Isis. So far we are not having much success. The mud from Vesuvius is so thick it will require blasting to break it loose. But blasting would most likely cause structural damage to buildings in Ercolano. So we are digging out very slowly. Sometimes less than a foot a day. But it has been rewarding—we have found many artifacts of priceless value."

"Like lost booty from Carthage?" Sam snapped at the Count, not sure if he had his history correct, but not caring, either.

The Count simply gave a slight chuckle. Sam's annoyance was of no interest to him. "If you're referring to the treasure of Marcellus, which came from Siracusa, not Carthage, the answer is no. My company turns all the artifacts it finds over to the National Archaeological Museum in Naples. You see, Mr. Harrison, my country has a rich history, but Italy has been raped of its rightful treasures."

"So that's why you terminated the *tambaroli?*"

"The ones we know about, yes. However, they are an ongoing nuisance. As soon as we rid the country of one or two of them, four more pop up in their place."

Later, Sam would only remember bits and pieces of what happened next as his rage finally overcame him. He recalled smashing the Count's nose into a bloody pulp while he screamed, "You son of a bitch!" But he had no memory whatsoever of slamming his fist into the Count's ear, a blow that left the old man permanently deaf. And he did not remember—even though the knuckles on his right hand were mysteriously lacerated—turning the Count's perfectly straight white teeth into useless stumps.

Sam did remember turning Ponytail into a eunuch, however. Before Pig-Pen could inject him with amobarbital sodium, Sam, pulled off the Count by Ponytail, slammed his right knee into the big man's groin. As if that weren't enough, Sam wound up and drove a haymaker punch into Ponytail's face as he doubled over. The big man flipped onto his back, landing in a gravel roadway. Adrenaline and rage still pumping through his body, Sam delivered one final blow, driving his right foot into Ponytail's groin, grinding unmercifully. "That's for the four hundred innocent victims you motherfuckers killed in Amsterdam!" he screamed.

Sam regained consciousness in a dark, damp room. He was tied to a chair, his mouth was gagged, and he had a splitting headache.

Chapter 28

Sorrento

Libra came to a stop at the top of a plateau overlooking a plush green valley. She had slipped away from the villa without attracting attention, but climbing down the mountain left her feeling dizzy and thirsty. Sam had not returned to meet her, and she feared the worst.

Libra scanned the horizon. The sun reflected off a mirror in the distance and she looked in the direction of the flash. The Positano to Sorrento bus. She could intercept it, if she hurried.

The terrain was uneven and rocky, and several times she tripped over rocks and branches hidden by the overgrown vegetation. She started waving her hands in hopes of getting the driver's attention. Just as she was about to give up, the bus started to slow down, its yellow warning lights flashing.

Libra slowed to a jog, out of breath and gasping. As she fought back the waves of fatigue. Libra looked to the sky. Something strange. Two horses, white stallions. Two boys clad in ancient war gear, mounted on the stallions looking down at her. Then as suddenly as they appeared, they vanished.

The doors on the bus opened, and she was greeted by a blast of cool air coming from inside the bus. Her dizziness was subsiding. "Can you drop me at the Hotel Bristol?"

"*Si, Signora,*" the driver responded. "It is three hundred lira."

She wondered how much longer her luck would hold out as she dragged herself to an empty seat in the rear of the bus. Another forty minutes passed before they reached the Bristol.

The elevator deposited her on the sixth floor, and she walked swiftly to Antonio's room. She could hear the television blaring and laughter from inside the room. Dominic and Antonio were watching an Italian soap opera as they ate their dinner.

"Libra! Where is Sam?" A worried look replaced Antonio's smile of welcome.

"I don't know, Antonio. He may be in trouble," Libra said as she grabbed a bottle of San Pellegrino from Dominic's dinner tray and filled a glass with the water.

She gulped it down, refilled the glass, and drained it again. The cool water cleared her head. She looked at Dominic.

"Dominic, I want you to take Antonio to a safe place. You must get him out of the hotel right away. There will be trouble."

Dominic looked up from his pasta. He exchanged worried glances with Antonio. "What is it?"

"The men I told you about. They will come here looking for me, and for Antonio. They have tried to kill Antonio twice. I don't think he will be as fortunate the next time. You must make arrangements right away."

Dominic nodded.

"Can you give me the telephone number for the car rental agency in Sorrento?"

Dominic gave her the number from memory. Libra punched it in. A woman's high-pitched voice answered. "Yes," Libra said. "I need a car right away. Do you have something available?"

"*Si, Signora.* But we are closing in five minutes."

"I will pay you an extra hundred thousand lira," Libra offered.

"Two hundred thousand is what it will take to make it worth my time."

"Okay, two hundred thousand," Libra said, too tired to argue. "But for that price, you have to deliver the car to the rear entrance of the Hotel Bristol within the next ten minutes."

Libra grabbed her bag and packed the clothes that Sam had brought her from Rome. She gave Antonio a hug and told him to take care of himself, and said that she would be in touch when this thing was over. She kissed Dominic on the cheek and thanked him for all his help. He blushed and flashed a big, crooked smile at her.

Libra hustled up the two flights of stairs to the rear entrance of the hotel. Just as she walked out the door, a dark blue Lancer pulled up the driveway, stopping at the door. At first Libra couldn't tell if the driver was a man or a woman. Slender, short body, like a teenager, bright red hair in a butch cut, wearing a beige raincoat. As the driver walked toward Libra, a strong scent of lilacs filled the air.

Libra handed her two rolled-up one-hundred-thousand-lira notes and signed the rental papers. Then she slid behind the wheel of the car and headed back down the winding driveway to Sorrento.

Ten minutes later she arrived at an outdoor pay telephone. She connected to the CIA switchboard and asked for Bannistar.

A sleepy Bannistar answered. "Libra! You okay? Where is Sam?"

"I don't know, Bill. I think they've got him." Libra gave Bannistar a rundown on the day's events.

"Oh, shit. First you, now Sam. You think he might be able to escape?"

"I doubt it. Now that I have gotten away from them, I suspect they may be a little more careful with their prisoners. What did you get on Count Montefusco?"

"The only thing we were able to dig up dates back to World War II. Got it from MI-6—they had to dig through an old warehouse in London to find it. This guy is dangerous. Very dangerous. He and a few of his buddies were the brains and the bucks behind Benito Mussolini. They put Il Duce in power and tried to ride Hitler's coattails in Europe. They thought that if Mussolini could establish an alliance with Hitler, they could take over parts of Europe using the German war machine to do their dirty work. The Count and his organization used Mussolini as a puppet. They were planning to take a piece of southern Europe and northern Africa for themselves, keeping the Third Reich at arm's length."

"Jesus," Libra said in astonishment.

"The whole thing blew up in their faces when Mussolini became enamored with Hitler and tried to emulate him. Up to that time, Mussolini was dedicated to the Count and his deep pockets. But somewhere around 1938, Mussolini jumped in bed with Hitler—lock, stock, and barrel—leaving the Count and his boys out in the cold."

"Is there more?"

"Yeah, but I haven't had a chance to look at the entire file. I just got it, and I've been wrapped up with the President and the Secretary of State on drug shipments from Afghanistan."

"Afghanistan. So they've opened up the drug routes again?"

"Yeah. Somebody assassinated Rham. We don't know who, but whoever it was has turned the drug situation around. They're back in production, and they've reestablished their shipping lanes. We've got a serious problem on our hands over here."

"There may be a connection between the Count and Afghanistan, but I'm still trying to fit the pieces together."

"That's the message I got from Sam, too, yesterday. Look, as soon as you've got something, get back to me. In the meantime, be careful of Montefusco—he's ruthless. This report claims that Montefusco sent thousands of Jews, Gypsies, and other non-Italians to their deaths in Hitler's concentration camps during the war. He also killed a lot of Mussolini's political opponents."

Libra cut in. "Bill, there are a couple more things. First, the British agent that went down with El Al 57. See if he was on Mossad's payroll. He may have had contact with the Israelis as well."

"Why are you asking?" Bannistar's voice showed his surprise.

"It's just a hunch at this point. Trust me on this one."

"Okay. What else?"

"At the American Express office in Paris—the one next to L'Opera—is an envelope that contains the key to a safe-deposit box at Banco Francais Nationale. The bank's address is with the key." Libra gave Bannistar the number. He committed it to memory.

"Who do we talk to at American Express to get the envelope?"

"The manager, Francois Overtran."

"What's in it?"

"There are two sets of Livy scrolls on microfiche—the originals. Have them delivered to your office in Washington, and get Professor Burrall from Hobart to translate them. Under no circumstance is anyone but Burrall to have access to them."

"Why Burrall?"

"Because he's clean. Montefusco and his moles have eliminated him as a possible threat. Plus, I owe him that much. If it hadn't been for him we'd have never broken Montefusco's spies in the Agency."

"Yes, ma'am," Bannistar replied, wondering who was in charge. "I'll have them picked up today. Anything else?"

"Yes. Can you get National Reconnaissance to take some pictures of the Count's villa in Sorrento and his island off Positano?"

"The last time I checked, I was still Director of the Agency, so I sure as hell can get the spy satellites to fly over Italy." Bannistar was a bit agitated by Libra's assuming control.

"One other thing, Bill. Under no circumstances are you to leave messages at Don Portico's apartment." Libra hung up.

Bannistar sat, the telephone still at his ear, trying to figure out what the hell she meant by that.

# # #

As Libra hung up the phone, she smelled lilacs. She turned around. The woman who had rented her the car was standing a few meters away, looking into one of the store windows. Probably going to blow her bribe all at once, Libra thought.

Suddenly the strange woman was standing over her...less than half a meter away. Her hand was raised in the air. A hypodermic needle was poised to strike. Blood trickled from the corner of her mouth. Her eyes were opened wide—lifeless—staring into Libra's. Libra stepped out of her path. The red-haired woman crashed to the sidewalk.

Standing behind her was a man in a chauffeur's uniform holding a small pistol. He looked vaguely familiar. Libra was puzzled. "Thank you, I think," she said.

"Boy, are you lucky I couldn't find the Bristol Hotel, Ms. L. I just happened to be looking for a telephone to get directions, when I saw this bimbo about to do you in."

The man walked up to Libra. "I think we met some years ago, when Mr. B. first took over the Agency. My name is Pug, Pug Williamson."

Chapter 29

Sorrento

"What on earth are you doing in Italy, Pug?" Libra asked as Pug headed the black limousine out of Sorrento down the Amalfi coast to Naples.

"Well, Mr. B. thought you and Sam would need some help. He said he couldn't tell me why he wouldn't send another agent, but I gotta guess he's having problems with moles in the organization. Bottom line is, he just doesn't trust any of the other guys. So he figures, what the heck, he'd send the next best thing…me!"

"Well, I can't fault your timing."

"Where do you think they took Sam?" Pug asked.

"Hard to say. I don't think they'll make the same mistake twice. They tried to keep me prisoner at one of their houses on the Amalfi coast. I got away. So I think they'll be more careful with Sam."

"So what are we gonna do?"

"Not exactly sure yet. For now we play it cool. They'll probably hold Sam for ransom once they learn he doesn't have all the information. He's their key to getting at me. I've got an idea that might force their hand. I'm going to need your help, though, to pull it off."

"I think that's what I'm here for, Ms. L."

"Another question for you, Pug. How well do you speak Italian?"

"Are you kidding? I learned Italian before I learned English."

"How is that?"

"I grew up in northern Italy. My family didn't move to America until I was thirteen. I'll spare you the details, but suffice it to say that my real name isn't Williamson."

"I suppose you're going to tell me that your first name really isn't Pug?"

Pug shot her a look.

"We need to do a little research on this Count Montefusco and his organization," Libra said. "Here's the role I'd like you to play…"

Pug nodded as Libra laid out her plan. He turned the car north on Autostrada A1 to Rome.

Chapter 30

Rome

Sunday

"I need another favor, Don Portico," Libra said respectfully, not sure she was using the right words. "I need to borrow that big man who works for you."

"He's at your disposal. I'll send him right away."

"I also need to know everything you've got on a Count Montefusco. He's got a couple of places. One in Sorrento, a villa. And one in Positano, a very large house on an island. Do you know him?"

The Don paused. "I remember him. It was long ago. During the War. He was seen here and there with Mussolini. He founded Tri-Color Industries. As far as I know, it is strictly legitimate. I will get you the information you want right away." He hung up.

Libra walked down the corridor to check on Mario, Figlio and the professor. She opened the door to the study and was immediately taken aback. The room looked like an operations center in Langley. Computer equipment was everywhere—two twenty-four-inch monitors, a laser printer and a fax machine. Libra couldn't believe her eyes.

Sitting in front of one of the monitors was Phil O'Brien. She recognized him immediately—his tall, lanky features, dirty blond hair, wire-rim glasses, bony face and blue eyes. One of Bannistar's high-priced "chip-heads," the guy could do just about anything with a computer.

Standing behind O'Brien were Mario, Figlio and Maria. The professor had his head stuck in one of the Livy scrolls, and he was writing notes furiously on a legal pad. Mario and Figlio hardly noticed Libra's entrance. They were fascinated by O'Brien's toys.

"You must be Maria?" Libra asked with amusement.

Maria smiled and extended her hand.

"What the hell are you doing here, Phil?" Libra asked.

"Bannistar sent me. Sam told him you needed help translating the Livy books. So we cut a deal with the Don. He lets us use his penthouse—for a fee, of course—and we translate the books. With a special software program I put together, we can translate these things ten times faster, and with better accuracy, than someone using paper and pencil." The professor grunted in the background.

"Yes," O'Brien continued. "You see, we have OCR—Optical Character Recognition—and with the use of a satellite uplink we can have the documents translated almost immediately back in Washington by the Encryption and Forgery experts. With the help of your friend Professor Burrall, of course. You see, all we have to do is place this scanner over the text, and away it goes!" He pointed to what looked like an old Xerox copier.

"Speaking of Sam, where is he? I thought he'd be with you," O'Brien asked suddenly.

"He had to take care of some matters in the south," Libra lied. She turned to the professor. "What have you guys got so far?"

The professor nodded at Mario. Mario took the cue. "We have found that one of Marcellus's great-grandchildren was one of the people trying to sabotage the empire during the reign of Augustus, around the time of Christ. Livy says he was trying to capture the southern port cities of Pompeii and Amalfi. Both of those cities were major trading ports with strong governments. They were wealthy cities, and so they played a significant role in the commerce of the empire."

Libra nodded for him to continue. "So we deduced that this Marcellus financed a private army with the stash his great, great-grandfather plundered at Siracusa in 212 B.C. We know that Marcellus was successful in his attempts to take over the two cities. What we are trying to determine is where he might have been keeping all this great wealth when it was taken by Augustus. Livy, in his epilogue, says the Marcellus family bequeathed the riches to the Caesars. It looks like Marcellus was killed by an army that we can't identify. But the professor and I are at odds here. My translation says Marcellus was killed by a rogue army. The professor says no, that Marcellus killed off the rebels."

Mario looked up again. "If I am right, and Marcellus was killed, then it is likely that Augustus took Marcellus's treasure and moved it from the south to somewhere in the north. If the professor is right, then it is likely that the treasure remains hidden in one of the southern ports, buried under two thousand years of piled-up earth. We think it might be Pompeii or Herculaneum, but we won't know until we get farther along in the translations. We are hoping the computer can settle the dispute between the two of us and come up with the accurate meaning."

O'Brien jumped in. "Yes. Well, we can clear up the discrepancy by having the computer not only translate the transcripts, but it can also tell us which theory is most plausible: the professor's or Mario's. We do this by putting all the Latin verb translations into the computer along with all of Livy's verb translations and then analyzing the probabilities…"

Libra tuned him out. O'Brien had a tendency to ramble on about his expertise in computers. She had more important things to consider. She caught Mario's eye and motioned for him to come into the hallway with her.

"Mario, I need to ask you something."

"What can I do for you, Libra?"

"I want you to take me to the place on the Palatine where you found the scrolls. I do not want you to tell Figlio or the professor or Maria that we are going there. This will be between you and me. Understood?"

Mario nodded.

"Listen very carefully…" Libra gave Mario a list of items she wanted him to bring to the Palatine.

As Mario ambled back to the study, the telephone in the living room rang. Libra walked into the room and picked it up. "Yes," she said curtly.

The Don's gruff voice came through. "I have some information for you regarding this Count Montefusco. I think it's important."

"Let's hear it."

"Montefusco made a fortune after the war. He had contracts from the Italian government, and from the Allies, for rebuilding many of the cities bombed during the invasion." The Don sounded a little envious. "He also has major holdings in a number of other companies in Italy and abroad. Chemicals, distribution, transportation—all service companies. Everything looks legal. But, Libra, I must say to you that there is something that bothers me about this report."

"What is it?"

"It's too clean. No mistakes. No foul-ups. All their annual reports show steady growth with high profit margins. The construction business is not like that. There should be more negative numbers. I am on the board of two construction companies myself. When I see financial statements like these, it tells me they're hiding something."

"Do you have a list of projects that Tri-Color Construction is working on now?"

"Yes."

"Read them to me."

"Rome, Tuscany, Dozza, Inola, Ercolano, Mobery, Florence, Pisa…You want me to continue? There are many more."

Libra didn't hear him. She was running the cities through her mind. Rome, Tuscany, Dozza, Inola, Ercolano. None of them had any relevance. "Where are the cities located?"

"Well, I hope you know where Rome is, Signora," the Don said facetiously. "Tuscany is northeast of Rome. Dozza and Inola are north of Rome. Ercolano is just south of Naples, on the Bay."

"Do the cities have anything in common?"

The Don thought for a few seconds. "Yes. They all have Roman ruins."

"Hold the line for a second, Don." Libra called Mario on the intercom.

"Mario, what were the names of the cities you just told me about. You know, the ones where the Carthaginian gold might be hidden?"

"Pompeii and Herculaneum."

Libra switched back to the Don. "Are they doing anything in Pompeii or Herculaneum?"

"They are digging under the city of Ercolano—that's where Herculaneum is."

"How far is it from Sorrento?"

"About two hours' drive, depending on the traffic on the Amalfi coast road."

"Are his crews digging at any other archaeological sites?"

"Let's see." There was a short pause while the Don flipped through a pile of computer printouts. "No. That is the only place Tri-Color Construction has a permit for working in the ruins."

That's got to be it. "Don Portico, I need Fiore right away."

"He is on his way to you as we speak. He should be at the apartment momentarily."

No sooner had the Don finished speaking than the doorbell rang.

"I think he just arrived," Libra said, walking toward the front door.

"You will know him when you see him."

Libra opened the door. In stepped Fiore.

"Don, can I call you back in five minutes? I have one more important question for you, but first I need to take care of some business."

"No problem, Signora." He hung up.

Fiore walked toward Libra with his hand extended. She was surprised at his pleasant, gentle demeanor, but she shuddered to think what it would be like to be on his bad side.

Libra walked over to Pug, who was sprawled out on the sofa, sleeping off his jet lag. She nudged Pug and he awoke with a start. The first thing that came into Pug's field of vision was Fiore. He jumped to his feet with a yelp.

Libra started to chuckle. "It's okay, Pug. He's on our side." She turned to Fiore. "I have a plan that I need you to carry out immediately." Libra gave the two men instructions, then she pulled Pug aside. "I want you to call Bannistar and give him this message." She scribbled several lines on a pad of paper and handed the note to Pug.

The two men left the building. Libra picked up the phone and dialed the Don.

"Do you have any connections at the Ministry of Building and Construction?" Libra asked.

The Don laughed.

The loud pop of skin hitting skin resounded in Sam's ears. He rolled his head to the right trying to lessen the impact of the blow. A shroud of blinding white popped into his eyes. He felt his jaw unhinge from its socket as the bone shattered. He held his head on his right shoulder, trying to make his face less of a target for the stump of a man who was administering the beating.

A woman grabbed him by the hair and snapped his head upright. Pain shot through his face and neck. The woman looked directly into his eyes. At another time and another place he might have found the woman attractive. Long, silky black hair fell around her shoulders. High cheekbones, crescent eyes, full lips. Good figure; slim, shapely hips.

"You maimed my father," she said, emotionless and matter-of-factly.

Sam braced himself for another blow. The woman dug her fingernails into his cheek and pulled them down along the side of his face. Sam started to scream, but the pain in his jaw prevented him from doing so. He felt the salty taste of his own blood.

"I will ask you only once, Mr. Harrison: What has your associate, Libra, done with the Livy scrolls she stole from the University of Paris?"

Sam tried to remember. Scrolls from the University of Paris? The only thing Libra brought from Paris was microfiche. There weren't any scrolls. What the hell is this woman talking about?

I don't know anything, he signaled with his eyes. An open-hand slap seared across the deep scratch marks.

"I'm sure you don't expect me to believe that, now, do you, Mr. Harrison? The truth…I want the truth," the woman screamed into Sam's right ear, leaving a dull buzzing in his brain.

The woman grabbed him by the hair and snapped his head up again. He thought his head would come clean off his neck. The pain was ghastly. She looked down at him. He could barely see her face. Her nostrils flared, and her eyes narrowed.

"The microfiche that Libra brought to you from Paris is fake. The Livy chronicles are intact. They are in one full scroll." The woman spat the words in his face.

How the hell do you know that? He tried to force the words out, but he couldn't.

"Professor Rinot's notes were very specific and very clear. The spoils from Siracusa were chronicled by Livy in one long document," the woman hissed the words through her clenched teeth. He could feel her hot breath on his swollen face.

Notes from Rinot? What notes? Sam tried desperately to think. To remember. *Remember what? Safe-deposit boxes…Nice…Negresco…. The pieces aren't falling into place.* His thoughts couldn't penetrate the pain.

"The pain…it is awful, yes, *Signore*?" Sam could sense her smile as she ridiculed him.

Sam rolled his head and grunted something inaudible. He was trying to tell her to go to hell, but the words still wouldn't come out of his mouth.

"Well, Signore, we have something for the pain."

She was a blur. His eyes were almost swollen shut. *What the hell is she doing? Shit! Chemicals.*

"In a matter of hours you will be begging to give me the information. The location of the scrolls will be insignificant to you. The only thing that will matter to you is another dose of this wonderful pain reliever." She injected the contents of a needle into Sam's right arm.

Sam felt the sharp pinprick. He watched the blur in front of him slowly back away. Within moments, the pain started to withdraw, gradually at first. Then, suddenly, he felt euphoric. He was ready to tell her anything she wanted to know. But he passed out.

Chapter 31

ROME

The fax machine next to Phil O'Brien rang twice. He looked down to see the machine spewing out a sheet of paper. He reached across and picked up the encoded message. He briefly scanned it, but could not make sense of the garbled words. He picked up the intercom and buzzed Libra.

"Got a fax here for you. Just came in."

"Who's it from?"

"Langley. It's coded."

"I'll be right down."

The fax was three paragraphs long. She broke the simple code in a matter of minutes, writing down the message on the legal pad. She studied it for a few minutes, then whispered, "Perfect." She ripped the page off the tablet and stuck it in her money belt. She folded the fax into quarters, ripped it into pieces, and discarded the pieces in a wastebasket in the kitchen.

#

Sam felt a pinprick on the left side of his face. His head started to clear from the drugs the woman had administered…how long ago? He couldn't remember. Her face was a blur in his mind. What was she saying? Something about the Livy chronicles? They're fake? No. The ones Libra brought were fake. How does she know that? He tried desperately to focus. His eyes fluttered open.

The pinprick in his jaw started to spread, slowly at first, then throughout his entire face. It wasn't a pinprick. It was pain. He remembered a stocky man hitting him. The other side of his face started to smart from the scratch wounds. *Can't talk. Pain spreading through my head. Red hot pain. Water. God, what I wouldn't give for some water. God, just a few drops.* His mouth felt like cotton.

Tears formed in his eyes. What had the woman been saying? Something about Nice. He was in Nice. *The Negresco. Jean Claude Rinot? He didn't have scrolls. He had notes! That was it. He had notes. Notes about what? Livy. Notes about the Livy chronicles. How the hell did she know Libra's were fake?* His head swirled. Pain was taking control of his body and his mind.

Light. Light from where? A door. A door is opening. It looks like slow motion. Two people coming through. Why are they walking so slowly? Shit. Woman and the beater. More punishment. Damn. Hold on. Don't tell them anything. Can make it through one, maybe two more beatings.

"Ah, so you are awake now. Did you have a good rest, Mr. Harrison?"

Give me some water, you bitch. He tried to form the words with his mouth. All it got him was a lightning bolt of pain that shot from his jaw to the top of his head and back down to his toes.

"I have brought you some juice. It will give you energy," the woman said.

The woman poured the juice into Sam's swollen mouth. The cool liquid iced his tongue, but it sent flames shooting through his face.

"Now, Mr. Harrison. Are you ready to tell me where the Livy chronicles are?"

I can't talk, you idiot.

"The pain is returning, yes?"

You know damned well it is.

"Untie his hands, Novo."

Yes, Novo. Untie my hands, so I can break your grubby, thick neck. He felt something rustling at his side. He tried to look down at his hands, but a lightning bolt seared through his brain with even so much as cursory movement. He held his head upright, not daring to look down again.

What are they doing? Massaging my hands. I can feel my hands.

"Now, Mr. Harrison, I know it is difficult for you to look down, so I will help you."

No, please… Ungodly pain shot through his whole body. The woman grabbed him by his hair and jammed his face downward. There was a pad and pencil sitting on the arm of his chair.

"Now we'll give you something for the pain," she turned and snapped her fingers. "In just a moment or two you will feel like your old self again."

It did not take long for the drugs to take effect. The pain withdrew. Despite the fact that his jaw was awkwardly detached from his mouth, he felt euphoric.

"I'm sure your hands will function very nicely. Please write in a word or two, Mr. Harrison, where the Livy chronicles are hidden."

At first he couldn't see the pad and pencil in front of him. Then it started to take form. He could see the pencil in his hand. He scribbled, "Do not have Livy chronicles."

"What do you have, Mr. Harrison?"

Sam moved the pencil to the notepad. "Have two sets of scrolls written by Livy."

Montefusco glanced at what he had written. "What is in the scrolls?"

Sam wrote slowly for the next few minutes, detailing what Mario and the professor had translated.

Montefusco picked up the pad and read what he had written. She grimaced. "Did you discover where the treasure of Marcellus was hidden?"

Sam started writing again. "Somewhere in southern Italy around Pompeii."

"That's all you know?" the woman screamed incredulously.

Sam nodded.

Ramona stood with her arms folded across her chest, a disgusted look on her face. "What did Libra bring from Paris?"

Sam started writing again. "Microfiche."

"What was in the microfiche?"

"Didn't translate it," Sam wrote slowly.

The questioning went on like this for another half-hour. All Montefusco got from Sam was more of the same. Her frustration mounted with every question.

The drugs were wearing off. Suddenly all Sam could see was white-white-hot searing pain blinding his eyes. His mouth filled with his own salty tears. He was on the verge of unconsciousness. He prayed for divine intervention. A miracle. Anything. His thoughts turned to Libra. *Where the hell is she when I really need her?* he said facetiously to himself, trying to numb the hurt.

"I will ask you one last time, Mr. Harrison. Where has Libra hidden the Livy chronicles?"

Sam stared at the pad, afraid to move any part of his body. He slowly lifted his hand. Stumpface had propped the pencil in his hand. Through his tear-filled eyes his hand looked like it was moving in slow motion. The only thing he could think of was a line from an old W.C. Fields movie where Mae West got mad at Fields and said, "I got two words for you, pal, and they ain't 'Let's dance.'" Sam's hand shook violently as he wrote West's two words on the pad, then sank back in his chair.

The woman picked up the pad and read. There was a delayed reaction. Sam suspected she wasn't prepared for profanity, especially from him. Then it hit her—rage that came with understanding. She slammed the clipboard to the floor and screamed in a ghastly voice, "Novo, teach him a lesson he will never forget."

Sam braced himself for the onslaught. He squeezed his eyes shut. He guessed it was a hammer, but he was never really sure. Whatever it was, it hit his right kneecap with a blinding impact. The pain in his jaw suddenly became insignificant. He tried to cry out, but his throat was filled with saliva, and his tongue swollen to incapacity.

He fought the pain with every ounce of energy he had left, but it was not enough. He let the blackness overtake him. It was a pleasant refuge.

Chapter 32

Northern Tuscany
Monday Morning

In the center of the Piazza di Spagna was a fountain with a sunken boat. Students were sitting around it singing. Libra looked over at the Spanish Steps. Rows of flowers lined the first step. At the top of the steps an Egyptian obelisk stood high against the pale-blue sky, offset by two spires from a cathedral in the distance. There were people, mostly tourists and students, sitting on the steps. Some were playing guitars, others just relaxing in the sunshine.

"In my next life I'm going to be a professional tourist," she muttered to herself as she approached the American Express office in the middle of the Piazza di Spagna. She walked in and found the manager's office. She entered without knocking. The manager was seated behind a large Formica desk, smoking a cigarette. He looked up from a magazine when Libra walked in.

"Yes? May I be of service?"

"Yes. My name is Libra. I believe you have a package for me."

"Ah, yes. It came only an hour ago, by special courier." He reached down under his desk and came up with an oversized green courier sack. "I must ask you to sign a receipt for it."

"Very well," Libra said, visually inspecting the large sack. The seal was still intact. She doubted that anyone at American Express would even think of disturbing it. She signed the form.

"I need an office with a telephone."

"Of course, *Signora*. You may use the Counsel Club. There are several private offices with telephones, fax machines, copy machines…I will walk you over. It is in the next building."

He escorted Libra out into another building and up the elevator to the top floor. Libra looked around a large, open room filled with leather sofas, chairs, and a number of circular tables, along with fax machines, copiers and an array of other communication devices. Libra signed the guest register, gave the receptionist her card number, then followed her to a private office. Libra opened the door to the office to find a desk, complete with a telephone, a fax machine and a copy machine.

Libra broke open the seal on the courier's bag. Inside were the file on Count Montefusco, several updates since she had talked to Bannistar, and an overview of the Italian Fascist Party since 1930. The file was classified under the British Secret Intelligence Service, the precursor to MI-6.

Libra opened the folder and started poring through page after page of old documents. Several of the pages were handwritten, with the date and location marked at the top of the page. For the next several hours she was transfixed by one of the most fascinating spy stories she had ever read.

Bernardo Feticcini walked out of the tunnel in wonder. Only hours ago, his crew had unearthed the lost Temple of Isis. The blast from Vesuvius and the ensuing mudslide had left the temple totally intact. The perfectly sculptured marble building was today as it was over two thousand years ago. His crew had even found the bones of what must have been the high priestess, lying at the foot of the altar.

Feticcini walked up the wooden-plank footbridge and turned to the parking lot. He fumbled in his pocket for his car keys. Reflected in the car window, he saw an enormous figure walking up behind him. Before he could turn around, the figure raised a fist in the air and brought it down onto the top of his head.

"*Prego*," Libra responded to a knock on the door.

The toothy woman from the reception desk entered. "Would you care for something to drink now, Signora?"

"Yes. Some water, please."

The dossier on Montefusco read like a spy novel. He managed to penetrate the highest levels of governments, one way or another, in Italy, Germany, England and Russia. Bannistar had been right: From the report, Montefusco had been the brains behind Mussolini's success, but even more significant, he had been the impetus behind Mussolini's disgrace and fall from power.

Libra began reading her notes:

"Country of origin: unknown, presumed to be Italy. Family of origin: unknown, the title of Count, believed to be self-imposed. Self-made millionaire before age twenty. Made fortune in cocaine and heroin. Smuggled drugs into western Europe and U.S.A. from East. Added to his fortune by smuggling alcohol into U.S. during the later prohibition years. Operated from Palermo, branched out to Naples, then Marseilles. Net worth, at time, estimated: excess/ten billion dollars..."

She was interrupted by a knock on the door. The receptionist walked in with a bottle of San Pellegrino and a glass filled with ice cubes. Libra thanked her and returned to her reading.

"Montefusco used his wealth and influence to grapple his way to the top of the Italian political structure, which, at the time, was racked by corruption. Cold and ruthless, he conned his way into Mussolini's inner circle. Those politicians he couldn't buy, he intimidated and manipulated with threats and 'late night visits' from his gallery of rogues and killers. Always twice-removed from the hardball tactics, he gained a reputation in Italian political circles as a man not to be crossed.

"Ties with Mussolini enabled him to expand his drug operations without the interference from the *carabinieri*—they turned a blind eye to his expanding drug businesses. Started Tri-Color Construction, won most of the major construction projects in Italy. His bids were rigged. Also, skimmed millions more from phony contracts and cost overruns.

"1938 Mussolini seduced by Hitler, Nazis…Montefusco out. Montefusco warned Mussolini about getting too close to Hitler. At first, Mussolini took the Count's advice and kept Hitler at arm's length. He refused to support Hitler's first attack on Austria, in 1936. In the second attack on Austria, in 1938, Mussolini backed Hitler, this time with armed forces. They forged an alliance, and Germany and Italy jointly attacked Austria.

"Montefusco fell out of Mussolini's inner circle, blamed Hitler. The Count faced the loss of construction contracts, and his drug business was in jeopardy.

"The demise of Hitler wrought the fall of Mussolini. Two days before Hitler shot himself in the head, Il Duce was shot in northern Italy with his mistress while trying to escape to Germany. The partisan ringleaders who assassinated Mussolini and dragged him to Milan were believed to be the Count's own handpicked men."

Libra paused and started to consider the cunning and baffling achievements of Count Montefusco, if indeed that was his real name. She remembered something from spy school: *Never underestimate the enemy. Let them underestimate you. It will give you a significant advantage.* She cursed herself for having done just that, underestimating the Count and his nefarious organization. The Count had wanted her to believe that they were not competent. Now they had Sam, and the advantage.

Chapter 33

Monday Afternoon

Libra walked into the apartment to find a long-faced Mario walking around the living room, hands in pocket and eyes watery.

"Why the glum face, Mario?"

Mario took a deep breath. "Signore O'Brien just finished running the Livy translations to find that the professor's theory has more probability than mine."

Libra wasn't sure if Mario was chagrined because of the mistranslation or because of losing the bet to the professor. But a little wounded pride would not hurt him for long.

"Have you heard from Sam?" Mario changed the subject eagerly.

"He's fine. Just taking care of a few loose details. He'll be back shortly," she fibbed. "Mario, I need you to do something for me. Run down to the corner and pick up the evening edition of the Rome paper. Be sure to get the late edition with the Borsa Valori di Milano trades."

Libra headed down the hallway to the study. Figlio and the professor were looking over O'Brien's shoulder at one of the computer monitors. They looked up at her as she walked in.

"Good news, Libra. I think we've cracked the dispute between the professor and Mario," O'Brien said.

"Yeah. I got the news in the living room. What does it mean, Professor?"

The professor took his eyes off the computer screen. "It means that somewhere between Pompeii and Amalfi there should be a vault containing the spoils of Siracusa. It should be filled with the Carthaginian Cresas. We are trying to determine right now where Marcellus the Younger lived during that time period."

She heard the apartment door opening in the other room. She excused herself and walked down the hall to find Mario just coming in with the newspaper.

"Did you get the equipment I asked you to get for going into the Forum tonight?"

Mario nodded again, puzzled. "Why do you want to go to the Palatine tonight?"

"I have a hunch that we may find something very interesting, but I can't tell you what it is, because I'm not sure myself. Trust me, okay?" she said with a wink. Mario's eyes lit up.

"I always trust you. What time do we go?"

"At three o'clock. Be ready. I will meet you at the elevator."

"Yes, Libra, three o'clock. I will be ready." He headed back to the study.

Opening the paper to the financial section, Libra looked up the closing prices for the day on the Borsa Valori di Milano stock market. She sat down on the sofa, scanning the listings.

"TCI, closing price $10, up three-quarters for the day." She frowned. She closed the paper and laid it by her side. She picked up the telephone and dialed the international operator. Libra gave the operator a number. Less than a minute later, the telephone rang in New York City.

"This is Kent," a friendly voice said.

"Becky here. I need some help."

"Becky! Nice to hear your voice again," came the warm reply. "God, I haven't talked to you in years. You going to the reunion?"

"Kent," she said very softly into the phone, looking over her shoulder toward the hallway, "I'm in Rome. I don't have time to talk right now. I need all the information you can dig up in a big hurry on a Tri-Color Industries, based in Rome, Italy. The symbol on the Milan market is TCI. Call me tomorrow at this number." She gave him the number of the American Express office and hung up.

She picked up the telephone and dialed the Don's private line.

#

Tuesday, Before Dawn

No sooner had the big grandfather clock in the living room chimed three o'clock than Mario stepped from his bedroom, holding a pair of running shoes in his right hand. He quietly pulled the door closed and tiptoed down the hall and out the apartment door to find Libra waiting at the elevator. She was dressed in black clothes, black running shoes and a black knit cap, with her hair pushed up under the cap. They stepped onto the elevator and Libra pushed the Lobby button.

"Do you have everything we need?" Libra asked.

"Yes. Everything you asked me to get is in a box at the entrance. The security man is holding it for me."

They walked out of the elevator into the lobby, retrieved the box, and stepped outside. The night sky was filled with stars. As they walked to the curb, a car flashed its lights on and off. They walked to the car and climbed in the back seat.

"*Buonasera*," the Don's driver said to Libra as she settled into the comfortable leather. "You are going to the Palatine? It is a nice night to see ancient Rome."

Mario gave the driver instructions. "On the east side of the Palatine, there is a hole in the fence. We can scale the hill to the top. It is an easy climb. We will not need the rope until we reach the hippodrome," he assured Libra.

"What about night security lights, Mario?" Libra asked. They would be exposed for several minutes while they walked to the gladiator's portico.

"It is not a problem. There are no lights, and the night security guards usually sleep through their watches. They work during the day, then come here to sleep."

"Mario, I have a question for you. Remember the afternoon when we escaped across the roofs of the ghetto, and you told me about your patron saint, Saint Anthony?"

"Yes. How could I forget? It was quite an afternoon!"

"How is it that your patron saint is Saint Anthony, when your name is Mario? I thought you had to be named after your patron saint."

"Ah. That is a very good question. You see, my first name is Anthony. It was also my father's name. There was so much confusion around our house that my mother decided to call me by my middle name, which is Mario. After my parents were killed, I never thought to change my name back to Anthony because everybody knew me as Mario. So you see, I was named after Saint Anthony."

"And you believe that Saint Anthony is the one watching over you and protecting you?"

"Yes."

"How can you be so sure?"

"I don't know. I just know he does. How come you are asking me these questions?"

"I'm not sure," Libra responded. "It's just that I've been experiencing some very unusual coincidences lately."

"What do you mean, coincidences?"

Libra thought for a moment. "Well, it's like this, Mario. It seems that just when I'm about to get into some kind of trouble, something comes along at just the right moment, and gets me out of it. I really can't explain it better than that."

"Ah," Mario said as his eyes lit up. "That is not coincidence. It is what the priest called 'the long arm of the Lord.' It is what I was telling you about…about Saint Anthony watching over me. He sent you to protect me and my brother. And if you are here to protect me, he must be protecting you, too."

Libra inhaled deeply. She shivered at the thought of a "higher power" intervening in her life. It was a concept she was never taught, let alone believed. She was about to bring up Castor and Pollux when the driver interrupted her thoughts.

"We are almost there," he said as he slowed the car. They approached the east gate of the ancient Palatine Hill. The streets were empty.

Libra and Mario snuck from the back of the car, crept across a sidewalk, and crawled through the fence. Mario had loosened one of the iron bars months before to facilitate his nocturnal visits. He pushed it aside, and Libra stepped through. He followed and carefully replaced the bar. The car slowly moved away.

Mario led Libra up a winding path. It was too easy to see in the moonlight, Libra worried. They'd be visible to anyone else who happened to be on the Palatine. They walked briskly through a patch of shrubbery to the top of the hill.

Mario turned to Libra. "Get down," he whispered. "I see a flashlight."

Libra hit the ground. The smell of fresh pine filled her nostrils.

"Hey, I thought you said these guys sleep all night…"

"They do. I know that one. He's only going to the lavatory. Quickly, before he comes out."

They ran into the Farnese Garden. "This is where Rome was founded, according to legend. It is also where all the Roman emperors lived. Back there," he pointed to a massive structure, "is Augustus's palace."

"Skip the history lesson, Mario. Let's get under cover before we get spotted by one of those guards. You can give me a full tour some other time."

Mario shrugged and beckoned for her to follow. "We will go in through the hippodrome, but there is another way out if we get into trouble. The well at the bottom of the hill connects with the catacombs, which connect with a tunnel that leads to the chambers of Augustus."

They walked past the Temple of Cybele and up a flight of ancient stone steps that brought them to the rim of a racetrack about twenty feet below. Mario secured one end of the rope to the guardrail and tossed the other end to the track below. He climbed over the railing and shimmied down to the ground. Libra was right behind him. He pulled the rope loose, coiled it, and hid it under a marble column resting on the infield. They sprinted toward the portico.

When they reached the wall, Mario started pulling the rocks away from the crawlspace. Soon they were standing in the room where Mario first discovered the scrolls.

"Jesus. This is one eerie place," Libra whispered.

"Not once you get used to it," Mario said smugly.

"Okay, show me where you found the scrolls and the coins."

Mario walked over to another pile of rocks. "The hole is behind these rocks." He started pulling the rocks away from the wall. Soon Libra could see a small hole, no bigger than a basketball hoop, just above ground level.

"Get me the hammer and the chisel," Libra said. He reached in his knapsack and handed them to her.

Libra widened the hole to the size of a manhole cover.

"What are you looking for?"

"In a few minutes, you will see…or, maybe, there will be nothing, and we will have wasted our time. But if my guess is right…"

Mario watched as half of her body disappeared through the hole in the wall. She was bent over on her knees, with her head and shoulders and most of her upper body inside. He then heard the sound of a hammer hitting a chisel. Libra was cutting through the next wall!

Mario waited for half an hour. Finally, Libra pulled back through the hole. Her face was covered with dirt and dust. "Okay, kiddo. It's your turn. You can see where I've been chipping at the inner wall. Damned Romans built things to last. I don't know how thick the wall is, but I guess it's going to take a while to break through it."

Mario bent his lanky body into the hole and started hammering. He wondered what Libra was up to.

They chipped away for over an hour. Libra looked at her watch. It was almost five o'clock. It would be daylight in another hour. As she took a drink from a plastic flask, Mario let out a yelp. He pulled back into the room. "I have broken through the wall. But something is not right. I should see daylight, or, rather, moonlight. But there is nothing—it is pitch black on the other side."

"Good," Libra said, letting out a sigh. "Let me take a look."

Mario pulled himself back into the room, and Libra took his place. She shined her flashlight through the small opening. She smiled and turned back to Mario.

"Okay. You look. Use the flashlight to see into the hole this time. But make it fast. We've got to get out of here before daylight."

Mario set his head inside and peeked through the hole. He let out a bloodcurdling yell.

Chapter 34

Rome
Tuesday Morning

Libra arrived at the American Express Counsel Club at precisely 9 A.M., opening time. She walked up to the toothy receptionist. "Excuse me, but can you recommend the name of a good stockbroker in Rome?"

"Certainly, Signora. We have two very good stockbrokers who are members of our club. I will give you their names and telephone numbers."

Libra thanked the woman and headed toward the office she had used the day before. No sooner had she settled in when the receptionist knocked on the door and handed Libra a slip of paper with the names of two brokers. One of them was within walking distance.

The shrill ring of the telephone startled Libra. She picked up the receiver; it was the receptionist announcing that she had a call. She pushed the button and heard a friendly voice. "Yeah, Becky. Kent. I've got some information on Tri-Color Industries. You got a fax machine?"

Libra gave him her fax number. "What's your assessment of the company?"

"Looks pretty solid on the surface. However, there's something funny about their businesses. They're into just about everything under the sun. Manufacturing, chemicals, transportation, construction, and some service businesses scattered throughout Europe. Annual revenue was a couple billion last year."

"So what's so unusual?"

"They should be producing a lot more revenue than they are. For example, the tonnage they're reporting from their shipping business doesn't add up; that is, unless they're skimming the revenues somehow. Like a shell corporation would do."

"Have you got a list of the officers and members of the board?"

"Hold on, let me look." Libra could hear him shuffling through some papers. "Yeah. They're in last year's annual report. Second page. The president's name is Ramona Montefusco. From the picture I'd guess she's about forty, forty-five. Directors come from a number of companies around Italy. Stock range for the last year was a high of twelve to a low of seven and a half. That's in dollars. You'd have to make the conversion to lira over there."

"What's the name of the accounting firm that audited the books?"

She wrote down the name of an accounting firm in Rome. "Thanks, Kent. I owe you one." She replaced the receiver. Moments later, the fax machine started spewing out page after page of information on Tri-Color Industries.

Libra placed a call to the first brokerage firm the receptionist had given her. The phone was answered by a secretary. "Signore Giuseppe Ronternaro, please."

"*Si*. May I tell Signore Ronternaro who is calling, please?"

"My name is Rebecca Arnason. I am interested in making a sizable investment."

The call was transferred. "*Prego*," a deep, scratchy voice answered.

"Signore Ronternaro. My name is Rebecca Arnason and I am interested in opening an account at your firm. Would it be possible for you to join me for a cup of espresso this morning? I am at the American Express Counsel Club. I believe you are a member?"

"Of course, Signora. In about one hour. Would that be satisfactory to you?"

"Yes. That will be fine. One other thing. I am considering a large transaction of Tri-Color Industries stock. I would be grateful if you would bring all the information you have on that company with you."

"I will do so. In an hour, then." He hung up.

Libra collected the sheets from the fax machine and started poring through the information. After half an hour, she picked up the telephone and called Don Portico's private line.

"Don, one more favor," Libra blurted.

"Certainly, my Libra. But you'd better be careful. You are going to owe me a lot of favors by the time we are through with this, how do you say, *caperi*?" the Don said, laughing.

"That's 'caper,' don, and thank you. I'm going to need the use of many of your men."

"They are yours. What is it you want me to do with my men?"

It took Libra more than half an hour to give the Don her instructions. As soon as she had finished, the receptionist knocked on the door and announced that Giuseppe Ronternaro was waiting in the main reception area. Libra saw a man in his mid-fifties sitting at the table smoking a cigarette and reading his notes. "Tell him I will be with him in a moment," Libra replied.

She picked up the phone and dialed the international operator and gave the number for CIA headquarters in Langley, Virginia. Bannistar was on the line in seconds.

"I've got some information for you…" were Bannistar's first words.

"I don't have time. I'll have to call you back. I need twenty million dollars deposited in the American Express Bank in Rome by tomorrow morning. Trust me on this, Bill. If I can pull this off, you'll have the money back with interest within forty-eight hours." She hung up before Bannistar could say anything.

"Twenty million dollars! Jesus, I've got Congress all over my case for spending as it is." Bannistar slammed down the phone and punched the intercom button.

Libra walked out to meet the stockbroker. Giuseppe Ronternaro put out his cigarette and rose slowly, a smile on his tan, leathery face. He extended his hand.

"I have brought you the information you requested on Tri-Color Industries. As a matter of fact, my firm does a lot of trading for Tri-Color. The president of my company is a financial advisor to the Chairwoman, Ramona Montefusco."

"And what is the name of your president?" Libra asked, pretending not to be too interested. Once again, she could not believe her good fortune. Was Saint Anthony watching from above?

"Thomoso Calamenti. You are interested in opening an account in my firm?"

"Yes. Actually, I am thinking of opening a trust account for my two nephews. I will, of course, manage the account until they are of age."

"I hope I'm not being too forward, Signora, but may I ask how much you are thinking of depositing?" he asked politely.

"Twenty million American dollars. Ten million per account."

Giuseppe choked on his cigarette smoke.

"Now, if you will excuse me, Signore, I have business to attend to." Libra rose from the chair and extended her hand to the speechless broker.

Libra walked back into the office and punched the numbers of the Don's private line into the telephone. "Don, please get me all the information you can on Thomoso Calamenti. He is the president of Dementia and Calamenti."

# # #

Bernardo Feticcini sat on the end of the bed in a third-floor room in the Hotel Excelsior in Naples, naked except for a bandanna stuck in his mouth. Fiore stood in front of the door, slapping an ax handle into the palm of his gigantic hand.

"I will ask you one more time, *Signore*. After that, I'm afraid I will have to let my partner ask the questions," Pug said as he pulled the bandanna from Bernardo's mouth.

"But I told you already. They do not tell me those kinds of things. I am but a construction superintendent. So I do not know what you ask," Bernardo said, trembling.

"Okay, okay," Pug said, holding the palms of his hands in the air. "Fiore, start with the kneecaps, and then remove his testicles."

Fiore's face brightened as he walked to the man on the bed. He raised the ax handle over his head, aiming for Bernardo's knees.

"No, no, please. I remember now," Bernardo cried out with a heart-rending scream. "I will tell you everything."

Pug sighed in relief.

# # #

Washington

You mean you don't have an inkling where the drugs are coming in?" Van Clevenson roared at Bannistar, who sat meekly in his chair and cast a glance at the President, hoping he would bail him out of this embarrassing situation. The President watched with fascination.

Van Clevenson was fifty-five years old, with a full head of blond hair and a body built like a spring. His face was red and twisted with rage as he attacked the Director's lack of results in rounding up the Afghanistan drug lords.

"That's right," Bannistar replied with a gulp. "We don't have the foggiest idea what ports the drugs will enter." Normally, Bannistar could handle Van Clevenson's bullying tactics, but he didn't feel like he was negotiating with a lot of leverage at the moment, especially since he was about to request a twenty-million-dollar advance from the President.

The Secretary of State shook his head in disgust. "You mean to tell me you've had your two best agents in Europe the past several days on a wild-goose hunt, when these rogues from Afghanistan are about to dump millions of dollars of heroin on the streets? And we don't even have a clue where or when the drugs are coming in?"

Bannistar took the heat and sighed in resignation. Van Clevenson walked around the table looking at the ceiling in disgust. "Jesus...Jesus...Jesus," he muttered, making Bannistar think of a bizarre revival meeting.

Nobody dared to speak for several moments. Finally, Bannistar turned to the President. "I have one more request. It's an unusual one, so I'd suggest you brace yourself."

The President looked at Bannistar with a raised brow.

"I need twenty million dollars wired to Libra at American Express in Rome within the hour."

"*What?*" roared Van Clevenson from across the room. "You want what? Did I hear you say twenty million dollars? Now I know you're out of your mind."

"Calm down, Warner," the President said. He shot a stern look at the Secretary.

"What's it for, Bill?" the President asked.

"I don't know," Bannistar replied, keeping his voice as low as possible.

"You don't know? *You don't know?*" Van Clevenson had both palms on the table.

"I told you to calm down, Warner," the President said.

Van Clevenson sat back down, crossed his arms and fumed.

"Jeff, Libra is on to something. I don't know what. But I'm afraid if we don't get the money to her, the whole thing is going to fall apart. I mean, look…she's been right about everything so far. She tipped us off about the fact that the MI-6 agent on the El Al flight was a double agent for Mossad. Libra has demonstrated impeccable judgment and incredible street smarts during this whole mess. I think if we don't send her the money, we'll all be sorry."

The President listened carefully to Bannistar's argument. He leaned back in his chair. "When those drugs hit the country, there'll be chaos in the streets. Crime will take off like a rocket. I'm already starting to hit rocky patches with the electorate. I can imagine the editorials in *The Washington Post* and *The New York Times* after the drugs have been on the street for a while. And *The Wall Street Journal*…God, there'll be no mercy from those bastards."

The President leaned forward. "Okay, Bill. I'll go along with it, but only because Libra has been right on everything up to this point."

The Secretary of State came roaring out of his chair.

Chapter 35

Pompeii, Italy
Wednesday

At 5:30 A.M. three flatbed trucks pulled out of the Tri-Color Construction yard in Naples, Italy. One truck carried a large crane, another a hydraulic cherry picker. The third truck was empty. They formed a convoy and headed south on the Autostrada A3 toward Pompeii.

An hour later the trucks rumbled down the ancient stone street of Via le di Villa dei Misteri, outside the towering walls protecting the ruins of Pompeii. They turned onto Via de Sepolcri and came to a stop at the guard station adjacent to the entrance of the city. The guard, an elderly man, checked his manifests for the day as he observed the big construction vehicles outside his window. There was nothing on the day's entry about construction activity. He walked out of the guardhouse and held his hand in the air, motioning for the trucks to stop.

The driver of the first truck climbed down from the cab. Dressed in khaki work clothes, a hard hat on his head and a clipboard under his right arm, he waved back to the old man. "*Buongiorno, Signore.* We have work orders for the House of the Faun this morning," he said, as he handed over the official work papers signed by the Minister of Building and Construction in Naples.

The guard took the clipboard and looked carefully at the order. It looked official enough. He nodded to the driver and waved him on through the chainlink gates. He gave a curt salute to each of the trucks as they rumbled on past him.

The trucks bounced down the narrow stone street and turned left onto Via della Fortuna Augusta. They drove another ten meters to the House of the Faun. The air brakes let out loud hisses and screeches as the trucks came to a stop in front of the concrete archway leading to the two-thousand-year-old residence of Publius Sulla, who was charged by Augustus Caesar to organize and reconcile the old and new interests of the Roman Republic at Pompeii.

The workers quickly cordoned off the house and began off-loading the heavy earthmoving equipment. The sun was rising over the mountains, lighting up what once was an enormous open-air villa. The remains of Corinthian columns bordered a lush garden, with palm trees shading the remains of a large, private bathhouse. Just beyond the entrance was a sunken pool the ancients used to collect drinking water. A bronze statue of a faun playing his lute stood in the middle. The crew quickly removed the faun and the top of the arch, a replica made of wooden beams. They moved the large crane through the garden, past the decaying columns to the rear garden and pool.

The crane operator cranked up the powerful diesel engine and swung the jaws of the shovel into the reflecting pool. It took him less than half an hour to dig up the old concrete and mortar, and the shovel began to chew into the dirt below. An hour later, when he had dug a hole ten feet deep, he heard the large shovel hit something that reverberated through the controls as though it were solid rock. He stopped the crane and jumped down from the cab to look. His eyes widened. He waved for the cherry picker.

An hour later, a large stone vault sat on the back of the empty flatbed truck. The workers quickly backfilled the hole. In another hour, a follow-up crew would rebuild the ancient pool. With the proper coloring and weathering, no one would know it was freshly built.

# # #

Rome

Libra willed herself to stay awake. How long had it been? She tried to remember the last time she slept. Her eyes swept around the large conference room. A dozen accountants were poring through piles of documents and spreadsheets laid out on a large mahogany table. They were in the cellar of the Don's modest house on the outskirts of Rome. The Don was snoring loudly in a corner. His head was resting against the back of a stuffed blue chair, his feet propped up on a matching blue footrest. His arms were sprawled out on the arms of the chair, and his mouth was open wide.

Two of the Don's top consiglieri pored through stacks of legal documents. Everyone in the room looked exhausted. They had worked all night. The Don's men had broken into the accounting firm of Besiglari and Besiglari and trucked out boxes and boxes of documents on Tri-Color Industries.

Libra looked at her watch. It was 6:00 A.M. and so far they had found nothing.

Suddenly, one of the accountants let out a yelp. He stood up with a big grin and snapped the suspenders holding up his baggy pants. "I have found it. Very clever. Very clever," he exclaimed.

"Found what?" Libra asked, her fatigue replaced by a surge of energy.

"It is very complicated and hard to explain. But they did a masterful job at hiding their real businesses. They made one small error, however. An error so tiny, in fact, that if we were not looking for something out of the ordinary, it never would have been noticed," the man said as he opened a long spreadsheet in front of Libra. The other accountants and the consiglieri rose and walked over, craning their necks to see what their associate had discovered.

The Don awoke with a start. He rubbed his face with the palm of his hand and blinked the sleep from his tired eyes, then walked over to the table to see what his man had found.

"This is something we should consider for our own businesses," the man said with a smile as he glanced across the table at the Don.

The man started a detailed explanation of how Tri-Color Industries had hidden the major portion of their profits that were derived from illegal businesses.

"Excellent…excellent," Libra said, softly, as the man walked her through the accounting procedures. She looked up at the Don. "And what have you learned about Thomoso Calamenti?"

The Don smiled. He handed Libra a brown folder. "This should give you the leverage you need."

At 8:30 A.M. Libra walked out of her room in the Don's apartment, dressed in a tailored navy blue business suit, a white silk scarf and navy high-heeled shoes. Mario's eyes lit up as he observed Libra walking down the corridor. "*Giorno, Signora.*" He had never seen Libra look so beautiful.

"*Buongiorno*, Mario. *Buongiorno*, Figlio. *Buongiorno*, Professor," Libra smiled at the three of them as they wolfed down breakfast.

"*Mama mia,*" Figlio whispered in awe as he saw Libra standing behind his brother. "You are magnificent."

Libra looked at her watch. "I must hurry. I have an appointment in twenty minutes." She gave Mario and Figlio a hug and a kiss on the cheek.

"I have this strange feeling that we're not going to see Libra for a while," Mario said glumly.

"Why do you say that?" Figlio asked.

"I don't know. Just a hunch. But, don't worry, Figlio. We will see Libra and Sam again."

Libra walked into the waiting limousine. The driver turned to Libra. "I have the briefcase with the documents you requested."

"The Don has begun his part of the plan?" Libra asked the driver as they headed toward the financial district in the center of Rome.

"Everything has started, Signora. It is a most ingenious plan. I have not seen the Don have so much fun in many years."

Ten minutes later the driver stopped the car at the entrance to Dementia and Calamenti, one of the most prestigious brokerage houses in Rome. The driver ran around the car and opened the door. Libra stepped out and walked into a lavish reception area. She was greeted by Giuseppe Ronternaro and Thomoso Calamenti.

"*Buongiorno*, Signora Arnason," the president of the firm said with a wide smile. "I am honored that you would consider our firm for your investments. If you would be so kind to follow me to my office. It is on the top floor."

Libra exchanged pleasantries with the men as they took the elevator to the top floor, and then walked down a lush hallway adorned with marble statues of ancient Romans. They entered Calamenti's office, which was furnished with fine oak and leather furniture.

A waiter greeted them as they walked in. "May I interest you in some coffee or some breakfast, Signora?" Calamenti asked.

"A glass of San Pellegrino will be fine." She turned to Giuseppe. "I would like to transact my business right away. I am pressed for time, and I would like to conclude this matter as soon as possible."

Giuseppe clicked his heels and gave a slight bow. They sat down at a small conference table. Libra opened her briefcase.

"I wish to make a transaction involving two million shares of Tri-Color Industries."

"We will be most happy to accommodate you," Calamenti replied.

"There are three conditions on which I will do business with your firm."

The men held their breath in anticipation.

"First, your fee: I will pay you six cents per share for the transaction."

The two men huddled on the opposite side of the table. Libra could hear their whispers as they dickered between themselves.

"We will take the trade at nine cents per share, Signora," the president offered.

"Seven cents. If that is not acceptable, then I will take the account to another firm."

Calamenti hesitated. "Agreed. Seven cents per share," he said, slapping the table with the palm of his hand. "And your second condition?"

Libra looked at Giuseppe and dismissed him with her eyes. She turned to Calamenti. "This will be between you and me only."

The president nodded at Giuseppe, who was already rising to leave.

"I am informed that you are not only a personal friend of Signora Ramona Montefusco, but that you manage her portfolio as well. You are to set up a meeting for me this afternoon at precisely two o'clock, with her, in her office."

Calamenti looked at Libra and said, "Under the circumstances, I hardly…"

The man stopped in midsentence as Libra placed a brown folder on the table.

"I am further informed that you have misappropriated over a million dollars of United States Treasury bills that you and your firm purchased at auction last week…"

"How dare you imply…" the man's eyes flashed in anger.

"…which you used to cover gambling debts…"

Perspiration broke out on Calamenti's forehead. He took a handkerchief and wiped his brow and his upper lip.

"…which amount to a million American…"

"Please, that is enough…"

Libra's eyes did not leave the man for a second. She opened the folder in front of her. Three Polaroid snapshots, facing Calamenti, were in the folder.

"And there is the matter of…"

"Stop. Okay, okay. What is it that you want me to do?" His face was gray with guilt and shame.

"Here are the exact words you are to use in setting up the meeting with Ramona Montefusco…"

The man's head nodded as Libra explained what he was to do.

"At precisely three o'clock this afternoon, you will receive, by courier, the photographs, provided, of course, that you do as instructed. Concerning your debts, I am afraid you will have to work out terms with Don Portico."

Libra stood and walked out of the office.

#

Libra walked into the Counsel Club and addressed the receptionist. "Get me the Maritime Commission in London, please."

She walked toward the office she had been using. The receptionist followed her down the hall and handed her a small green sack and a pink message slip. "This came for you early this morning by courier," she said, "and there was a call for you from a man named Pug."

Libra punched in the number. "How did it go?"

"All taken care of. We have everything you wanted. Our little bird sang like a canary."

"I need you and Fiore to take care of one more detail." Libra opened the courier's sack and pulled out aerial photographs of the Count's villa and his island home.

#

SORRENTO

At quarter to two that afternoon, the familiar brown UPS truck pulled up to the tall iron gates protecting Count Montefusco's villa. The driver pushed the intercom buzzer hidden under the ivy that covered the brick archway. Inside the house, a security camera monitor showed the new driver standing at the gate, backing away from the three Doberman pinschers racing down the driveway.

"Where is Fabio?" a deep voice came from the speaker under the ivy.

"He is on holiday this week and next. The Dobermans reached the gates. "I am the temporary driver," Pug Williamson said into the speaker. "I have a very heavy package for Count Montefusco. I will need help carrying it into the house."

The dogs stopped barking and retreated back to the house. A buzzer sounded and the gates started to open. Pug jumped back into the truck and drove it to a delivery entrance at the rear of the villa. He turned to Fiore in the back of the truck. "Okay, we are at the delivery area."

Fiore checked the tape wrapped around Bernardo Feticcini's head and mouth. He tightened the rope binding the man's hands and legs. The truck came to a stop and the rear doors opened. Pug stood at the back of the truck. Fiore picked up a long flat box. He extended the end out to Pug. Pug almost fell to the ground under its weight.

Fiore stepped out of the van. His UPS uniform was about three sizes too small. What the heck, Pug thought, it was the best we could do under the circumstances. UPS probably won't even know their truck and drivers are missing until they are due to return from their runs.

Fiore carried his end of the box as if it were a feather. "Hey, Fiore. Slow down, will you? If I go any faster, I'm going to have a hernia," Pug said, his face a bright red from the strain. They walked up to the door. It was opened by a man dressed in a suit.

"Hey, buddy, we're going to need some help getting this thing into the house. We can barely lift it as it is. Had to use a forklift back at the shop to get it on the truck."

The man nodded, then disappeared into the house. Pug counted to five very slowly, then took off after the man. He pulled out his service revolver.

The man walked through a gigantic kitchen, a lavish dining room and out a set of patio doors that led to a large verandah. He put two fingers in his mouth and whistled to the eight men working in the orchard. He held up four fingers. The men looked at each other, deciding who would go; four dropped their rakes and jogged toward the house.

The man in the suit turned back to the kitchen. He stopped, his eyes open wide. He reached inside his coat pocket for his gun. Before he could get his hand to the holster under his left arm, a bullet penetrated his chest, passed through his aorta and came out his back. He was dead before he hit the ground.

Pug jumped up from his firing position with Fiore right behind him. Pug ran to the patio doors. Fiore dragged the dead man into the kitchen. Pug positioned himself in a corner of the patio, his back against the wall. Fiore stood to the side of the kitchen door.

Four men dressed in gray work uniforms walked through the dining room into the kitchen. The first two men were knocked unconscious with one swift blow from Fiore's right hand. The other two turned to get out of the kitchen, only to run into Pug, who slowed them long enough for Fiore to put them both out of commission.

Pug turned back to the patio, revolver in hand. He slid open the screen door, crouched on his knees, extended his arms and let go four rounds. The four men in the orchard fell to the ground. Pug turned back to Fiore. "Okay, he's got to be upstairs."

They sprinted up a long circular staircase two steps at a time. Pug turned toward an open door on the right of the landing. He held the pistol to his chest, took a deep breath, stopped outside the door, and turned ninety degrees into the room. A large man with slicked-back hair spotted Pug and reached for his gun. He didn't stand a chance. The bullet from Pug's gun smashed into the man's face and out the back of his skull, leaving a splash of blood on the neatly patterned wallpaper.

Pug looked to his right. The Count was lying in bed. Bandages covered his nose, and a tube ran from his left ear. His face was puffy, with large black and blue marks under his eyes. A man in a white lab coat stood at the side of the bed, his hands extended in the air.

"I am a doctor. Please do not shoot," he cried, with a terrified look on his face.

Pug slipped his gun back into his jacket. He walked to the Count's side. The Count's eyes flashed in anger and surprise.

Fiore walked down the hallway to an open door. He stuck his head inside the room. A woman—very pretty, very tiny—sat on the edge of the bed, arms folded across her chest, her hands on her shoulders. She was shaking violently. Fiore walked over to her and gently placed his hand on her head. "It is okay now. We are here to take you back to your family in Rome. These people will never bother you again."

The woman, her face streaked with tears, looked up at the big man and nodded. "I will get the children," she said, as she rose from the bed and crossed to an adjoining bedroom. She woke her two sleeping children, a boy and a girl. "Come…we are leaving now."

Fiore walked from the room, cradling a child in each arm. They looked like dolls against his massive frame. Their mother followed.

Pug stepped out of the Count's room, carrying the old man in both arms. Behind him the doctor protested, "He is very sick and cannot be moved." Pug shot the doctor a look that suggested he would regret any attempt to interfere.

Pug and Fiore swiftly descended the stairs, stopping just short of the back door. Three Doberman pinschers stood on the asphalt surface, snapping their white teeth at the intruders coming from the house. Pug put the old man down on a chair.

Fiore turned the children away from the dogs so they would not be frightened. Pug took his revolver, fired three shots, and slipped the gun back in its holster. Fiore nestled the children's faces into his chest as he stepped over the dogs.

Pug picked up the Count, who was furious but couldn't move, and headed for the long garage on the far side of the driveway. He kicked in the door. With his free hand he pushed the green automatic switch attached to the wall. Eight doors opened simultaneously.

"Wow," Pug said out loud. His eyes gazed over a chauffeur's utopia—two Rolls Royce Silver Arrows, a Bentley, and five other models Pug had never seen. "Let's take the Bentley. It'll be easier to maneuver along the coastline road."

Fiore gently set the children down on their feet, then took the Count from Pug and deposited him in the front seat. He put the two children in the back seat and motioned for their mother to get in beside them. Pug climbed into the driver's seat as Fiore headed toward the UPS truck. The key was in the ignition.

Fiore picked up Bernardo Feticcini, slung him over his shoulder and walked to the Bentley. Pug saw in the rear-view mirror where he was headed and pressed the button that latched the trunk. Fiore deposited Bernardo in the trunk and slammed down the lid. He jumped in the front seat, squeezing the Count between himself and Pug.

Pug headed the big car with its five passengers and live cargo back down the mountain to Sorrento.

Chapter 36

ROME

Libra stepped out of the limousine and looked up at the twenty-story glass building. She entered the main lobby. Glossy color photographs hung on all the walls of the main reception area. The floor was polished white marble. She saw a picture of a Caterpillar tractor, marked "Tri-Color Construction" in bold white lettering, moving earth, and a picture of a freighter with the "Tri-Color Shipping" logo.

Libra walked up to the information desk. "The offices of Ramona Montefusco, please," she said to a bored security guard behind the counter.

The uniformed guard looked up and gestured at a nearby elevator. Libra walked into the elevator and rode it to the top floor. She stepped out into a reception area adorned with fresh flowers, where a large oil portrait of Count Montefusco hung on the far wall. Next to it hung a portrait of Ramona.

Libra walked up to a reception desk. A young woman smiled up at her. "*Prego, Signora?*"

"I have an appointment with Ramona Montefusco."

"*Si, Signora.* You are Rebecca Arnason?"

Libra nodded.

"I will let her know that you are here. Would you like something to drink while you wait?"

Libra shook her head and took a seat. After a short wait, a man entered and escorted her into Montefusco's private reception area. He informed her that Signora Montefusco would be out momentarily.

The room was filled with antique furniture; a sofa covered in bright multicolored silk rested against the wall. Large plate-glass windows provided a picturesque view of Rome. Libra could see three truck trailers entering the Roman Forum in the distance.

Libra walked to an overstuffed chair and sat down on the edge. There was a matching chair on the opposite side of the small table. She reached into her briefcase, removed a brown folder and put it in the center of the table. She reached into the briefcase a second time and removed a small cellular telephone.

Less than two minutes later a woman walked from an inner office into the reception area. Her silky black hair fell to her shoulders. She wore a black silk skirt with a red silk jacket and beige blouse. She had high cheekbones and a no-nonsense look on her face.

"Welcome, *Signora*. It is indeed an honor to have a stockholder who invested such a large sum in Tri-Color Industries visit us here at our corporate headquarters," she offered with a detached smile. She extended her hand.

Libra ignored the artificial greeting. She shifted her eyes to the folder in the middle of the table, leaving Montefusco awkwardly standing over her with her hand outstretched.

"As a large stockholder in your company," Libra started, "I have serious reservations about your capability to manage the businesses." She brought her icy brown eyes to bear on Montefusco's face.

Montefusco did a double-take. She looked at Libra with a puzzled expression. She slowly dropped into the chair directly across from Libra, locking her eyes on Libra's.

"Then what is it that you want?"

Libra paused briefly, then began, "First, you can donate thirty million dollars to the El Al Survivors Fund in retribution for the 360 people you and your father murdered."

"Thirty million dollars? What—what on earth are you talking about?"

"Forty million," Libra countered.

Montefusco paused, then leaned back in her chair, steepling her fingers. Her cobalt eyes narrowed. "You…you are the woman called Libra," she said through clenched teeth. She stood up abruptly. Her jaw taut and her eyes flashing anger, she raced to the telephone.

"I would not do that," Libra snapped.

Montefusco stopped dead in her tracks, then slowly turned to face Libra. "You understand that with one telephone call, my men will be here in seconds. You will not leave this office alive." A smirk came to the corners of her lips as she stood with her arms folded.

"But you won't make that call." Libra's eyes conveyed the rest of the message: Move another inch, and you're dead.

Montefusco's face turned ashen. She carefully backtracked to her chair and sat down.

Libra slid the brown folder across the table toward Montefusco. It stopped at the edge, less than an inch from the chairwoman's knees.

"What is this?" Montefusco asked hoarsely.

"Read it." There was an unconditional tone to Libra's statement.

Montefusco leaned forward and picked up the folder. Her hand had a barely discernible tremble as she brought the single white sheet of paper in the folder to eye level and started to read. Her eyes furtively scanned the pinched handwriting. She swallowed hard.

"A signed confession, Signora. Bernardo Feticcini, a Tri-Color Construction superintendent from Herculaneum, has confessed to the bombing of El Al Flight 57. It is very precise. Signore Feticcini has spared no detail of how he planted the bomb on the plane. In point of fact, he has made it very clear that you and your father conspired to kill over three hundred people—most of them Israelis."

Montefusco's eyes narrowed. She leaned back and folded her arms across her chest. A defiant look crossed her face. She suddenly burst into raucous laughter.

"You think anyone will believe this?" She tossed the confession back on the table.

Libra flinched. Time to call Montefusco's bluff. "By itself, perhaps, perhaps not. However, at seven-thirty this morning, one of your construction crews unearthed a vault beneath the House of the Faun in Pompeii."

"So?" Montefusco asked nonchalantly, not sure where this was going. "What has this to do with your preposterous accusations? There was nothing wrong with what my crew did in the old city. They had the appropriate papers signed by the authorities, as well as the proper permits for the work in Pompeii. I can assure you that everything was legal."

Libra removed another brown folder from her briefcase. "In point of fact, your men used forged documents to enter the city of Pompeii. The building permit, too, was a clever forgery." She pushed the folder across the table. "You will find your forgery in that folder. Your construction crew is now in jail in Naples."

"How did…" Montefusco caught herself. She bit her lower lip and paused for a few moments. Then an insidious smile formed on her lips, her body loosened. "You are a reasonable woman, Signora. I'm certain that you are aware that these documents, while having no legal basis, would cause my company some embarrassments. So I am willing to make you a most generous offer in return for these documents and all copies."

"What is your offer?"

"I will give you a third of the contents of the vault that my men recovered at the House of the Faun in Pompeii. I must advise you that this offer is worth millions of dollars. You would have enough money to be secure for the rest of your life."

Right after you stuck a knife in my back. "And what would I do with thirty-three percent of architectural plans and civic orders from the emperor Augustus for rebuilding the city of Pompeii following the earthquake?" Libra asked, with mock puzzlement.

Montefusco's eyes flared and her face turned crimson. "Inside that vault is the treasure of Marcellus. You are a fool if you turn down what I am offering you."

"You mean, *you think* the vault holds the treasure of Marcellus."

"What do you mean?" Montefusco's breathing was becoming labored.

"You compromised Professor Rosolinni by taking his daughter and grandchildren, then holding them hostage at the Count's villa in Sorrento. You forced him to give you information for the safe return of his family. The professor pieced together a shredded fax from Washington and broke the code. He passed that message on to you in the hope that you would release his family. The message read, in part, that Augustus buried the treasure in the house of his consul Sulla in Pompeii, the House of the Faun. The information in the message the professor received was fabricated in the hope that you would take the bait. And you did! Your donation to the El Al Survivors Fund has now been raised to fifty million dollars." Libra's voice cracked like a whip.

"You are..." Montefusco caught herself. Libra's eyes were contemptuous, unyielding. It was clear she had the upper hand. Montefusco thought for several moments.

"Look," she offered as she leaned across the table toward Libra. Their faces were only inches apart. "The evidence you have will never stand up in any court. What you have in these folders is worthless. But, as I have stated previously, I do not wish to have a scandal burdening my company, so I am willing to make a contribution of say, a million dollars to the El Al Survivors Fund."

"Sixty million." Libra's voice was low and murderous.

"No plane crash is worth sixty million dollars!" Montefusco came roaring out of her chair.

"Seventy million." Libra leaned back in her chair, casually looking at her fingernails.

Montefusco's face had a complex look of worry, fear and disbelief. After several moments she tried to speak, but the words caught in her throat.

"You are to call the Banco di Roma, this minute, and have a cashier's check for seventy million dollars, payable to the El Al Survivors Fund, drawn against Tri-Color Industries' account."

The corners of Montefusco's mouth tightened. Finally, she rose from the chair, her body taut with resignation, and stepped toward the phone on the opposite side of the room. Libra stopped her with a dismissive wave and extended her arm, offering her cell phone. "Push the redial button. Your personal banker, Avanti Chervello, is awaiting your call."

Montefusco's nostrils flared and her eyes flashed again in surprise. "It would appear that you did your homework. You are every bit as good as your reputation says. You could have made a fortune working for me. Seldom am I as outwitted as I am today. I do not lose in negotiations, especially a negotiation with such consequences for the loser."

Libra ignored the compliment.

Montefusco grabbed the cell phone from Libra's outstretched hand. She pushed the redial button.

"*Si, Signora Montefusco,*" a nervous voice answered.

"You are to make out a cashier's check in the amount of seventy million dollars, payable to the El Al Survivors Fund."

"*Si, Signora.* I will do that right away." Chervello rang off.

"Now, if that is all, I have other things to attend to," Montefusco said. She rose from her chair. "If the treasure of Marcellus is not in Pompeii, then where is it?"

Libra reached in her briefcase and pulled out a roll of sheepskin parchment. She tossed it on the table. "The answer to that question is contained in this document."

"Livy," Montefusco whispered. The word stuck in her throat, partly from admiration, partly from surprise. She reached for the scroll. Libra stopped her.

"Not so fast. If you want the document, you must pay a price for it."

"I have just paid you seventy million dollars!"

"There is an ambulance parked in the street in front of the building. You are to release my partner, Sam Harrison, to the paramedics waiting in the ambulance."

"And how do I know you have not already taken the spoils from Siracusa?" Montefusco's eyes narrowed.

"You don't."

"Do you take me for a fool? I will turn Signore Harrison over to you after I have verified that the treasure is safe, and not a moment before."

"There is a car coming down from the mountains of Sorrento as we speak. That car is headed to the seaport below the Hotel Excelsior. Docked in the port is an Israeli gunboat. There are a dozen Mossad agents on it. If I do not call the car in five minutes, it will stop at the port and deliver your father to the Israelis. He will be taken to Israel, where he will stand trial as a war criminal for the murder of hundreds of Jews in the Second World War."

Montefusco was speechless. Libra could see the rage welling in her face. After several moments she said, "Very well." She took the phone and punched in a set of numbers. "Bring the American to the front entrance of the building—unharmed—and release him to the ambulance waiting there."

Montefusco placed the telephone on the table. She had lost, and she knew it. "One thing, Signora. Why did you buy so much stock in my company when it was your intent to ruin me?" she asked.

"I did not buy stock in your company. That is what you were led to believe by your miserable stockbroker. In point of fact, I sold short two million shares of Tri-Color Industries stock. By the time the market opens in Milan tomorrow, your stock will be worthless."

The woman leaned back and looked to the ceiling, the blood draining from her face. She slowly looked back to Libra. "What do you mean?"

"An audit of Tri-Color Industries' books has been sent to every major news organization in the world. It documents how you have built a paper empire whose sole product is the manufacture and distribution of narcotics. Every one of your ships is in the process of being seized as we speak, and I will make a healthy profit at your expense."

Libra walked out of the office, leaving the woman shattered. She crossed the corridor and stepped onto the elevator waiting on the top floor.

Ramona Montefusco looked out of the windows. Her eyes scanned the Eternal City below. A crowd of people was gathering at the Roman Forum. Television crews were filming something. Whatever it was, it didn't matter. She walked over to the ancient document lying on the table. She picked it up and stretched it out in her hands. No sooner had she started reading the ancient Latin text than the door to her office opened and two men in baggy suits walked in.

"Ramona Montefusco?"

"*Sì*, I am Ramona Montefusco. What is it you want?"

"You are under arrest for stealing artifacts belonging to the nation of Italy."

#

Libra met the red-and-white ambulance at the curb. She stopped at the rear doors. "How is he?"

One of the paramedics looked up. "He's in shock, but there are no life-threatening injuries." Sam was laid out on a stretcher, his head wrapped in bandages and a brace protecting his jaw. "He's dehydrated, and he has a broken jaw. They broke one of his knees, too. We have given him a sedative. He will be sleeping shortly."

Libra smiled down at Sam. *What the hell took you so long?* his eyes asked. He motioned with his hands, indicating that he wanted something to write with. Libra pulled a pencil and pad from her briefcase.

"How did U know?" Sam struggled to write the words on the pad.

Libra pulled an Alitalia in-flight magazine from her briefcase. "When you're well enough to read, here's a good article on 'Augustus, The Master Builder of Rome.' I've underlined the part that dovetails with what Mario told us about the hidden room."

No, no. I mean, how did you know I was in the building? Sam's eyes screamed at her. He fell asleep before Libra could answer.

She bent down and brushed his brown hair from his forehead. She kissed him affectionately, then turned to the paramedic. "Take him to Leonardo da Vinci. There's an Air Force plane waiting to take him back to the United States."

The paramedic nodded as Libra turned away. Twenty minutes later, she walked through the doors of the brokerage firm of Dementia and Calamenti. She ignored the receptionist and walked directly to Giuseppe Ronternaro's office. She found him talking on the telephone.

Giuseppe excused himself, then put down the telephone. "Ah, *Signora*. Please come in. Can I get you something to drink?"

"No, thank you. I am here to close out my accounts."

"But you just opened them this morning," he protested.

"Please give me the trading numbers for Tri-Color Industries."

Giuseppe punched the symbol into his computer. His eyes nearly popped out of his head. "Something must be wrong with my computer, Signora. It says the stock is trading for only one dollar." He looked closer at his monitor. "It has just dropped another fifty cents. I will make a telephone call to see if this is correct."

"There is no mistake, Signore. By my accounting, that's a thirty-nine-million-dollar trade. Nineteen-million profit, less your commissions. Please wire twenty million dollars to this account in Washington, D.C. And nine-and-a-half million dollars to each of these two accounts—one for Mario and one for Figlio." She handed Giuseppe three slips of paper, each with the corresponding account and dollar amount. "I will wait here while you make the transactions. I will need receipts."

Giuseppe disappeared down the hallway. He returned fifteen minutes later. "Thank you so much for your business, *Signora*," he said.

Before he finished speaking, Libra had walked out of the room. She left the building and headed across the Piazza di Spagna and into the Counsel Club office. The receptionist met her.

"*Signora*, you are missing all the excitement. They have found treasure on the Palatine!"

"Oh?" Libra said, in mock surprise.

"Yes. You know the great historian, Livy? They have found his lost…"

Libra cut her off. "I would like you to send these three letters for me—this one by courier to Washington, D.C., and these two to the address here in Rome." She handed the woman three white envelopes. "In addition, I would like you to purchase two open first-class tickets on Alitalia to Palermo from Rome for me, and have them sent to my two nephews whose address is on the envelopes. Please make the charges to my account."

"I will take care of it immediately."

Libra handed her five one-hundred-thousand-lira notes.

"*Grazie!*" the woman said, astonished.

Libra walked out into the piazza. The Don's chauffeur pulled up. On the back seat of the car was a bouquet of red roses and a note from the Don. Libra then tore open the letter.

"My dear Libra," it read, "I will miss you. You will always have a place in my family. I have enclosed a small wedding gift for you and Sam. May you be blessed with many bambinos. Fondly, Don Portico."

Libra reached for the small gift-wrapped box sitting next to the flowers. She carefully removed the wrapping and opened the felt box. Inside were two polished gold coins bearing the bust of an ancient warrior—Carthaginian Cresas. Libra chuckled. She admonished the Don not to skim any of the treasures from the Palatine.

Libra wiped a tear from her eye.

She looked up at the driver, whose eyes were also moist. "The Don says the two boys may stay in his apartment until they find another home. He said for you not to worry about them. And I will miss you, too, Libra."

"Let's get to the airport before I change my mind," Libra said, touching the driver's arm.

Chapter 37

Washington

Bannistar leaned forward in his chair, lit a cigarette, and unfolded the morning edition of *The New York Times*. On the front page was a grainy picture of two young boys being presented with a key to the City of Rome. He turned his eyes to the adjacent column:

"Livy's Lost Works Unearthed in Rome

"In what is being described as the single most important historical discovery in modern times, the city of Rome today announced that it had discovered the lost works of the ancient historian Titus Livius (Livy). Livy wrote *From the Founding of the City* during the reign of Augustus Caesar. His works cover the time frame from the beginning of Roman civilization in 753 B.C. to the reign of Julius Caesar in 10 B.C. According to a spokeswoman in the mayor's office, the remaining ninety-eight books of Livy's work, considered to have been destroyed in antiquity, were recovered on the Palatine Hill. The works, written on sheepskin scrolls, were found encased in a foundation wall of what once was the palace of Augustus Caesar. In addition, the city announced that it had recovered priceless artifacts and a hoard of gold coins believed to have been looted from the ancient port city of Siracusa (Sicily) by the Roman general Marcellus, in 212 B.C.

"The lost works were discovered by two young boys who were exploring the many catacombs that run underneath both the ancient city and what is now modern Rome. Architects and classical scholars expressed surprise that the ancient historian's works had remained hidden for so long beneath their noses…"

There was no mention of Libra in the article. Bannistar breathed a sigh of relief. He turned his attention to column one, where a bold headline read "El Al Bombers Captured: Sorrento, Italy. An Israeli gunboat…"

He turned to the international section. "Afghanistan Government Overthrown…"

Bannistar hit the intercom: "Betty, cancel all my appointments this afternoon." He was finally going to get in a round of golf.

"Yes, Mr. Bannistar. A courier is here with a delivery from Rome."

"Bring it in…"

Betty handed him a small white envelope. Bannistar tore it open. The message read, "I quit." There was no signature, only a pencil sketching of the astrological sign for Libra.

Chapter 38

Siracusa, Sicily
Four Weeks Later

"How did you know I was being held hostage in Tri-Color's corporate headquarters and not at the Count's villa in Sorrento?" Sam wrote on a legal pad and handed it to Libra. His jaw has been wired shut since the surgery.

"The construction superintendent in Herculaneum—the one Pug and Fiore intimidated into giving us the details on the El Al bombing. He told Pug they were holding you in Rome. He didn't know where in Rome, but by the process of elimination, it had to be in Tri-Color's building."

Sam reached for a diet Coke in a cooler next to his beach chair. "How did you figure they didn't take me to the Count's villa?" he scribbled.

"Bannistar's spy satellites," Libra replied. "Pug gave me the head count for the number of people staying at the villa, including the professor's daughter and kids. Heat-sensing pictures showed that there were no extra live bodies anywhere on the grounds, so I figured you weren't there. Also, the pictures showed the house on the island off Positano was deserted. Does that satisfy your curiosity?"

Sam nodded.

Suddenly they heard their names being called from the ocean. They looked up to see Figlio running along the blue-green surf, dodging the foamy waves as they crashed to the beach. Figlio turned and ran toward their large beach umbrella. He came to a stop between the two of them.

With both hands on his knees, he gasped for breath.

"What is it, Figlio?" Libra asked pleasantly.

"You will never guess what Mario has found in the ruins…"

Sam and Libra fell back in their chairs and let out a collective groan.

Headwaters
by Jerry Leppart
What's worse than a terrorist with nuclear weapons? A terrorist with nuclear waste. Jerry Leppart's fiction thriller tells of a bombing gone wrong, turning a brilliant surgeon into a terrorist who threatens the very existence of the American people. Too clever to bomb or hijack, this terrorist turns to something even more devastating—nuclear waste in the nation's water supply. Full of twists and turns, heart-stopping scenes, and three-dimensional characters, this page-turner will leave you asking for more.
1–880090–66–X   6 x 9
256 pgs. $14.95

Pest Control
by Jerry Leppart
Someone is killing attorneys in Minnesota. At each murder scene is a business card with the term "Pest Control" and the mysterious numerals, II, VI, 4, 2. The killer uses a variety of techniques with military precision, a real assassin. And it's up to Billy "Two Bears" Simpson to find him.
1–880090–95–3   6 x 9
272 pgs. $14.95

To order these books, please send full amount plus $4.00 for postage and handling for the first book and 50¢ for each additional book. Foreign orders please call for s&h. Send orders to Galde Press, Inc., PO Box 460, Lakeville, Minnesota 55044-0460.
Credit card orders call 1–800–777–3454.

To Slay a Demon
by John Wayne Kennedy

CIA agent Mark loses his beloved daughter to cocaine. He embarks on a trail of vengeance aimed at the destruction of the drug cartel. Although fiction, *To Slay a Demon* clearly and accurately depicts how current technology can be used to destroy the major coca plant production, the source of cocaine and its derivatives entering the United States. Governments could even now be using the technology described here in an operational program. The rage experienced by Mark has been felt by millions who have lost loved ones to drugs. In this breathtaking novel, a very dangerous man leads a determined band of far-from-helpless people against one of the greatest empires on earth—the drug cartel.
1–880090–97–X   6 x 9
224 pgs.   illus. $14.95

To order this book, please send full amount plus $4.00 for postage and handling for the first copy and 50¢ for each additional copy. Foreign orders please call for s&h. Send orders to Galde Press, Inc., PO Box 460, Lakeville, Minnesota 55044-0460.
Credit card orders call 1–800–777–3454.